Praise for Erica James

'Erica James' sensitive story . . . is as sparklingly fresh as dew on the village's surrounding meadows . . . thoroughly enjoyable and fully deserving of a place in the crowded market of women's fiction' *Sunday Express*

'This book draws you into the lives of these characters, and often makes you want to scream at them to try and make them see reason. Funny, sad and frustrating, but an excellent, compulsive read' *Woman's Realm*

'There is humour and warmth in this engaging story of love's triumphs and disappointments, with two well-realised and intriguing subplots' *Woman & Home*

'Joanna Trollope fans, dismayed by the high gloom factor and complete absence of Agas in her latest books, will turn with relief to James' . . . delightful novel about English village life . . . a blend of emotion and wry social observation'
Daily Mail

'Scandal, fury, accusations and revenge are all included in Erica James' compelling novel . . . this story of village life in Cheshire is told with wit and humour' *Stirling Observer*

'An entertaining read with some wickedly well-painted cameo characters. It's a perfect read if you're in the mood for romance' *Prima*

'An engaging and friendly novel . . . very readable'
Woman's Own

'A bubbling, delightful comedy which is laced with a bittersweet tang . . . a good story, always well observed, and full of wit' *Publishing News*

Erica James grew up in Hampshire and has since lived in Oxford, Yorkshire and Belgium. She now lives in Cheshire. She is the author of twelve novels, including *Gardens of Delight*, which won the 2006 Romantic Novel of the Year Award.

Tell it to the Skies

ERICA JAMES

An Orion paperback

First published in Great Britain in 2007
by Orion
This paperback edition published in 2008
by Orion Books Ltd,
Orion House, 5 Upper Saint Martin's Lane,
London WC2H 9EA

An Hachette Livre UK company

1 3 5 7 9 10 8 6 4 2

Copyright © Erica James 2007

A CIP catalogue record for this book is available
from the British Library.

ISBN 978-0-7528-9336-5

Typeset by Deltatype Limited, Birkenhead, Merseyside

Printed and bound in Great Britain by Clays Ltd, St Ives plc

The Orion Publishing Group's policy is to use papers
that are natural, renewable and recyclable products and
made from wood grown in sustainable forests. The logging
and manufacturing processes are expected to conform to
the environmental regulations of the country of origin.

www.orionbooks.co.uk

To Edward and Samuel
who make it all worthwhile

Acknowledgements

While digging deep to write this book I was fortunate indeed to be supported and encouraged by some wonderful friends.

Endless gratitude to Ray Allen for his many words of wisdom and for making me laugh with such regularity. Who'd have thought he'd be such a wise sage?

My sincere thanks to Sheila and Alan Jones. Alan, whilst we will happily never agree on all manner of subjects, I congratulate you on being married to one of the nicest people in the world.

Thank you to Max and Keith for adding to my enjoyment of Venice last year. Especially for the extravagant bunch of red roses – a gesture I couldn't resist pinching for this book!

Thanks, too, to Kathleen, my 'English Teacher' in Venice.

I wouldn't be the first author to take a few liberties here and there, but hopefully no one will notice. Or if they do, they'll be accepted as the artistic tweakings of a creative mind.

'Men never do evil so completely and cheerfully as when they do it from religious conviction.'

BLAISE PASCAL 1623–1662

'And now these three remain: faith, hope and love. But the greatest of these is love.'

1 CORINTHIANS 13:13

Now

Chapter One

It happened so quickly.

She had been hurrying from the market side of the Rialto Bridge, trying to avoid the crush of tourists in the packed middle section of shops, when a single face appeared in the crowd as if picked out by a bright spotlight entirely for her benefit. She turned on her heel to get a better look. And that was when she missed her footing and ended up sprawled on the wet ground, the contents of her handbag scattered.

Any other time Lydia might have been appalled at this loss of dignity, yet all she cared about, whilst a voluble group of Americans helped her to get back on her feet, was the man who had caused her to slip. She scanned the crowded steps for his retreating figure in the fine, drizzling rain. But he was long gone.

If he'd been there at all, Lydia thought as she relaxed into the chair and felt the downy softness of the cushions enfold her. The doctor had left ten minutes ago, promising the delivery of a pair of crutches in the morning. Her ankle was now expertly strapped and resting on a footstool. *Dottor* Pierili's parting words had been to tell her to keep the weight off her foot for as long as possible. He'd wanted her to go to the hospital for an X-ray, just to be on the safe side, but she'd waved his advice aside, politely yet firmly. Bandages, rest and painkillers would suffice.

'I still don't know how you managed to get home,' Chiara said, coming into the living room with a tray of tea things. She put the tray on a pedestal table between a pair of tall balconied windows that looked down onto the Rio di San Vio. The weak, melancholy December light had all but faded and the spacious room glowed with a soft-hued luminosity. Strategically placed lamps created a beguilingly serene atmosphere, making it Lydia's favourite room in the apartment. She was a self-confessed lover of beautiful things; it was what brought her to Venice in the first place. Living here she was surrounded by beauty on a scale she had never encountered anywhere else. Venice's glorious but crumbling architecture together with its proud history combined to produce a profoundly sad and haunting sense of identity that appealed enormously to Lydia. It was the apparent isolation of the place that touched her; it was somewhere she felt she could be separate from the rest of the world.

She would always remember her first glimpse of Venice. It was early evening and as the *vaporetto* entered the basin, the city was suddenly there before her, floating like a priceless work of art in the distance, the low sun catching on the gilded domes and *campanili*. It was love at first sight. From then on she was a willing victim to Venice's trembling beauty and the spell it cast on her. Even with the myriad challenges that the city was forced to cope with – the growing threat of *acqua alta*, the ever-increasing crowds that were choking the narrow *calli*, and the graffiti (almost worst of all to Lydia) that was spreading endemically through Venice – it was still a place of dreams for her. Even the relentless chorus of 'Volare' and 'O Sole Mio!' coming from the gondoliers as they cruised the waterways with their cargo of nodding and smiling Japanese tourists could do nothing to diminish her love for her adopted home.

'You're either the bravest woman I know or the stupidest,' Chiara said as she handed Lydia a cup of tea.

Lydia smiled, noting that Chiara had gone to the trouble of digging out her favourite bone china cup and saucer. 'Undoubtedly the latter,' she replied. 'That's certainly what your father would have said.'

'You probably did more damage walking on it than when you slipped.'

'He would have agreed with you on that point too. And said that for a forty-six-year-old woman I should have known better.'

Chiara crossed the room for her own cup then came and curled up in the high-backed chair next to Lydia. It was where Marcello always used to sit, his hand outstretched to Lydia as he quietly read the *Gazzettino*.

'I want you to know that this arrangement will only go on for a day or two,' Lydia said, keen to establish that she would soon be back at work, business as usual.

Chiara, all twenty-four years of her, gave Lydia a quelling stare, her eyes dark and shining in the muted light. 'Oh, no you don't. We can manage perfectly well without you.'

'That's what I'm worried about. I don't want you getting too used to my absence.'

'Now there's an idea. A boardroom coup.'

The shrill ring of the telephone in the hall had Chiara getting to her feet. Within seconds it was obvious the call wasn't for Lydia. Selfishly she hoped it wasn't one of Chiara's friends inviting her out for the evening; she could do with the company.

This neediness had nothing to do with her sprained ankle, and all to do with not wanting to be alone. If she was alone, she might dwell on that face in the crowd. And that was definitely something she didn't want to do. An evening with Chiara would be the perfect distraction.

It was a matter of pride to Lydia that she and Chiara didn't have the usual mother and daughter relationship. For a start Lydia wasn't actually Chiara's mother: she was her stepmother. It was a clumsy label Lydia had dispensed with at the earliest opportunity. Chiara had always called her by her Christian name, anyway.

Lydia had never told anyone this, but it had been Chiara who she had fallen for first – her love for Marcello, Chiara's father, had come later. They had met fifteen years ago, when Chiara was nine and Lydia had been employed to teach the little girl English. She received a phone call in response to one of her advertisements offering her services, and three days later a distinguished-looking Signor Marcello Tomasi and his only daughter arrived at her apartment in Santa Croce. She was a painfully shy, introverted child and it didn't take long to realize why: her mother, as her quietly spoken father explained, had died last winter. Nobody could have empathized more with the young girl. Lydia knew exactly how it felt to have your world turned upside down and inside out. Every ounce of her being made her want to take away Chiara's sadness, to make her face light up with a smile.

The lessons always started at four o'clock on a Saturday afternoon and took place in Lydia's tiny kitchen. She thought it would be a less intimidating environment for this fragile child than to sit at the formal desk in the sitting room. There would always be a pot of freshly made hot chocolate on the table, along with a box of delicious almond biscuits from her local *pasticceria*. Lydia's other students were never offered more than tea or coffee, or fruit juice if she happened to have any in the fridge. Gradually her young pupil began to grow in confidence, which meant she looked less likely to burst into tears if she got anything wrong.

Without fail Marcello Tomasi would return for his daughter as the bell from San Giacomo dell'Orio struck five. He would hand over the agreed amount of money, check that they were still on for the following Saturday and then wish Lydia a pleasant evening. However, one day, just as Lydia was opening the door for them to leave, Chiara did something that changed everything. She beckoned her father to bend down to her, cupped her hand around her mouth and whispered into his ear. Straightening up, he cleared his throat, rubbed his hand over his clean-shaven chin and said, 'Chiara would like to invite you to her birthday party next week.'

The thought of a roomful of over-excited, noisy Italian

children held no appeal for Lydia. As if reading her mind, Marcello Tomasi said, 'It will be just a small party. I think Chiara would very much like you to be there. And so would I,' he added.

The party was bigger than Lydia had been led to believe, but it was very much a family affair with the only children present being a handful of Chiara's cousins, most of whom were younger than her and blessedly well behaved. After six months of teaching this man's only daughter and forming a strong, protective relationship with her, but exchanging no more than a few words with him, it was strange to be in his home; it felt oddly intimate. She was suddenly seized with the urge to snoop and pry, to find out more about this immaculately dressed, taciturn man. She knew that he worked on the mainland in Marghera, the nearby industrial zone that was generally considered to be the Beast to Venice's Beauty. She also knew, from Chiara, that he was *very, very* important and had *lots* of people working for him. Judging from the house – a two-storey, stylishly restored property a stone's throw from Ca'Doro – he had excellent taste and lived in a degree of comfort. But this scant amount of detail wasn't enough for Lydia; she wanted to know what he did for pleasure. Did he read? If so, what books did he read? What music did he listen to? What did he eat for his supper? More to the point, who cooked his supper? Did he cook it himself, or did he have help? Chiara had never mentioned anyone.

Even if she had had the nerve to carry out any actual unseemly rifling through Marcello's personal effects for answers to her questions, there was no opportunity to do so. Chiara took her excitedly by the hand and introduced her in overly rehearsed English to her many relatives, one by one. 'This is Miss Lydia, my very nice English teacher … This is Miss Lydia, my very nice English teacher.' The responses were all in Italian, which was fine by Lydia; she had been speaking Italian since she was eighteen. She might only have been in Venice for two years but she could manage a passable version of *la parlata*, the local dialect, which seemed to her to be entirely made up on a whim solely to vex outsiders.

Everyone at the party was very welcoming and took it in turns to press plates of tempting food onto her as well as top up her glass of Prosecco. But she took pains not to outstay her welcome; this was a family affair, she reminded herself. Shortly after the children had been called upon to sing for the adults, accompanied on the piano by Fabio, Marcello's brother – apparently a family tradition – she tried to make her exit as discreetly as possible, but Chiara was having none of it and announced to everyone that her *very nice English teacher* was leaving. Endless goodbyes then ensued until at last she was rescued by Marcello who, having instructed Chiara to offer her sweet-toothed great-grandmother another helping of *dolce*, steered Lydia away.

'I hope that wasn't too awful for you,' he said when they were standing outside in the courtyard garden, the cool night air making her realize how warm she'd been inside and how much Prosecco she'd drunk. She could feel the heat radiating from her cheeks.

'I had a lovely time,' she said truthfully, thinking how much she really had enjoyed herself.

'It wasn't too overwhelming?'

'Not at all. It was good to see Chiara so happy. She's a delightful child; you must be extremely proud of her.'

'She is and I am. I don't know if you're aware of it, but she's grown very close to you.'

'The feeling is mutual. She's charming company.'

'Are you busy tomorrow evening?'

'I don't think so. Why?'

'Will you have dinner with me?'

And that, six months after losing her heart to his daughter, was the start of her relationship with Marcello. A man who, ten years older than her, in no way fitted her idea of a typical Italian. He wasn't one of those rumbustious Italian men who constantly argue about politics and corruption in high places and claim they could change everything overnight if only given the chance. Nor did he have the infuriating habit of shouting '*Ascoltami!*' ('Listen to me!') every other sentence. And not once did he grab her arm to make sure he had her full attention during a conversation. Instead there was a quiet and intelligent reserve about him. He was courteous to a fault and very astute. He realized and accepted that there was a part of her he would never know or understand. 'Your life is like a photograph album with occasional blank spaces where some of the pictures have been removed,' he said on the day he asked her to be his wife.

'Does it matter to you?' she replied.

'No,' he answered. 'I think it's those mysterious gaps I love most about you.'

Perhaps if he had pressed her, she might have shared more of herself with him.

The sound of Chiara's happy laughter, as she continued talking to whoever it was on the phone, broke through Lydia's thoughts and, not for the first time, she wondered how the painfully shy child she had met fifteen years ago had grown into this confident, carefree young woman, a young woman who had had to cope with the loss of both her parents before she'd turned twenty-one. Lydia liked to think that she'd played a part in Chiara's recovery from the death of her mother – Marcello always believed she had – but all she'd done was give the child what she had never experienced when she was that age: love and stability.

Having children had never been something Lydia had particularly craved. However, having Chiara in her life had felt exactly the right thing to do.

That night she slept badly, her sleep disturbed by a host of fragmented dreams. In one dream the siren sounded, signalling *acqua alta*. Venice was sinking. The water was lapping at her feet as she tried desperately to make it home to Chiara. But she was lost; every *calle* she ran into was a dead end. The siren continued to ring out. The ancient wooden supports creaked and groaned and finally they gave way and the buildings crumbled and slid slowly but surely into the lagoon.

She woke with a start and lay in the dark remembering a Bible story from her childhood, about the man who built his house upon the sand. Pastor Digby had his long, bony finger raised accusingly to her; he was asking if she understood what the story was teaching her.

Once she'd allowed one memory to enter her thinking, others began flooding in too. Her next mistake was to attach too much meaning to the dream. Was her life disintegrating? Had she built her life on foundations that were about to give way?

She pulled the duvet up over her head, blaming that wretched face in the crowd. Who was he? A ghost?

Chapter Two

The following morning the promised pair of crutches arrived, as did a succession of visitors throughout the day, all of whom had been despatched by Chiara to entertain Lydia.

'Another one who's been sent to keep me company, I presume,' Lydia said tiredly after she'd buzzed up Marcello's brother, Fabio. His wet, bedraggled appearance was a clear indicator of the kind of day it was outside. The lower edges of his overcoat were drenched, his furled umbrella was dripping onto the marble floor, and his trousers were tucked into a pair of black, knee-high rubber boots.

'Would you rather I left you to rest?' he asked. From his coat pockets he retrieved a bag of *biscotti* and a bottle of Vin Santo. Smiling, he dangled them in front of her. 'I could always keep these for myself.'

'Well, seeing as you've gone to so much trouble, perhaps I'll let you stay.' She watched him take off his coat and boots, then set off awkwardly down the length of the hallway on the crutches, negotiating the rugs with care. Fabio followed behind in his stockinged feet. 'What dear, well-meaning Chiara forgot,' Lydia said, conscious that she was sounding less than gracious, 'in her attempt to keep me occupied for the day, was that I would have to be up and down like a yo-yo to let you all in.'

'In that case, I'd better stay until she returns so you won't be further inconvenienced.'

'Now you're just making me feel like an ungrateful bitch.'

He laughed. 'And with so little effort, *cara*.' He put

his gifts down on the coffee table and helped her to get comfortable on the sofa.

'So why aren't you hard at work?' she asked.

'I'm the boss; I can take time off whenever I want.'

'I'll tell Paolo you said that.'

He laughed again. 'It was Paolo who insisted I drop everything and come and see you after Chiara called.'

'Hah, so he's to blame.'

'I think you need a drink to sweeten that sour tongue of yours.' He fetched a pair of glasses from the kitchen and poured out two generous measures of Vin Santo. He opened the packet of *biscotti* and passed it to Lydia. Of all her visitors that day, Fabio was probably the most welcome. As Marcello's younger brother, there had only ever been a vague physical resemblance between the two men, but the bond between them had been a strong one, had marked them out as being cut from the same cloth.

'So how did you hurt yourself?' Fabio asked after he'd chinked his glass against Lydia's and sat down.

'Too silly to say.'

'Oh, come on, I could do with a good laugh.'

'I thought you were here to make *me* laugh?'

'I know a lost cause when I see one. What did you do, kick some poor tourist out of your way and lose your balance?'

She smiled, but didn't say anything. Instead she dunked a biscuit into her drink then sucked on it, aware that Fabio was watching her closely. She knew all too well that he could spot the slightest change in her a mile off.

'What is it, *cara*?' he said. 'You don't seem yourself. You look distracted.'

She wished that her brother-in-law wasn't so sensitive and perceptive. After Marcello's death from a heart attack four years ago it was his shoulder she had cried on, just as it was his hand, along with Chiara's, that she had held during the funeral service. He had always been there for her. She had joked once that it was as well he was gay or people would certainly have got the wrong idea about them. But right now she would give anything for him not to care so much for her.

'It's being stuck here,' she said, pointing at her ankle. 'I feel so useless.'

Looking far from convinced by her explanation, Fabio sat back and crossed one leg over the other. 'It's nothing to do with Chiara, is it?' he asked.

She took a sip of her drink, enjoying its dry, sweet warmth on her throat. 'Chiara's fine,' she said. 'And anyway, didn't I just say what's wrong with me?'

Fabio stared at her doubtfully. 'So if it's not Chiara,' he persisted, 'is it work? You've built up quite a business there; it's not becoming too much for you, is it?'

She shook her head. 'Work's fine.' Again, she was telling the truth. The business she and Marcello had started together had never looked in better shape. Shortly after he'd proposed to her, Marcello announced his intention to leave the chemical company where he was the research director. He had always felt that the nature of his work was at odds with his love for Venice – given the environmental effect the industrial zone was having on the lagoon – but he had eased his conscience by saying it was better that someone like him had a say in how things were done, than someone who didn't care. 'I want to do something new,' he told her. 'And it has to be something we can do together.' They soon came up with the idea of running a lettings agency, initially acting on behalf of private and individual owners, but eventually investing in property themselves. Before long, they had an impressive portfolio of apartments to offer clients, most of whom were British, American, French and German. After Marcello's death, and as a direct result of working the worst of her grief out of her system, the agency became even more successful. She now had a reliable team of girls working for her in the newly expanded office, including Chiara who joined the agency when she had finished her studies in Bologna two years previously. As architects, Fabio and his partner Paolo had played their part by helping with any restoration work that was required in the properties. They had also overseen the work carried out on this very apartment, which she and Marcello had moved into only eighteen months before his death.

The irony of her line of work was not lost on Lydia. Like so many Venetians who complained bitterly about the number of visitors to Venice, she actively encouraged tourists to pour in for the sake of her livelihood. There was also the more controversial matter of Venice's dwindling population. Hardly a day went by when there wasn't a piece written in the *Gazzettino* about the plight of young locals being forced to live on the mainland because they couldn't afford the sky-high prices here in Venice. Prices that had been inflated by outside investors. It was a problem that had everyone in agreement: something would have to be done. But meanwhile, life had to carry on and people made their living the best way they knew how, by welcoming tourists with open arms and giving them a thorough fleecing.

'If it's not Chiara or work that's bothering you,' said Fabio, 'is it loneliness?' He paused, and Lydia could see he was choosing his next words with care. 'Do you think it's time to move on?'

For a while now Fabio had been discreetly hinting that she ought to find someone to take Marcello's place. Lydia smiled. 'Oh, Fabio, I know how you worry about me, and I appreciate it, really I do. But it's not that. Not that at all.'

'*Sei sicura?*'

'Yes, I'm sure. To be honest, I'm usually too busy to give it a thought.'

'That's not healthy.'

'It's the way it is.'

'Then perhaps it's time you changed your ways. When was the last time you had a holiday?'

'Don't be ridiculous. What would I do with a holiday?'

He shook his head in what she hoped was defeat, but taking her by surprise, he said, 'Sometimes I think you go out of your way to punish yourself. For the life of me I can't think why.'

You don't know the half of it, she thought grimly.

Chapter Three

Chiara came home from work early and straight away Lydia sensed there was something different about her. From the moment she had hung up her coat and put her umbrella to dry, the walls of the apartment seemed to reverberate with the sound of laughter and chatter. She greeted Fabio with her customary warmth, but the hug definitely went on for longer than usual and the grin on her face never slipped. She was joyful. Exuberant.

Now that Fabio had gone, Lydia watched Chiara move about the apartment, drawing the curtains, tidying away the debris of a day's worth of visitors, and all the while humming to herself. She was in a world of her own. No doubt about it. But what could have put Chiara into such an exceptionally happy mood?

After pondering on this for several minutes on her own, Lydia went to find Chiara in the kitchen. She was standing in front of the full-length window, staring absently at her reflection in the glass. On the hob, the kettle was boiling furiously, sending up a cloud of steam. Realizing that Chiara wouldn't notice the ceiling falling down on her in her current frame of mind, Lydia went over and switched off the gas.

Chiara slowly turned around to face her. 'Can I ask you something, Lydia? Something personal?'

'Of course,' said Lydia. 'What is it?'

'Have you ever had a real moment of epiphany? When you knew with absolute certainty that a certain thing was meant to happen to you? Or a certain person was meant to be in your life?'

Of all the things she might have expected Chiara to ask her it was not this. Her response was to think of her own life-changing moment and the subsequent terror it had filled her with. It had happened a long time ago, yet she had never forgotten how resolute she had been. Or how utterly convinced she had been that it was the right thing to do.

'I don't know how it happened,' Chiara went on, not seeming to notice that Lydia hadn't answered her, 'but I was looking into his eyes and I knew that nothing would be the same again. Does that sound crazy? Do *I* sound crazy?'

'Well,' said Lydia, the wind taken out of her sails, 'this sounds like something I should be sitting down to hear. Tell me more. And exactly whose eyes are we talking about?'

Splashing hot water over a peppermint teabag in a mug, Chiara said, 'You promise you won't overreact and tell me I'm being silly?'

Settled at the table now, her crutches propped against the back of another chair, Lydia said, 'Have I ever behaved like that before with you?'

Chiara tossed the dripping teabag into the bin. 'No, but there's a first time for everything. Do you want me to make you a drink?'

'No, I'm fine, thank you. But come and sit down and tell me who's had such a devastating effect on you. He must be quite something.'

Chiara laughed and came and joined her at the table. 'Yes, that's exactly how I'd describe it. I knew you'd understand. His name's Ishmael, and I met him today, and he's ... well, he's just, oh, I don't know, he's the first man to knock me off my feet. I can't even tell you exactly what it is about him that's so amazing. But I do know this: he's *Quello Giusto*.'

The One. Lydia didn't know whether to be delighted or alarmed. It was wonderful that Chiara had met someone who could make her feel this way, but a complete stranger? Trying desperately not to pour cold water on

Chiara's excitement, she said, 'How did you meet this extraordinary man?'

'He came into the office this morning; he's one of our clients and is staying in Ca' Tiziano. Maria Luisa was supposed to take him to the apartment but she had an emergency with Luca and had to fetch him home from school because he had a fever, so I stepped in. And—' She paused for breath and Lydia half expected a drum roll to follow. 'And there he was, standing the other side of my desk, and my heart nearly somersaulted clean out of my chest. I swear I'm not exaggerating. It was just as well I was sitting down as otherwise I'm convinced my legs would have gone from under me.'

'Goodness,' Lydia said inadequately. 'Do you think he realized the effect he had on you?' She hated the thought of Chiara wearing her heart so openly on her sleeve and leaving herself exposed to being hurt. But presumably if this so-called *The One* was staying in one of their apartments, his presence in Chiara's life would be no more than transient. He would leave Venice and Chiara's heart would be left relatively unscathed. No sooner had she articulated this thought to herself than Lydia wondered if she was reacting in this negative way because she was frightened of Chiara leaving her. There had been no previous boyfriend who had got anywhere near to threatening their close relationship, so could it be that Lydia was jealous, that she saw Chiara as her best friend and was afraid to lose her? She flinched at this uncomfortable insight and forced herself to join in with Chiara's enthusiasm.

'I'm not sure if he noticed anything,' said Chiara, 'but after I'd shown him round the apartment he asked if it was against company policy to mix business with pleasure, and would it be all right for him to take me for a drink. He said he'd never been to Venice before and would appreciate any local knowledge he could get.'

'Well, we can't fault him for seizing the moment,' Lydia said.

Chiara stared at Lydia over the top of her steaming

mug, her dark eyes flashing defensively. 'You sound dis-approving.'

Lydia offered up what she hoped was a reassuring, conciliatory smile. 'I think I'm acting like a very boring middle-aged woman who's just looking out for you. After all, what do you know of him?'

'Quite a bit as it happens,' Chiara said with a show of spirit. 'He's English and arrived in Venice two days ago and has been staying at the Monaco before moving into Ca' Tiziano. He's here to do a crash course in Italian at the Institute because he's starting a new job in Padua in the spring. And don't forget, if he can afford to stay in Ca' Tiziano, he's not exactly a pauper.'

Hardly sufficient evidence in Lydia's opinion to allay her fears. 'When are you having that drink with him?'

For the first time during the conversation Chiara looked awkward. She raised a hand to her long, dark hair and twirled a curly lock of it around her finger, just as she had as a child when she'd been holding something back. 'If it's OK with you, that's if you don't mind being on your own, I was hoping to meet him in half an hour. I thought I'd take him to the Christmas market, you know, to show him a bit of local colour.'

'Of course it's OK with me,' Lydia said. 'You go and have fun. You've earned it putting up with me whilst I've been such a misery.'

'Really?' The dear girl was practically out of her chair.

'I always mean what I say,' Lydia said.

Within minutes, Chiara had made a call on her mobile and was tying a scarf around her neck and buttoning her coat. 'You're sure you'll be all right?'

Lydia smiled. 'Scram! Go on, get out of here! And don't forget your umbrella.'

'*Ciao, ciao.*'

Laughing happily, Chiara slammed the door after her.

In the silence that followed, Lydia could hear one of Renzo's music students playing the violin in the apartment below. Outside, a motorboat was chugging slowly by, the water slapping against the sides of the canal. Further away, the bells of the Gesuati were pealing the hour.

She closed her eyes and pictured Chiara – breathless and smiling – meeting this unknown man a short walk away in the prettily lit Campo San Stefano. She saw them browsing the specially erected wooden chalets of the Christmas market, a cup of mulled wine in hand as they sampled the many varieties of salami, olives and cheese on offer. Chiara would probably introduce him to her friend, Felice, who was there every day selling his black and white photographs of Venice. Afterwards they would go on to a bar for a spritzer and probably meet more of Chiara's friends. You couldn't go anywhere in this small city without bumping into someone you knew.

Or perhaps they would want to be alone …

She reached for her crutches and stood up decisively. This pathetic behaviour had to stop. Chiara was a grown woman who could fall in love with whomever she chose. Lydia couldn't protect her for ever. Hadn't she made that mistake before, thinking that she alone carried the world on her shoulders and was entirely responsible for those she loved?

Chapter Four

Four days later and Lydia was climbing the walls. Mentally, that was. Her ankle was on the mend but she still couldn't tackle the four flights of stairs that would take her to the outside world. As undignified as the process would be, she was tempted to make her escape on her bottom, but Chiara wouldn't hear of it. The most she had been able to negotiate out of Chiara was the right to work on her laptop at the kitchen table. Really, that girl was turning into quite a tyrant!

Waiting now for Chiara to come home from work, Lydia was bored rigid. She was on edge, too. Chiara was bringing Ishmael back with her for the first time. 'You'll love him,' Chiara had said at breakfast that morning. 'I just know you will.'

Lydia had done her best to walk the fine line of showing a healthy interest in what was making Chiara so happy, and keeping a tight lid on the many questions she was longing to ask. Not that Chiara had given her much of a chance to be interrogated: if she wasn't at work, she was out with Ishmael, often not coming home till late when Lydia was in bed. Frustratingly, she knew no more about this young man than she had four days ago.

Countless times she had had to fight off the urge to go behind Chiara's back and speak to the girls at the office to see if they knew anything about the client staying in Ca' Tiziano. It was the fear of Chiara finding out that she had done something so sneaky that stopped Lydia from picking up the telephone. That and knowing there was a line a parent never crossed: Chiara's privacy had to be respected.

At the sound of a key in the lock, Lydia roused herself from the sofa. Armed with just the one crutch, she stood to attention, a welcoming smile firmly in place.

If Chiara's reaction on meeting Ishmael for the first time had been a somersaulting heart, Lydia's was all-out shock.

While her mind was making wild panicky leaps, her body had lost all of its strength. She leaned heavily on her crutch and felt the blood drain out of her. Her shock must have shown because, mid-introduction, Chiara said, 'Lydia, are you all right?'

'I'm fine.' But she was far from fine. How could this be? How could she be standing in the same room with the man who had caused her to slip on the steps of the Rialto Bridge ... the very man who had meant the world to her?

Except it wasn't the same man. It couldn't be. It wasn't possible. A lifetime had passed since she last saw him; there was no way he couldn't have aged. Yet, to all intents and purposes it *was* him. The dark, intelligent eyes were the same, as was the narrow face, its features delicately etched as if by a great master. His short, fine hair was instantly familiar too, light brown and highlighted with flecks of burnished gold. And just as familiar were his faded corduroy jeans and black polo-neck sweater. She dropped her eyes to his shoes – that all-important indicator of someone's personality. What else, but well-worn black and white baseball boots? Just as she'd known. He was exactly as she remembered him, even down to the angular, insubstantial build of him.

That had been her initial impression when she'd first set eyes on Noah at the age of nine. He'd seemed so insubstantial, quite incapable of taking care of himself. She hadn't known whether to despise him or feel sorry for him. He'd had a strange unearthly quality, which she later came to realize was a formidable inner strength. It was to prove more powerful than any name-calling or fist-waving threats, to which she and their peers frequently resorted.

But that was *Noah*, Lydia reminded herself. This carbon copy's name was Ishmael. He had to be a handful of years older than Noah had been when she'd last seen him. There could be only one explanation for what she was seeing, but could it be?

'I know this will sound like a cliché, Signora Tomasi, but you look as if you've seen a ghost.'

Once again she was assailed by shock. His voice was the same. It was the kind of voice that could convince you nowhere was safer than by his side, that together you could take on the world no matter what it threw at you.

'Please,' she said, conscious that Chiara was staring at her, 'call me Lydia.' She held out her hand. He took it and as their eyes met, she said, 'I don't recall Chiara mentioning your surname to me; what is it?'

'Solomon,' he replied with a beguiling smile – another trait she had seen before. 'I know,' he shrugged. 'I have the most biblical name going: Ishmael Solomon. It's down to my father, who has a weird sense of humour. The name was his choice. He said he'd been similarly afflicted as a child with the name of Noah, and saw no reason to let me off.'

Through a pounding in her ears, Lydia could hear Ishmael talking as if from a great distance. Further and further away his voice was drifting as the years rolled back and the memories struggled to take flight on the wings of incredulity. For twenty-eight years she had consigned Noah Solomon to the darkest, most unreachable depths of her old life. And what courage and heartbreaking effort that had taken. But now, here was a young man who could change all that. Was it coincidence, his being in Venice? Surely it had to be. Yet what were the chances of that happening?

Questions tumbled through her head, but now wasn't the time to deal with them. Perhaps irritated with her odd behaviour, Chiara had taken Ishmael over to one of the windows. Despite the cold, she'd opened it so the two of them could stand on the balcony overlooking the narrow *rio*. She began pointing out the landmarks across the water on the Giudecca where lights twinkled invitingly in the darkness. 'That's the Rendentore,' Chiara was explaining, 'a church built by Palladio to celebrate the end of the plague in 1576. Redentore means redeemer. And over there,' she said, warming to her theme and glancing up at Ishmael, 'is the Mulino Stucky.' Lydia caught the soft, lost smile on Chiara's face and the dazzling one Ishmael gave her in return. Almost imperceptibly, the gap closed between them.

Lydia left them to their mutual absorption and hobbled out to the kitchen. She needed time alone. Time to think what the consequences of this evening might be.

'Lydia,' whispered Chiara, 'what on earth's the matter with you? Don't you like him?' Chiara had now joined Lydia in the kitchen, giving Ishmael some privacy to take a call on his mobile.

'Don't be silly, I like him very much. He's an engaging young man.'

'So why all the dramatics earlier? As he said himself, you looked like you'd seen a ghost.'

Lydia had often stretched or skirted round the truth when she thought the occasion warranted it, but never had she told a full-blown lie to Chiara. Now, though, she wanted to lie until she was blue in the face. 'He reminds me of someone I used to know,' she said. 'That's all.'

'Really? Who?'

'Oh, just someone.'

'Is that why you asked what his surname was? To see if there was a connection?'

'My, you are sharp today.'

Chiara threw her arms in the air. 'Sharp? *Stai scherzando!* You're kidding! A deaf, one-eyed drunk would have noticed your reaction. I can't begin to think what Ishmael must have thought of you.'

'I doubt he noticed. He's much more interested in you than—'

'Sorry about that.'

They both spun round to see Ishmael standing in the doorway; he was slipping his mobile into his pocket. 'It was my mother,' he said, 'checking that I was wearing clean underpants.'

Once again the unexpected sight of him caused Lydia a moment's alarm. She laughed politely at his joke but was concerned by the frown on Chiara's face.

'*Ti vedrò più tardi*,' Chiara muttered under her breath, with more than a hint of Wait-till-I-get-you-home to her tone. '*Parleremo*.' To Ishmael, in English, she said, 'Ready?'

'*Sì*,' he replied. 'But I wish you'd speak to me in Italian. It's why I'm here, don't forget.'

From the sitting room window, Lydia watched Chiara and Ishmael walk along the *fondamenta* in the direction of the Zattere. They'd known one another for no more than a few days, but already she could see by the way they shared their umbrella, their heads inclined towards each other, their pace evenly matched and Ishmael's hand at the small of Chiara's back, that they looked like a couple who'd been together for some time. There was a comfortable ease about them that Lydia knew all too well. She sighed and leaned her forehead against the cold glass. Why was he here? What had brought him to Venice? There were any number of language schools in Italy he could have attended; what was so special about the institute in Campo Santa Margherita?

She drew the curtains and chided herself for her paranoia. It was obvious why he'd come here. Venice was one of the most beautiful places in the world. Millions of visitors descended on the small city every year, far outnumbering its 62,000 inhabitants. For all she knew, Noah may well have been one of these tourists; she could have passed him in a *calle* and never known it. She shook her head. Inconceivable. She would have known he was there. She would have felt his presence as keenly as a pinprick.

Standing in the middle of the room, she wondered what to do next. What would best settle and calm her mind? Some work?

Who was she fooling? How could she contemplate working when she had just met Noah's son?

It was risky, given the state of her ankle, but unable to stop herself, she lifted the latch on the door of the store cupboard in the hall and hauled an aluminium stepladder out from the junk. She hobbled slowly to her bedroom, positioned the ladder in front of the built-in wardrobes, and, letting her crutch drop to the floor, made her way painfully up the steps.

Steely determination finally got her to the top, and perspiring and aching, she rewarded herself with a short rest, carefully shifting her balance so as not to put too much strain on her ankle. There were three locker-style cupboards in all, and opening the middle one she prayed that she'd made the right choice, that her memory hadn't failed her. She had to stretch to reach all the way inside the cupboard, and her hands fumbling blindly, she pushed aside a plethora of old handbags, scarves, hats, belts, coat hangers, and unwanted gifts of table linen. Finally her fingers touched what she was hunting for.

With the wooden box tucked under her arm, she descended the stepladder with excruciating care. She was exhausted when she reached the bottom and sat gratefully on the edge of the bed, the olive wood box on her lap. When she'd caught her breath, she ran her hands over its carved surface, released the two small brass clasps and lifted the lid; it swung smoothly on its hinges.

She removed the protective layer of discoloured tissue paper and put it to one side. The first item she picked out was a cheap tarnished powder compact. She pressed the catch on it at the front and the top flipped open. It was more than forty years old but the smell that escaped was instantly evocative of Lydia's mother. She snapped it shut and moved on to the next item, a long thin jewellery case covered in faded dark blue velvet. Inside, nestling in the folds of white silk, was a necklace, a single pearl hanging like a tear from a delicate silver chain. Next was a slim leatherbound book of poetry – *The Complete Works of Christina Rossetti*. All that now remained in the wooden box was a ripped and battered manila envelope. She put the box on the bed and tipped the contents of the envelope onto her lap.

The first photograph she looked at was a small black and white snap of her parents. Her mother was wearing a pair of white-framed Jackie Onassis-style sunglasses and her hair was backcombed to resemble a cloud of candyfloss. Her father was in his shirtsleeves and had one arm round his wife's belted waist.

The next photo was of Lydia sitting on a doorstep. For such a young child she had surprisingly thick, bushy hair and a pair of dark eyebrows that almost met in the middle. With her lips pressed tightly together, her chin jutting forward as she squinted into the lens, her face was stormy. She was an odd-looking child, the kind of child people didn't always warm to. Cradled in her arms was a much prettier little girl: Lydia's baby sister, Valerie. Valerie was too busy chewing on the foot of a doll that was almost the same size as her to be concerned about the camera.

The remaining photographs were in colour, the smaller of the two showing a pair of grinning teenagers – Lydia and Noah – larking about for the camera. They were in a kitchen, wearing saucepans on their heads.

Lastly there was a picture of Noah on his own and of all the photographs, this was the one in the worst condition. Every crease and rip reminded Lydia that for a while she hadn't let it out of her sight; she had carried it with her everywhere she went, tucked inside a pocket, or sometimes hidden within her bra for fear of losing it. She turned it over. The ink was faded, but she could still make out the shape of a heart and the single word written within it: Noah. She turned it over again and tilted the photograph to catch the light so she could see it more clearly. And yes, her memory hadn't played a trick on her; Ishmael's face could be perfectly superimposed on Noah's. She stared at the fineness of his features, the introspective intensity of his gaze, the suggestion of a smile concealed beneath the solemnity of his expression. She recalled the day she'd taken the photo. A day, like so many, when they had sworn nothing would ever part them.

But part they did.

One by one she spread the pictures out on the bed, and though it had been a golden rule never to do so, she allowed herself to think of all that she had lost. When tempted to do this in the past, knowing that it would only leave her feeling hollow and bereft, she had resisted the urge by bringing to mind everything she had gained instead – Marcello and Chiara, and the love and support of the Scalatore family. She was lucky, she always reminded herself.

But today was different. Today the golden rule was irrelevant. She felt like the game was up and she could finally give in to the profound sense of loss that had haunted her for most of her adult life. But mixed in with the pain was a new emotion – the cruel sting of jealousy and betrayal. Noah had led a life without her. He had married. He had had a son. All without her. She was being irrational, she knew. What else was he supposed to have done?

Tears filled her eyes and the photographs swam and became blurred. Eventually she could no longer see them. Crying without restraint, she lay on the bed and pressed her face into the bedspread.

The sound of the intercom buzzing had her jumping off the bed. Too late she remembered her ankle and let out a loud yelp as a bolt of pain ripped through her.

The intercom buzzed again. She wiped her face with her hands and reached for her crutch to go and see who it was.

When she heard Fabio's cheerful voice asking if he could come up, she panicked. 'It's not really convenient at the moment,' she said into the intercom, not wanting to be seen by anyone right now, 'I'm not feeling very well.'

'*Davvero?*' he said. 'I've just bumped into Chiara and she never said anything.'

'It's nothing serious.'

'In that case, and if it's not contagious, let me in and I'll pamper you for a couple of hours. I'm at a loose end; Paolo's deserted me and gone to Milan.'

Lydia knew it was useless to argue with Fabio.

'*Dio mio!*' he exclaimed, after he'd bounded up the four flights of stairs and she'd opened the door to him. 'You do look ill.' And then, '*Cara*, you've been crying, haven't you? What's wrong? What's happened?'

She opened her mouth to make a rush of denials, but all that came out was a strangled cry. Fresh tears were a blink away. She took a step back and instantly regretted it. Her ankle was throbbing with renewed vigour.

Without another word, in one impressive movement, Fabio lifted her off the floor and carried her through to the living room and set her gently on the sofa. He shrugged off his coat, tossed it onto a chair and knelt beside her.

'Of all the people to find me like this,' she said, 'why did it have to be you, Fabio? If it was anyone else, I'd be able to pull the wool over their eyes.'

'I think you rate your ability as an actress just a little too highly,' he said with a smile. 'Now while I decide what my line of attack will be to get to the bottom of what's upset you, why don't you tell me who the good-looking *ragazzo* is I just met with Chiara. Where's he sprung from? They make a handsome couple, don't you think?'

The connection was too great and once more, much to Lydia's mortification, she couldn't hold back the tears any longer. Aware that Fabio was looking helplessly around for a box of tissues, she said, 'My bedroom, next to the bed.'

It was only when he'd left the room that she realized her mistake: she stopped crying in an instant, picturing her bedroom – the open cupboard, the stepladder ... the photographs.

When he reappeared, he had a box of Kleenex in one hand and the photographs in the other. He passed her the tissues and while she blew her nose, he laid out the photographs on the coffee table in front of them as if he were about to play a game of patience. 'You should never have been on that stepladder,' he said, 'you could have hurt yourself.'

'I agree; it was very silly of me.'

'But I must say you look *bellissima* wearing the saucepan.' He smiled. Then pointed to the picture of Lydia holding Valerie. 'And is this you with the *piccolina*?'

She nodded.

'And these people?'

'My parents.'

'And if I didn't know better,' he said, 'I'd say this was the handsome *ragazzo* I've just been talking to with Chiara.' He turned and looked at her. 'You don't have to tell me if you don't want to, but is he your son? A child you've never told us about?'

She almost laughed. 'No! But I strongly suspect,' she indicated the picture of Noah, 'that he's the father of Chiara's new friend.'

'Without a doubt,' Fabio said. 'Did he mean something to you a long time ago?'

Lydia hesitated before replying. Did she really want this conversation to go any further? Or was it too late? In her heart she knew it was. Ishmael Solomon's presence here in Venice was a catalyst for something she couldn't stop. To lie now to Fabio would be plain stupid. 'Yes,' Lydia said. 'He meant everything to me. We thought we'd always be together.'

'What went wrong? Or was it just a case of two young sweethearts growing up and drifting apart?'

'Something like that.' It was the best answer she could give. To tell the truth was far too complicated. Moreover, even after all this time, she still felt that it was better that only she and Noah were the keepers of that particular truth. But what if Ishmael and Chiara became seriously involved? What then? Could Lydia go on pretending that there was no history between Ishmael's father and herself? It would never work, because once it came out that she had deliberately concealed her relationship with Noah, Chiara would want to know what she had been hiding.

'Lydia,' Fabio said, 'you know I'd never force you to do anything against your will, but Marcello made me promise that if anything ever happened to him I would always be more than just a brother-in-law to you.'

'And you are. You've been the best friend I could have wished for.'

He suddenly looked serious. 'Marcello told me something I've never forgotten. He said he thought you'd spent all your life carrying an impossible burden. My brother was right, wasn't he? And it has something to do with these photographs you've kept hidden away all the time I've known you. Why don't you tell me what that burden is? That way I'd know I'd honoured my brother's wishes to take good care of you.'

That's not fair! Lydia wanted to scream. You can't use Marcello like that. All the same, she felt a chink in her resolve. And then another. Dear sweet Marcello. So caring and intuitive. 'I'm sorry, Fabio,' she rallied, 'I wouldn't know how to. I wouldn't even know where to start. It's such a long story.'

'I disagree. I think you know exactly where to start; you've probably written every word of it in your head a million times over.'

Lydia looked around her, comparing the elegant charm of her home here with its silk damask wall coverings, antique furniture and ornate Murano glass chandeliers to the stark, loveless house in which she'd grown up, the very walls of which had been permeated with hatred and tension. She shivered, feeling the chill as if she were back there now.

She felt Fabio's hand on her arm and knew that if there was one person in the world she could trust, it was him.

THEN

Chapter Five

Lydia always blamed herself. If she hadn't pestered her mother for that ventriloquist's dummy none of it would have happened.

It all started when Diane Dixon's parents had given her one for being 'brave' when she'd had her tonsils out. Lydia didn't know what all the fuss was about – you were fast asleep when the doctor removed your tonsils and when you woke up you were allowed to eat nothing but ice-cream. What was so brave about that? When Diane was well enough to return to school, she brought the dummy in with her and they'd all crowded round to take a look at it. Its eyes moved from side to side and its mouth clunked open and shut with a jerky snap, depending on how well you operated the lever hidden in its back. Dressed in a smart red suit with a black bow tie and shiny black shoes, its legs and arms dangled loosely like lanky sausages from its hard body. Lydia didn't think Diane did the voice very well, especially when she tried to make it sing that silly song by The Beatles, something about them all living in a yellow submarine – but maybe that was because Diane didn't have her tonsils any more. Lydia thought she could do a much better job.

With her ninth birthday coming up, Lydia got to work on her mother, dropping hints and reminders whenever she could, saying how she'd give anything in the whole wide world to have a ventriloquist's dummy just like Diane Dixon's. Every time they went shopping she would make a point of lingering in front of the toyshop where Diane had said her parents had bought the dummy, and where there was one actually displayed in the window, propped up in a box padded with tissue paper. She pointed it out to her mother and from then on whenever they passed the toyshop she would make sure there was always a reason to hang about and look in the window. She would suddenly notice that her shoelace needed tying, or that her sagging socks needed pulling up, and while she was crouched on the pavement she would will her mother to see the dummy looking out at them through the glass, its eyes wide and staring, just begging to be taken home with them.

Home now was a flat in Mr Ridley's house. Lydia didn't like Mr Ridley; he had a weird way of looking at her mother, like he was hungry. He was always licking his lips. He came upstairs to their flat nearly every day saying that he had to make sure everything worked. 'There!' he'd say, as he fiddled with the bath tap. 'I guessed as much: it needs a new washer.' He seemed very concerned that nothing should ever leak – gas or water – and regularly checked for anything that might be faulty. He said he would be failing in his duty as a landlord if he didn't take good care of his tenants. 'And your mother's a very special tenant,' he told Lydia one day when Mum was at the doctor's and Mr Ridley had offered to watch Lydia and her sister while she was gone. 'It's not right that your mum's all alone,' he said, poking around at the back of the electric fire in the lounge, his enormous bottom sticking up in the air.

'She's not alone,' Lydia said indignantly, tempted to give him a kick up the bum, 'she's got me and Valerie.'

'Children are all very well, but what she needs is a man.'

It was when Mr Ridley – Creepy-Ridley, as Lydia secretly called him – said things like that, that she wished her father was still alive. Before he died they'd lived in a pretty house with a garden and a small fishpond which one day her father had covered with green netting. 'We don't want your baby sister falling in, do we?' he said.

'Didn't you worry that I might fall in when I was a

baby?' Lydia had asked him. Babies got all the attention, she was fast learning.

'We didn't live here when you were a baby.'

Babies were dull, in Lydia's opinion. Valerie did nothing more exciting than lie in her cot making funny squawking noises when she wanted her bottle. It was difficult to imagine her getting down the stairs and out to the garden and fishpond when she couldn't even crawl to the end of her cot. Everyone had told Lydia it would be fun having a baby sister. Well, it wasn't.

Their father was killed when a lorry drove into him and knocked him off his motorbike on his way to work. It was raining and the lorry driver said he hadn't seen him, and when he did, it was too late. Lydia had overheard the policewoman telling her mother all this from the top of the stairs. 'Is there anyone who could be with you, Mrs Turner?'

'No,' was her mother's faint reply. 'There's no one.'

It had never seemed odd to Lydia that her parents didn't have any friends or family, although she had once questioned her mother's insistence that they weren't to get too friendly with their neighbours. According to Mum, the last thing they needed was a street of busybodies knocking on the door every two minutes scrounging a bowl of sugar.

'Why would they ask for sugar?' Lydia had wanted to know. 'Why not something nicer, like biscuits or crisps?'

'It doesn't matter what they're asking for, it's so they can poke their noses into our business.'

'Your mum's a very private person,' Lydia's father had often told her, usually when she'd asked if a friend could come to play. He explained that it was because Mum had grown up in an orphanage. Her parents both died when she was very young and being constantly surrounded by other people had made her learn to keep herself to herself. 'Your mum doesn't like a lot of fuss, love.'

Dad had parents but Lydia had never even seen a photograph of them. For some reason Dad hadn't spoken to them since he'd married Mum.

The day after Dad died, the telephone rang and from her permanent position at the top of the stairs – where she could listen out for Valerie in her cot and her mother crying downstairs – Lydia listened to the one-sided conversation. To begin with Mum's voice was trembling with little choking sounds, but then suddenly she became cross, her words coming out loud and snappy. 'I just hope you're happy now. You wished your son dead when he married me, and now he is!' The phone was banged down hard.

Happy. Why would anyone be happy that Dad was dead?

A few days later, for the first time ever, Lydia and Valerie got to go inside a neighbour's house. It was the day of Dad's funeral and Mum had said Lydia and her sister couldn't go with her, and that Mrs Marsh next door had offered to look after them. Mrs Marsh was nice. After she'd settled Valerie in her pram outside by the back door for some fresh air, she tied a frilly apron around her waist and told Lydia they were going to do some baking. She didn't seem at all the kind of person Mum had warned her about, the sort of scrounging, nosy parker who would want to know everything about them.

Lydia was disappointed when Mum arrived to take her and Valerie home: Mrs Marsh had just sat her down at the kitchen table with a cup of milky tea and an iced fairy cake. Mrs Marsh offered Mum a cup of tea but Mum shook her head. 'Well, how about taking some of these cakes with you?' Mrs Marsh asked.

'No thank you.' Mum's voice was clipped and short.

'If there's anything else I can ever do, you've only got to ask.'

'We'll be fine, thank you.'

'Suit yourself.' Now Mrs Marsh's voice sounded like Mum's.

From then on Mum was never the same. She began staying in bed until gone lunchtime, leaving Lydia to feed and change Valerie. When she did come downstairs she would lie on the settee in her nightdress staring up at the ceiling.

Luckily it was the summer holidays and Lydia could take care of her sister. With each day that passed she hoped her mother would get better, but she didn't.

Lydia missed her father so much it hurt deep inside her, but she also missed her mother. She missed her kisses, even the messy ones that left red lipstick on her cheek. She missed her mother's singing and the way she used to spend hours in front of the mirror doing her hair. To try and make Mum feel better, Lydia would kneel on the floor next to the settee and stroke her limp, dry hands, whispering to her that everything would be all right soon.

One morning when Lydia was standing on a chair in the garden hanging out the nappies she'd just washed in the kitchen sink, she heard voices. They were coming from the other side of the fence, from Mrs Marsh's garden. Lydia could hear Mrs Marsh saying that things were definitely sliding at number ten. Another woman's voice said, 'The curtains are pulled across for most of the day. She's probably gone to pieces.'

'But will she ask for help? Not on your Nellie! She's a stuck-up madam, for sure. Thinks she's so much better than the rest of us. It's the children I feel sorry for.'

'She was quick enough to leave them with you for the funeral, wasn't she?'

Lydia hurriedly finished pegging the last of Valerie's nappies on the line, but when she stepped down from the chair she saw that some of them were still dirty. Torn between needing clean, dry ones for Valerie, and giving something else to the neighbours to gossip about, she yanked the worst ones off the line and carried the chair back inside the house. She threw the nappies into the sink to wash again later and after making her mother a cup of tea in the hope it would encourage her to get out of bed, she went upstairs. Valerie was awake in her room and gurgling noisily like a bath emptying, but her mother was still asleep.

'I've brought you some tea, Mum,' Lydia said, putting the cup and saucer on the cluttered, dusty bedside table.

Her mother stirred but didn't open her eyes. Lydia was about to pull back the curtains and let some light in when she changed her mind. Instead she tiptoed over to the dressing table and, holding her breath, she pulled out her mother's purse from her handbag. Very quietly she opened it and took what she hoped would be enough.

Half an hour later, with Valerie sitting up in the pram with a crumbling pink wafer biscuit in her chubby hand, they set off for the shop. The pram was large and bouncy and Lydia could only just see over the top of it. Dad had always been telling her to eat more so that she'd grow big and strong.

She'd come top in her class for arithmetic at the end of term and so she had no trouble adding up the cost of things at the corner shop – some Cow and Gate milk powder for Valerie, a tin of Spam, a packet of Smash, a loaf of Mother's Pride, a pot of jam and a packet of strawberry-flavoured Angel Delight. She hovered by the bottles of drink but decided against a bottle of Tizer. Mum only let her have that on special occasions.

Mr Morris rang up the items on the till and placed them in the red string shopping bag Lydia had brought with her. 'All alone?' he asked after she'd handed over the money and was putting the shopping in the wire tray under the pram.

'No. My mother's at the post office.' The lie slid off her tongue like butter off hot toast.

'Give her my best wishes,' he said, and holding the door open for Lydia, added, 'and tell her I was sorry to hear about your dad.'

Lydia manoeuvred the pram out onto the street and was just thinking how men were always nicer to her mother than women were, when she realized she was almost level with the post office. She slowed her speed and, glancing back over her shoulder, she saw Mr Morris still standing at the door of his shop. She stopped the pram and made a conscious effort to look as if she was waiting for her mother.

There were many more days like that. They were the easy ones. By the start of the new autumn term, they were no longer living at number ten Larch Road. It was something to do with money. Just as Lydia had learned that babies got all the attention, she was now learning that money was the key to everything.

Their new home was Flat A, sixty-four Appleby Avenue. Number sixty-four was a large semi-detached house with a paved garden to the front and back, and the owner, Mr Ridley, had turned the upstairs part of the house into a flat. The day they moved in, he offered to help carry what little furniture they had upstairs. Lydia was so used to hearing her mother say, 'No thank you, we can manage on our own,' she was surprised to see her mother smile and say, 'Thank you, that's very kind of you.'

It didn't take them long to unpack; they had so little. Valerie's cot hadn't made the move with them and Lydia had to share her bed with her sister now, top and tail style. Even the big old pram that had been Mum's pride and joy had been sold and replaced with a second-hand pushchair that stank of sick until Lydia scrubbed it clean with disinfectant. Now it smelled like the toilets at school.

Back at school, everyone treated her differently. She heard them whispering about her in the dinner queue. Her best friend, Jackie, had also moved during the holidays, but to somewhere a long way away. She hadn't written to Lydia as she'd promised. There was no one to play with during break time and no one to talk to about what had happened during the summer. Instead she wrote it all out for their new teacher, Miss Flint, after she told the class that the best way for her to get to know them was to hear all about what they'd got up to during the holiday. So very carefully, as they'd been instructed, Lydia put that day's date – 4 September 1968 – at the top of the page of her brand new exercise book and didn't stop writing until Miss Flint told them to. But when it was Lydia's turn to go up to the front of the class and read out her work, Miss Flint's face turned red. 'Thank you, Lydia,' she interrupted, even though Lydia had only read a tiny bit of what she'd written. 'That was ... yes, that was ... Goodness. Perhaps you'd like to sit down.'

The subject of money was seldom far from Lydia's thoughts. This was mainly down to her mother constantly reminding her that they didn't have any. 'Our situation has changed,' was a frequent remark, along with, 'We're poor now, Lydia, so please don't even think of asking me for anything trivial.' Bang went the new shoes Lydia desperately needed as well as the school trip to the swimming baths. 'Maybe school will let me go for free if we tell them we can't afford to pay for it,' Lydia had suggested. She received a sharp slap for her comment and was told that no one was to know they had no money. With what she thought was a flash of helpful brilliance, Lydia's next suggestion was: 'I know what the answer is! Why don't you try getting a job?' She was clearly missing something because her mother took another swipe at her.

It couldn't have been such a daft idea because shortly afterwards her mother announced that she'd found herself a job. The following Monday she would start work at the local off-licence. It was owned by a man called Mr Russell and Mum would have to work there from six o'clock until ten. 'Who's going to look after us while you're not here?' Lydia had asked.

'You're a big girl, Lydia; you don't need anyone looking after you.'

'I'm only eight.'

'You'll be nine in a few months' time. And anyway, Mr Ridley will be downstairs if there's a problem.'

Creepy-Ridley had dirty fingernails and was always running them through his greasy, dandruff-speckled hair. She wrinkled her nose at the thought of him. Her mother said, 'You could at least look pleased for me. After all, it was your idea for me to get a job.'

To begin with it was great with Mum going out to work. There were no more comments about being poor. No more cuffs around the ear. And best of all, Mum brought home the occasional bottle of Tizer and packets of salted peanuts. She was looking much more like her old self, too. Her hair was done nicely and she'd started wearing perfume and make-up again, regularly opening and shutting her powder compact with a businesslike click. They even had a small turkey for Christmas and Lydia was allowed to decorate the plastic tree all on her own.

But then in the New Year, at the end of January 1969, it all went wrong. Lydia had just put Valerie to bed when she heard the front door slamming downstairs. She went to see what was going on. Peering over the banister, she saw Mum leaning back against the front door and then Creepy-Ridley appeared in the hall. Mum was crying.

'What's the matter, Bonnie?' Creepy-Ridley asked. Lydia hated it when he called Mum by her Christian name; it didn't seem right.

'I've been sacked.'

'Why?' Creepy-Ridley was now standing next to Mum.

Her crying got louder and Creepy-Ridley moved closer still. 'Women can be so spiteful,' she spluttered through her tears. 'Mr Russell's wife had no right saying those things to me. As if I'd want her husband! And now I won't be able to pay you this week's rent.'

Creepy-Ridley put his hand on Mum's arm. 'Now don't you go worrying your pretty head over a little thing like that. I'm sure we can come to some other arrangement.'

Chapter Six

Once again they were officially poor. Hardly a day passed without Mum burying her head in her hands and saying how shameful it was to be on the dole. 'Being on the dole' was a new phrase to Lydia and she couldn't understand what the fuss was all about. If someone was prepared to give Mum money for free, surely that was a good thing? Her mother was insistent that no one should ever know that she had to go to the Labour Exchange and stand in line with a lot of other people and wait patiently to be given a cheque which she could then exchange for real money at the post office so she could buy that week's food. When it was a dole day, she always wore her big sunglasses and a chiffon scarf tied under her chin to cover her hair.

Mum was constantly worried about what others thought of her. Every night she made Lydia spend twenty minutes polishing her school shoes. Apparently you could tell a lot from someone's shoes. Especially if they weren't polished. Mum said people would think she didn't care about Lydia if she couldn't see her face in them. Lydia would have preferred a dirty, scuffed pair of shoes that fitted her properly to the gleaming pair that pinched and squashed her toes, but she kept her head down and her hand busy with the polishing brush.

Occasionally Mum took time out from worrying about the state of Lydia's shoes and lay in bed claiming she couldn't get up because the sleeping pills the doctor had given her made her feel too groggy. And if she wasn't groggy from the pills, she had what she called one of her thundery headaches coming on. Then one day she started to smell different. Whenever Lydia got close to her mother, her breath reminded Lydia of happier times, when there was something special to celebrate, and Mum used to have a glass of sherry and Dad always had what he called a tot of whiskey. But what was Mum celebrating on her own when Lydia was at school?

It did at least mean that her mother was often in a better mood. When it was a Good Mood Day, Lydia would come home from school to be given a handful of loose change and told to run down to the chip shop for their tea. Other treats began creeping into their lives, like Arctic roll for pudding, or trips to the sweet shop where Lydia could spend as long as she liked choosing from the glass jars of pink shrimps, white sugar mice, traffic light gobstoppers and mint humbugs. She was allowed to stay up late too, so long as she was quiet while Mum listened to her Engelbert Humperdinck records – 'Please Release Me', 'There Goes My Everything', and 'The Last Waltz' played over and over. Sometimes, if Mum was in a really happy mood, she would make Lydia dance with her, twirling her round the small room, not caring about the furniture and saying that very soon their uppsy-downsy life would all be sorted out. She would hug and kiss Lydia goodnight, reassuring her that their luck was about to change. With her mother's sweet sherry breath making Lydia's eyes water, she wanted desperately to believe that this was true.

It was during a week of late-night Engelbert Humperdinck sessions that Lydia decided she wasn't getting anywhere with her hints about the ventriloquist's dummy. Her birthday was only a few days away; the time had come for her to catch her mother in one of her 'good moods' and ask her outright for the present. Now seemed as good a moment as any – Mum had just been downstairs to the dustbin with an empty bottle and she was now coming in to kiss Lydia and Valerie goodnight. Humming to herself, she sat down heavily on the bed, not noticing that she was crushing Lydia's feet. Lydia tried to slide her feet out from under her mother's bottom without her noticing. 'Mum, you know it's my birthday on Friday? Well, I was just wondering if you'd remembered what it was I said I really, *really* wanted.'

She must have totally misjudged her mother's mood because suddenly Mum was slumped forward, her head in her hands and crying. 'How can you ask for a present when we don't have any money?' she cried. 'How can you be so selfish?'

'But I thought we had money. I thought the dole money—'

'It's not enough!' her mother shouted at her. She then jumped off the bed, her arms wrapped around herself. 'And if you really want to know, there's nothing left in my purse and there won't be any more until next week.' She shuddered and sniffed.

Lydia wriggled her toes, confused. Where was all the money going? At the other end of the bed, sensing the change in atmosphere, Valerie had also started to cry.

Mum whipped round on Lydia. 'Now see what you've done!'

Lydia was horrified. Was she selfish? Was it wrong of her to want a present for her birthday?

An hour later when Valerie was sleeping soundly, Lydia heard the bedroom door creak open: light flooded in. 'Are you awake, Lydia?'

Lydia closed her eyes and lay very still.

'Lydia?'

She opened her eyes. Maybe her mother was going to apologize and say that somehow she'd find the money for a present. 'Yes, Mum?' she whispered.

Her mother came in and stood next to the bed. 'Don't be cross with me,' she said. Her voice was thin and wobbly. 'You know how difficult it is for me. Why don't we pretend your birthday's next month? I'll save up some money and buy you whatever you want. How does that sound?'

Lydia said nothing. She simply stared at her mother and thought of all those sherry bottles rattling around in the dustbin downstairs.

The next day when Lydia was walking home from school she stopped to look in the window of the toy shop. Her heart sank. The ventriloquist's dummy had gone. It had been there in the morning, but now in its place was an enormous blonde-haired doll in a shiny pink dress with a yellow sash tied around its waist.

Lydia pushed open the door, setting off the tinkling bell, and went inside. 'Do you have any more ventriloquist's dummies?' she asked the woman behind the counter.

'I'm afraid not. I sold the last one this afternoon. I was glad to see it go, to be honest. We had it in the window gathering dust for weeks. What about a nice dolly?'

A nice dolly? Dolls were for babies! Disgusted that she'd been mistaken for a baby, and furious that there was no hope now of her having what she wanted for her birthday, Lydia stomped home, her satchel banging against her hip. She was about to dig under her school shirt for the door key she wore round her neck on a piece of string, when she saw the dustbins beneath Creepy-Ridley's front window. She glanced up at the top window, then back to the dustbin.

Minutes passed.

Then, throwing her satchel to the ground, she lifted off the lid of their bin, the one with '64a' painted on it. The rubbish stank, but she didn't care. She rummaged through it until she had everything she wanted and when she was finished, she put the lid back on the bin and let herself into the house. From the other side of Creepy-Ridley's door she could hear him speaking on the telephone.

Upstairs, Valerie was asleep on the settee, her thumb tucked inside her mouth, her tongue and cheeks moving rhythmically.

'Is that you, Lydia?' The question coincided with the closing of a cupboard door. With new understanding, Lydia recognized it as a guilty sound and one she'd heard for several months now every afternoon when she'd come home from school.

Her mother appeared in the doorway of the lounge, one hand smoothing her hair, the other covering her mouth. 'How was school today?' she asked.

'I want to show you something,' Lydia said.

'Oh, something you made at school?'

'No. Come with me. It's downstairs.'

'How mysterious you are. Is it a surprise for me?'

Just you wait, Lydia thought nastily. She opened the front door and stepped outside ahead of her mother. She wanted to be able to look back and see the expression on her face. 'There,' she said, 'that's the reason you won't let me have my birthday on the proper day.'

Her mother gasped, then made a strange whimpering sound. But Lydia ignored her. Months and months of keeping her feelings to herself, of missing Dad, and of not saying anything in case she upset her mother, suddenly exploded inside her. 'That's why you wouldn't buy me the only present I ever really wanted,' she screamed. 'I hate you and I wish it was you who'd died and not Dad!' She kicked out at the row of sherry bottles she'd carefully lined up and sent them flying; three of them crashed against the brick wall, and the rest toppled and spun on their sides.

For a split second she was frightened at what she'd said and done. She felt her stomach drop to her knees. As she looked at her mother's shocked face, a tremor ran through her and her breath came out with a shudder. But there was no undoing what had happened and all she could think to do was to run; run from that look on her mother's face. She took to her heels and sprinted down the road. She didn't know where she was going, only that she could never go home again. Never! With tears nearly blinding her, she felt the pain of bottling up all the hurt of wanting Dad to be alive again. Why did he have to die?

She did go home, though, when it got dark and started to rain and her rumbling tummy wouldn't stop reminding her that she hadn't had any tea. She didn't like the way

48

people were staring at her either, probably wondering why she was out so late.

She quietly closed the front door behind her and bumped straight into Creepy-Ridley coming down the stairs. He was smirking and hitching up his trousers. He looked very pleased with himself. He'd probably been fixing something in the flat again. 'Like a bad penny you've turned up, then?' he said.

Mum was already in her nightdress and shabby old candlewick dressing gown when Lydia let herself in. Funny, Mum didn't usually get ready for bed this early. She was shredding a tissue, letting the pieces drop onto the carpet at her feet. Once again Lydia felt guilty at what she'd done. 'I'm sorry, Mum,' she said.

'So am I,' her mother said tightly. 'More sorry than you'll ever know. I just hope that one day you'll realize what I've done for you and understand how hard it's been for me.'

It's always about her, Lydia thought when she was lying safe and warm in bed with Valerie. Why didn't her mother ever think that it was difficult for her too?

On the morning of her ninth birthday, despite knowing the day wouldn't be any more special than any other, Lydia woke with a sense of anticipation. She couldn't help herself. It was habit. Dad had always made such a big thing of birthdays; he said they were something to enjoy and celebrate. Thinking of her father made her instantly sad. How different their lives were since her last birthday when she'd been eight and Val wasn't yet two. Dad had been alive then and they were living in their lovely house. Everything had been lovely. Now everything was horrible.

Valerie was already out of bed and playing on the floor with Lydia's satchel, the contents of which now lay scattered over the small threadbare rug. She beamed proudly at Lydia, a pencil sticking out of her mouth. Lydia tried to look sternly back at her but found she couldn't. Not with Val smiling at her like that. She gathered everything together, put on her school uniform and took Valerie through to the kitchen where she sat her in her highchair. For once Mum could change Valerie's first nappy of the day. She would be glad when her sister was properly potty trained. She was sure she hadn't still been in nappies at this age. Within minutes Valerie was protesting, and as if sensing she was being used to get even with their mother, she started to wriggle and cry, her face puckered like an old lady's.

'Oh, all right,' Lydia relented. Ten minutes later, the soaking wet nappy had been replaced. Lydia hadn't been able to find any clean ones so she'd used a hand towel from the kitchen drawer. She wasn't bothered what Mum would say. If she couldn't get out of bed today of all days, then why should Lydia care about anything?

She'd just got Valerie settled back in her highchair and put two slices of bread under the grill when Mum shuffled into the kitchen. She wasn't dressed, but in her hands was a large, badly wrapped box; there was a gap on one side where the paper edges didn't quite meet. 'Happy birthday, Lydia,' she said.

Lydia didn't know what to say. Perhaps she was dreaming. Any minute she would wake and the day would begin again. Yet she knew she wasn't dreaming and what's more, she was sure she knew what was in the box. She would know its shape and size anywhere. She felt her face burn with shame and regret. How could she have doubted her mother? How could she have been so mean to her?

'Don't you want it?' prompted her mother.

'I thought we didn't have any money,' Lydia murmured awkwardly.

After a pause, during which Lydia noticed her mother was looking anywhere but at her, she said, 'You have Mr Ridley to thank. He … gave me the money.' She held out the present. 'Take it, then.'

Lydia didn't hesitate. She didn't care where the money came from, so long as she finally had what she'd been wanting all this time. 'Thank you,' she said, remembering her manners. She placed the box on the table and picked at the sticky tape carefully. She never frantically ripped presents open; she liked to take her time, to make the moment last as long as possible.

But when she had the paper off she could have cried. It wasn't the ventriloquist's dummy – it was the ugly blonde-haired doll she'd seen in the toy shop window the other day.

From behind her came the smell of burning toast.

Chapter Seven

It was the summer school holidays and they'd spent the afternoon at Dad's grave. It was exactly a year since Dad had been knocked off his motorbike. Mum cried for most of the bus ride home and then went to bed. It was only six o'clock, but she said she had a headache. Which meant Lydia and Valerie had to be quiet. Valerie was three now and while she wasn't much of a talker – she was more of a watcher – she could kick up a right storm with the pots and pans in the kitchen. Turn your back for two seconds and she'd have the cupboard door open and would be crashing saucepan lids together like cymbals. So while their mother slept off her headache, Lydia didn't dare let Val out of her sight. She kept her occupied with jam sandwiches, a bath, and a very long bedtime story before she finally snuggled her down under the bedclothes with Belinda Bell. Belinda Bell was the ugly doll Mum had bought for Lydia on her birthday; Val had claimed it for herself and rarely went anywhere without it now.

Lydia didn't know how long she herself had been asleep in bed when she was woken by a noise. She sat up, expecting it to be Valerie wanting to be taken to the toilet. She peered into the darkness but at the other end of the bed, Valerie was sleeping soundly. No sooner had she put her head back down on the pillow when she heard the noise again. It was somebody singing. Mum? Lydia sat up again and listened properly. The singing stopped abruptly and the door opened. No light flooded in, but Lydia could just about make out her mother in the darkness. She was still dressed in the clothes she'd worn during the day, but for some strange reason she was wearing her sunglasses and chiffon scarf.

'I want you both to come with me,' her mother whispered urgently.

'Why? Where are you going?'

'Don't argue with me, Lydia. Not today of all days.'

When Lydia started reaching for her clothes on the floor by the side of the bed, her mother said, 'Don't bother getting dressed; there isn't time. Just put your shoes on and a cardigan over your nightie.'

At her mother's impatient insistence, Lydia then carried a still sleeping Valerie downstairs and tucked her into the pushchair with a blanket.

Her mother quietly unlocked the front door and they stepped outside. The road was quiet; nobody was about. In the light cast from the street lamp, Lydia looked at her watch to see what time it was: it was ten minutes past one in the morning.

'Come on,' her mother whispered. Her breath was sticky sweet. Sherry.

'But where are we going?'

'You'll see.'

'Is it far?'

Without answering her, her mother set off down the road, her high heels clicking in the silence. Lydia chased after her with the pushchair.

They'd been walking for what felt like for ever. A few cars had passed them and one had actually slowed down and the driver had stared hard at Lydia as she ran to keep up with her mother. They were now in an area that Lydia didn't recognize, but at least Mum wasn't walking so fast. Instead she was singing again and making herself angry because she kept getting the words to 'Please Release Me' all muddled up. Each time she got it wrong she would stamp her foot and go back to the beginning and start again. If Lydia hadn't been so jumpy with apprehension, she would have sung along to help her mother.

There were no street lights and the only houses were

set miles back from the road. It was difficult to see where they were going; several times she'd come close to losing Valerie in a ditch. Worry had now turned to fear. What if they got lost and couldn't find their way home?

When they came to what looked like a small bridge, Mum stopped unexpectedly. 'We're here.' She spoke as if suddenly everything made sense, and pushed through a gap in the hedge. Nearly losing control of the pushchair, Lydia found herself sliding down a slope, brambles and twigs scratching at her legs as she tried to stay upright. Oblivious to her daughter's struggle, her mother waited for her at the bottom of the slope. Dizzy with exhaustion, Lydia was close to tears. Why was her mother doing this? Why couldn't she be normal like other mothers?

'Please, Mum, can we sit down for a while and then go home?' she asked.

'Oh, do stop whingeing, Lydia. We're having an adventure. Don't you want an adventure you'll always remember?'

'Y-es,' she said uncertainly, 'but why here?'

'Don't you think it's pretty?'

Lydia looked around her doubtfully. 'It's too dark to see anything.'

Her mother started to poke the grass with her foot as though she was looking for something. 'Your father and I used to come here before you were born. We would lie here and stare up at the stars. Come on, let's do the same.'

Beginning to shiver with the cold, but glad of the chance to rest, Lydia lay in the cushiony, damp grass alongside her mother. Within seconds she felt herself drifting off to sleep, but then a hand was shaking her roughly. 'Look,' Mum said, sitting up beside her now. 'I bought you your favourite, a Marathon bar. It is your favourite, isn't it?'

'Yes, Mum,' Lydia said sleepily, 'it is. Thank you.'

'Aren't you going to eat it?'

Lydia unwrapped the slightly squashed chocolate bar and took a bite. She then offered it to her mother.

Her mother shook her head. 'It's for you. Eat it up.

When Valerie wakes, I've got some chocolate buttons for her.' She took off her sunglasses and worked at the knot of her scarf. She must have done it too tight because she gave up on it. Chewing on a mouthful of chocolate and peanuts and watching her mother staring up at the sky, Lydia wondered how she had managed to find her way here in the dark with those silly glasses on.

'Isn't the sky beautiful?' Mum's voice was suddenly soft. So was her face. Lydia thought how young and pretty she was. She wished that she might be as pretty one day. That people would turn and stare at her the way they did with Mum. Or the way they used to. Recently she'd noticed people often looked away. 'It's like it goes on for ever and ever,' Mum murmured, her face still turned up towards the sky. 'Your father used to tell me that if you have a problem, you shouldn't keep it to yourself; you should tell it to the skies. I want you to promise me something, Lydia.'

Lydia didn't like it when her mother asked her to make promises – they were usually impossible to keep.

'It's important that you remember this moment and what I'm about to say. You must promise you'll always look after your sister for me. Do you promise?'

With her eyelids feeling so heavy nothing in the world would keep them open, and the warm, dreamy sensation of sleep wrapping itself around her, Lydia murmured that of course she would take care of Val. It was an easy promise to keep. Hadn't she been doing exactly that ever since Dad died?

'And something else I want you to remember—'

But Lydia didn't hear what else she was supposed to remember. She was dreaming of Dad. He was carrying her off into the dark night sky, above the trees, over the roof tops and chimney pots, flying higher and higher. He was telling her everything would be all right now. 'Just tell it to the skies, Lydia, and everything will be all right.' It was good to be in his arms again. She felt so safe and happy.

*

Lydia read about it in the newspaper. Nobody knew that she had – they thought they'd hidden the papers – but she'd found one and had read it so many times she could have recited it from memory.

> A twenty-seven-year-old mother of two, not long since widowed, threw herself in front of a train whilst her children slept on the embankment.
>
> The train driver, a father of two children himself and from Crewe, who wishes to remain anonymous, said there was nothing he could do. 'There was no way I could avoid hitting her,' he said of the tragedy, which took place shortly before five a.m. and approximately two miles from Maywood station. 'I don't think I'll ever get over what happened,' he further added. 'It was horrific.'
>
> It is believed the woman, Mrs Bonnie Turner, of 64a Appleby Avenue, Maywood, had never recovered from the death of her husband, who died in a motorcycle accident a year ago. Neighbours claim that her mental state had been unbalanced for some time before she took her life.

Her mother would have hated for everyone to read about her this way. Lydia hated it too. But then there was so much for her to hate now. Like the people in the children's home who wouldn't listen when she told them she and Valerie didn't need to be there, that they could manage perfectly well on their own back at the flat. She had tried to explain to them that she was perfectly capable of taking care of her sister. But they kept saying she and Valerie couldn't live on their own, that it wasn't allowed; it was against the law. 'And what about school?' they asked. How would she go to school *and* look after Val? And who was going to pay the rent?

Sitting in the back of the car with Valerie and Belinda Bell on her lap – two women from the children's home in the front – Lydia stared out of the car window, watching the blurry scenery fly by. They were on their way to a place called Swallowsdale in Yorkshire. It was where Dad's parents lived and it was to be their new home. She had read stories about children losing their parents and going to live with complete strangers. They always ended up having exciting adventures.

She rammed her clenched fists against her eyes, remembering her mother's words: 'Don't you want an adventure you'll always remember?'

Chapter Eight

She was sure she had only slept for a few minutes but when Lydia opened her eyes, she awoke to a completely different world. They must have travelled an unimaginable distance. She had never seen anything like it. There was so much of it. Emptiness. Miles of it. It went on and on as far as she could see, nothing but sloping green fields criss-crossed with funny walls that didn't look as if they'd been made properly. They weren't made of bricks like normal walls; they were made of dirty grey stones. Some of the fields had sheep in them. She pointed them out to Valerie, but Valerie wasn't interested; she was clinging to Lydia, her warm, flushed face pushed against Lydia's neck, her mouth making a cool damp patch on her skin.

The road they were driving along kept on twisting this way and that. It went up and down too; it was a bit like that time Dad took her on a ride at the funfair. She'd been sick afterwards. She hoped she wouldn't be ill when they arrived at their grandparents' house.

She closed her eyes and listened to the two women talking in the front: one was telling the other they were almost there. Lydia always made a point of listening hard to other people's conversations now. It was the only way she could find out what was going on. She'd discovered that Dad's parents didn't really want to have Lydia and Valerie living with them. Well, join the club! Lydia didn't want to live with them either. Not if they were the kind of people who could be happy that Dad was dead. She fought the aching tightness in her throat. She would not cry. Not when she knew it would upset Valerie.

She opened her eyes and concentrated on looking at the passing scenery. It had changed. The fields were sort of grubby and patchy and the walls were tumbling down in places. It didn't look a friendly place. In the distance, crouched like a black cat in a hollow, she could see what looked like a town. The buildings all seemed to have been built higgledy-piggledy. Five tall, blackened chimneys puffed out smoke into a dreary grey sky. There was a church slap bang in the middle of the chimneys and its spire looked as though it should have been smoking too. Further into the distance, the ground rose up into a hill that seemed to watch over the town disapprovingly. Dotted across the hillside were clumps of trees and houses, and more of those funny walls. As the car dipped down towards the town, Lydia saw a sign on the side of the road: Swallowsdale.

They came to a stop in front of a house that stood at the end of a long row of terraced houses. Every one of them seemed to have been built with the same sooty stones the rickety walls in the fields had been made with. Hadn't they heard of bricks here? Behind the row of houses was a bump of a hill.

Lydia stared at the house they were parked in front of. It seemed to be bigger than all the others. A twitch of net curtain at one of the downstairs windows made Lydia's stomach churn.

'Well then,' said the woman in the front passenger seat in a stupidly jolly voice, 'here we are.' In the last couple of weeks Lydia had noticed that grown-ups had an irritating habit of stating the obvious when they were nervous and didn't know what else to say.

The front door was opened by a skinny woman with hair the colour of a grey, rainy day. It was scraped back from her pale face into a scruffy bun. Pin-prick eyes skimmed over Lydia and her sister. 'You're later than I was told to expect you,' she said, her hands crossed in front of her.

'Yes, we're sorry about that, Mrs Turner,' said the

woman who had driven them here. 'It took us longer than we thought it would.' She held out her hand. 'I'm Janet and this is my colleague, Deirdre. And of course, these are your grandchildren, Lydia and Valerie.'

Once more Lydia felt the pin-prick eyes skim over her and Val. Lydia suspected they were the kind of eyes that missed nothing.

They were shown through to the lounge. For a few moments no one seemed to know what to say, then Deirdre suggested that 'the girls' might like a drink of orange juice after the long journey.

Their grandmother pursed her lips. 'We don't throw money away on extravagances like orange juice in this house,' she said, 'not when the good Lord provided us with water to drink.'

'I'm sure water will be fine, Mrs Turner.'

Lydia caught the two women exchanging glances when they were left alone. As well as listening to grown-ups, Lydia now made it her business to watch them closely.

'Well then,' Janet said. 'This is nice, isn't it, Lydia? What do you think of your new home?'

Lydia looked round the gloomy room. Cold. Dull. Miserable. Plain. Those were the words that described it best. There was nothing nice to look at, not in this room anyway, just two brown upright armchairs either side of the fireplace, a small brown upright settee that Janet and Deirdre were sitting on and a glass-fronted bookcase that was almost empty. On top of this was a wooden cross and the largest book Lydia had ever seen. The floor was covered with a sludgy green carpet. There was no television in the room, no record player, no ornaments, no pictures. Nothing like the cheerful things Mum used to treasure – her red balloon glass vase, her picture of the gypsy woman playing the guitar, and her collection of Engelbert Humperdinck records. She wondered what these people did in the evening if they didn't watch the television. Without answering Janet's question, she said, 'What do I call them?'

'Who, Lydia?'

'Mr and Mrs Turner. My father's parents. My grand-parents.'

The two women exchanged another look. 'That's probably best sorted out between you and them after we've gone,' Deirdre said.

Lydia went over to the window. She lifted the net curtain and stared out at the small front garden. She hadn't noticed much about it between the car and the front door, but now she saw that everything was extremely neat and tidy. A thin border of blue and white flowers ran up either side of the short path. Two circular beds, each with red roses in them, were edged with orange marigolds. Here at least was some colour, she thought. She didn't know why, but the sight of it made her want to rush out there and stamp on every single flower, crushing the petals till there was nothing left of them.

Mr Turner – their grandfather – appeared within minutes of Janet and Deirdre leaving. After a brief conversation with his wife in the kitchen, he returned to the lounge where Lydia and Val had been told to wait.

He instructed Lydia to stand in front of him, and looming over her he stared down, examining her. Like his wife, he was grey-haired, but he wasn't anywhere near as thin as her. He was tall with big shoulders. He looked strong and powerful, like a giant. He had faded, unfriendly blue eyes and his hair, parted at the side, was oily and glued down close to his scalp. He didn't have a particularly big nose, but from where Lydia was standing, he had the biggest nostrils she had ever seen; great caverns of dark hairiness. How could such a horrible-looking man be her father's father? Dad had always had a smile on his face. He had been the kindest, funniest man she knew. This man was none of those things. He was cold. Cold as winter.

As his silent examination of her continued, she became conscious of her thick unbrushed hair, and her clothes that were rucked up from being in the car for so long. She suddenly remembered her shoes. Not daring to lower her eyes, she couldn't recall when she'd last polished them. Mum would have been furious with her.

Taking her by surprise, the man bent down and pushed his face almost into hers. 'You look just like your mother,' he announced. He spat out the word 'mother' like it would leave a nasty taste in his mouth if he let it stay there for a second longer. It took all of Lydia's willpower not to shrink back from him. 'It remains to be seen if you've inherited her ungodly ways as well,' he added, straightening up. He clicked his fingers and waved her away dismissively, then turned his attention to Valerie, who was cowering behind Belinda Bell on the settee.

He made no comment on Val's appearance other than to clear his throat and tell them tea would be ready soon.

Tea was poached fish, boiled potatoes and cabbage. No one spoke during the entire meal, other than at the start when their grandfather bowed his head and thanked God for the food on the table. Before now, Lydia had only ever heard grace said at school. A clock on the mantelpiece ticked loudly in the unnerving silence. The fish was chewy and bland – not like the lovely cod in batter Lydia used to fetch from the chip shop – and the potatoes were rock hard and covered in something that could have been grass cuttings. What was wrong with chips? Or Smash? Afraid to leave anything on her plate, Lydia forced it down, at the same time trying to help Valerie feed herself. But Val was having none of it. Wobbling on her cushioned seat – there was no highchair for her – she kept her mouth tightly shut, only to open it finally to whisper to Lydia that she needed the toilet.

When the ordeal of tea was over, their grandmother showed them upstairs to their bedroom and told them to unpack their two small cases before putting themselves to bed. Left alone with Val, Lydia got on with the job straight away, but the sight of their few clothes hanging in the big wardrobe that smelled of something not very nice made her see them with new eyes – they were old and worn, in tatters some of them. She knew what her grandmother would think when she saw them: that Mum hadn't been a good mother.

Was that what her grandfather had meant about 'ungodly ways'?

Chapter Nine

'It's *my* hair and you can't cut it if I won't let you.'

Lydia's grandfather came towards her, the scissors in his hand. 'Close the door, Irene. Let's get this over with.'

They were upstairs in the bedroom; Lydia and Valerie were still in their nightdresses. They'd only been awake a few minutes when the door had opened and their grandparents had come in and found them in bed together. 'But we always sleep together,' Lydia had begun to explain when their grandfather demanded to know what was going on. Ignoring her, he'd pulled back the sheet and blanket as though checking to see if there was anyone else in the bed: all he'd found was Belinda Bell. A woman at the children's home had tried to stop them from sleeping together, but after Val had made herself sick from crying so much, the woman had given in.

'Don't just sit there,' their grandfather had said. 'We haven't got all day.'

What had they done wrong? Had they slept too long? Only then had Lydia seen that her grandmother was holding a pair of scissors and a hairbrush. A cold shiver had run through her. She'd put a hand to her hair, which was wild and tangled after being in bed. She had forgotten to plait it the night before.

Their grandmother had stepped forward. 'I won't have you living under this roof running around like a couple of savages. Shorter hair will be easier to keep clean.'

'But I don't want my hair cut,' Lydia had said. 'I like my hair the way it is.' This wasn't exactly true. She never gave her hair a second thought; she couldn't remember the last time she'd had it cut. Mum used to trim it when the mood took her, often giving her a fringe as jagged as crocodile teeth.

Her grandfather had sucked in air through his nose, then let it out slowly through his mouth.

'It's *my* hair and you can't cut it if I won't let you,' Lydia had asserted.

That was when her grandfather had taken the scissors from his wife and told her to close the door. 'One thing you're going to have to learn,' he said, addressing Lydia, 'is that what *you* want doesn't count. You're living in *our* house now and by *our* rules. If I say you're having your hair cut, that's exactly what's going to happen. Do I make myself clear?'

With the door now shut, Lydia knew there was no escape. With equal understanding, she realized that the best way to get through this was to act as if she didn't care. Her grandparents could do whatever they wanted and it wouldn't matter to her.

So she stood in the middle of the room, between the two single beds, deliberately facing the mirror on the dressing table so that she could watch her grandfather cut her hair, her chin jutting forward to prove that he didn't scare her. She didn't even flinch when he made the first cut level with the top of her ear and a long, thick hank of hair dropped to the floor. She gritted her teeth, her lips pressed tight, and stared hard at her reflection, telling herself that it didn't matter. It was only hair. She would grow it again one day. For Valerie's sake too, she would stay quiet and calm, as though everything was perfectly normal. Snip, snip, the scissors went. But not a flicker of movement did she make.

When her grandfather had finished and the floor all around her was covered in hair, he said, 'You still look more like a child of Satan than of God, but it's a start.'

I look like a boy, Lydia thought. An ugly, skinny boy. Everything about her face seemed bare and bigger. Her cheekbones were wider apart, her chin was pointier, her eyes greener, her skin paler. Worst of all her eyebrows looked thicker and darker. She put a hand to the stubby tufts of coarse hair that were sticking up all over her head. She imagined the nicknames she would be taunted with. Hedgehog. Toilet brush. Coconut head.

She was so preoccupied with staring at her reflection – this new person that wasn't her – she didn't notice that behind her Valerie was now having her hair cut. 'No!' she cried, spinning round. 'Not Valerie!' But it was too late; her sister's lovely silky baby-blonde hair lay in wispy ribbons on the floor.

Lydia's heart slammed shut against these people. She had never hated anyone so much in her life.

Two things were decided during breakfast. The first was that Lydia and her sister were to call these hateful strangers Grandfather and Grandmother. Grandma was also allowed. But not Nanny, Nan, Granddad, Grandpa or Gramps. No reason was given. Just as no reason had been given when Lydia had referred to the lounge and was instantly reprimanded and told to call it the front room.

The second decision was that their grandmother was to take them shopping for some new clothes. This, at least, was something to look forward to.

They were instructed to wait at the bottom of the stairs while their grandmother got ready to take them into town. Their grandfather had already left the house to go and do God's work. Lydia didn't have a clue what that meant. Was there an office nearby where her grandfather sat with other men dressed in suits doing God's work? And what exactly was that work? And why couldn't God do it himself?

Sitting next to Lydia on the bottom step, Valerie was stroking Belinda Bell's long, matted hair. Lydia put a hand to her own hair. She wondered how long it would take for her to get used to it being so short. She missed the weight and warmth of it. Mum would hate it.

Wrong! Mum *would have* hated it.

As she continued watching her sister stroking Belinda Bell's hair, she thought of Valerie's lovely blonde hair now lying in the dustbin along with hers. She felt hot and sick. And bad. Very bad. This was all her fault. If only she hadn't pestered Mum for that stupid ventriloquist's dummy none of this would have happened. If she hadn't been so selfish and greedy she would never have upset Mum so much that she had to borrow money from Mr Ridley and then go and ...

She swallowed and tried again; it was important to punish herself with the truth. Her mother had killed herself because of her. There. She'd said it. Her mother had thrown herself in front of that train because of *her*. And Lydia would remind herself of that every day of the rest of her life so that she never forgot what a bad, bad daughter she'd been. To make up for it, she would keep her promise to Mum. She would do her absolute best to look after Valerie.

She felt a hand touching her. It was Valerie. Her pretty little face was screwed up into a frown and she was running her fingers over the top of Lydia's head. Lydia forced herself to smile. 'Do you like it?' she asked.

Valerie shook her head sadly, her blue eyes big and anxious.

Mum had always said that Val was slow to speak because Lydia had never let her get a word in edgeways. But since Mum had died Val had almost stopped talking altogether. It worried Lydia. What if Val forgot how to do it?

There was a bus stop at the end of their grandparents' road. While they waited for the bus in the warm summer sunshine, Lydia noticed that everyone in the queue seemed to know each other and they were chatting happily amongst themselves. The women wore brightly coloured sleeveless dresses, and some had shiny handbags that matched their belts and stiletto-heeled shoes. They reminded Lydia of her mother before Dad died. An older woman with painted-on eyebrows that shot up and down as she joked and laughed was wearing a pink headscarf; a row of hair-curlers peeped out from underneath it. Lydia had the feeling they were talking about her grandmother, who was dressed in a navy-blue pleated skirt with a grey, long-sleeved cotton blouse buttoned up to her chin. She wore no make-up, except for a dusting of chalky powder, and with her flat black lace-up shoes and a large shopping bag clutched in both hands, she looked so dull she was almost invisible. None of the other women spoke to her, but they all had a good gawp at Lydia and her sister. Never had Lydia been more conscious of what she looked like. Two buttons were missing from her cardigan and both of the cuffs were frayed, the hem on her dress was much too short and the sole on her left sandal was flapping open at the front. Ashamed, she slid behind the pushchair, where no one could see her shoes. A pity there wasn't a way to hide her head.

They were hardly on the bus before they were clambering off. Lydia was disappointed; she had been enjoying the ride. Seeing all that open space with the sun shining down on it had made her want to pull off her socks and sandals and run and run until she was so breathless she would have to lie down in the grass to recover. Then she'd roll down one of the steep slopes and scream and laugh at the top of her voice.

The town was busy. 'Is it always like this?' she asked her grandmother as people jostled around them.

'It's Saturday; market day.'

Lydia had already caught sight of the market stalls with their brightly coloured awnings. Pointing across the road to the stalls of clothes, she said, 'Is that where we're going, to the market?'

'Stop pointing! And no, we're not doing our shopping with the heathens.'

'What's a heathen?'

'An ungodly person.'

'What's an ungodly person?'

Her grandmother came to a stop and stared at her sternly. 'An ungodly person is a person who asks too many questions. Now do as you're told and be quiet.'

Lydia was just turning this thought over when her grandmother took a sharp turn to the right and led them down a narrow street. At the end was a scruffy building with a corrugated iron roof and a large cross above the door with a sign that said: The Church of The Brothers and Sisters in Christ. Her grandmother headed straight for it.

Just inside the door an old woman with glasses and teeth like a rabbit was sitting behind a small trestle table; in front of her was a Quality Street tin and a book of tickets. 'Hello, Sister Irene,' she said, while Lydia's grandmother rummaged around in her purse for some money. She tore off a ticket and after staring at Lydia and Valerie, said, 'Are these the—' she lowered her voice, 'the children you told us about?'

'Yes, Sister Muriel. As you can see, they're badly in need of some decent clothes.'

The goofy woman stared again at Lydia and Valerie through her thick lenses. Especially Lydia. Lydia wanted to cover her head with her hands and shout that it wasn't her fault she looked so awful. 'Sister Vera and Sister Joan are in charge of children's clothing,' the woman said. 'You'll find them next to Pastor John's bookstall.'

Curious, Lydia looked around the hot, stuffy hall. It was packed with people pushing and shoving in front of tables piled high with all sorts of junk. Mum used to say that she would rather die than wear other people's filthy cast-offs from a jumble sale. 'You never know what germs you might catch from wearing someone else's old clothes,' she would say with a shudder. Lydia took a cautious sniff. The air smelled stale. To be on the safe side, she decided to hold her breath whilst they were here.

With her grandmother already moving ahead, Lydia followed behind with the pushchair. Several times she caught the backs of her grandmother's heels and received a furious look each time. When they made it to the table of children's clothes, Lydia once again found herself flinching under the scrutinizing gaze of two more women. She heard her grandmother greet them as Sister Joan and Sister Vera. They were talking to her grandmother when one of them, a big woman with bosoms as big as pillows, said, 'Is there something wrong with that child? Should she be that colour?'

All three women stared at Lydia. 'Lydia?' her grandmother said. 'Glory be, whatever is the matter with you?'

Lydia couldn't hold on any longer. She let out the breath she'd been holding and coughed and spluttered and breathed in hard. If there were any of those germs here that her mother had warned her about, she'd probably got them now.

Her grandmother tutted and turned away, disgusted. 'That tramp of a mother taught them no manners at all.'

'Praise the Lord that they're now in your hands, Sister Irene.'

'Praise the Lord indeed,' echoed the other woman, who unbelievably had what looked like a moustache growing above her pink, rubbery lips. 'One day they'll thank you.'

'They need to be washed in the blood of Christ; that'll see them right.'

'Amen to that.'

'The youngest one doesn't look too much of a handful,' the big bosomy woman said. 'She has an innocence about her.' Knowing she was being talked about, Valerie hugged Belinda Bell, tucked her chin into her chest and closed her eyes. 'But the other one has a very sour look about her.'

'That's because she takes after her mother.'

Sister Vera and Sister Joan shook their heads. 'We'll pray for you, Sister Irene,' they both said.

Lydia edged away from them. For something to do, she picked up a dress from the pile of clothes. It was a delicate shade of apricot with a cream collar. How could anyone have parted with it? It was just the kind of dress Lydia would love to wear to a party. 'You can put that down for a start,' her grandmother said, snatching the dress from her hands. 'It's much too fancy. There'll be no vanity in our house. Here, try these on. Go on, go behind the table.'

Lydia was horrified. Not only because the clothes she was being given looked as dowdy as her grandmother's, but because everyone would see her trying them on. 'I'm sure they'll fit,' she said in desperation.

'Your feckless, spendthrift mother may have been stupid enough to fritter away good money on clothes that didn't fit you, but I'm not. Now do as you're told and go behind the table.'

Her face as scarlet as a pillar box, Lydia did as she was told. When she was down to just her knickers, the holey ones with a safety pin holding them up, she wished she could catch some of those lethal jumble-sale germs her mother had warned her about and die right there on the spot.

'She's a bit thin, isn't she?' was one of the comments she heard as her grandmother pushed her head roughly through the neck of a scratchy, red woollen jumper. Next she was forced into a pair of even scratchier blue and green tartan trousers. A heavy grey duffle coat was added to the outfit. It came down well below Lydia's knees and her hands were lost within the miles of sleeves.

While Lydia thought she might faint from the heat, her grandmother stood back to take a better look. 'It'll do for the winter. Maybe even two winters if we're lucky. Now, take it all off and try these on.'

When her grandmother had at last finished with her and had turned her attention to Valerie, Lydia escaped to the bookstall. 'Do you have any children's books?' she asked the man running the stall, wondering if he was the man the woman at the door had referred to as Pastor John.

'Over here,' he said, leading her to the middle section of the long table.

'Are they all stories about God?' she asked after she'd hunted through the box and hadn't found anything of any interest.

He gave her the friendliest smile she'd seen in ages. 'I had some Enid Blytons earlier,' he said, 'but they've all gone. Don't you like Bible stories? I've got plenty of those.'

She'd never really thought about enjoying Bible stories before. She knew the Christmas and Easter stories and the one about a man being in a lion's den, oh, and the one about Noah's Ark, but liking them had never come into it. It was what they did at school. 'I like some of them,' she said politely. Then noticing a book on the top of a pile at the back of the table, a thought occurred to her. 'Can I look at that one, please?'

He passed the dictionary to her. 'You're a girl of discerning taste, I can see.'

'What does discerning mean?'

He laughed and tapped the book in her hands. 'Why don't you find out for yourself?'

She turned the pages steadily, and when she'd got as far as *disaster* she said, 'How do you spell *discerning*?'

He spelled it out for her. 'D-I-S-C-E-R-N-I-N-G.'

She moved her finger slowly down the page. '*Discern: to see or be aware of something clearly*.' She read on. '*Discerning: having or showing good judgement*.' She thought about this before looking up from the page. 'That sounds like a good thing to be,' she said.

'It is.'

'Are you Pastor John?'

'I am. And with whom do I have the pleasure of talking?'

She blushed. 'I'm Lydia Turner.'

He held out his hand. 'Hello, Lydia, pleased to meet you. I heard you and your sister would be arriving soon.'

Lydia had never shaken hands with anyone before. Embarrassed, she did what she thought she was supposed to do and then said, 'Is Pastor your name? Your Christian name?'

'Strictly speaking it's my title. You know, like a vicar, a Reverend Somebody or other. Officially I'm in charge of the church here.' He laughed. 'Though not everyone would agree with me on that.'

Confused, Lydia said, 'Is it a real church?'

'Oh, yes, as real as any you'll find.'

Lydia wasn't convinced. She was sure churches had to have a proper spire or a tower with bells in it and windows made of coloured glass. 'Why do my grandmother and her friends call one another Sister?'

'It's how we address each other here, because we're all brothers and sisters in Christ. Would you excuse me, please? I think I have another customer.'

He moved away, down to the other end of the table, and remembering the word she wanted to look up, Lydia flicked almost to the end of the dictionary. *Ungodly: wicked; sinful.*

She shut the book. That didn't sound such a good thing to be. Was she wicked? Whilst sitting at the bottom of the stairs with Valerie earlier that morning she had called herself bad. Had she got it wrong? Was she worse than bad?

She said the word several times over inside her head.

Wicked.

Wicked.

Wicked.

The more she said it, the more she knew that it was true. She *was* wicked. Look what she'd made her mother do.

As though to prove just how true it was, she slipped the dictionary under her cardigan and walked away with it.

Chapter Ten

The next morning Lydia saw another bit of herself disappear. Standing in front of the mirror, staring at her exposed, unfamiliar face, she did the buttons up on a stranger's short-sleeved shirt. She wondered who had worn it before her. The buttons were on the wrong side, so it must have been a boy. What kind of a boy? A nice boy? A snivelling, cry-baby boy? Or a mean, nasty bully? The navy-blue shorts her grandmother had picked out for her had a white anchor on each pocket. They were much too big and baggy for her and made her legs look like white sticks. After she'd pulled on a pair of ankle socks, she slipped her feet into a pair of brown sandals with a soft rubbery sole; there was about an inch of free space beyond her toes – growing room, her grandmother had said. They were so comfortable after the torture of her last pair of shoes, Lydia didn't care who had worn them before, or how ugly they were.

Next she helped her sister to get dressed. Lydia was glad that their grandmother had chosen some pretty clothes for Valerie. The pale yellow smocked dress and white cardigan made her look sweet enough to eat and Lydia couldn't resist kissing her smooth cheek in the way Mum used to press her lips against her own cheek.

When they'd got back from the jumble sale yesterday, their grandmother had dragged out the twin-tub washing machine from the corner of the kitchen and hooked it up to the tap at the sink and while their new second-hand clothes – including vests, socks and pants – had been left to stew in a milky brew of Tide and steaming water,

Lydia and Valerie had been told to gather their old clothes together so that their grandfather could make a bonfire of them later that evening. They'd gone to bed with the smell of smoke and ashes in their nostrils and a fear of what else might be taken from them to be burned – Valerie wouldn't let Belinda Bell out of her sight now and Lydia had hidden the only photographs she had of Mum and Dad and Valerie, along with Mum's powder compact. She'd climbed onto a chair and hidden them on the dusty curtain pelmet.

Today they were being taken to church. Sitting in the back of their grandfather's car with her legs sticking damply to the sun-warmed vinyl seats, Lydia thought about the dictionary she had stolen from Pastor John. Was there a chance he had seen what she'd done? If so, would he be there today and tell everyone that she was a thief?

She'd smuggled the book home in Valerie's pushchair, under her seat cushion, and had put it in her bedside drawer. When she'd stolen the dictionary she had felt a tingle of excitement, like the time she had once stuck two fingers up behind Creepy-Ridley's back. But the tingle had only lasted a few minutes. When it had gone she'd been left with a bad feeling inside her.

The hall was hot and stuffy just as it had been yesterday, but unlike yesterday, there were no trestle tables to be seen, just rows of wooden chairs laid out in two blocks with an aisle down the middle. Most of the chairs were occupied. There didn't seem to be any other children. Trailing behind her grandparents, Lydia felt everyone's eyes on her. Was it her hair? Or was it because they all knew who she was? Hadn't Pastor John said he'd known that she and Val would be coming here? Or was it far worse than that? Had he told them about the dictionary?

Halfway down the aisle, Lydia recognized Sister Muriel and Sister Joan. Recalling how Sister Joan had seen her in nothing but her tatty old knickers yesterday, she lowered her head and kept her eyes on the wooden floorboards.

When they'd taken their seats, right at the front, Lydia saw another familiar face. And body. Sister Vera was sitting behind an upright piano not five feet away from them and banging out a loud, jangly piece of music that made Lydia want to cover her ears. Next to her, with Belinda Bell on her lap, Valerie did exactly that. With each crash of her massive hands on the keys, the woman's enormous pillowy bosoms shook and wobbled.

Lydia had never been taken to church before. Their father had been dead against it. He'd said that he'd rather walk over hot burning coals than set foot in a church; he'd said he'd had enough of that when he'd been growing up. She supposed this was the church he'd come to as a child. Maybe he'd sat in this very chair. God wasn't something that Lydia had ever heard her parents talk about, but her grandparents seemed to talk about little else. And if it wasn't God, it was Jesus.

Something that had been bothering Lydia for a while now was what the teachers in assembly used to say: that when you died, if you'd been good and believed in God, you went to heaven. But to believe in God properly, did you have to go to church regularly? If that was true, Mum and Dad wouldn't have been allowed into heaven, because they never went to church. And supposing Lydia and her sister were made to go to church every week with their grandparents, would that mean they would go to heaven when they died and not be with Mum and Dad?

The more Lydia thought about that, the more she thought it would be better to be bad. She thought of the stolen dictionary in her bedside drawer and hugged the badness to her.

During the service Lydia looked at anything except Pastor John's face. She stared at the woman who banged a tambourine whilst Sister Vera bashed the keys of the piano. She stared at her unfamiliar sandals, wriggling her toes in the roomy, soft leather. She picked at the anchors on her shorts. She turned the pages of the hymn book looking for something interesting to read. When everyone else had their heads bowed and their eyes shut to say the Lord's Prayer, she twisted round and watched in fascination as a bald man at the back of the church got to his feet and, with his hands in the air, babbled something she couldn't understand. Was he foreign? When he sat down Lydia heard her grandmother mutter the word 'unhinged'. Lydia made a mental note to look it up in her stolen diction-ary. But even with all these distractions, she couldn't stop worrying about Pastor John. She was so convinced that he knew what she'd done, she wished he'd put her out of her agony and get on with whatever punishment he had in mind for her.

At the end of the service, a shutter went up with a clatter-ing rattle and revealed a counter of cups and saucers and a plate of biscuits. Behind the counter, with a large brown teapot in her hands, was a smiling woman wearing a bat-tered little hat decorated with flowers. When Lydia looked closely, she could see there was a tiny pretend robin hidden in amongst the flowers. She was just wondering how many biscuits she could sneak off the plate and into her pockets to share with Val later, without anyone seeing, when she felt a firm hand on her shoulder. 'How did you like the service, Lydia?'

Startled, she looked up to see Pastor John staring down at her. He'd come for her, at last. She stuck out her chin and put on her best stormy face – the one Dad used to say could stop a pack of wild dogs in its tracks. 'It was OK,' she said.

He smiled. 'I expect you found it a bit boring, didn't you?'

The smile wasn't fooling her. Or his friendliness. She knew what he was doing; he was softening her up with some silly conversation before telling her off in front of everyone. Well, if that's what he wanted, she could play along. 'Who was that peculiar man who stood up when we were saying the Lord's Prayer?' she asked. 'Is he

foreign? Or is he—' she decided to try out that new word
– 'unhinged?'

The smile got bigger. 'Brother Walter was speaking in
tongues. It's a gift from God. Not everyone is given it.
And not everyone here appreciates it. I thought you might
enjoy these.'

Lydia had been so intent on protecting herself with her
stormy face, she hadn't noticed what Pastor John had been
holding. He held out a pile of books to her.

'After you'd gone yesterday I found these Enid Blytons
in a box under the table. They're not in very good condition, I'm afraid. There's also a children's Bible for you.'

She jammed her hands into her pockets and stared at
the books suspiciously. 'But I don't have any money. I
can't pay for them.'

'I'm not expecting you to pay for them; they're a present
from me to you.'

'But ...'

'But what, Lydia?'

She looked away, down at the floor. 'I don't deserve
them,' she said, wishing that he wasn't being so kind. Or
was he playing a cruel trick on her? Get her to take these
books and then accuse her of stealing them as well? Or ...
or was he being genuinely nice and hadn't seen what she'd
done yesterday? Was it possible she'd put herself through
all that worry for nothing?

'You're not thinking of that dictionary, are you, Lydia?'

Thump! There went that hope.

When she didn't say anything, he said, 'You only had to
ask me, and I would have given it to you anyway.'

She looked up and her insides shrivelled. He had such a
kind, friendly face. Shame trickled through her like sand
in an egg timer. 'Are you going to tell anyone what I did?
My grandparents?'

He bent down to her so that his kind, friendly face was
level with hers. 'Do you want me to?'

She shook her head, unable to speak.

'Then it will be our secret. Now why don't you take the

books and go and get yourself a drink and a biscuit?'

'Thank you,' she managed to say. She took the bundle from him and was about to go when she thought of what had been bothering her earlier. 'Can I ask you something?' she asked.

He was standing up straight now. 'Of course.'

'If someone doesn't believe in God and they don't go to church every week, where do they go when they die?'

He scratched his ear and looked thoughtful. 'I wouldn't worry yourself about that, Lydia. Better to think about how much the Lord Jesus loves you and what a wonderful friend you have in him.'

She didn't know about Jesus, but Lydia decided Pastor John was quite a nice friend to have.

Chapter Eleven

There were lots of bits of their grandparents' long thin garden that were out of bounds – the raspberry canes, the strawberry patch, the shed, the bonfire bin, the chestnut tree and the compost heap. Apparently compost heaps were dangerous; if you fell into one on a hot sunny day you could get badly burned. Lydia and her sister had been ordered never to go near these areas, which made them all the more tempting. When nobody was looking, Lydia deliberately crossed the invisible boundaries and helped herself from the strawberry patch or the raspberry canes. She had even prodded a stick into the compost heap to see if it would burn, but disappointingly it didn't. What she really wanted to do was to unlock the padlock on the shed at the end of the garden and snoop around inside. One day when her grandmother had been standing guard over the twin-tub and her grandfather had been out at work – he had a proper job with the council as well as the Lord's work that kept him busy most evenings – she had stood on tiptoes and peered in through the grimy window. She didn't know why her grandfather bothered to keep the door locked when there didn't seem to be anything valuable in there. From what she could see it was just lots of tools hanging from hooks above two messy shelves. On the top shelf she could see a rusty tin with a picture of a rat on the front and the words 'Rat Poison' underneath it. There was a folding camping stool on the floor next to a stack of dirty old clay pots and a brass lamp suspended from the roof. The lamp was similar to the smelly kerosene one Dad used to have in the shed where he kept his motorbike.

On the floor, under a pile of sacking cloth, Lydia could see what looked like the corner of a magazine poking out. In the two weeks she and her sister had been living with their grandparents, Lydia had only ever seen her grandfather read the Bible, which he did every morning before getting into his car and going off to work, and then again in the evening after supper when Lydia helped her grandmother do the dishes. So what did he read here all on his own?

Today, while Valerie was having her afternoon nap and their grandmother was hammering out wrinkles and creases with a hot spitting iron and complaining about the extra work she now had to do, Lydia was once again breaking her grandfather's boundary rules and climbing the chestnut tree next to the compost heap. It was the first time she'd ever climbed a tree – the children in the books she liked to read were always doing it – and to her delight and amazement she found it was the easiest thing in the world to do. It was as if the branches had been perfectly placed for her to pull herself up onto them; she felt as light and springy as a monkey. Within minutes she was high above the garden, astride a thick solid branch, pretending she was riding a horse, galloping across all that countryside the other side of the garden wall. She still hadn't got used to the big, wide open spaces. Or how different it could look depending on the weather. In the sunshine, the sloping hills and fields appeared green and soft and welcoming, but when it rained they became harsh and wild. Some of the fields weren't fields at all, but moorland; she hadn't worked out which yet.

She opened her mouth wide and gulped back a mouthful of air that was sweet and milky with the smell of freshly mown grass from one of the neighbouring gardens. The air didn't always smell as nice. Some days, when the wind blew in from a different direction, it brought the bitter, sooty smell of the town with it.

Gripping the branch with her legs, she imagined herself galloping far away, leaving behind her the sadness of Mum and Dad and the cruel strictness of her grandparents. She decided this would be her special place, where a secret sun would always shine down on her through the dancing leaves of the tree.

She wondered how old the tree was. Had her father climbed high into its branches when he'd been a boy? If she looked hard enough, would she find his name carved into the bark somewhere? If she did, she'd carve her name right next to his. The thought that she might be following in her father's footsteps filled her with a mixture of happiness and emptiness. To feel closer to Dad, she often went round the house touching things that he must have touched when he was little – the door knobs, the handrail on the stairs, the bathroom taps, the light switches. It didn't really work. There was nothing to remind her of Dad in the house. No photographs. No old games or jigsaw puzzles he used to play with. No favourite books. It was as if he'd never been here.

Off in the distance she could see an area of woodland that crept up the side of the hill. It looked somewhere interesting to go and play. She wondered what was on the other side of the hill. Were there houses there where other children lived? There was no one the same age as her in her grandparents' road. She'd seen a gang of spotty teenagers hanging around the bus shelter or phone box kicking a tin can between them, cigarettes dangling from their lower lips, but no one she could be friends with. She longed for school to start. All she'd had for company so far had been the books Pastor John had given her.

Her grandparents hadn't approved of the books. They said the only one she needed to read was the one the Good Lord had written. When she'd reminded them that it had been Pastor John himself who had given her the books, her grandfather had banged his fist down hard on the dinner table – so violently even her grandmother had started. Sometimes Lydia thought her grandmother was as scared of her husband as Lydia was. 'You will never answer me back again, young lady,' he'd roared, his huge nostrils flaring. 'Now go to your room and pray that God will save you from your wickedness.' Lying on her bed, her stomach growling for her supper that lay untouched downstairs, she had tried to make sense of what had just happened. Surely Pastor John, as the leader of their church, was like God and was never wrong? If Pastor John thought Enid Blyton was all right for her to read, why didn't her grandparents?

When she'd woken in the morning, she'd discovered that all her books had disappeared. She'd dashed across the landing to the bathroom and opened the window that looked down onto the garden: smoke was coming out of the blackened chimney of the metal bonfire bin. Downstairs she found that not all of the books had been burned: two had escaped. On the breakfast table there was the children's Bible Pastor John had given her, along with the dictionary. She pushed them casually to one side and got on with her breakfast. She wouldn't give her grandparents the satisfaction of knowing they'd upset her.

Changing her position on the branch, Lydia swung one leg over to join the other and swivelled round to peer into next door's garden at the washing that hung on the line. It was very different from the stuff her grandmother put out to dry. It looked expensive and what Dad, with a wink, would have called racy. Stockings, petticoats and slinky knickers fluttered and rippled like silky flags in the sunshine. There was a black see-through nightie too, along with several lacy brassieres and a girdle. Her mother had worn a girdle after she'd had Valerie; it had made her tummy as flat as a chopping board. It had also made her breathless and Dad had said he preferred her without it.

According to her grandmother, the woman who lived next door was a floozy. Lydia had checked the word in her dictionary and discovered that this meant she was disreputable. Further reading revealed that disreputable meant The Floozy had a bad reputation. But a bad reputation for what?

Lydia had overheard her grandmother talking to Sister Vera about The Floozy at church. Between them they had a long list of complaints that Lydia didn't understand. What was wrong with having a breakfast bar in your kitchen and a patio made of crazy paving, or buying a fake leopardskin coat from a catalogue?

Lydia now knew that The Floozy was one of the women she had spotted at the bus stop the first time they'd gone into town to buy clothes at the jumble sale. Since then she had dyed her hair an even brighter shade of yellow. Lydia had never seen her without make-up. She wasn't married, but Lydia didn't think she was lonely because now and then, late at night when Lydia couldn't sleep, she could hear music and laughter coming through the wall from next door.

The following Sunday in church, Pastor John reminded everyone that it was the last day to get their money in for the Brothers' and Sisters' Weekend away. 'What weekend away?' Lydia asked her grandmother when the service was over and cups of tea were being passed round. She sensed that people were excited about something; tea and biscuit time wasn't usually this noisy. It was more like a party.

'I've told you before; speak when you're spoken to, child.'

'Oh, go on, Sister Irene, tell the dear girl where we're going.'

This encouragement was from a funny little pink-faced woman who was smiling and nodding so hard she was spilling tea into her saucer. Her hat was sliding about on her head, too. Lydia had learned that Sister Lottie was famous for her hats. She had dozens of them, all decorated with flowers and fruit and tiny birds or animals.

Her grandmother narrowed her eyes to slits and Lydia knew she was far from pleased about something. 'It's nothing to lose one's head over,' she said dismissively to Sister Lottie. 'It's only a weekend in Scarborough.'

'Where's Scarborough?' Lydia asked, forgetting that she was supposed to wait until she was spoken to.

Her grandmother shot her a furious look, but Sister

Lottie beamed and placed one of her white plimsolled feet over the other. Lydia had never seen an adult wear plimsolls before. 'We're going to Yorkshire. To the seaside. Won't that be fun?'

During the drive home Lydia thought of nothing but splashing about in rock pools, throwing herself into waves, building sandcastles and licking chopped nuts off the top of an ice-cream cornet. Sister Lottie was right; it would be fun. She'd been to the seaside before, with Mum and Dad. She'd ridden a donkey and eaten so much candy floss her mother had scolded her and said she'd probably wake up pink in the morning. That was the day Dad had taken her on the ride that had made her sick.

In the days that followed Lydia was careful not to put a foot wrong. Her grandfather was constantly on at her, saying that if she didn't do exactly as he said, she could forget about going to Scarborough. So she helped her grandmother around the house as much as she could, dusting, polishing, ironing, scrubbing out the toilet, as well as taking care of Valerie. Every night she knelt at the side of her bed – making sure the bedroom door was open so that her grandparents could hear – and prayed out loud as they'd taught her. 'God forgive me for my sinful nature. God take away my sin and make me a better person. Thank you, God, for my lovely new home and the kindness of my grandparents, even though I don't deserve it. Amen.' Before hopping into bed, she would silently add: 'Please, please, *please*, God, let me go to the seaside.'

The weekend away blazed like a bright light at the end of a very dark tunnel and she was prepared to do and say whatever it took to be allowed to go.

But then, the day before they were due to leave, and after she'd laid out her and Valerie's clothes to pack later that evening, she did something wrong. Whilst Valerie had been having her usual nap and her grandmother was having a Tea and Sisters Scripture meeting in the front room, Lydia was down at the bottom of the garden. It was a scorching hot afternoon. There hadn't been any rain for ages and the air was thundery, as thick and sticky as syrup. All the strength seemed to have been sucked out of her body and she couldn't even be bothered to climb the chestnut tree. Instead, she found a stick and played with the compost heap, pretending the sweet-smelling rotting grass cuttings and vegetable peelings were the ingredients for an enormous cake that needed stirring before going in the oven. With the sun beating down on it, the heat from the steaming layered mixture was extraordinary – hot enough to use as an oven itself. She was so absorbed in what she was doing, she didn't hear her grandfather's footsteps approaching, not until she heard him fitting the key into the padlock on the shed door. She held her breath and kept perfectly still in the hope she would be invisible to him. It didn't work. He'd just opened the door and was pulling something out from inside his jacket when he saw her. At first he looked startled, as though he was the one who had been caught doing something wrong. Then his expression hardened and she knew she was in for it. In a flash, before she'd had time to make a run for it, he'd disappeared inside the shed and was back out and coming for her. He towered over her, hands on hips, blocking her way. Gripping the stick, she did her best to look him in the eye, to disguise how terrified of him she was.

'I warned you about playing with the compost heap,' he said. 'What did I say could happen if you weren't careful?'

There was something scary about the slow, steely tone of his voice and she had to look away from him. 'I can't remember,' she lied.

He took the stick from her. 'Do you want me to remind you?'

She kept her eyes on the stick and shook her head.

'So you do remember what I told you?'

She swallowed. 'I'm very sorry. I won't do it again.'

He prodded her chest with the dirty end of the stick, pushing her back against the boarded side of the compost heap. 'No, you won't do it again. And do you know why you're not going to come down and play in this part of the garden again?'

'Because I'll get into trouble if I do?'

'You most certainly will. But to make sure you do as you're told, I'm going to have to teach you a lesson that will make you mend your ways. Hold out your hands.'

Her whole body clammy with sweat, her heart beating frantically, Lydia did as he said and braced herself, her eyes closed.

Her screams tore apart the still silent afternoon. On a branch above her head, a startled wood pigeon clattered its wings and flew off into the sultry sky.

Chapter Twelve

She was lucky. That's what people had said yesterday. Lucky that she hadn't hurt herself more. Lucky too that she was well enough to go to Scarborough.

In the back of their grandfather's car, with Valerie on her lap and a suitcase bumping against her shoulder whenever they went round a corner, Lydia kept telling herself that the moment she could smell the tangy sea air, the pain would magically stop. Her hands and arms were bandaged from the elbow down to her fingers and if she concentrated hard on reciting her times tables in her head, she could forget the stinging pain that made her want to rip off the bandages and plunge her arms into two imaginary buckets of icy water.

Grandmother had been furious when her grandfather had taken her into the house and interrupted her Tea and Sisters Scripture meeting. He had explained what had happened – that he'd come home early from work and found Lydia mucking about on the wall behind the compost heap, despite having been expressly forbidden to play in that area of the garden. He told everyone that she'd lost her balance and fallen in when he'd asked her to get down. Her grandmother had been all for sending Lydia – still covered in grass cuttings and rotting peelings – straight to bed without any tea, but then Lydia had felt the room spin and had been sick over the carpet. Sister Lottie had dropped her Bible and knocked over her cup of tea as she rushed to help. 'It's shock!' she cried. 'If she's badly burned we must get the poor girl into a bath of cool water.'

'She certainly requires washing,' said Sister Vera, her face puckered with disgust.

'She's lucky she didn't break her neck,' Sister Joan said. 'She should count herself lucky she didn't kill herself!'

When Lydia was sick again, The Sisters were hurriedly shooed out of the house. Twenty minutes later, shivering with cold, she had begged through chattering teeth to be allowed out of the freezing bathwater. Her grandmother had then rubbed margarine into her rapidly reddening arms and wrapped them roughly in bandages. 'There, that's the best I can do,' she said. 'You should give thanks to the good Lord that it was only your arms you burned.'

As the windscreen wipers scraped backwards and forwards – the weather had finally broken in the night with the loudest thunderstorm Lydia had ever heard – she caught her grandfather looking at her in the rear-view mirror. No longer brave enough to stare back at him, she closed her eyes and tried to pretend he didn't exist. That he was buried deep at the bottom of the compost heap.

In those few short seconds when she had waited for that stick to come cracking down on her hands, she'd found herself suddenly being lifted off her feet and her arms being pushed into the compost heap. Surprise had made her cry out but then, as she'd wriggled to break free from his strong grasp, she'd screamed louder and harder because of the fiery heat that was spreading up her hands and arms. But he'd ignored her cries, saying the punishment was for her own good, that the heat she was experiencing now was nothing like the fires of hell that awaited her if she continued to disobey him. When he eventually put her down, he said, 'Tell anyone about this and I'll punish you again. Do you understand?'

Tears streaming down her cheeks, she'd promised him she wouldn't tell anyone.

For the rest of the journey Lydia kept her gaze glued to the dreary, rain-soaked scenery through the steamed-up side window. Anything but catch her grandfather's glinty eye in the mirror. Anything but wonder why he hated her so much. Or why she hadn't been brave enough to tell anyone what had really happened to her.

The sky was blue and the sun was shining brightly by the time they arrived in Scarborough. Pastor John greeted them at the boarding house where they were staying. When he saw Lydia, he crouched down in front of her. 'Poor Lydia,' he said, 'Sister Lottie told me about your accident. How do you feel?'

Through a dry raspy throat, and conscious of her grandfather standing behind her – one of the cases he was carrying was digging into the backs of her legs – she said, 'I feel much better now, thank you.'

'She's fine,' her grandfather rumbled, pushing forward with the cases, 'a lot of fuss about nothing. It'll teach her to be more careful in the future. Now then, where are our rooms?'

Lydia and Valerie had a room to themselves. It smelled of cigarette smoke and something fishy. There was no window to let in any fresh air or light, and the only furniture was a pair of bunk-beds. There was a notice pinned to the back of the door that read: 'No sand to be left in the bedrooms or public rooms. No wet towels or bathing costumes put out to dry on the window ledges. No guests back before four o'clock. The front door will be locked at ten thirty p.m. sharp.'

With no chest of drawers to put their clothes in, Lydia explained to her sister it would be best to keep their things in their case under the bottom bunk, which would be Valerie's. With no unpacking to do, they crept quietly back out onto the dimly lit passageway. The door to the right of theirs was shut but Lydia could hear her grandparents' voices. She moved a little nearer to the door, her ears straining to hear what they were saying. They seemed to be discussing Pastor John.

Suddenly the door opposite opened and Sister Lottie appeared. 'Isn't this grand?' she said, clasping her hands in front of her. She was wearing a pair of lacy gloves and another of her hats covered her curly grey hair. It was made of straw and decorated with real flowers – drooping buttercups and daisies – and was held in place with a yellow ribbon tied under her chin in a large bow. She patted Valerie's head. 'Sweet, darling angel,' she cooed. Then to Lydia: 'And how are your arms today, dear? You gave us all such a terrible fright yesterday. Really you did.'

'They're much better, thank you.'

'I'm so pleased.' She smiled a dimply smile and bent forward. 'Shall we be very naughty and go for a walk before tea?' she whispered. 'I expect you're like me and can't wait to see the sea.'

Much as Lydia wanted to race down to the beach straight away she wasn't sure it was such a good idea to go without letting her grandparents know. Yet she knew that if she asked them for permission to go they would be sure to say no.

Sister Lottie was already off down the passageway with Valerie's hand in hers. 'Come on, Lydia,' she called over her shoulder. 'Let's go and have some fun!'

They passed Sister Joan and Sister Vera on the stairs and grabbing a way to stay out of trouble, Lydia said, 'Could you tell my grandparents Sister Lottie's taking me and my sister to the beach, please?'

'Sister Lottie, you do realize tea is in an hour, don't you?'

'Oh, yes, Sister Joan. We'll be back in plenty of time, won't we, girls?'

Lydia suspected that Sister Joan and Sister Vera didn't really like Sister Lottie. They think they're better than her, Lydia thought as she followed behind Sister Lottie and Valerie. True, there was something perhaps a little batty – that was the word Mum would have used – about the woman, but so what? Sister Lottie and Pastor John were the only really nice people she'd met since coming to live in Swallowsdale.

*

The sun was low in the sky when they made it to the beach and people were packing up their things to go home. Valerie had only been a tiny baby when Mum and Dad had taken them to the seaside and she held on to Lydia's hand tightly as she looked anxiously around her. Staring out to sea, Sister Lottie was standing perfectly still. 'Isn't it beautiful?' she said, her arms stretched out in front of her, her palms held high, a joyful smile on her parted lips. 'This is why I love God. He's so good to us. Alleluia and praise the Lord!' Her voice had risen and around them people had stopped what they were doing and were gawping. They gawped even harder when, without warning, Sister Lottie gathered up her skirt and ran towards the water's edge. Someone sniggered and said, 'Crazy old woman.'

Another said, 'Probably soft in the head and let out from the loony bin for the day.'

'Has to be as nutty as a fruitcake to be wearing that awful hat and those ankle socks and plimsolls.'

Lydia felt her cheeks redden. Part of her wanted to creep away, to pretend she didn't know the woman they were discussing. But something far stronger than embarrassment made her want to stand up for Sister Lottie. So what if she wore a funny hat and children's plimsolls? So what if she was a bit soft in the head? If soft in the head made you kind and nice, then Lydia knew whose side she was on.

'Come on,' she said to Valerie, 'let's go and see what Sister Lottie's doing.'

Valerie looked doubtfully at the sand and pebbles and held up her arms to be carried. 'Sorry, sweetheart,' Lydia said, 'I can't. Not today. Maybe tomorrow.'

By the time they had joined Sister Lottie at the water's edge, she had removed her socks and plimsolls. 'We must have a paddle,' she said.

'But we don't have a towel.'

'Oh, Lydia, we don't need a towel. Don't worry so.'

She's more of a child than me, Lydia thought as she sat down and took off her socks and sandals. Valerie shook her head when Lydia tried to undo the buckles on her sandals. 'Then you must sit here like a very good girl and don't move. Can you do that for me, Val?'

Valerie nodded. But she didn't sit down. 'Dirty,' she whispered, looking around her.

The water was cold and made Lydia suck in her breath and stand on tiptoe. She let the waves wash over her toes and then ventured in further. She felt the pull of the water and laughed when a rush of sand and stones tickled her feet. She breathed in the salty air, tipped her head back to let the sun stroke her cheeks and felt a tiny chink of happiness burst through the clouds inside her.

'I said it would be fun, didn't I?' Sister Lottie said. The hem of her skirt was wet, but either she hadn't noticed or she didn't care. Lydia was glad she was wearing shorts – at least there was no danger of getting them wet and being told off for it. Looking out at the sea, the waves sparkling in the lowering sun, Lydia realized this was the first time since coming to live at number thirty-three Hillside Terrace that she had been properly alone with someone other than her grandparents. Better still, this was someone who might be able to answer some of the questions she had.

'Sister Lottie?'

'Yes?'

'Have you known my grandparents for a long time?'

'Ooh, I should say so. I knew them when they married.'

'Did you know my father?'

'Of course I did. He was a dear, sweet boy. The apple of your grandparents' eye. Valerie looks a lot like him, you know.'

'Really?'

'Well, not when he was grown up, but when he was little. He had the same lovely blond hair.'

'Do you know why my grandparents were happy when my dad died?'

The old woman gasped and turned round. 'Oh, dear me! Dear, dear me. How could you say such a terrible thing?'

93

'Because it's true. I heard my mother on the telephone the day after he died.'

'Well ... oh, precious child, you're much too young to understand these things.'

'What things?'

Sister Lottie sighed and, with a trembling hand, touched the silver cross she wore at her neck. 'You have to remember that your grandparents loved their son very much and they wanted the world for him.'

'I don't think that's true. I've never heard them talk about him. They don't even have a photograph of him in the house. I've looked and I can't find anything that belonged to my dad.'

A wave larger than any of the ones before rolled in fast and crashed at their legs. Sister Lottie hitched up her skirt but was too late. Drenched to the waist, she plucked the wet folds of now transparent cotton off her thin legs and began squeezing out the water. 'What a silly goose I am,' she said with a cheerful laugh.

'So why aren't there any pictures of my dad in the house?' Lydia pressed on, at the same time keeping an eye out for any other big waves.

'They used to have lots of photographs of him,' Sister Lottie said, 'all round the house, but then ... but then he changed.'

'How? How did he change?'

'He disappointed them. He met your mother, and I'm afraid to say he turned away from God.'

'Is that all?'

'It meant everything to them.'

'And is that why they hate me and Valerie?'

Sister Lottie looked shocked. 'Wherever did you get that idea? How could they not love you and your sister?'

Lydia wanted to hold out her bandaged arms and say, 'Could someone who loved me do this to me?' But she didn't. She clamped her mouth shut and shrugged.

Chapter Thirteen

They ran all the way, Sister Lottie carrying Valerie and
Lydia frantically urging her to go faster. But they were still
late for tea. They would have been even later had Lydia
not begged Sister Lottie to stop kicking through the waves
and put her socks and plimsolls back on.

Her grandmother was waiting for them in the doorway
to the dining room. Her thin body looked as taut as a
stretched rubber band about to go ping. 'You've delayed
tea by twenty minutes,' she said, arms crossed in front
of her, eyebrows drawn. 'And for the sake of proprieties,
Sister Lottie, you might like to tidy yourself up before
eating.'

With her flushed face, her hat tipped to one side and her
wet skirt beginning to show a salty tide line, even Lydia
had to admit that Sister Lottie did look a bit of a mess. But
Sister Lottie didn't seem in the least concerned. 'We had
such a glorious time, Sister Irene,' she said breathlessly,
her eyes shining. 'Simply glorious. You should have been
there with us. We had such fun.'

How wonderful it must be to be Sister Lottie, Lydia
thought enviously, so completely unaware that anyone
could be cross with her. But all too aware of her grandmother's mood, and anxious to get in her good books,
Lydia said, 'I'll take Valerie upstairs so we can wash our
hands, shall I?'

'Yes,' her grandmother said snappily. 'Five minutes,
mind. And make sure you comb your hair. No messing
about up there.'

*

Tea was a dollop of gloopy shepherd's pie with tinned peas and watery cabbage. For afters there were tinned peaches with evaporated milk. Lydia and Valerie weren't allowed to have any evaporated milk. Their grandmother said it was too rich and would make them sick. 'And the last thing I need, on top of everything else,' this was said with a look in Sister Vera and Sister Joan's direction, 'is another episode like yesterday.' Lydia's ears pricked up at the words *on top of everything else*. What did that mean? She searched her grandparents' faces for clues, then looked about the room.

Sitting at the nearest table was a group of people she didn't know. Apparently they were from their sister church here in Scarborough. There were only two churches like theirs in the whole of the country, but by coming here to spread the word, they hoped to get more people to join and maybe start up a third church. On another table, Pastor John and Sister Lottie were chatting with more unknown people, including a man with silvery-grey hair, deep dark grooves either side of his mouth and a black eye patch. Lydia stared in fascinated horror. What lay behind that patch? A gruesome hole that went straight through to his brain? She shivered and popped a piece of squishy peach into her mouth. Then wished she hadn't.

'What have I told you about staring?'

'Sorry, Grandma,' Lydia said meekly. 'Who's that man with the eye patch?'

'His name's Brother Digby and a man more full of the Holy Spirit you will never meet. He's a truly righteous and scripturally led man. Now stop mythering me with your questions and finish your tea.'

The next morning they were up early and immediately after breakfast they marched in single file down to the beach with a box of tambourines and hymn books, as well as a stack of leaflets inviting people to let Jesus into their lives.

Lydia and Valerie had been given the task of handing

the leaflets out whilst the congregation sang 'Onward Christian Soldiers', 'All Things Bright and Beautiful', and 'For All the Saints'. With it being so early and with a strong wind blowing in off the sea, there weren't many people about. Lydia soon noticed that if she persuaded her sister to offer the leaflets to the few who were on the beach, more people took them. Probably because Valerie looked so sweet. Unlike Lydia, she wasn't cringing with embarrassment and wishing she could dig a big hole in the sand and bury herself.

Brother Digby – his full name was Brother Digby Pugh – led the service and he was very different from Pastor John. He had the loudest voice ever. Several times Lydia jumped out of her skin at his shouted words. She noticed others doing the same, including Sister Lottie. He roared and bellowed at them above the wind about how sly and dangerous the devil could be, that he was the most infectious disease known to mankind. He warned them to be alert and constantly on their guard. Then he thumped his opened Bible with his fist and read from it: 'Finally, brethren, be strong in the Lord, and in the power of his might. Put on the whole armour of God, that ye may be able to stand against the wiles of the devil. For we wrestle not against flesh and blood, but against principalities, against powers, against the rulers of the darkness of this world, against spiritual wickedness in high places.' He jerked his head up, slapped the Bible shut, and with his one piercing eye swept the faces of the congregation as if searching for someone in particular. 'Which of you,' he hissed, his hand raised and a long bony finger pointing, 'has allowed the evil one to feast on the demons within?' Lydia gulped and slid to her left to hide behind Sister Vera. When she thought it was safe to come out, she saw that Brother Digby's eye and bony finger had settled on Pastor John.

Pastor John had turned very pale.

By tea-time it was all anybody could talk about. The Brothers and Sisters in Christ were in crisis. Hovering in doorways, taking her time over handing out Bibles, lurking behind corners, or pretending she was praying, Lydia gathered information from the rustle of gossip like a thieving magpie.

Shocking!

Disgusting!

Who'd have thought it?

A man we trusted!

He's betrayed us all!

He'll burn in hell for this!

He could have taken us all down with him!

Lucky for us Sister Irene was on to him!

These were just a few of the snippets Lydia overheard until finally she got to the bottom of it. Pastor John was being kicked out of the church, for something to do with indulging in ungodly relations with a married woman in Keighley.

Having been told by her grandparents to go and amuse themselves – they had important business with Brother Digby to discuss – Lydia took Valerie upstairs with her to look for Sister Lottie. They found her sitting on her bed, crying.

'I can't believe the dreadful things they're saying about Pastor John,' she sobbed, flapping her handkerchief. 'He was such a good man. Always so patient and understanding. The kindest man I ever knew. The church won't be the same without him.' She crushed Lydia and Valerie to her. 'Promise me you won't think too badly of him. You mustn't turn against him like everyone else.'

At breakfast the next morning not only did Lydia find out that Pastor John had packed his case in the night and left without saying goodbye, but she learned that Brother Digby was to be their new pastor in Swallowsdale.

Chapter Fourteen

The start of a new term had always made Lydia feel anxious, but the start of a new term in a new school was keeping her awake at night and making her head ache and her tummy tie itself into knots. Dad would have said she was suffering from an attack of the collywobbles. She'd always thought that having the collywobbles sounded like it should be fun, something that made you laugh.

But as she sat at the breakfast table in her second-hand blue and grey uniform, trying to force down a mouthful of toast, and reminding herself that a few weeks ago she had been longing for school to start, she wasn't laughing. It wasn't only herself she was worrying about. This was the first time in ages that she and Valerie would be apart. Lydia was so used to doing everything for her sister, she couldn't imagine how Valerie would cope without her around. Nor could she imagine their grandmother being patient enough to tease out what it was that Val wanted when she would sometimes do nothing more than speak through her eyes.

With her stomach all topsy-turvy, Lydia gave up on the toast and looked at Valerie, who had hardly eaten any of her cornflakes; they were either sticking to the side of the bowl or floating like soggy scabs in the milk. 'Come on, Valerie,' Lydia encouraged her, 'try and eat some more.'

Valerie turned her eyes meaningfully to Lydia's uneaten piece of toast.

'That's different,' Lydia said, 'I don't need to do as much growing as you. Now promise me you'll be good for our grandmother whilst I'm at school.'

Valerie blinked. It was a slow, deliberate movement, just the way Belinda Bell blinked when you tipped her slowly backwards.

From the hallway came the sound of letters being pushed through the letterbox, followed by their grandmother's thwacking footsteps hurrying from the kitchen to the front door. Their grandfather had already left for work; he rarely ate breakfast with them. He complained that they interfered with his routine.

Helping her sister down from her cushioned seat, Lydia kissed her briskly on the forehead. 'I'll be home before you've even missed me.'

There was a queue at the bus stop. Lydia recognized the spotty gang of teenage boys; they looked different in their black blazers and grey trousers, bigger and not so scruffy. They all had the same bristly short haircut with a white rim of pale skin above their ears and round their necks. A group of girls in black blazers and short grey skirts showed off long legs in knee-high white socks and carried duffel bags slung over their shoulders. When they saw Lydia they stopped talking and looked her up and down. For days now Lydia had been practising for just such a moment. Concentrating hard, she narrowed her eyes and stared back, pretending she was casting an evil spell on them. The tallest of the girls, inhaling hard on a cigarette, said, 'Cheeky little tart! I've a good mind to thump her one. She needs to learn to respect her elders. Oi, Tufty, what yer staring at?'

'Give over,' one of the boys said. 'She's nowt but a baby.'

Lydia bristled. She knew she was small, but she wasn't *that* small.

Someone else said, 'Isn't she the granddaughter of them religious loonies? Mad as snakes, my mum says.'

Grateful that the gang of teenagers thundered upstairs to the top deck of the bus, Lydia claimed a seat downstairs next to the window. She had been told by her grandmother to stay on the bus until the other children with the same uniform as her got off. After a few minutes she risked a glance to her right and then over her shoulder to the seats behind. A blur of blue and grey confirmed she was at least on the right bus. For the rest of the journey she willed her churning, queasy stomach to settle. To distract herself she thought of the good luck card Sister Lottie had made for her. She had given it to Lydia in church yesterday morning. This was after Pastor Digby had put one of his bony hands on her head in front of everyone and prayed that she would be a good child of Christ and that she wouldn't be infected by the ungodly at her new school.

The first thing Pastor Digby had done when he came to Swallowsdale was to walk up and down the aisle of their church sweeping the floor with a broom. It was a symbol of his ministry, he said. He had been sent to them to sweep away the old and to make room for the new. He had then read out a list of changes he wanted to put in place. There was to be no gambling of any sort, not even the buying or selling of raffle tickets. No alcohol was to be drunk. Television was banned, as was smoking, the reading of horoscopes, perms, make-up, perfume and hair colouring, and the wearing of jewellery. Wedding rings were allowed, but nothing in the way of unnecessary accessories. Only hats of a modest and unadorned nature could be worn. Sister Lottie had let out a little gasp at this. Lydia had later looked up the word unadorned and understood her gasp.

According to Pastor Digby these were all instruments of the devil and he was ridding the church of them. 'They encourage the sin of pride and vanity, the sin of slothfulness, and worse, the sin of greed,' he roared at them, making the windows rattle in their frames. He explained that under Pastor John's guidance, the church had been allowed to become flabby and vulnerable to attack. If they were to be a godly church, tough leadership was required. He vowed he would make street evangelists of them all.

Lydia had only found out recently that there had been a question mark over her being allowed to go to school.

She'd overheard her grandmother telling Sister Vera that she was concerned that Lydia would pick up the ways of the heathen at school, that maybe she would be better staying at home. Pastor Digby had then been asked for his opinion on the matter and he'd ruled that as Lydia was the only school-age child in their flock, she would be their secret weapon. It would be her job, on behalf of the Brothers and Sisters, to spread God's Word at school.

As she'd known they would, the lessons flew by and the break times dragged. Out in the playground the boys screamed and ran around like idiots and the girls huddled together, their arms linked, telling Lydia what she already understood all too clearly: friendships had long since been formed and no one needed a new one thank you very much. She'd tried talking to them during morning break, but when one of them had asked her why she had her hair cut like a boy's, she'd scowled and walked off.

For something to do she went for a walk round the field. She took off her cardigan and tied it around her waist – just as her grandmother said she wasn't supposed to do – and pushed up her sleeves. The burns on her arms had healed. She'd been disappointed that she wasn't left with some really good scars that she could show off, but all that remained was a faint blush on the inside of her arms.

Above her, the sun shone down from a pearly blue sky and birds sang in the trees. It was a beautiful day, still very much like summer. Instead of making her feel happy, though, it made her feel uglier and more alone. But perhaps that was how she was meant to feel. Pastor Digby said God saw and heard everything and that he punished those who did wrong. Pastor Digby hadn't said how God punished people, but maybe he just made them unhappy, like her.

In the days and weeks that followed, Lydia gradually got to know some of her classmates, particularly the ones who had been made by their teacher, Miss Dillinger, to take it in turns to sit next to her. The first had been a blonde girl called Zoe Woolf who spoke in a fancy lah-di-dah voice. She was originally from somewhere in the south of England and said words like bath and glass as though they had an r in them. She already wrote with a fountain pen and was considered one of the cleverer ones in the class. She could ask for directions to the toilet in French, whereas the rest of them were only just learning to count and say *bonjour* and *au revoir*. She had thought she was the only one in the class who had her own dictionary, until Lydia pulled hers out of her satchel.

Next to sit with Lydia was a boy called Peter Day, who had been born with a hole in his heart. Everyone called him Bena, as in Ribena, because he was a funny purply-blue colour. He was excused all games and PE lessons but was never teased.

Then there was a boy called Jimmy Dodson, who was nicknamed Jimmy Fumble because he was so clumsy. Everyone dreaded it – '*Oh, Miss!*' – if he was ever picked to be milk monitor.

After Jimmy came Lisa Fortune, of whom Lydia was secretly terrified. Apparently when she was still inside her mother's tummy, her mother had been given some tablets by her doctor and when Lisa was born she only had one hand. She wore an artificial limb with a hook on the end of it and Lydia had had nightmares about Lisa chasing her round the playground with it.

She'd discovered that there was a girl in the other class in their year who was definitely one to be avoided. She was a big, tall girl with a long ponytail of dull, mousy-brown hair and she never went anywhere without her gang of friends. Her name was Donna Jones and just yesterday she had approached Lydia wanting to know who she was and how much money she had on her. After putting her scowl to good use once again, backed up by an imaginary evil spell, Lydia had walked off as though Donna hadn't spoken. Within seconds she regretted what she'd done and next playtime, despite the awful smell, she'd hidden in the outside toilet block until the bell rang.

Today, wandering round the school field during morning break, she was keeping an eye out for Donna Jones and her gang. She found trouble sooner than she expected when she came upon a crowd of chanting girls and boys. Curiosity made her draw nearer. When she was close enough she realized that they had a girl pinned down on the grass. Donna Jones was sitting on top of her, undoing the poor girl's blouse. From listening to the chants Lydia soon understood why: it was because the poor girl was wearing a bra for the first time and they wanted to see what she had to put in it. Lydia felt sick at the unfairness of it and badly wanted to do something to stop it. But what? What could she do against all of them? Perhaps they'd do something equally cruel and embarrassing to her. Like ... pull her knickers down.

To her shame, knowing it was the wrong thing to do, she walked away before anyone saw her.

Chapter Fifteen

It was a week later, on a cold, crisp October day, when life at school changed for Lydia.

After morning assembly she and the rest of her class found Miss Dillinger waiting for them in their classroom. She wasn't alone; a pale, thin boy with darting eyes was with her. The most noticeable thing about him was that he was wearing an ugly leg brace, all metalwork and leather straps. Lydia had seen one before, but not close up like this.

'This is Noah Solomon,' Miss Dillinger announced once they were in their seats and sizing up the unknown boy. 'I want you all to make him feel very welcome.'

The only empty chair in the classroom was the one next to Lydia, so it was no surprise when Miss Dillinger instructed the new boy to sit with her, saying, 'Lydia only recently joined the school, so she's the best person to look after you and help you with anything you need to know.'

Lydia watched him make his agonizingly slow way between the desks, the leg brace clanking and squeaking. Sniggers broke out from the other side of the classroom: the word 'spastic' ricocheted off the walls. Jack Horsley and Alfie Stone were immediately told to be quiet. He finally made it and plonked himself down on the chair, his leg sticking out into the narrow aisle. Pretending to give all her attention to turning the pages of her exercise book for that morning's maths lesson, Lydia watched him out of the corner of her eye as he lifted the lid on his desk. A sheen of sweat had appeared on his top lip and he looked paler than ever. He had the darkest eyes she'd ever seen. It didn't take him long to organize himself. All he seemed to have in his satchel was a notebook and a metal tin. When he opened the tin she could see three pencils, a rubber, a pencil sharpener, a clear plastic six-inch ruler and a pen: a fountain pen like Zoe Woolf used. He caught her looking at his things and flipped the lid shut.

For some reason it was OK for a girl to have something wrong with her, but it wasn't the same for a boy. Jimmy Fumble was always being made fun of for his clumsiness, but Lisa Fortune with her hook was never bothered. Peter Day was the exception. They all knew that because of the hole in his heart, Bena could die any minute just by someone snapping their fingers too loudly. So unless this new boy could prove he had something as impressively wrong with him, he was in for some serious trouble. As the day wore on and the taunts – spaz and spacky – came thick and fast, Lydia soon felt that the task given her by Miss Dillinger was beyond her. How could she possibly look after this new boy? It was hopeless. Everything was against him. From his clanky leg, to his brand new shoes and uniform (ridiculously too big for him), to his posh voice. He rarely spoke, but when he did, he sounded like Zoe Woolf. And why didn't he try and help himself, instead of just standing there with that strange, slightly puzzled expression on his face?

The next day, during morning break, Donna Jones and her gang appeared. 'Go on, then, spacky,' Donna said, 'show us how yer can run with that thing on yer leg.'

'I can't run,' he said simply.

Donna and her friends laughed and crowded round him. 'Then yer'd better learn. If yer not too busy building an ark, that is!'

Lydia couldn't bear to see him standing there so help-less and vulnerable. She went over to make her presence known.

Donna saw her and laughed. 'I see you've got yerself a

midget-sized girlfriend to protect yer. But if that's the best yer can do, yer'd better learn to run extra fast, cos you're gonna need to.' She tossed Lydia a snarling look. 'Yer an all.'

Their point made, Donna and her gang sauntered off to pick on someone else.

'I don't need looking after.' These were the first words this strange new boy had spoken directly to Lydia.

'Could have fooled me,' she retaliated.

'And you're not my girlfriend,' he added sullenly.

By home time, Lydia felt the full sting of his words. He was nothing but an ungrateful snob! As far as she was concerned, he was on his own from now on. Why should she care about him? He could get into whatever trouble he wanted and it was nothing to do with her. Besides, it would be better for her all round if she wasn't seen with him too often. She didn't want anyone else accusing her of being his girlfriend.

But as the days went by she couldn't stop looking out for him. Right now, despite not knowing a single thing about him, he was the nearest she had to a friend. She'd got used to him sitting like a silent shadow next to her in class and having to share books with him. For some reason he never put his hand up to answer any of Miss Dillinger's questions, although Lydia was sure he knew the answers because he was always getting ten out of ten for his work and being awarded gold stars to go on the wall chart. His handwriting was good too, better even than Zoe's. All his letters sat perfectly on the line and slanted evenly to the right; nothing he handed in was ever smudged, creased or torn. When he wasn't looking one day, Lydia had stolen a piece of work from his desk and had tried copying it at home so that she could learn to write neatly and be allowed to use a real pen instead of a pencil. He was better at art than anyone else in the class, too; when he drew something you could easily recognize what it was.

The truth was, even if he didn't have to wear that ugly

leg brace, he would still stick out from the rest of the boys in the class, none of whom was interested in getting to know him because he couldn't play football or bulldog. Bena wasn't interested in him, either. He kept his distance, probably sensing that no good could come of being his friend.

But if Noah was her silent shadow during lessons, Lydia was his secret shadow in the playground. She spied on him round corners and kept her ears pricked not just for the clunky squeak of his brace, but for the name-calling that followed him wherever he went. She suspected that he was on borrowed time, that any day soon the taunts would turn into something worse.

She was proved right.

After lunch one day she came across him at the back of the portable classrooms. He was surrounded by Donna and her gang. They had his blazer and were going through the pockets, tipping whatever they found – mostly bits of paper and loose change – onto the grass. Somebody had already broken his fountain pen and added it to the pile.

'And what have we here?' Donna crowed. 'A drawing of someone? Hey, I know who this is; it's that ugly midget girl with the bog-brush hair and the eyebrows, in't it? Do yer fancy her, then? Is that why yer've drawn her?'

When Noah didn't answer, Donna screwed the picture up and tossed it onto the ground. After another poke around in a pocket she pulled out something else. 'Oh, how *sweet*!' she said sarcastically. 'It's a photo of Mummy and Daddy! Look, everyone!'

'Please give it back,' Noah said quietly.

'Ooh, *please* give it back,' Donna mimicked him. Like sheep, everyone else followed her example.

'If yer want it that badly,' Donna taunted, 'why don't yer come and get it, yer cissy spaz?' She held the photo just out of his reach and when he took a step nearer to take it, she snatched it away.

It still shamed Lydia down to the tips of her toes when she thought of the day when she'd walked away from that poor girl who'd needed her help in this very same spot, and so when she saw Donna suddenly shove Noah to the ground and rip up the photograph, letting the pieces flutter over him as he struggled to get to his feet, Lydia knew she couldn't make the same mistake twice. She stepped out from her hiding place and with a massive surge of energy, knowing she had the element of surprise on her side, she threw herself at Donna and knocked her flying into a patch of long grass.

Bang! went Donna's head on the soft ground.

Bang! it went again.

Bang!

Bang!

Filled with a violent rage, Lydia could have gone on doing it for ever. Never had anything felt so good or so satisfying. She could hear herself screaming at Donna as she held onto the girl's ears but had no idea what she was saying. She knew, though, that her anger wasn't just about Donna picking on Noah.

Finally the worst of her fury subsided and Lydia released her hold. 'Come after me or my friend again,' she hissed, 'and I'll spread the word about what I've just done to you. And you wouldn't like that, would you? A girl my size embarrassing big tough Donna Jones in front of all her mates?' She pinched Donna's ears hard. 'Got it?'

Donna nodded.

'Good.' Lydia stood up, and knowing it would humiliate Donna further, offered her hand to her so she could pull herself upright. Rubbing the back of her head, Donna refused her help.

'You didn't need to do that,' Noah said when they were alone.

'Somebody had to, or they would have gone on for ever making your life miserable.'

'There's nothing they could do to make my life any worse than it already is,' he said gloomily.

She followed the direction of his gaze. He was staring at

the scattered pieces of the photograph on the ground.

'It would be less embarrassing for me if you would push me over so I could get down there to pick them up,' he said. 'I hate asking for help.'

'So what's wrong with your leg?' she asked after she'd gathered together the pieces of ruined photograph and he'd put them in his pocket.

He looked her square in the eye. 'Are you asking if I'm a spastic? And would it make a difference if I was?'

'I'm only asking you what's wrong with your leg, you idiot.'

He shrugged. 'It was an accident.'

'Are you stuck like that for always? You know, with that thing on your leg?'

He shrugged again. 'I don't know.'

His eyes had now settled on the screwed-up ball of paper. Lydia said, 'Do you want that as well?'

'Not really. It wasn't very good.'

'Can I see it?'

'I'd rather you didn't.'

'Why, because you've made me look even uglier than I am?'

'You're not ugly.'

'Liar.'

'So far you've called me an idiot and a liar. Anything else you want to say?'

She picked up the ball of paper. 'Yes,' she said with a smile. 'Can we be friends?'

Chapter Sixteen

It was the second day of half-term and Lydia was missing Noah.

She had decided to keep quiet about him at home, to keep him as her very own special secret. He was the one really good thing to happen to her in ages and because of that she was frightened he might be taken away from her. Having lost so much already, she hated the thought of losing him as well.

They spent all their break times together at school, usually playing hangman and noughts and crosses, but she still didn't know that much about him. One thing she did know was that he was a Roman Catholic. Every Friday morning he and about nine other children were excused from assembly so that a man in a black dress could come into school to talk to them.

He'd moved to live in Swallowsdale only recently and had had hundreds of operations on his leg, spending ages in hospital because of it. The glimpse of that ripped-up photograph was all Lydia had to go on about his family and she assumed Donna had been right, that it was a picture of his parents. It seemed an odd thing to carry round with you at school – like bringing in your favourite teddy. It was asking for trouble. Sometimes she thought he deliberately made himself a target. He was either very stupid, which she didn't think he was, or he just didn't care what anyone did to him. For all his quiet thoughtfulness and his smashed-up leg, she'd decided he was a lot tougher than she'd initially thought.

But something he'd said that day at the back of the

portable classrooms niggled. *There's nothing they could do to make my life any worse than it already is.* What had he meant by that? His life didn't seem that bad to her. OK, he had to wear that awful contraption and couldn't run about like the rest of them, but was that really so bad? So what that he couldn't play football or go on the climbing frame? He could draw and paint better than anyone else she knew. Compared to her – having to live with her grandparents because both her mother and father were dead – a mangled leg wasn't exactly the end of the world.

She'd deliberately not told him much about her life or her grandparents. She wanted him to think she was as normal as everyone else. If he knew the truth he might not want to be her friend any more. Anyway, it was better to keep everything separate. Their friendship was perfect just as it was. No point in jumbling it all up.

She had kept the crumpled picture he'd drawn of her and at first she hadn't known what to think when she'd looked at it. Her eyebrows certainly stood out, but instead of the cross expression she'd been expecting, he'd made her look ... well, less cross and a bit nicer. Curious, she had asked him when he'd drawn it. With his face turning slightly pink, he'd said he'd done it from memory at home. She felt doubly flattered that he'd not only wanted to draw her, but that he'd been thinking of her outside of school. She now had the picture smoothed out and hidden inside the children's Bible Pastor John had given her.

Lydia was missing Pastor John, too, although she hadn't known him for long. She often wondered where he was. Was he still having 'relations' with that married woman from Keighley? Referring to her dictionary, she'd discovered that this was a way of saying that Pastor John had been having 'sexual intercourse' with the woman. She knew about all that stuff because when Mum had Valerie growing inside her tummy, she'd explained how Valerie had got there – Daddy's 'thingy' had gone inside Mummy and had planted a tiny seed. Lydia also knew that the words 'sexual intercourse' were two words that were guaranteed to make a grown-up go bright red and change the subject. And because she was bored, bored, *BORED*, she thought it might be interesting to see what kind of reaction she would get if she said those two words now.

She was helping to pass round cups of tea during her grandmother's Tea and Sisters Scripture meeting. As a result of Pastor Rigby's new rules, the Sisters were dressed even more plainly than they used to be. Sister Vera wasn't wearing her beaded necklace or amethyst brooch on her huge wobbly bosom any more and Sister Hilda's hair was no longer that strange mauve colour: it was snowy white. Sister Mildred's hair was also different. Before it had been like a see-through doily of rigid white curls – now her pink, baldy scalp was even more visible through the wisps of hair that lay flat on her head. Lydia felt embarrassed to look at her. And poor old Sister Lottie looked all wrong in her sad flowerless hat. Only Lydia's grandmother looked exactly the same as before.

Whilst concentrating hard on not spilling any tea as she moved amongst the Sisters, Lydia was listening to what was being said, waiting for exactly the right moment. It came just as she was handing Sister Joan her cup and saucer: over by the door, in a hushed tone, Sister Mildred mentioned Pastor John's name. When the tutting and shushing had died away, Lydia said, 'What does sexual intercourse mean, Grandmother?'

Her question was like a bomb going off. In the commotion that followed Lydia immediately regretted what she'd asked. What had got into her? As if seeing it all in slow motion, Lydia watched Sister Joan's cup and saucer slip out of her hands onto the carpet, while next to her Sister Vera started choking on a Rich Tea Finger, causing her bosom to shake so violently Lydia feared it might burst out of her dress, sending buttons popping. Meanwhile, Sister Hilda, who had Valerie sitting on her lap, covered Val's ears with her hands and Sister Mildred quivered like a jelly. Sister Lottie had turned the colour of beetroot and looked as if she was trying not to giggle.

But Lydia's grandmother looked like thunder. Down on her hands and knees at Sister Joan's feet, she was scrubbing furiously at the carpet with a paper napkin. 'Go to your room at once, Lydia. You're not fit to mix in decent company.'

Closing the door after her, Lydia heard her grandmother say, 'I blame that whore of a mother of hers. She painted her nails red, you know.'

Upstairs, Lydia lay on her bed, her hands clasped behind her head. What *had* got into her? What had made her say something so stupid that was bound to cause trouble? Afraid to think how she might be punished, she swung herself off the bed and went to look out of the window. It had started to rain; in the distance she could see it slicing the air at an angle that was almost horizontal. Down in the road, she could see The Floozy tottering along on her high heels, her short mac belted tightly at her waist, an umbrella protecting her beehive hairdo, her bottom swinging from side to side. When she was out of sight, Lydia wondered what Noah was doing. Whatever it was he had to be having more fun than she was.

She went back to lying on the bed. Disappointed, she had half hoped that Valerie would come upstairs after her and keep her company. Since Lydia had started school back in September, Val had changed. There were times when her sister seemed happier to be with their grandmother than with Lydia. She had become everyone's favourite at church and the Sisters couldn't stop cooing over her or chucking her under the chin. Sometimes they squabbled over whose turn it was to have her sit on their lap.

Lydia certainly wasn't jealous – who wanted to sit on Sister Vera's lap and risk being suffocated by that enormous bosom! – but occasionally she did feel left out. At least Valerie was happy and had started to talk more and was sleeping in her own bed with only Belinda Bell for company. But Lydia missed doing things for her, missed being the only one who could understand her nods and blinks. It upset her that she wasn't as important to Valerie as she used to be.

'Your grandmother's worried about you.'

Normally Lydia didn't have to think too much about where to look when she was being spoken to, but with Pastor Digby it was different. She couldn't stop herself from switching between his good eye and his sinister black eye patch. It was like a game of ping-pong – good eye, black eye patch, good eye, black—

'Lydia, are you listening to me?'

The rapping sharpness of his voice made Lydia concentrate extra hard and stand up straighter. Definitely the good eye. 'Yes, Pastor Digby,' she said.

'Your grandmother has asked me to talk to you because she's concerned that you're succumbing to outside influences.'

'Um … I'm not sure what you mean, Pastor Digby,' she lied. She knew exactly what this was about. Just hadn't expected Pastor Digby to be the one who told her off.

He rose from his chair, his tall thin body looking like a scarecrow silhouetted in the light from the window as he stood with his back to her. 'I'm talking about wicked people putting filth into your mouth, Lydia. Your grandmother told me that yesterday you uttered words no child of your age should know or dare to say out loud. And I think you know to which words I am referring.'

'I only asked what they meant.'

Pastor Digby slowly turned round. 'But where did you hear such wicked words? That's what your grandparents and I want to know.'

Thinking fast and concerned that he might take her dictionary away if she told him the truth, Lydia said, 'It was the older children at the bus stop.'

His good eye glittered back at her. Did he believe her? Or had she just cooked her goose? Would he now ban her from going to school? Her gaze slid to the black eye patch. From the other side of the closed door she could hear her grandmother singing to Valerie that Jesus wanted her for a sunbeam.

'Some children are born bad, Lydia. Did you know that?'

She shook her head, wondering where the conversation was going next. He came and sat down again. 'Unfortunately, it's true,' he said. 'Do you have bad thoughts, Lydia?'

She was having one right now. Why couldn't he drop dead and leave her alone?

'Tell me the truth, Lydia.'

'Sometimes,' she said warily.

He leaned forward, resting his elbows on the shiny fabric of his suit trousers. 'I thought as much. What kind of bad thoughts do you have?'

Hoping to shock him into leaving her alone, she said, 'I sometimes wish I was dead so I could be with my mum and dad.'

His good eye bulged like a full moon and he snapped to attention in the chair. 'Only God can decide who lives and dies,' he said sternly. 'That's why what your mother did was such a sin. It was selfish and wrong of her. Surely you don't want to be like her, Lydia, an evil unbeliever who abandoned her children on a railway line?'

Lydia suddenly wanted to run from the room. Why was he saying these things to her? Her mother hadn't been evil. She'd been unhappy. And it was all Lydia's fault that she had been unhappy – that's why she did what she did. That's why she killed herself.

'You know what happens to evil people like your mother, don't you, Lydia? They don't go to heaven to be with our Lord; they go to hell. Is that where you want to go? Lydia? Answer me. Is that where you want to go?'

Tears filled her eyes. She wanted to say yes, if it meant she could be with her mother again and tell her how sorry she was. But she knew that Pastor Digby would only leave her alone if she gave him the answer she thought he wanted to hear. 'No,' she tried.

'Louder, Lydia. I can't hear you.'

'No,' she said, 'I don't want to go to hell.'

'Then you must change. You must be the child God wants you to be, not this wild, disrespectful, feral, devil-child your grandmother tells me your mother allowed you to become. You must put that wretched to-be-pitied person behind you, Lydia. Can you do that?'

She swallowed and nodded.

'When I ask you a question I expect a proper answer, Lydia.'

'Yes, Pastor Digby,' she said. 'I will try to be a better person.'

That Sunday at church it was decided that Lydia would take the leaflets left over from their weekend in Scarborough in to school with her to distribute. She couldn't help but feel this was her grandmother's petty way of punishing her for ruining her Tea and Sisters Scripture meeting. Not that she had any intention of doing anything so embarrassing. She would simply dump them all in a bin.

Chapter Seventeen

Lydia was disappointed when there was no sign of Noah at school the next morning. She had been so looking forward to seeing him after a week of being apart. At first break, having offered to stay behind and help get the classroom ready for their art lesson, she asked Miss Dillinger if she knew what was wrong with Noah.

'His uncle phoned to say he had a hospital appointment,' Miss Dillinger said as Lydia stood at the sink filling jam jars with water from the tap.

'Has he got to have another operation on his leg?' she asked, concerned.

'As far as I'm aware his uncle didn't say anything about that.'

The last of the jam jars filled, Lydia began placing them carefully on the tables that Miss Dillinger had covered with newspaper. Something struck Lydia as being odd. Why wasn't it Noah's mother or father who had left the message? She thought of the photograph he had been carrying round with him, and because Miss Dillinger seemed to be in a chatty mood, she said, 'Is Noah's uncle taking him to the hospital?'

'I assume so.'

'Not his mum or dad, then?'

Miss Dillinger, counting out sheets of grey sugar paper, stopped what she was doing but didn't say anything. Lydia watched the woman's face closely; the hesitant expression was one she had come to know well. She had seen it a million times in other adult faces. If Miss Dillinger didn't want to answer Lydia's question, it could mean only one thing: she had stumbled across something she wasn't supposed to know about.

'Good heavens,' Miss Dillinger suddenly exclaimed, 'just look at the time, Lydia! We're nowhere near ready. Quick, go and get the paintbrushes; they're on the middle shelf next to the glue.'

The next day another cross was put against Noah's name in the register. As soon as the opportunity arose, Lydia approached Miss Dillinger.

'Sorry, Lydia,' the teacher said. 'I have no idea where he is today; there's been no further message. Don't worry. I'm sure he'll show up tomorrow.'

But Lydia was worried. She was convinced something terrible had happened to Noah and as the day wore on her anxiety grew to the point that by the time she was on the bus going home, she imagined the absolute worst: she would never see her friend again.

The following day there was still no sign of Noah and once again Miss Dillinger claimed not to know where he was. Lydia decided the woman was lying. Nothing else for it; she would have to find out the truth for herself. Knowing that the headmistress insisted on fresh air swirling around every room of the school, no matter what the weather was, she went and hung about outside the open window of the staff room during afternoon break. For ages she breathed in the smell of cigarette smoke and listened to the teachers complaining about some of the children. Alfie Stone and Jack Horsley got the most mentions. As did Donna Jones.

With only a few minutes left before she knew the bell would ring, Lydia was ready to give up, but then she heard her own name being spoken. Jamming herself as near to the window as she dared without being seen, she held her breath and listened hard. They were talking about her and Noah. 'It's easy to see why they took to each other the way they did,' someone said. 'You know, having so much in common.'

'But that's the weird part. I get the distinct feeling Lydia doesn't know anything about Noah's background.' Lydia recognized Miss Dillinger's voice. 'She wouldn't have asked me what she did if she knew.'

'Why, what did she ask you?'

'She wanted to know if his parents had taken him to the hospital. Clearly Noah hasn't told her anything.'

'You're right, that is weird. You'd think he'd want to confide in someone, especially a kindred spirit.'

'Or maybe what happened to his parents is just too awful for him to talk about. Who could blame him?'

The bell rang and somebody inside the staff room sang, 'Hi bloody ho, it's off to teach we go.'

Yet again, the next day Noah's chair remained empty. At first break Lydia went to look for the person most likely to be able to help her. In the short time she had been at the school she had heard many stories about Mr Darby, the school caretaker. You always knew when he was nearby because he stank of disinfectant; it was rumoured that he dabbed it on like aftershave to cover up the smell of the gin that he drank all day. Depending on who you listened to he was either one of the Great Train Robbers who'd managed to escape the police and was hiding here until everyone had forgotten about the robbery, or he was a Russian spy on a secret mission. But the two things he was really famous for were knowing everything that went on in the school, and his stash of lost property pens, especially fountain pens. Some said he went round the classrooms when everyone had gone home and helped himself to them from the desks. If you wanted your pen back, you had to go and see him and pay a forfeit for being stupid enough to lose it in the first place. Lydia had heard that he made the boys hand over a whole sixpence to get a pen back, but made the girls show him their knickers. She had yet to speak to any girl who had actually done this, but perhaps that was because they were too embarrassed to admit it.

As she knocked on Mr Darby's door, Lydia hoped that

she wouldn't have to pay anything in exchange for asking for information.

'Not been with us long, have yer?' Mr Darby said, when she stepped into the dim, fuggy atmosphere of the boiler room. 'Aren't yer the lass who lost her mother?'

She wobbled her head in a yes-and-no kind of way, at the same time fighting the urge to cover her face with a hand. The pong of disinfectant made her want to gag.

'What's the matter? Cat got yer tongue?' He hauled himself from his chair and Lydia was shocked to see two enormous breasts staring back at her from the page of a newspaper laid out on a table he'd been sitting at. Her grandmother said that women who showed their naked bodies like that were filthy, nasty tarts. But Lydia thought the woman looked extremely clean and not at all nasty. In fact she was smiling in a very friendly way. Her breasts must have been quite heavy because she was holding them up with both hands and sort of pointing them towards whoever had taken the photograph.

'So what can I do for yer?' he asked, at the same time turning the page of the newspaper. 'Lost a pen? Is that it?'

Steeling herself, Lydia said, 'I want to know something,' she said.

'Oh, aye?' Staring at her, he scratched his chin; Lydia could hear the scrape of his nail on his bristly skin. 'And what might that be?'

'It's about a friend of mine, Noah Solomon.'

'And what made yer think I'd know owt about him?'

She shrugged helplessly. 'I just thought ...' Her voice trailed off. How could she politely accuse him of knowing everything that went on at school because he was such a nosy parker? She began to think coming here hadn't been such a good idea after all. She took a step back towards the door.

He suddenly started to laugh at her. 'It's OK, lass, don't look so scared. I'm not about to eat yer. There's not enough on yer bones to feed a sparrow any road. So what is it yer want to know about this friend of yours?'

'I want to know what happened to his parents.'

'Do yer indeed?'

'Yes I do,' she said with as much conviction as she could. 'It's very important to me.'

He laughed again and sat down. 'Hark at yer with your posh cut-glass voice! "It's very important to me,"' he mimicked.

Lydia had never been called posh before. To her surprise she felt a rush of pride.

'OK, then,' he said. 'I'll tell yer what yer want to know. Sit yerself down.'

Lydia looked around the boiler room, noticing for the first time that the place was a giant slag heap of mess and clutter. Mops, brooms, buckets, tins of polish, grubby towels, boxes of soap, newspapers, punctured footballs, cans of disinfectant and a stack of wastepaper bins gave the impression of swallowing up the room whole. But nowhere could she see another chair.

'Go on,' Mr Darby said, 'pull up a drum. Or are yer too fancy for that?' He pointed to a large drum of cooking oil.

'Shouldn't this be in the kitchens?' she asked when she'd got herself settled.

'Yer accusing me of sommat?' he said sharply.

Aha! So the rumour about him pinching stuff was true. 'Tell me about Noah Solomon,' she said.

'Pushy little thing, aren't yer? Let's hope yer've got a strong stomach, because the way I see it, yer gonna need it. Aye, it's a grim tale and all. Are you sitting comfortably?'

She nodded.

'Then I'll begin.'

Chapter Eighteen

Lydia heard Noah before she saw him. She was hanging up her duffel coat whilst trying to stop Jack Horsley messing about with her hair when she caught the unmistakable sound of clanking footsteps.

Since visiting Mr Darby in his smelly boiler room yesterday afternoon – and escaping without having to give him anything! – she had been wondering what to say to Noah when he did finally return to school. She badly wanted him to know that she *knew*, but had no idea how he would react if she so much as hinted that she did. Now that he was here, though, she felt unexpectedly shy of him and playing for time, she pretended to hunt through her coat pockets for something vitally important whilst listening to the others dishing out their welcome-back comments. 'Look who it is – it's old spacky! ... Not floated off in your ark, then, spaso?'

Not a word did Noah say in response and when everything eventually went quiet and she was sure it was just the two of them left amongst the coats and plimsoll bags, Lydia turned round. He had his back to her and appeared to be doing what she'd just finished doing – hunting through his coat pockets for something vitally important. 'Hello,' she said awkwardly. 'How's your leg?'

He stopped what he was doing and faced her with a puzzled expression. 'My leg? It's the same as ever. Why do you ask?'

'Miss Dillinger said you were at the hospital on Monday. With your uncle.'

'Oh, that. It was nothing.'

The careless flatness of his reply smarted. After all the worry she'd gone through, how could he be so off-hand with her? Didn't he realize how much she cared about him? Her head buzzing with indignation and not minding how he would react, she said, 'Why didn't you tell me about your parents?' Straight off she could see she'd surprised him. And was glad.

'Why didn't you tell me about *your* parents?' he said with a frown.

Two could play at that game! 'You never asked,' she said, quick as a flash.

'Well, neither did you.'

Only then, as she tried to think of something else to fire back at him, did Lydia realize what he'd just admitted: that he knew about Mum and Dad. But how? It certainly wasn't something she had ever discussed with anyone at school. There again, Mr Darby seemed to know all about her.

She watched Noah pick up his bag from the floor and, regretting her outburst, she said, 'Can I ask you *now* about your parents?'

'What? Right now?'

'No, not *now*, silly. Later.'

He gave her a long, hard look. 'OK,' he said, 'after lunch, on the far side of the field. Under the beech tree.'

The morning dragged on. Who cared about long division or what boring old Monsieur Bertillon and his stupid family were getting up to in their *maison* when there was Noah's family to hear about? Break time had passed with Lydia helping him to catch up on the work he'd missed, and although she was brimming over with questions, she kept her mouth firmly shut.

But now, here they were beneath the copper beech tree, the chilly November wind swirling the fallen leaves on the ground at their feet. Noah seemed happy enough just to stand with her in the rustling silence, but Lydia wasn't. She decided to be the one to get things moving, to loosen that tongue of his. 'My mother killed herself by jumping in front of a train,' she blurted out. She poked at a stone in the dusty hard ground with the toe of her shoe. 'My sister and I were sleeping on the embankment when she did it.'

'I know,' was all he said.

'Who told you?'

'Does it matter?'

'Was it Mr Darby, the caretaker?'

Noah shook his head. 'No. It was Donna Jones.'

The stone popped out of the ground and Lydia gave it a kick. She wished chicken pox, mumps, German measles, tonsillitis, and verrucas the size of golf balls on Donna Jones. All at the same time and with a dose of diarrhoea thrown in. She had no idea how Donna had found out about her mother, or why she hadn't said anything to Lydia, but for now that wasn't important. 'If you knew, why didn't you ask me about it?' she asked Noah.

'Because it would have led to us talking like this.'

'Is that so very bad?'

'Perhaps not for you, but for me, yes. I don't like to talk about what happened.'

'You think it's any easier for me, telling people about my mum's suicide?' As soon as the word was out, Lydia wanted to snatch it back. Never before had she uttered the word 'suicide' aloud. She began poking at another stone in the ground with her shoe, conscious that her cheeks were burning with something that she thought was embarrassed shame, although she couldn't really understand why.

'Was it very bad for you?' Noah asked.

No one had asked Lydia this before. Decisions and assumptions had been made on her behalf because of what her mother had done, but not one single person had actually asked her how she'd felt at the time. Now that someone had, she wasn't sure how to answer. 'There was too much going on to stop and think about it,' she said without looking up. 'Besides, I had my little sister to take care of.'

'You were lucky. I had nothing to distract me.'

She risked a glance at his face. 'Did you have any idea it was going to happen?'

'There'd been lots of arguments and all that kind of thing, but nothing to warn me that one day I'd come home from school and find—' He broke off, his eyes sliding away from hers.

Lydia waited patiently for him to carry on. And waited.

Flexing his clanky leg, he eventually said, 'Mum didn't answer the back door when I knocked so I looked in through the kitchen window and saw my father lying on the floor with his head in the oven. It seems stupid now when I say it, but I thought he was trying to mend it. He was always tinkering with stuff that had stopped working or was broken. I didn't even think it was odd he was home so early from work. I knocked on the window to attract his attention but he didn't seem to hear me.'

'Didn't you notice he wasn't moving?'

Noah shot her a dark look. 'I'd never come across any-one who had killed themselves by sticking their heads in a gas oven before, so perhaps I was a bit slow to act.'

Lydia could have kicked herself for her clumsiness. It had sounded as if she was criticizing, or worse, blaming Noah. How would she like it if he told her she might have been able to save her mother if she hadn't agreed to go for that walk in the middle of the night? 'I'm sorry,' she said. 'Just ignore me and my big mouth.'

He flexed his knee again and took up the story once more. 'I knocked and knocked and when I finally realized something was seriously wrong I smashed a pane of glass in the back door and let myself in. I switched off the gas and dragged my father out to the garden. I tried to give him the kiss of life, the way I'd seen it done in a book, but he was dead ... I was too late.'

Lydia pictured the scene: Noah struggling with his clanky leg and trying to heave his father's heavy body outside. She felt so sorry for him. But something else, too. Envy. There had been no opportunity for her to try and save her mother. No last touch. No final goodbye. Only the terror of being woken from a deep, fuzzy sleep by the unearthly sound of metal screeching on metal. She'd had a vague feeling that fear had made her let out a scream, but she couldn't be sure. What she had instinctively known at the time was that her mother was in danger. She had leapt to her feet and scrambled pell-mell down the slippery bank towards the railway line. She hadn't given a thought to Valerie who was still strapped into her pushchair on the embankment. It was a while before anyone spotted her and when they did, someone yelled, 'For God's sake, don't let her see!' A man and a woman came and led her away. She'd tried to wriggle out of their grasp, but they wouldn't let go of her. She'd shouted at them: 'But my mother's down there, don't you understand? I have to go to her!'

'God help you, that's not your mother, dearie,' the woman told her. Initially this had given Lydia hope. She'd got it wrong! How silly of her to think her mother would do such a terrible thing, that she would want to kill herself, leaving Lydia and Valerie all alone. But her relief was soon shattered when she understood that the woman had meant something altogether worse: the body she wasn't allowed to see was no longer recognizable as Lydia's mother.

A cold gust of wind brought her back from that dawn morning and a shower of leaves fell like huge pieces of copper confetti at her feet. Her throat had tightened and tears were filling her eyes. Embarrassed, she worked at trying to loosen another stone in the ground. If Noah could tell his story without crying, so could she. 'When did you find your mother?' she asked.

'When I knew there was nothing more I could do for Dad I went looking for her. I found her upstairs on their bed. She'd been ... Dad had strangled her.'

Despite having heard this from Mr Darby, Lydia was still shocked to hear Noah say it. She couldn't imagine her father ever having wanted to do that to Mum. Not even when she accidentally knocked over his motorbike and ruined the paintwork. You'd have to be very cross with the person you were married to, to want to kill them like that. Curious, she said, 'How did you know she'd been strangled?'

'I didn't at the time. I found that out afterwards. And that it was Dad who had killed her. He wrote me a letter.'

Lydia felt another pang of envy. Her mother hadn't left her a note. 'Do you still have the letter?' she asked.

He hesitated, as if he regretted what he'd just told her. 'I do,' he said slowly, 'but you must swear not to tell anyone.'

'Of course I won't tell anyone. Who would I tell, anyway?'

'You swear?' He suddenly seemed jumpy and anxious.

'I swear on ...' Not her mum or dad's life, so whose? 'On my sister's life,' she said, hoping that she wasn't tempting fate. 'So what did the letter say?' she asked.

'Not much. Mostly that he was sorry for the mess he was leaving behind him and that he hoped I wouldn't hate him for what he'd done.'

'And do you?'

'How can I hate him? He just went a bit crazy, that's all.'

That's all. Lydia wondered about this. Was that what had happened to her mother that night? Had she merely gone a bit crazy? Did it happen to everyone? Would she and Noah go a bit crazy one day? 'What did the police think of the letter when they read it?' she asked.

'I never showed it to them. It was *my* letter. It was private ... between Dad and me. That's why you mustn't tell anyone about it.'

'Could *I* read it?'

One of his eyebrows shot up. 'Why would you want to do that?'

The honest answer was that the more Noah shared with her, the better she felt. It was as if his own dark experience was shining a light on hers. But thinking he wouldn't understand this, she said, 'We're best friends, aren't we? And best friends share everything.'

When he didn't reply right away, Lydia began to worry. Supposing she had got it wrong and Noah didn't consider her his best friend?

'OK,' he said. 'I'll let you read it, but you must remember your promise.'

Suddenly the letter didn't matter to her. All that was important was that he hadn't denied their friendship.

Chapter Nineteen

Noah was very clear about two things.

The first was that Lydia must keep the promise she had made not to tell anyone about the letter and the second was that she had to meet him somewhere outside of school to read it. He said he couldn't risk taking the letter into school and someone getting their hands on it. She suspected he was thinking of Donna Jones's hands in particular. But since that day round the back of the Portakabins, Donna hadn't come near either of them. Lydia had had a heart-stopping scare just the other afternoon, when she'd caught sight of Donna going into a house at the other end of Hillside Terrace – the cheap end, as her grandmother called it. It turned out that Donna had an aunt who lived in the road and that was probably how she'd got to hear about Lydia's mum killing herself.

Following that day in the field beneath the beech tree when Noah had told her about his parents, Lydia had told him more about herself, about Dad, Creepy-Ridley, her mother's sweet sherry breath, and the ventriloquist's dummy. In exchange, he had told her that his parents' deaths had made it into the newspapers, and not just the local ones in Lincoln where he used to live, but into the big papers read by the whole country. Knowing that Noah was sort of famous made Lydia proud to be his friend. His cleverness – which he never showed off about – was something else she was proud of. Secretly she wanted that same cleverness for herself and she had started to work extra hard in class. Nothing pleased her more than when she got a better mark than Noah. Apparently, when he'd spent so much time in hospital, he'd done nothing but read from a set of encyclopaedias his father had bought for him.

Lydia was glad that her mother's death hadn't made it to the big newspapers – just two paragraphs in the *Maywood Gazette* – as she hated to think of so many people knowing how Mum had died. Particularly people at school. Yet Noah wasn't worried about anyone at school finding out who he was. He said his name and photograph had never appeared in the papers, so why would anyone think he had anything to do with the story? But he wasn't happy that the headmistress and teachers at school had been put in the picture by his uncle. 'I don't like knowing that they're watching me,' he admitted one day. 'They're probably worried I'm going to go loopy and fly off the handle.'

Lydia was fascinated by this remark. 'Do you think you *will* go loopy?' she asked.

'Who knows?'

Something else that fascinated Lydia was Noah's uncle. Noah rarely spoke about him in any real detail, so in the hope he would tell her more, she had thought she could trade with him by telling him about her grandparents and the Sisters and Brothers and their church. Disappointingly, all she'd got in return was that he thought the church she went to sounded a bit weird and that it wasn't like the one his uncle occasionally took him to.

How and where to meet up with Noah to read his letter was proving to be almost impossible. Apart from school and church and the end of the garden, Lydia didn't go anywhere where she could be alone with him.

There's always a way, her father used to say, and a week into December, when every day the sky was the colour of dirty dishwater, an opportunity to meet with Noah outside of school fell into Lydia's lap.

Sister Lottie was ill in bed with bronchitis. The Sisters had been praying for her and taking it in turns to visit with Pyrex dishes of nourishing meals, most of which she was too ill to eat. It was decided that Lydia should also take her turn to pay a call on Sister Lottie and so on Sunday afternoon she was loaded up with a flask of hot vegetable soup and a copy of Pastor Digby's sermon, which he had written out specially for Sister Lottie. Seeing this as a golden opportunity, Lydia hatched a plan to meet Noah at his uncle's house when she had finished her visit to Sister Lottie.

What she hadn't bargained on was how long it would take her to reach Sister Lottie. From the back of her grandfather's junk-piled wooden garage, a heavy, rusting old bicycle emerged. It was the first thing Lydia had seen which had actually belonged to her father. Despite the half can of oil squirted at the gears and chain, the bicycle still made a deafening racket when the pedals went round. The saddle was as hard and pointy as a rock with a rusting metal spring bursting through the split leather, and there was also the small matter of the crossbar to negotiate.

Ker-lunk, *ker-dunk*, *ker-lunk*, *ker-dunk* went the pedals. Downhill wasn't too bad, but uphill was a nightmare. Several times she had to jump off and push the bike. Eventually, twenty minutes late, she made it to Cuckoo Lane where Sister Lottie lived. Exhausted and steaming like a hot pasty in her enormous duffel coat, she unhooked the basket from the handlebars, left the bike leaning against the gate and panted up the short path to the little terraced house. She'd been told how to let herself in and after slipping her hand through the letterbox, she found the key on the end of a long piece of string. Once inside, she called out to Sister Lottie. 'Up here,' came a faint reply, followed by the sound of coughing.

Feeling a bit like Little Red Riding Hood as she went upstairs with the basket, Lydia held on tightly to the banister; the narrow strip of shabby stair carpet was thin and coming away dangerously in places. Balls of dust and fluff had collected in the corners of the varnished steps. Knowing how fussy her grandmother was about housework and how she was always telling Lydia that cleanliness was next to godliness, she wondered why no one from church, including her grandmother, had offered to flick a duster round Sister Lottie's house since she'd been stuck in bed.

The poor woman didn't look at all well. She was propped up in bed in a shabby pink bedjacket, her pale face almost lost in the whiteness of the pillows. She smiled when she saw Lydia. 'What a lovely surprise,' she said. 'Is your grandmother with you? Is she downstairs?'

'No. I came on my own. I cycled all the way,' Lydia said proudly, 'on my father's old bicycle.'

'Goodness! What an adventure! But I'm afraid I'm not very good company at the moment.'

'That's all right. I've brought you something to eat. Oh, and Pastor Digby's sermon. I'm supposed to read it to you while you have your soup.'

'That doesn't sound much fun for you. I'm sure you'd rather be somewhere else.'

Lydia thought of Noah. The plan had been to get her visit over and done with as quickly as possible, but here now with Sister Lottie and seeing how unwell she was, Lydia's heart softened. This funny old woman had always been so kind to her. 'I've come here specially to see you,' she said brightly, shrugging off her coat and setting the basket down on the end of the bed. 'Shall I fetch a bowl from the kitchen for your soup?'

Sister Lottie's house was so small it reminded Lydia of a doll's house. The kitchen was particularly tiny; there wasn't even room for the smallest of tables. There was a white china sink with a wooden draining board, a green and yellow gas cooker, two shelves that contained a tea caddy and a small collection of tins and jars – pilchards, butter beans, rice pudding, custard powder, Shippam's paste. A refrigerator hummed noisily in the corner and next to it was a cream cupboard where Lydia found a bowl and a spoon.

On her way back to the stairs she stopped to push open the door to the only other room downstairs and peeped in. It was the front room and was jam-packed with furniture, big and small. With its flowery wallpaper, fancy frilled and fringed lampshades, doilies and antimacassars, books and ornaments everywhere, it looked a busy sort of room. The framed pictures on the walls were old-fashioned black and white photographs. Some were very old, Lydia decided, judging from the funny clothes the people were wearing. She closed the door after her and carried on carefully up the stairs with the tray. Now that she had taken off her coat and had cooled down she realized just how cold Sister Lottie's house was. Surely that wasn't good for someone so ill?

After she'd poured out the bowl of soup and rearranged Sister Lottie's pillows so she could sit up comfortably, she noticed that behind the chair she was about to sit on there was the teeniest-weeniest fireplace. 'Would you like me to light a fire for you?' she asked. 'It's very cold in here.'

Sister Lottie's pale face brightened. 'Would you? Oh, that would be marvellous. How good you are to me. What an angel you are!'

Lydia had never actually made a fire before, but she didn't let on to Sister Lottie. She gathered up all the equipment she thought she needed – the coal scuttle from the front room, along with a pair of tongs, some kindling in a box by the back door, and a box of matches from the windowsill behind the cooker. Something was missing though. 'I need some paper,' she said to Sister Lottie. 'Do you have any old newspapers?'

Sister Lottie shook her head, and then right at the same time, their eyes fell on Pastor Digby's ten-page sermon, which Lydia had yet to read. 'That will do,' Lydia said decisively.

Sister Lottie gasped, and then coughed painfully, her face turning pink. 'Do you think we ought to?' she croaked when she'd caught her breath.

Already screwing up the sermon into loose balls, Lydia shrugged. 'I won't tell him if you don't. And anyway, I can tell you word for word what his sermon was about.'

Sister Lottie relaxed back into the pillows. 'Of course you can; you're the brightest little girl I know.'

Lydia suspected that apart from Valerie, she was the *only* girl Sister Lottie knew. 'I'm not that little, you know,' she said, adding one last lump of coal to the fire and striking a match.

'You are to an old woman like me. What's more, you're a very special girl whom I'm immensely fond of.'

It was so long since anyone had said anything so nice to her, Lydia didn't know what to say.

Strange, she thought later as she pumped away on the *ker-lunky*, *ker-dunky* pedals, that an unexpected kindness like that should make her feel sad. You'd think it would have the opposite effect.

It was getting dark when she found herself on the road that, according to the map Noah had drawn for her, would lead directly to Upper Swallowsdale House. He had told her that he lived in the middle of nowhere and that she had to watch out for a stile in the drystone wall on the right and then a large house made of dirty grey stone.

She saw the stile and, finding the hill too steep, she swung her leg over the crossbar and jumped off the bike, pushing it the last few yards. Noah had explained that his uncle would be out, which meant they would have the place to themselves.

Noah was waiting for her at the front door. 'You're late,' he said irritably. 'I thought you weren't coming.'

'Sorry, but I stayed with Sister Lottie longer than I thought I would.'

He instantly cheered up at her apology. 'Oh, well, you're here now, that's all that matters. Let's go up to my bedroom.'

Lydia had never seen Noah tackle stairs before – everything at school was on one level – and she found herself having to look away as he struggled with the steps. Lagging behind, she discreetly looked back down to the gloomy hallway. While it was the largest she had ever seen – in fact she had never been inside such a big house – she could see the tell-tale signs of something that Noah had kept quiet about: Noah and his uncle were poor. There weren't any carpets anywhere and the floor wasn't even properly made; it was just slabs of worn, shiny stone. They couldn't afford electricity either, by the looks of things. Instead of proper lights there were white candles fixed onto the walls with funny little mirrors behind them. Melting wax was dripping onto the stone floor beneath them as well as making a mess on the top of a scruffy wooden chest. There were strange unframed paintings on the walls. She couldn't really work out what they were pictures of, but it occurred to her that maybe someone had made a mistake and they were actually hanging upside down.

There were more paintings covering the walls on the landing upstairs. One seemed to have been painted with chunks of blue and purple paint and showed a naked woman sprawled across a fancy settee that had only one end to it. But it wasn't the kind of woman Mr Darby had been looking at in his newspaper in the boiler room. This one had two eyeless heads on the end of long thin, bendy necks. Lydia turned away from it quickly. 'You get used to them after a while,' Noah said.

Annoyed that she'd been caught out, she said, 'Who's it of?' She didn't want him to think she was childish enough to be embarrassed.

'My mother.'

'Your mother! She had two heads?'

He smiled. 'No, silly. It's called abstract art.'

'Oh, that,' she said airily. She made a mental note to look up the word 'abstract' when she got home.

'This is another painting of my mother,' he said when they had reached the end of the landing, which was about a mile long and lit with yet more candles. 'It's her on her eighteenth birthday. Do you like it?'

This painting was much more normal. It was a picture of a pretty fair-haired girl wearing a low-necked dress and a necklace. She was sitting on a chair and behind her was

136

a mirror with the fuzzy reflection of a man in it. The style was very different from the other picture. A lot less paint had been used and the colours were soft and delicate. Lydia decided she liked it.

'See the man in the mirror?' Noah said. 'That's my uncle. He and Mum were twins.'

'So it was both their birthdays?'

'Yes. My uncle says it was the first picture he'd painted that he was actually proud of.'

'Your uncle did it?' Lydia couldn't keep the surprise out of her voice. 'Did he also do the other one?'

Noah nodded. 'All the paintings in the house are his.'

She thought of the upside-down pictures downstairs. 'Is he a proper artist?' she asked doubtfully. 'You know, one who gets paid for his paintings?'

'Oh, yes. He gets paid stacks of money. I'm thinking of being an artist like him one day.'

Thinking of the bare stone floors and all the candles, Lydia kept her mouth shut. For once she felt she knew something that Noah didn't: that her uncle couldn't possibly be rich. Only poor people used candles; that's what had happened to them when Mum ran out of money for the electricity meter.

Noah's bedroom was also lit with candles. There were four lined up along the window ledge, three on the mantelpiece, two on the desk next to his bed and another two on the bookcase that was packed full with books and board games. Shadows played against the walls and the room smelled pleasantly of used matches. But best of all, there was a fire burning in the grate; behind a blackened metal guard logs spat and popped noisily. Drawn to it, she stared into the flickering flames, wanting to say how brilliant it was that he was allowed his very own fire in his bedroom. But she didn't dare. If this was normal for Noah, she didn't want him to think she was so easily impressed. Instead she said, 'You're lucky to have such a big room all to yourself. Mine's much smaller and I have to share it with Valerie.'

'I expect it's better than being on your own all the time.'

'But at least you have your uncle. He sounds as if he's—' She was going to say fun, but remembering the picture of Noah's scary two-headed mother out on the landing, she quickly changed her mind and settled for, 'interesting.'

'He's that all right. Do you want something to eat?'

'What have you got?'

From the bottom drawer of the desk he pulled out a battered old Crawford's biscuit tin. He took the lid off and offered her the tin. Other than in a shop, Lydia had never seen so many sweets all together. There were Spangles, Smarties, Rolos, Opal Fruits, Curly Wurlies and Milky Way bars. 'Help yourself,' he said. 'Or would you rather have something else? I can make you some toast in front of the fire if you'd prefer.'

The idea of making toast by the fire sounded like fun to Lydia, but not if Noah had to go all the way downstairs for the bread and then back up again. 'This will be fine,' she said. She helped herself to a packet of Rolos, took one and returned the packet to the tin.

'No,' he said, 'take them all.'

'Really?'

'Of course. I've got some Tizer if you'd like it.'

She hesitated. 'Will you have to go downstairs for it?'

'I have everything I need up here.' He went over to the massive wardrobe on the far side of the room and opened one of the doors. She stared open-mouthed at what was practically a small larder. Noah had more food in his wardrobe than Sister Lottie had in her entire kitchen. 'Good, isn't it?' he said. 'I'm what you call self-sufficient. But then I have to be; my uncle sometimes forgets I'm here.' He poured out two mugs of Tizer, handed her one and then pointed for her to sit on the bed. 'When you've finished your drink I'll get my dad's letter for you.'

Lydia sipped her Tizer slowly, letting the bubbles fizz up into her nose. She glanced round the comfortably untidy room, taking in the candlelight and the fire, the well-stocked larder in the wardrobe, the telescope in front of the window, the plastic model aeroplanes hanging on threads of cotton from the ceiling, the chemistry set and spinning globe of the world on his desk, the posters of Concorde and Neil Armstrong on the moon, the shelves of books and games – Mousetrap, Twister, Monopoly – and wondered if she was dreaming. Noah's world was so different from hers. He seemed to have so many interesting things all to himself and so much freedom. There was no one like her grandparents constantly watching over him, stopping him from having fun.

'Where's your uncle?' she asked.

'London. He went down there last night.'

'London? You mean you're here alone?'

'I often am. That's why I couldn't make it to school after half-term.'

'So you didn't have a hospital appointment?'

'Oh, I had that, but the next day Uncle Brad had to be in London to exhibit some of his pictures. Which meant I couldn't get to the bus stop for school.'

'Didn't anyone from school telephone to find out where you were?'

'The phone did ring, but Uncle Brad had left me strict instructions not to answer it, just in case school found out I was here alone. The last thing he wants is them poking their noses in and making things difficult for us.'

'Why didn't you tell me this before?'

'I never think those kinds of things are important.'

'I do. I was worried about you.' Lydia blushed at her own confession and then let out a loud, Tizer-fuelled burp. She slapped a hand over her mouth and giggled.

Noah grinned. 'Bet you can't do that again.'

'I bet I can.' She flexed her throat and belched satisfyingly loudly.

They spent the next ten minutes out-burping each other until their sides ached with laughter. Lydia couldn't remember the last time she had felt so ridiculously happy.

They were making so much noise, they didn't hear the sound of footsteps or the door opening.

'Fee fie foe fum, I smell the unmistakable whiff of fun,' said a man's voice.

Chapter Twenty

In Lydia's imagination Noah's uncle had been a friendly, jolly, absent-minded, tubby man with spectacles and a beard. She supposed she had wanted to think that her friend had someone nice and kind taking care of him.

Uncle Brad – as Noah had referred to him for the first time that afternoon – was far from being tubby. He was tall. Lanky tall, and as skinny as a drainpipe. His hair was a dull blond colour and Lydia's grandparents would have been disgusted by how long it was; it all but touched the shoulders of his pink and white flowery patterned shirt. He was wearing a purple scarf knotted at his neck and purple trousers made of velvet. They were embarrassingly tight until just below the knee, where they suddenly flared out. Lydia had never seen anything like him before. She'd heard of hippies and something called a beatnik and wondered if he was one of them. She tried not to stare, but he really was so peculiar, like a brightly coloured daddy-long-legs.

'Who's the groovy little friend, Noah?' he asked from the doorway where he stood with one shoulder resting casually against the frame. His voice was not altogether clear. It sounded a lazy can't-be-bothered kind of voice.

'Her name's Lydia.' Unlike Lydia, who was blushing and standing nervously to attention, Noah was still lying on the bed, propped up on one elbow.

Uncle Brad waved at Lydia, just one sweep of his hand, as though wiping a window clean to peer through it. 'Hi, Lydia,' he said. 'Nice to meet you.'

Lydia blushed an even deeper shade of red.

'Why are you home so early?' Noah asked his uncle. 'I thought you weren't coming home till late tonight.'

'I'd had enough. Everyone I met was beyond tedious.' He yawned hugely, not even attempting to cover his mouth with his hand. 'Ma-*a-a-an*, but I'm starving. Don't suppose you have any odds and ends I could scrounge, do you? There's a zero-food situation downstairs.'

'Help yourself.'

Uncle Brad came into the room and ambled over to the wardrobe. He helped himself to a couple of biscuits. 'God knows what I'd do without him, Lydia,' he said as he munched noisily and sprayed crumbs into the air. 'He's a saint for putting up with me. I must be the worst uncle ever. Isn't that right, Noah?'

'You're not so bad,' Noah said with a faint smile.

'See what I mean, Lydia? He's a saint. Anyone else would have told me to sling my hook and buy my own biscuits. Not this boy. Heart of gold.' He pushed a hand through his long blond hair and moved back towards the door. 'Well then, I'll leave you two groovesters to get on with whatever it was you were doing. Sorry to have interrupted you.'

'It's getting late,' Lydia said when they were alone. 'I ought to go.'

'You don't have to go just because my uncle's home.'

'No really, I should. I don't want to be too late and make my grandparents suspicious that I've been some-where other than Sister Lottie's.'

Rolling off the bed, Noah got awkwardly to his feet. 'Will you come again?'

'If I can find a way, yes.'

'I don't understand why you don't just tell your grand-parents about me. Then you could come any time you wanted.'

Lydia picked up her coat from the floor and thought of how they would react to Noah's extraordinary uncle. 'It's better that I don't,' she said. 'Anyway, secrets are fun.'

It was only when she was riding the *ker-lunk, ker-dunk*

beast home in the dark that she remembered Noah had forgotten to show her his secret letter.

The next day at tea-time, to Lydia's delight, her grandparents announced that seeing as everyone at church was busy in the run-up to Christmas, with the strict rota of street evangelizing they had to do, she was to make herself useful and keep Sister Lottie company after school each day. Whilst she wasn't glad that Sister Lottie was ill, it did mean, as she discussed with Noah at school in the morning, she would now be able to see him secretly after every visit she made to the old lady.

Sister Lottie really did seem to be quite poorly. Lydia could see that everything was an effort for her. Perhaps she was bored. The few times Lydia could remember being ill in bed she had always been bored.

While she cleared the ashes out from the grate, made another fire and gave Sister Lottie a bowl of her grandmother's pearl barley soup, she tried to think what might cheer up the old woman.

'Do you still have all your lovely hats, Sister Lottie?' she asked.

'Don't tell anyone,' the woman whispered, as though she was frightened somebody might hear, 'but I didn't throw them away as I was supposed to. I know Pastor Digby says it's a sin to value anything too much but I just couldn't part with my dear old friends. They're in a box under the bed.'

'Shall we get them out and check they're all right? We could try them on, just to be sure.'

Sister Lottie's face broke into a small smile.

It was dusty under the bed and the box was larger than Lydia had expected. When she'd got the lid off and peeled away the layers of tissue paper, she realized she had seen only a tiny part of Sister Lottie's precious collection. 'Can I try this one on?' she asked, very taken with a pale green hat complete with a veil. She went over to admire herself in the three-way mirror on the dressing table. 'I've never seen you wearing it,' she said, catching her profile this way and then that way. The veil did a fantastic job of hiding her eyebrows. 'Why's that?'

'Sister Vera once told me it was too grand for church. She was probably right.'

Lydia kept her thoughts about Sister Vera to herself and went back to the box. 'Which one do you want to try on?' she asked.

'You choose for me.'

Lydia searched for the hat that she remembered Sister Lottie wearing most often, the one with the tiny robin peeking out from behind the flowers. 'How about this one? I always liked you in it.'

Sister Lottie put her bowl of soup on the bedside table and took the hat. Lydia fetched the hand mirror from the dressing table. 'See, it makes you look more like your old self. Doesn't that make you feel better?'

Staring at her reflection, Sister Lottie tilted her head from side to side. She put a hand to the bedraggled flowers sewn onto the floppy brim and stroked them gently. Something sad and faraway washed over the old woman's face and Lydia knew then that she had made a mistake. The hats weren't making Sister Lottie feel better at all.

Ten minutes later, guilty that she was rushing away so soon, Lydia said goodbye and set off for Upper Swallowsdale. It was pitch-black and with no street lamps and hardly any cars on the road, she was dependent upon the faint glow of light from her bicycle lamp to guide her to Noah's house.

As before, he was waiting for her at the front door. The candles in the hall flickered and spluttered in the cold draught when he swung the heavy wooden door shut. She could see from the look on his face that he was pleased to see her. Her heart swelled.

'Is your uncle here?' she asked.

'Don't worry about him; he's in his studio working on a new painting. Come on, let's go upstairs.'

Noah's bedroom seemed even more magical than Lydia remembered it. Laid out on a blanket in front of the roaring fire was a plate of sliced white bread, a pot of jam and a packet of butter. 'I'm going to make us some toast,' he said, getting down awkwardly onto the floor. He picked up a long fork and hooked a piece of bread onto it. 'Can you take the guard away for me?'

Lydia did as he said and sat next to him. Within no time at all they were biting into hot toast, their lips shiny with jam and butter. I never want this moment to end, Lydia thought. This is perfect. This is how I want my life to be. Always. 'I wish I could live here with you,' she said shyly when they'd finished eating and were licking their fingers clean.

He smiled. 'You'd soon change your mind after living with my uncle for a week.'

'He seems OK to me. He lets you do whatever you want and he's not at all strict.'

Noah shrugged. 'Sometimes it's as if he's the child and I'm the adult. There are days when I get tired of it.'

'Do you have any grandparents?'

'Nope. All dead. It's just me and Uncle Brad. Do you want to read my dad's letter now?' Without waiting for her to answer, he got to his feet and went over to the desk. She watched him root around in the bottom drawer until he found what he was looking for. She decided to save him the trouble of getting back down onto the floor and went and sat on the bed. Then, very carefully, as if he was handing her the Crown jewels, he gave her the letter. Almost afraid to read it, she unfolded the single sheet of paper. The writing was messy and shaky, almost unreadable in places. Out of the corner of her eye Lydia was aware of Noah moving aimlessly round the room.

> *Dear Noah,*
> *I'm sorry. Sorry for everything. Please, PLEASE believe me when I say I never meant to do it. I loved your mother but she was going to leave us.*

*I couldn't let that happen. She was my world. All I
ever wanted. Forgive me if you can. Don't hate me
for leaving you on your own but I can't live without
her. Or with what I've done.*
   Goodbye, Noah.

Lydia folded the letter and passed it back to Noah, who
had now come to a stop and was sitting on the bed beside
her. 'When did he write it? I mean, when did it happen?'

'Earlier this year. The third of April.'

A few months before she lost her mother, Lydia thought.
'Did it make you feel angry?' she asked.

'Yes. Was it the same for you?'

'A bit. But I didn't think it was right. If someone dies
you're supposed to feel sad, aren't you? Feeling angry with
Mum, because of what she'd done, felt like wearing the
wrong clothes. Sort of scratchy and too tight.'

He nodded. 'Uncle Brad was angry. So angry he drove
his car into a brick wall. He said it made him feel better.
But only for a while. He gets drunk quite often. He says
it helps.'

Lydia thought of her mother and all those empty sherry
bottles. Her mother had only been trying to make herself
feel better. 'Do you think we should try it?' she asked, half
joking but half curious.

'I already have.'

Lydia was impressed. 'What was it like?'

'Foul. I was sick and woke up with a terrible headache.
I don't know how my uncle does it.'

They sat in silence for a few minutes. Lydia was just
thinking how much she and Noah had in common, and
how that thought made her feel better, kind of happier and
less cold and prickly inside, when a painful stab of guilt
stopped her short. She had no right to start feeling better
or happier, because unlike Noah, who couldn't be blamed
for what his father had done, it was entirely her fault that
her mother had killed herself. And nothing could ever take
away that feeling inside her.

A sudden bone-jumping bang at the door had Noah snatching the letter out of Lydia's hands. He'd just managed to put it safely back in the desk drawer when Uncle Brad burst in, crashing the door against the wall. 'And who might you be, young lady?' he demanded, his hair wild and his face splattered with paint.

'This is Lydia,' Noah said. 'Don't you remember her?'

Uncle Brad staggered into the room on his long, spidery legs. He came right up to the bed where Lydia was still sitting. He stared hard at her, bent down and took her chin in his rough hand. It smelled oily. 'Actually, now you mention it, there is something familiar about her.' Terrified, Lydia allowed him to turn her head slowly to the right and then slowly back to the left. 'Interesting profile,' he said, his breath coming at her in a fiery blast. 'I could do something with that.' He pressed his thumb into her chin. 'What's more, young lady, you're going to be a beautiful woman one day.' He straightened up abruptly.

Lydia's face burned. Was he drunk and making fun of her?

For days afterwards, Lydia replayed Uncle Brad's words in her head. A beautiful woman. She was going to be beautiful one day. A tiny part of her began to believe it and she would often find herself standing in front of the bedroom mirror searching her face for signs of what was to come. Yet the more she studied her reflection, the more she decided Noah's uncle was mad. She was ugly and always would be.

Chapter Twenty-One

In the year Lydia turned eleven four things happened.

It was 1971 and in February everyone in the country had to stop using pounds, shillings and pence and convert to decimal currency. Lydia's grandparents thought it was disgraceful that people were abbreviating the word *pence* to *pee*. Sister Lottie had been so anxious about the new system of money she had begged Lydia to go shopping with her. 'Just until I've got the hang of it,' the old woman had said. 'You know how flustered I get.'

Then during the summer holidays, a few days after Uncle Brad had brought home a television for Noah to watch the astronauts driving round on the moon in a moon buggy, Noah was given the news that he no longer had to wear his leg brace. His leg was nowhere near perfect – he still walked with a bad limp – but without the heavy contraption strapped to it, he could get around much more easily.

A month later in September, Lydia and Noah, along with all of their classmates, started at Swallowsdale Comprehensive. It was very nearly the end of the new autumn term when Lydia came home from school to learn that her grandmother had been taken into hospital for an operation and would be staying there for some time. 'With your grandmother not here, you'll have to look after your sister and take over the running of the house,' her grandfather told Lydia before she'd even got her coat off.

'What's wrong with her?' Lydia asked.

'Never you mind! Just make sure you have her in your prayers. Now out of my way; I have things to do.'

Lydia went upstairs to find her sister. Valerie was five now and with her sweet, angelic face and fine blonde hair – which she had been allowed to grow – she had become the apple of their grandmother's eye. She didn't have a naughty bone in her body and she behaved as perfectly as she looked. Which of course made Lydia, who had grown a whopping five inches in the last year, appear even more of an awkward, gangling tomboy. Unlike Val, she wasn't allowed to grow her hair and she regularly had to sit on a kitchen chair and watch her dark curls drop to the floor as her grandmother wielded the scissors. She didn't care. Nothing that went on at home was of any interest to her. She had long since accepted that what really mattered was what went on beyond the walls of number thirty-three Hillside Terrace. The real Lydia Turner only existed inside her head or when she was away from her grandparents. She was happiest when she was with Noah. Or Sister Lottie, whom Lydia secretly considered to be her proper grandmother.

It was after Lydia had confided in the old lady about Noah being her only real friend that Sister Lottie suggested Lydia bring him to church one Sunday morning. Lydia knew the suggestion was kindly meant, but she couldn't imagine anything worse than letting Noah experience the full embarrassing horror of the Brothers and Sisters. Not wanting to hurt Sister Lottie's feelings, she had said she didn't think he would be interested.

She was wrong. When Lydia asked Noah if he'd like to come to church with her, explaining that if he came her grandparents might approve of him and decide he was a suitable friend for her, he'd said he would but wanted to know why they might think he wasn't a suitable friend.

'Because they only want me to mix with believers,' she'd told him

'What's a believer when he's at home?'

'A believer is someone who believes in God.'

'And do you?'

'Sometimes I do and sometimes I don't.'

'Sounds OK to me. But I thought you wanted to keep our friendship a secret?'

'There's no point in it being a secret if I can only see you at school.'

So it was arranged, and the next Sunday Noah asked his uncle to drop him off in the town centre, having made no mention of where he was going. Lydia had made Noah swear he wouldn't let Uncle Brad come anywhere near the Brothers and Sisters, not when there was no knowing what they would make of him. Sister Lottie was the first to welcome Noah and within minutes of his arrival others were buzzing curiously around him wanting to know who he was. Lydia was amazed how relaxed he was around grown-ups. He seemed to know exactly what to say to get on their right side and gain their acceptance. Throughout the service he sang loudly and said Amen and Praise The Lord with such sincerity she could have believed he'd always been a member of their church. She felt proud that he could put on such a convincing performance for her benefit.

His only blunder, so it seemed, was to cross himself in front of the altar, which was actually nothing more than a table with a wooden cross on it. Lydia had no idea why such a simple gesture should have provoked the reaction it did, but Pastor Digby's swivelling eye nearly popped out of its socket and her grandmother muttered something about Popish nonsense. Even so, everyone was polite to him during tea and biscuits and said they hoped he would come again. He later joked with Lydia that the Brothers and Sisters' acceptance of him was because adults can never resist a crippled child – this had been just before he'd had his leg brace removed.

'Was it very awful for you?' she asked him.

'It wasn't as bad as I thought it would be. They're a weird bunch, though. But then my uncle says most churches are made up of people who don't fit in anywhere else. Misfits, he calls them.'

Lydia thought about this for a few moments. 'But that's

what *we* are, aren't we?' she said. 'We're misfits who don't really fit in with everyone else.'

'I suppose you're right.'

'Does it bother you?'

'Why? Who wants to be the same as everyone else? I'm happy being who I am. By the way, did I pass the test with your grandparents?'

'They haven't said anything bad about you, so hopefully, yes. Will you come to church with me again?'

'I don't think so. That one-eyed coot Pastor Digby gave me the creeps. And anyway, Uncle Brad would rather I went to St Joseph's. He doesn't go regularly himself, but when he does, he insists I go with him.' St Joseph's was the red brick-built Catholic church next to the cinema and Lydia had recently discovered that for some strange reason anyone who went to that church was known as a left-footer. She had never asked Noah why this was, or what it meant, for fear of appearing stupid. Something she was always keen to avoid with him.

'You don't really think God made the world in only seven days, do you?' he once asked her.

He had asked the question with such dismissive authority, she'd said, 'Of course not. That's just a story for little children like Valerie.' She'd said nothing about quite liking the idea of a God who had that much power. That with a click of his fingers he could do whatever he wanted and make everything right.

Valerie, on the other hand, believed every word Pastor Digby said about God and Jesus as well as everything their grandmother taught her. 'She's full of the Lord's grace,' their grandmother would say with pride. 'A true child of God.' Every picture Valerie drew or painted portrayed some Bible story or other. The stories she wrote at school – she was now at infant school – always contained characters with biblical names and whenever she sang, it was always a hymn. The Sisters said she had the voice of a heavenly angel and often encouraged her to sing to them during their Tea and Sisters Scripture meetings. Valerie was nothing like the silent, anxious child she'd once been; she was confident and chatty and completely devoted to their grandmother.

Lydia had learned the hard way to be careful what she now said to Val. Saddened that her sister couldn't remember their mother, she had made the mistake of trying to bring back some of the memories for her. Val had immediately got out her crayons and drawn a picture of their mother from the description Lydia had given her. Their grandfather had been furious when he'd seen it and walloped Lydia on the side of the head so hard her ear had rung for days afterwards. She was accused of brainwashing her sister and sent to bed without any tea. Being punished for the slightest thing was something Lydia was quite used to. There were days, weeks even, when she didn't seem able to do anything right.

When Valerie started becoming aware of the difference in the way they were treated and got upset by it, she was told by their grandmother that Lydia had to be punished for her own good, that it was what God wanted. It was also God's wish that Val's clothes were brand new and Lydia's were all bought from jumble sales because it was pointless wasting good money on new clothes for her while she was growing so fast.

Lydia found Valerie in their bedroom. She was sitting at the dressing table, her head bent in concentration. She looked up when she saw Lydia. 'I'm making a card for Grandmother,' she said. 'She's in hospital.'

'Do you know what's wrong with her?' Lydia asked, at the same time admiring her sister's handiwork. Val had drawn a bed with presumably their grandmother sitting up in it and in the top left-hand corner was a smiling angel, her hands clasped together in prayer.

'Grandfather says she has to have an operation.'

'Did he say what kind of operation?'

'No. There, I've finished. Do you like it?' Valerie held the card up for Lydia to see. 'I want it to be really special so it makes her feel better.'

'It's lovely,' Lydia said. 'And you're a very clever and kind girl to go to so much trouble.' She meant what she was saying, but she hated the way Valerie's kindness always showed up her badness. It made her feel petty and mean-spirited.

But, she reminded herself, if her grandparents treated her the same way they treated Valerie, then maybe it would be different. As it was, Valerie was the favourite and Lydia was the nuisance. And that, she told herself firmly, was not Valerie's fault. She must never, *ever* blame her sister. Valerie was simply too young to understand what was going on.

Over the following days, before and after school, Lydia cooked, washed and ironed. She swept and mopped, she vacuumed and she polished. Valerie did her bit by helping with the washing-up and making the beds while Lydia did her homework. But heaven help Lydia if their grandfather came home from work and found the brass door knocker and letterbox not polished enough or the cushions not straight. And all the while, not a word did he say about when their grandmother might come home.

At church that Sunday everyone said a prayer for Sister Irene's full recovery and afterwards, while her grandfather was busy talking to Pastor Digby, Lydia asked Sister Lottie if she knew what was wrong with her grandmother. Her voice low, Sister Lottie said, 'She'll be home soon. Try not to worry. The Lord has her safely in the palm of his hand.'

'But what's wrong with her?'

Sister Lottie bobbed her head, checking that no one was listening to them. 'It's a woman's operation.' She fluttered a hand over her right breast. 'There was a lump. The doctors thought it was cancer. But thank the Lord, it wasn't. It'll take a long time for your poor grandmother to convalesce and fully get over the drastic surgery she's undergone. We must all pray extra hard for her. Can you do that, Lydia?'

Pray for a woman who hated her so much? Lydia didn't think so. But what was the alternative? If their grandmother died there would be no let-up for her. She would have to carry on doing all the housework as well as suffer her grandfather's worsening temper.

So pray she did. For herself as much as her grandmother.

Chapter Twenty-Two

Their grandmother didn't come home until the beginning of February of the next year. During the time she had been away she had lost weight and her face had sort of caved in. Her skin was the colour of ash. She held herself differently too; her thin shoulders were hunched and her arms seemed to be wrapped around her body as if holding it together. Lydia had wondered many times about the 'drastic surgery' Sister Lottie had referred to, but she had no idea what it could really mean. Whatever it was, she decided as she watched her grandmother make her way slowly upstairs to get into bed, it had to be bad.

Over the following days, whilst their grandfather was at work, a steady flow of visitors came to the house. A nurse came first thing in the morning to check on their grandmother, and from then on the Sisters took it in turns to come in pairs and sit with her upstairs. Listening at the closed bedroom door, Lydia would hear them praying and singing hymns. But one afternoon, when Sister Lottie and Sister Joan arrived for their shift, they were turned away before Lydia had even got the kettle on to make them some tea. 'Your grandmother's weak and depressed,' Sister Lottie whispered to Lydia as she was leaving. 'We need to be very patient with her.'

The one person their grandmother seemed willing to have around her was Valerie, and so the moment she came home from school, Valerie would rush upstairs to be with her. Only she could tempt their grandmother to eat the lunch their grandfather came home at midday to make specially for his wife.

But the patience they needed to deal with their grandmother was nothing compared to what Lydia needed to cope with her grandfather. The longer their grandmother remained in bed, the worse his temper became. She had the bruises to show for it. Nothing was ever right for him. The cups of tea she made for him were too weak or too strong. The meals she cooked were inedible, fit only for the bin. The shirts she ironed for him had the crisp creases he insisted on in all the wrong places. He didn't seem able to be in the same room as her without calling her a lazy slut or accusing her of something she hadn't done. Through it all, Lydia held her tongue. Until finally she forgot herself and answered him back.

She was in the middle of cooking tea when he arrived home early and announced that he wanted corned beef hash for his tea and not the mince and onions she was preparing.

'But we don't have any corned beef,' she said.

'Then go and buy some,' he roared. From his trouser pocket he pulled out a handful of change and threw it at her.

She ran all the way in the pouring rain to Gorton's corner shop, launching herself over puddles and hanging onto the hood of her duffel coat, which was much too small for her now.

Mrs Gorton was about a hundred and ten and as deaf as a post. She took ages to serve the customers who were ahead of Lydia in the queue and when at last she stepped back out onto the street the rain had almost stopped. She'd got as far as the phone box when she heard her name being called. Not her real name, but the nickname the gang of older boys and girls had given her on her first day at junior school. Now that she was at the same school as them, she saw even more of them.

'Oi, it's Tufty!' one of the lads yelled. 'Got anything to eat for us?'

Two lads came over. One flipped back her hood and messed up her hair whilst the other checked her pockets.

All he found was the tin of corned beef. Blowing smoke in her face, he said, 'Got any money?'

'No,' she lied.

The other lad grabbed Lydia's clenched fist behind her back and prised her fingers open to reveal a ten pence piece. 'Ta very much,' he gloated.

'Please don't take it,' Lydia said. 'I'll get into trouble if you do.'

'Tough! Yer shouldn't have lied to us. How's your witch of an old gran? I 'eard she had one of her baps cut off. She must look a right sight in t'buff. Bet her old man won't want to do it with her any more.'

Running the rest of the way home, Lydia felt sick. Surely it couldn't be true? How could *that* part of a woman's body be removed? As for her grandparents doing 'it', that was disgusting rubbish. They were much too old.

Out of breath, she let herself in at the back door. Her grandfather was standing at the sink washing his hands. There was no sign of Val. She was probably upstairs with their grandmother. 'What took you so long?' he demanded.

'Sorry,' Lydia panted, pulling the tin of corned beef out of her pocket and shrugging off her coat.

Drying his hands now, he said, 'Where's my change?'

'I'm sorry,' Lydia apologized again. 'But one of the boys outside the phone box took it. I tried to stop him but he wouldn't listen to me.'

He glared at her, his nostrils flaring. He slowly put down the towel. 'You expect me to believe that? You've taken it for yourself, haven't you? You lying bitch. You probably squandered it on sweets and ate them on your way home. That's why you were so long!'

'I didn't. Honestly. One of the boys took—'

'Don't answer me back!'

'I'm not! I'm just telling you what happened!'

The glare intensified and then with a suddenness that took Lydia completely unawares, her grandfather cracked her on the side of her head with the open palm of his hand. The blow was so powerful, her head whipped round and she staggered, lost her balance and banged her head on the hard, cold floor.

She could feel herself being lifted. Roughly. As though she were a heavy bag of potatoes. There were voices. She tried to open her eyes, but it was too much effort. She didn't know why, but she felt sick and dizzy. Like she'd been spun round too much. A woozy blanket of sleepiness began covering her and she slid deeply beneath its comforting warmth. She saw herself floating away, far, far away. There in the distance she could see her mother beckoning to her. Oh, and there was her father, smiling and holding out his arms for her. They weren't dead after all! The last couple of years had been nothing but a horrible dream. She ran to her father and he swung her round. They were spinning together, high in the sky, so high they were right above the snowy-white clouds. How wonderful it was to know that she would never have to live with those nasty parents of his again. His arms tightened around her and he spoke her name. Over and over. 'Lydia ... Lydia ... Lydia ...'

Except it wasn't her father. The voice was all wrong. Whoever it was, they were spoiling her lovely dream. She reached out to cling to her father, but he'd vanished and she was falling from the sky. And there was no one to catch her.

She snapped open her eyes.

'Ah, there you are,' said a voice she didn't recognize.

Lydia blinked in the bright light and tried to focus on her surroundings. She was in a bed with a brown and orange curtain around her. There was a strange woman in a uniform looking down at her.

But why?

Feeling groggy and confused, she was just about to ask where she was when she heard voices and a gap opened in the curtains at the end of her bed. A man wearing a white coat appeared. Right behind him was her grandfather.

Lydia hardly knew him for the expression of concern on his face.

'Well, young lady,' the man in the white coat said, 'it looks like Nurse Davies has done what I couldn't; she's woken you up. Perhaps now I can get a proper look at you.'

At his request they were left alone. 'You've had a lucky escape,' he said, when he was flashing a light into her eyes. 'You gave your head quite a bump. Not to mention some hefty concussion. You're now the proud owner of nine stitches, every one of them put in by my own fair hand. Your grandfather says you're constantly getting into mischief, that it's a wonder you haven't hurt yourself more seriously before now.' He put his stethoscope to her chest and moved it about.

Lydia swallowed and ran her tongue over her dry lips. 'Did my grandfather say how I hurt myself?'

'I'm afraid not. All he knows is that he came home from work and found you lying on the kitchen floor. Lucky he came home when he did, or who knows what might have happened.' Then, hooking his stethoscope round his neck, he said, 'I don't suppose you can fill me in on the details, can you? For instance, what's the last thing you remember?'

'I ... I'm sorry, I can't remember anything.'

'Not to worry. Temporary memory loss is quite common in these situations. It should return before too long. Meanwhile, I'm going to keep you in overnight and take another look at you in the morning. With any luck you should be sleeping in your own bed tomorrow night. Home's always the safest place to be in my opinion; you never know what you might catch in hospital.' He laughed at his own joke.

But Lydia didn't laugh with him. A tiny, shivery tweak of fear told her that being at home was the last place she would feel safe.

Chapter Twenty-Three

Lydia's grandfather arrived to take her home after he'd finished work. To the doctors and nurses he was all smiles and politeness, thanking them for their help and apologizing for his careless granddaughter who'd put them to so much trouble. But when he was alone with Lydia in the car the smile was gone. With his hands gripping the steering wheel, his expression rigid, he said, 'Have you remembered what happened yet?'

She hesitated, wanting so much to say the right thing. She sensed it was important not to make a nuisance of herself. Or any more of a nuisance than she already had been. Her grandfather probably thought she was pretending to lose her memory just so she could attract attention to herself. But the truth was, she really couldn't remember what had happened. All she had to go on was a hazy picture of being in the kitchen getting tea ready. From then on it was a blank.

When she didn't reply, her grandfather said, 'If you know what's good for you, you won't go causing any trouble. Your grandmother isn't well and the last thing we need is you making life more difficult for her. Do I make myself clear?'

As clear as mud, thought Lydia. What trouble did he think she might cause? 'Yes, Grandfather,' she said dutifully. Turning her face to look out of the side window, she put a hand to her bandaged head, willing it to start working properly. The doctor had assured her that her memory could return at any moment, that all she needed was the right trigger and that it could come in a flash all at once, or steadily like a dripping tap. There wasn't anything to worry about, he'd said. But she *was* worried. How could you lose a part of yourself like that and not worry? She didn't believe for a single second that she had fallen off a chair reaching for the biscuit tin in one of the high kitchen cupboards as her grandfather had suggested to the doctor. For a start, there weren't any biscuits in the cupboard any more because their grandmother only ever used to buy them for her Tea and Sisters Scripture meetings, and since her operation last year everyone now met at Sister Vera's house.

They were almost home now, and as her grandfather drove past Gorton's corner shop at the end of the road, Lydia saw that the usual gang of teenage lads was hanging about; they were lazily kicking a can to each other across the road. Her grandfather gave the horn a loud blast to make them get out of the way. The two cocky boys who had stolen her money yesterday stayed exactly where they were. When her grandfather banged his fist down on the horn again, they jabbed two fingers in the air and dragged themselves to the kerb. Her grandfather revved the engine noisily and drove on.

Lydia twisted round sharply in her seat, stared back at the gang of boys through the rear window and realized that she had remembered something from yesterday. The two lads … she'd had some money in her hand … one of them had taken it. She must have either been on her way to the shop or leaving it. What shopping had she been sent out to do?

Facing the front now, Lydia squeezed her eyes shut and held her breath. This was the trigger the doctor had told her about; she mustn't let it slip away from her. Very gently she tried to tease out these fragile new memories to see what else would come to her. It had been raining … she'd run home feeling sick about the awful things the boys had said about her grandmother … her grandfather was in the kitchen … he was the one who'd sent her to the shop ... he was angry and accusing her of stealing from him ... he ...

Lydia opened her eyes. Her grandfather had hit her. Not some sharp little prod or slap as she was used to, but a real hard blow that had knocked her off her feet. She shuddered, recalling how much it had hurt, and knowing that it had been no more of an accident than that time her grandfather had claimed Lydia had fallen into the compost heap. Then she'd been burned; this time he'd given her concussion and nine stitches. She supposed she had at least to be grateful that he had taken her to the hospital. Had he been scared into doing that because he couldn't wake her? Had he thought she might die? And that he could be blamed?

The car jolted to a stop. They were home. A tremor of fear ran through Lydia. Watching her grandfather getting out of the car, she wanted to say, *I know what you did to me; I've remembered everything. I know that you lied to the doctor and that you'll lie to everyone else. But I know the truth.* But to her shame she was too frightened of him. Who knew what else he might do to her if she made him angry? Better to keep quiet and let him think he'd got away with it. Because he had, hadn't he?

That night at bedtime, Valerie made Lydia promise she would never do anything to upset their grandparents, especially their grandmother.

'Grandma's very worried,' Valerie whispered when they'd switched off the light. 'She thinks we might be taken away from her.'

Lydia turned over to face Valerie in the dark. 'Why does she think that?'

When Valerie didn't reply, Lydia realized her sister was crying. She went and knelt beside her bed. 'What is it, Valerie? What's wrong?'

'Grandma thinks you're going to go and spoil everything by telling people lies about her and our grandfather.'

'What sort of lies?'

'That they're unkind to you.'

'But they *are* unkind to me.'

'Only because you do wicked things and they're trying to save you from provoking the Lord to anger. She says that if you spread bad lies about them someone will knock on the door one day and make us live somewhere else. Somewhere a long way away and not so nice, where we'll never see our friends from church again.' Valerie's cries grew louder. 'I couldn't live anywhere else, Lydia. I couldn't live without Grandma. She says you don't love her. You do love her, don't you, Lydia?'

Lydia hugged her sister and hushed her with a kiss. 'Don't be silly, of course I love her. And we'll live here for ever and ever. Just you see.'

'You promise you won't do anything to upset her?'

'I promise.'

Chapter Twenty-Four

They were playing Monopoly. Lydia was winning. By miles. She had all the best properties and Noah's racing car had just landed on Mayfair with four houses on it. 'Pay up! Pay up! Pay up!' she chanted.

Noah started counting out his money. It was obvious he didn't have enough.

'Tell you what,' she said, 'I'll let you off if you give me Fenchurch Street Station and King's Cross.'

He eyed her long row of property cards. 'That gives you the set.'

'Really?' she said innocently. 'Oh, so it does.'

He laughed and tossed his money onto the board. 'I give in. You win. Again. How about some toast? I'm starving.'

'OK. You get toasting and I'll put this away.'

'Sure you don't want to count your winnings first?' he teased. 'Just to rub in your victory?'

'I don't need to,' she said with a smile. 'I know exactly how much I have: eight thousand, four hundred and seventy-five pounds.' She waved the thick bundle of cash under his nose.

He smiled too and went over to the wardrobe, bringing back a loaf of Mother's Pride, a plate, a knife, and a pot of jam. As she tidied away the board game, Lydia watched Noah light the candles on the mantelpiece and thought how this room, with its every cluttered, shadowy nook and cranny, was so comfortingly familiar to her. It was her absolute favourite place in all the world. Nowhere was she happier.

Right now Noah and his uncle weren't the only ones using candles. According to Lydia's grandfather, the lazy Neo-Marxists who worked in the mines and power stations were holding the country to ransom by making sure there wasn't enough coal and electricity to go round. Some days at school they didn't have a cooked meal and the dinner ladies gave them sandwiches to eat. But according to Noah, who got his information from his uncle, the miners needed their support and what was a little inconvenience compared to fighting for a good cause and bringing down such a useless government? Ted Heath, who in Uncle Brad's opinion was nothing more than a poncy sailor and a social-climbing jackass for signing Britain up for the Common Market, would be the first to be put against the wall if he had his way.

Lydia had understood some time ago that she'd got it wrong about Uncle Brad. He wasn't poor at all. His weird paintings really did sell for lots of money down in London and his preference for candles over lightbulbs was just one of his many peculiarities.

'Would you mind nipping downstairs to get some butter?' Noah asked.

'Is your uncle around?'

'You're not scared of him, are you?'

She stuck out her chin. 'I'm not scared of anything.'

He smiled. 'I know; that's why I think you're so great.'

Lydia absorbed the unexpected compliment like a thirsty sponge and set off, candle in hand, on the trek down to the kitchen. Along the shadowy landing with its strange paintings and rucked-up rugs she went, down the wide staircase, across the hall, and through the freezing cold narrow passageway with Adolf the stag's head looking down on her from his lofty position on the wall. Hooked onto one of his enormous antlers was a policeman's helmet which Noah said Uncle Brad had stolen during a drunken brawl in a pub when he'd been a student.

Noah had been right to tease Lydia about being scared of Uncle Brad: she was. But not in a bad way, like she was with her grandfather. It was just that he was so unlike anyone she knew. He could be friendly, glamorous and grumpily aloof, all at the same time. She never knew what he was going to say or do next. Sometimes he would greet her with the words, 'Hey, here's the cool cat I'm going to paint one day!' Other times, even after all this time, he treated her as if they'd never met before. That was when he'd been knocking back the drink, Noah said. Or when he'd been smoking one of his special cigarettes.

There was no sign of Uncle Brad in the kitchen, but the sound of music blaring from his studio told Lydia he was nearby. She found an unopened packet of butter in the fridge and hurried back upstairs. One day, she told herself, she was going to live in a big house like this. Just as soon as she was old enough, she would leave Swallowsdale. She would work hard and earn so much money she'd be able to surround herself with lovely things and all her clothes would be new and beautiful. It was why she always concentrated during lessons at school and made a point of doing her homework and revising for any tests they had. Being rich and clever wasn't about being born lucky. She'd learned that from Noah. You only had to see his collection of books – she'd give anything to have all those fantastic encyclopaedias – to know that knowledge was a choice to be grabbed. And it was a choice she had grabbed ages ago, when she'd first tried to copy Noah's handwriting. She didn't do that now, of course. But she was always conscious that the better impression you gave people of yourself, the better they treated you. It was just as Mum used to say: polishing your shoes really did make a difference. It was why she'd taught herself to polish up the way she spoke by secretly mimicking the way Noah spoke. She didn't do it too much at home, not when she'd be accused of getting above herself, but she had it hidden up her sleeve ready for when the time came to leave Swallowsdale. If you wanted to be treated as a lady, you had to sound like one. And that's what she aimed to be one day.

What about Noah and Valerie? a voice inside her head

asked. Where will they be when you're waving goodbye to Swallowsdale?

Oh, that was easy. They'd have to come with her. She couldn't leave them behind. She'd earn enough money to look after all three of them.

Since her 'accident' two weeks ago, Lydia had taken extra care not to put a foot wrong with her grandfather. For Valerie's sake, she did everything that was asked of her, no matter how difficult or unreasonable. But the worst part was knowing that her sister now lived in constant fear of being taken away from their grandmother if Lydia didn't toe the line. How cruel and cunning their grandfather had been to twist the truth round to his advantage. What lies had he told their grandmother to make her put those fears in Val's head? Or had their grandmother, while she lay in bed with the curtains drawn, still too depressed to get up, worked it out for herself? Had she guessed what had really happened and worried what Lydia might tell people? Had she immediately come up with a way to make Lydia keep her mouth shut? Or had the pair of them put the idea together? This thought was doubly chilling because it meant that her grandmother was prepared to let her vicious, foul-tempered husband do whatever he wanted.

At the moment her grandfather's favourite punishment was to force Lydia to stand in the corner of the room during mealtimes and make her watch him and Valerie eat. 'It's for your sister's own good,' he would tell Valerie, while helping himself to another portion of apple pie and custard. 'She's growing too fast because she eats too much. She's a gluttonous pig that needs to have its appetite curbed. You must pray for her.'

And Val did pray for Lydia. Down on her knees at bedtime she would pray aloud for Lydia to be released from Satan's grip. She also prayed that she herself wouldn't be tainted by Lydia's refusal to bow to God's will. It broke Lydia's heart that her sister had been turned against her. What would their poor mother say? And what of the promise she had made Mum to look after Val?

As close as she was to Noah, Lydia never shared with him what went on at number thirty-three Hillside Terrace. Her pride just wouldn't let her. She didn't want him knowing just how shabby her life was compared to his. She'd hate it if he started feeling sorry for her. So she lied to him to stop him finding out. She lied about why her clothes were too small for her – they were her favourite and she couldn't bear to part with them. She said that the bruises she had on her arms and legs were from falling out of bed in the middle of the night, or from slipping on the stairs.

As to how she'd ended up with nine stitches in the side of her head – she'd had them removed last week – she used her grandfather's lie and told him she'd fallen off a chair. She even joked with him that she had turned into a clumsy idiot because she was growing so fast. Which wasn't entirely untrue. Taller than Noah by an inch, she was now the tallest girl in their year at school. For a while she had tried to make herself appear smaller and less obvious, but then one day she'd decided there wasn't any point. With her looks she was always going to stand out.

Just as Noah did. Nobody cared less about his appearance than Noah. His school uniform was smart enough, but his home clothes were scruffy and thrown on any old how, and he never noticed if they were too big or too small or if a button had dropped off. He was proud of the fact that he cut his own hair and made such a poor job of it. 'Oh, clothes,' he'd say with a shrug. 'Who gives a monkey's?'

Whilst Lydia hated lying to Noah, she never had a problem lying to her grandparents, so long as she was sure she wouldn't be found out. The most regular lies she told them were the ones that enabled her to spend time with Noah. Today she was supposed to be playing in an after-school netball match. Later in the week it would be a drama lesson that kept her late at school, or recorder practice.

*

'I've been thinking,' Noah said when she was back in his room and warming herself in front of the fire, 'why don't we make a pact?'

She glanced up from the piece of toast she was buttering. 'What kind of a pact?'

He looked at her steadily, his face glowing in the flickering firelight. His expression was thoughtful with just a hint of eyebrow-raising puzzlement to it. She called it his Question Mark Face. 'A pact that means we'll always be friends. That nothing will ever part us.'

Just as she usually did these days, Lydia took the short cut home from Noah's by climbing over the wall at the end of his garden and making her way across the mile or so of sloping moorland that separated their houses. She could cover the distance far quicker during daylight, but in the dark it took her longer. It didn't frighten her, not now she had perfected her route and knew how to avoid the boggiest, steepest or rockiest areas. The first time she had done it in the dark, she had been petrified and had imagined countless ways she could meet with her death – vampire bats, dangerous prisoners on the run, werewolves, or those strange men she'd heard about who just wanted to unzip their trousers and show her their 'thing'. She'd used Noah's torch on that first occasion, but now she didn't bother; she let instinct and experience guide her, having discovered that the darkness was rarely total.

At the halfway point, at the entrance to the wooded dell, which she and Noah had nicknamed the Dell of the Dead, Lydia shifted her school bag on her shoulder and paused to let her eyes grow accustomed to the gloom; the dreary afternoon light had all but faded. In the freezing February air, her breath formed a ghostly vapour, then vanished. It was always here that her heart skipped a beat and she felt the urge to make a run for it. It was a matter of honour that she didn't, that she kept her nerve and her pace unchanged. It was equally important to keep a lid on her imagination and not dwell on who or what might be hiding amongst the trees. Normally she hummed 'What Shall We Do With The Drunken Sailor?' inside her head, but this time, as she plunged in, she thought of the pact she and Noah had just made. Using his Swiss Army knife, he'd made a cut in the middle of their palms, then pressed their hands together to share their blood, saying the words, 'No matter what, we'll never be parted.'

Kicking through the thick layers of fallen leaves, within yards of the outer edge of the dell, Lydia touched the plaster Noah had put on her hand. She hoped she'd have a scar to remind her how much Noah meant to her.

A sudden rustle over to her left made her stiffen. Every hair on the back of her neck stood on end. Holding her breath and straining her ears, her heart nearly leapt out of her mouth when a bird with the biggest wingspan she'd ever seen flew out of the trees and swooped by right in front of her. When she heard its screeching call, she relaxed. If an owl was the scariest the Dell of the Dead had to offer, then she had absolutely nothing to fear.

Chapter Twenty-Five

The summer holidays were dragging for Lydia. It was over a week since the end of term, when she'd last seen Noah.

She was sitting in the garden making daisy chains with Valerie, wishing she could find a way to slip over the wall without anyone missing her and go and see him. When she and Noah had worked out that all that separated them was a wooded dell and a stretch of moorland, Lydia had remembered the day she had climbed up into the branches of the out-of-bounds chestnut tree for the first time and wondered who might live on the other side of the sloping hill. Little had she known that her very best friend would soon be living there.

With a sudden uncanny feeling that they were being watched, Lydia turned to look back up at the house. Sure enough, staring down at them through a gap in the bedroom curtains was their grandmother. She was dressed as she always was, in a nightdress and dressing gown. Lydia couldn't remember the last time she had left the house. Other than in March when she'd gone back into hospital for another operation. Just before this had happened she had started to feel better. She had been managing to get dressed and come downstairs for a few hours a day. She'd even had Pastor Digby and the Sisters round for tea a couple of times and was talking about being well enough to go to church again. But apparently the first operation hadn't been done right and there had been complications. When she came home this time, she was even more depressed and Lydia often heard her crying at night, a sort of low wailing sound. Their grandfather moved into the spare room around this time. He'd been sleeping in there ever since.

Another change to the routine was that unlike before when his wife had come home from hospital, he didn't come back during the day to make her lunch. Instead, the Sisters had been encouraged to pop in for an hour or so each day. Lydia had overheard him telling Pastor Digby that his wife might say she didn't want any company, but what she wanted and what she *needed* were entirely two different things. Pastor Digby had agreed and said, 'Sometimes a firm hand is what is needed.' He'd then quoted from the Bible about the importance of wives submitting to their husbands.

Lydia knew all about her grandfather's firm hand. He hadn't lashed out at her anywhere near as badly as he had earlier in the year, but there had been moments when she'd genuinely feared that he might. He seemed to take pleasure in knowing that he could so easily make her cower from him. It was as if it was a game for him, to raise his hand sharply and then watch her reaction. He would laugh at her cruelly, saying she would be scared of her own shadow next.

'Look, Val,' Lydia said, pointing up to the window. 'Grandmother's awake. Do you want to go in and see her?'

Scrambling to her feet, Valerie scooped up the daisy chain necklace she'd been making. 'I'll take this in for her, shall I?'

'Yes, go on, she'll like that.'

Lydia watched her sister skip up the garden path and disappear inside the house. She had only been alone a couple of minutes when Sister Lottie appeared at the back door. Wiping her hands on her apron she called out to Lydia. 'I'm putting a picnic lunch together. Do you want to help bring it out to the garden while I take some sandwiches upstairs to your grandmother?'

Lydia didn't hesitate. Sister Lottie's picnic lunches were the highlight of the day.

Having insisted with their grandfather that Lydia and Valerie couldn't possibly be left alone every day while he was at work during the long summer holiday, Sister Lottie's Morris Minor arrived outside the house every morning bang on ten o'clock. It was wonderful having her around. She was always so kind and cheerful, baking them lovely cakes and biscuits and telling them not to fret, that their grandmother would soon be well again and everything would be back to normal.

Was it so very wrong of Lydia to hope that things never went back to being normal? With their grandmother permanently 'resting' upstairs, life was so much more fun with Sister Lottie around. It was just a shame their grandfather couldn't lock himself away in the spare room as well.

Deliciously full of sardine and tomato paste sandwiches, cheese and onion crisps, fairy cakes and iced gems – something their grandmother would never have approved of – Lydia lay back on the grass and let out a contented sigh. 'Why is a picnic in the garden always so much nicer than sitting at the table inside the house?'

But before Sister Lottie could answer her, a sound Lydia hadn't heard since coming to live in Swallowsdale rang out. It was the sing-song chime of an ice-cream van. She even recognized the tune it was playing: 'Edelweiss'. Her father used to sing it to her. She remembered him telling her edelweiss was the name of a flower that grew in the mountains of Switzerland. The connection with her father, coupled with the excitement of something new and unexpected going on, had her leaping to her feet and racing from the end of the garden, down the path alongside the garage and round to the front garden. Yes! There it was. An ice-cream van parked right outside their house. It was blue and white with chrome so shiny the sun was bouncing off it. High up on the van's roof, lying on its side, was a large light-up plastic ice-cream cornet with a plastic chocolate flake sticking out of it. In red looping writing, the name 'Joey' was written on the cornet. The music suddenly stopped and the window on the side of the van slid open to reveal a man with a head of curly black hair. He had a thick black moustache and his skin was the colour of brown sugar. He spotted Lydia straight away. 'Hello,' he said. 'And what would you like on thissa beautiful day, leetle girl?'

How strange he looked and sounded. She started to back away.

'Pleeasse, do not run away. Come anda choose somezing. I have everyzing. Nats, spreenkles, strawberry seerop, weefers, cornots, and lallies. So many lovelee lallies.'

'I don't have any money,' she said, trying not to laugh at his funny pronunciation.

He shook his head of black curls. 'Ah, zat eesa beega problema. Maybe you go inside your lovelee house and aska your mama for money.'

'My mother's dead.' Lydia often said this just to see what reaction she got. It always interested her to see how awkwardly it made people behave.

This man's reaction was different from anyone else's, though. He put a hand to his forehead, then touched his chest and then both shoulders. Just as Lydia had once seen Noah do. 'Oh, *Mama mia*! I ama so sorry, leetle girl. Me anda my beega moutha. For that you can ave what you wanta. Pleeasse, come ana choose somezing.'

Lydia hesitated. 'I don't think I'd be allowed to do that.'

He nodded and was about to say something when footsteps approached. 'Ah, more customers,' he said, rubbing his hands together. 'Ziss isa good. It was a pleasure to meeta you, leetle girl. Bye, bye.'

Lydia watched her neighbours cluster round the van and then turned on her heel and ran straight to the back garden. 'Sister Lottie, can we have an ice-cream, please? Oh, please say yes! It's such a hot day. Wouldn't you like one, too? It would be the perfect end to our lovely lunch.'

Lydia knew Sister Lottie wouldn't let her down and in no time at all, the three of them – Lydia, Valerie and Sister

Lottie – were standing in front of the open window of the ice-cream van. The other customers had all gone. 'So, leetle girl,' said the funny curly-haired man, 'eeza zissa beautiful lady your grandmother?'

Sister Lottie giggled and put a hand to her face.

'No,' Lydia said, 'she's my friend. And this is Valerie, my sister. She's six.'

The man smiled. 'Anda may I know *your* name?'

'Lydia. Lydia Turner.'

'I ama very pleased to meeta you, *Signorina* Lydia Turner. I ama Joey Scalatore. I ama from Italy. Have you heard of Italy?'

'Is that the country that's shaped like a boot?'

'*Sì! Brava!* And my home cana be founda near Napoli. Butta please, you have not introduced me to your beautiful friend.'

'This is Sister Lottie.'

'I ama pleased to meeta you, Sister Lottie. You are a nun?' Lydia noticed the ice-cream man's face had turned serious, sort of respectful. She also noticed that peeping out from his open-necked shirt and dark hairy chest was a gold necklace with a crucifix hanging from it.

'Oh, no,' Sister Lottie laughed, her face now the colour of beetroot. 'I'm much too ordinary for anything like that.'

But she is a saint, Lydia thought when they had said goodbye to the nice man and were licking their double ninety-nines to the sound of 'Edelweiss' tinkling away down the street.

What a perfect day.

Chapter Twenty-Six

For the next fortnight, the sun shone brightly from a clear blue sky and the sound of 'Edelweiss' could be heard every afternoon between two and three o'clock on Hillside Terrace.

Joey Scalatore was just like Sister Lottie, always so cheerful. His real name was Giuseppe but he said Joey was easier for British people to say. She loved it when he called her his *bella* leetle friend in his funny voice. He'd explained to her that *bella* meant beautiful. He was teaching her Italian by giving her a different word to remember whenever he saw her. So far she knew the Italian for hello was *ciao*, or *buon giorno*, and that *arrivederci* meant see you soon. She knew that *va bene* was the same as saying OK, that *gelato* was ice-cream, and that thank you was *grazie*. Oh, and *sì* was yes. She could also count from one to ten and was practising rolling her Rs, just like Joey had taught her, but she didn't think she did it very well. It was quite different from French.

Joey must have decided that Sister Lottie couldn't really afford to buy ice-creams every day, so when he'd finished serving all the other customers from their road, he often gave them the broken lollies he said he couldn't sell. Yesterday he'd promised to bring Lydia some photographs of where he came from in Italy, and now, as she waited her turn at the back of the queue, she hoped he hadn't forgotten. She was curious to know what Italy looked like. The only pictures she'd seen were in a book at school and one of them had showed a tower that was leaning over so much it looked like it was about to topple over.

The Floozy was at the front of the queue and was taking for ever. Perhaps Joey was teaching her some Italian words as well. She was looking particularly smart today, wearing a tight-fitting white halter-neck dress and a pair of red high-heeled sandals. Lydia would have loved a pair of shoes just like that, all pointy and strappy. She could see that The Floozy had been sunbathing; her shoulders were pink and striped with pale white strap marks. From an overheard conversation at the corner shop, Lydia knew that The Floozy had recently changed jobs and was now working shifts at one of the mills, which meant she slept during the morning, had the afternoons free and then went to work at night. Lydia had never once heard anyone mention a husband – not even a dead one – which puzzled her. She would have thought an attractive woman like The Floozy would definitely have had a husband at some time. She certainly didn't seem to be short on men friends. In fact, Lydia had seen any number of different men turning up on a Saturday evening to take her out. Some brought bunches of flowers with them, or boxes of Milk Tray. Lydia couldn't imagine her grandfather ever bringing home a box of chocolates for his wife. He hadn't even done it the two times she'd come out of hospital. So maybe The Floozy had it right, that it was better not to be married. This way, she was independent, earned her own money and could have as many boyfriends giving her presents as she wanted.

The Floozy turned from the hatch with an ice-cream in her hand and exchanged a few words with the other women in the queue. Laughing huskily, she said, 'He could lick my cornet any time he wanted.'

'Mine too,' someone else said.

'For a foreigner, he's a bit of all right, in't he?'

'I'll say. Have yer copped a look at his hairy chest?'

Embarrassed by their talk, Lydia stared hard at the ground. She hoped Joey couldn't hear what they were saying. Or if he could, that he didn't understand it.

'What yer staring at down there, then?'

Lydia started. It was The Floozy. And she was talking to her.

'How're yer getting on? That grandfather of yours taking good care of yer and your sister while your grandmother's getting over her operation?'

'Um … yes. We have a friend who spends the day with us during the holiday while he's at work.'

'I'm glad to hear it. And yer've only got to knock on my door if yer need sommat. Yer could come in and watch a bit of telly if yer fancied it. I know yer don't have a set. For now, have this. Ta-ra.'

Lydia watched The Floozy tick-tacking away on her high heels, her curvy hips swaying. This was the first proper conversation Lydia had ever had with the woman. She then looked at the money she had just had pressed into her hand: a shiny fifty-pence piece. She decided The Floozy couldn't possibly be any of the bad things her grandparents had said about her.

At last it was Lydia's turn.

'*Ciao*, my leetle *bella* friend,' Joey greeted her.

'*Ciao*,' she replied shyly, even though they were alone.

He wagged a stubby dark finger at her. 'No, no. You musta say it louder anda with more passion. Remember, there is no sucha person as a shy Italiano. Especially not from Napoli, where I ama from.'

Self-consciously she tried the greeting again, then asked if he had remembered the photographs he'd said he'd bring for her to see.

He raised his hands in the air. 'Oh, I ama so sorry. Iya forgot all abouta zat. Forgeeve me, please, but I have hada many zings to zeenk about. I ama to be, how do you say, homeless? Yes, as of next week I will have nowhere to leeve. My landlord says he does nota like my van parked outside zee 'ouse.'

'Does that mean you have to go back to Italy?' Lydia scarcely knew Joey but she couldn't imagine the rest of the summer holidays without him.

'No, but if I cannota find somewhere to leeve, I will have to sleep in zee van.'

Lydia had a thought. Sister Lottie had a spare room – perhaps she'd like a lodger. 'I have an idea,' she said. 'Can you wait here a few minutes?'

'*Sì*. For you, my leetle *bella* friend, I have all zee time in zee world.'

Within minutes, Lydia had put her idea to Sister Lottie and they were outside talking it through with Joey. 'It's only a small room I can offer you,' Sister Lottie explained, 'so I wouldn't charge you too much rent.'

'Anda mya van, eet is nota problema for you?'

'I have a garage I never use, so you can put it in there.'

The next thing, Joey was out of the van and kissing Sister Lottie on each cheek. 'Sucha kindness! And if zere are any jobs you needa doing in your house, I cana do zem for you. Oh, *Dio mio*, what a lucky day zees is for me! Zank you, zank you!'

Pink-faced and hair all ruffled, Sister Lottie emerged from Joey's dark, hairy arms like a cork popping from a bottle. 'Don't thank me,' she said breathlessly, her voice all wobbly. 'Thank Lydia; it was her idea.'

But it was Sister Lottie who, in Lydia's opinion, came up with the best idea of the day. They were sitting in the garden with the broken strawberry Mivvies Joey had given them – Valerie had gone inside to share hers with their grandmother – when Sister Lottie said, 'I've been thinking, Lydia. You must be getting very bored here with only Valerie and me for company. Wouldn't you like to spend some of the holiday with your friend, Noah?'

'I'm not sure my grandparents would agree to that,' she said carefully, at the same time licking a dribble of melting ice-cream off her thumb.

'Oh, I think your grandparents have much too much on their minds to be bothered with the details of what we get up to during the day. We don't want to make a nuisance of ourselves by burdening them with anything unnecessary, do we?'

About to turn a few cartwheels inside her head, Lydia

suddenly thought of her sister. Val told their grandmother just about everything that went on. Choosing her words with care, not wanting to appear as though she was being disloyal and criticizing her sister, Lydia said, 'But what about Valerie? She might, well, you know, she might just happen to mention it to Grandmother.'

Sister Lottie smiled and patted Lydia's hand. 'You leave little Valerie to me.'

Lydia could hardly believe her luck.

The next morning she climbed over the wall at the end of the garden and set off across the hard, dry ground. It was ages since it had last rained. In the distance the heather was in full bloom and if she squeezed her eyes almost shut, all she could see was a mysterious smoky haze of purple. Sister Lottie had made her a cake to take with her to Noah's and she had this wrapped in foil inside her duffel bag. 'It wouldn't be polite to turn up empty-handed,' Sister Lottie had said. She'd also made several rounds of cheese and pickle sandwiches and slipped in a bag of crisps. Valerie had promised to keep Lydia's visit to Noah a secret because she'd been told that anything out of the ordinary might upset their grandmother, and she didn't want that, did she? Lydia had had no idea that Sister Lottie could be so sneaky.

As they'd agreed on the telephone yesterday afternoon, Noah was waiting for her on his side of the Dell of the Dead. 'I thought we could go up to the beck,' he said. He indicated the small rucksack on his back. 'I've made us a picnic.'

'Snap,' Lydia said. 'Sister Lottie's made us a cake as well.'

They set off through the heather and bracken for the beck and Lydia told Noah all the latest news; about Sister Lottie coming every day and about Joey Scalatore and him teaching her Italian. 'I've decided I'm going to visit Italy when I'm old enough,' she said. 'Joey says I'd love it. He says the weather is always warm and sunny where he's from and that the food is the best in the world.'

'If it's so great there, why's he here in Swallowsdale, then?'

Taken aback by Noah's question, and the flat tone of his voice, Lydia didn't know what to say. Thinking that maybe she had gone on too much and had bored him with all her chatter, she said, 'So tell me what you've been up to.'

'Not much. Uncle Brad's been away this last week.' His voice still sounded flat and uninterested.

'It must be great having the house all to yourself,' she said, trying to sound enthusiastic to cheer him up.

'It doesn't really feel that different from when he's around.'

'Do you have enough to eat?' she asked, concerned, knowing that he didn't have a shop on the doorstep like she did.

'Oh, yeah. My uncle stocked the fridge and cupboards before he went. And now that I'm more mobile and can get to the bus stop, he's left me a stack of money if things get low.'

'Where's he gone?'

'Bolivia.'

'Bolivia? Where's that?'

'Next door to Brazil and Peru.'

'Blimey, what's he gone there for?'

'Usual thing: inspiration for his paintings.'

'How long's he away for?'

Noah shrugged again. 'Not that long. Just a couple of weeks.'

They walked in silence for a while, and, always conscious that Noah couldn't walk too far or too fast, Lydia slowed her pace and pretended to be interested in watching a buzzard circling overhead. He didn't limp as much as he used to, not compared to this time last year when the brace had been removed, and he never made a fuss about it, but she knew his leg wasn't that strong. Maybe it never would be.

They were almost at the beck when Noah came to an abrupt stop. He put a hand on her arm. 'Lydia,' he said, 'I just want to say that I'm glad you phoned yesterday. I really—' His gaze and words fell away and he suddenly looked awkward and shy. To her surprise his face was turning pink.

'What is it, Noah?' she asked. 'What's the matter?'

'Nothing's the matter,' he said, his eyes coming back to hers. He swallowed. 'It's no big deal, it's just, well, the thing is, I've missed you. Really missed you. And I'm sorry I was so miserable earlier, but I was jealous. You sounded like you'd been having a lot more fun than me. I wish you'd phoned me before.'

'I wanted to, but—'

'It's OK,' he interrupted her, the pressure of his hand increasing on her arm. 'I know you don't want your grandparents to think that I'm anything more than someone who just happens to go to the same school as you. I don't suppose there's any chance they could both conveniently drop down dead, could they? It would solve a lot of your problems.'

She laughed. 'What do you mean? It would solve *all* my problems!'

Except of course, as Lydia knew all too well, it wouldn't. It would just create a whole load of new problems. Such as what their grandmother's death would do to Valerie. But she kept quiet about that and said, 'Anyway, never mind my horrible grandparents, tell me what you've been doing all on your own. You must have done something interesting.'

He took his hand away from her and pushed it down inside his trouser pocket. 'Oh, just the usual messing about stuff. Remember I said I wanted to have a go at making a crystal radio set? Well I have, and it works pretty well too.'

She gave him a light punch on his shoulder. 'Knowing how modest you are, that probably means it works brilliantly.'

'Hey, can I help being a genius?'

'Listen to Einstein!'

Laughing, with all trace of the awkwardness that had passed between them now gone, they walked on.

At the beck, when they were lying on their backs staring up at the puffy white clouds in the sky, Lydia pictured the rest of the summer holiday spent just like this. How blissful it would be.

So long as Sister Lottie kept looking after her and Valerie and their grandmother stayed in bed for ever and ever.

Chapter Twenty-Seven

When their grandmother did finally get out of bed nothing was as it had been. Physically she may have been stronger, but mentally she was very different. Exactly a year after her grandmother's first operation Lydia noticed that she was acting strangely, although with hindsight she realized it had been going on for a while. It was just little things to begin with, like refusing to answer the door or telephone, drawing the curtains during the day or hiding things at the back of the airing cupboard. Things started to disappear with such regularity that if Lydia couldn't find the peg bag, a saucepan lid or the potato peeler, she would go straight to the airing cupboard. Just as strangely, no one but Lydia seemed to think that it was odd. Neither her grandfather nor Val ever said anything about it. Which meant Lydia didn't either. As with so many other things, it was politely swept under the carpet and ignored.

But by the following Christmas, their grandmother's bizarre behaviour had escalated to the point that it was impossible for anyone to ignore it. Now if there was a knock at the door or the telephone was ringing, she would hide, quaking behind the settee, sometimes forcing Valerie to hide with her. Yet it was the fear of catching something that really filled her with the most anxiety. With germs as her number one enemy, she alternated between wearing rubber gloves and using the wooden tongs from the twin tub to pick up the post from the doormat. She was constantly washing her hands – sometimes scrubbing them so hard they bled – and would spend hours disinfecting the pavement outside their house with a mop and bucket.

Some days she would mop the path as well, going right up to the gate. She was getting through so much disinfectant that Lydia and Valerie were always being sent to the shop to buy more. Which was preferable to their grandmother going herself, because the corner shop was now owned by Mr and Mrs Khan, a Pakistani couple. During their first week of taking over from old Mrs Gorton, their grandmother had been embarrassingly rude to them about the colour of their skin.

It wasn't until she started burbling aloud in church on Sunday – just like the people she used to condemn as being unhinged – that their grandfather finally seemed to admit, if only to himself, that something was wrong. On Monday morning, after Lydia overheard him losing his temper with his wife and what sounded like a hard slap, he drove her to Doctor Bunch's surgery. Lydia had no idea what took place there, but in the weeks that followed their grandmother definitely seemed less agitated.

But not for long. By the summer of 1974, their grandmother's moods could switch as easily as turning the pages of a book – one minute she would be sitting calmly with Valerie and the next she would be rampaging round the house, throwing things and shouting at the top of her voice. It was the aggression that frightened Lydia most. Having caught enough of that from their grandfather over the years, Lydia was frightened that she might now have to put up with her grandmother lashing out at her. Or worse, what if she turned on Valerie?

Lydia knew that Valerie must be worried and confused about their grandmother, but try as she might she couldn't get her sister to talk about it. She had tried just now, but Valerie had rebuked Lydia by saying it was disrespectful to talk about their grandmother behind her back. For eight years old she could be remarkably – not to say annoyingly – stubborn and condescending.

Home from school, they were out in the garden, playing a game of jacks. It seemed such a trivial thing to be doing after the news Lydia had heard that morning. During assembly the headmaster had announced that Bena, who hadn't been at school that week, had died the day before. Everyone had instantly stopped fidgeting or kicking the chair in front of them. Even now, in the warm July sun, Lydia felt a shiver when she thought of it. Fourteen years old. Dead. Bena's heart had finally done what they'd all said it might. It had simply stopped working.

At the sound of raised voices, Lydia caught hold of the small ball and looked up. Their grandmother was arguing with their neighbour; she was pointing over the fence at The Floozy's underwear, which was hanging on the washing line. 'You're nothing but a dirty, filthy whore!' she screeched at the top of her voice.

Lydia had frequently heard her grandmother refer to The Floozy in this way, but she couldn't believe she was actually saying the words out loud to the woman's face.

Removing a cigarette from her red-painted lips, The Floozy shouted back, 'Better than a barmy, dried-up old hag who can't please her old man.'

Riveted by the angry exchange, but sensing it was something Valerie shouldn't witness, Lydia said, 'Why don't we go inside and get a drink, Val?'

They'd got as far as the back door when there was a blood-curdling cry from The Floozy. 'That's it! That's bloody done it! I've had enough. You're gonna cop it now, good and proper. Just yer wait and see.'

Lydia gasped: her grandmother had gone berserk and was throwing soil at The Floozy's clothes line. Great handfuls of it.

Pushing her sister inside the house, just in case Val had any ideas about joining in to defend their grandmother, Lydia wondered what on earth would happen next.

What happened next was that their grandfather arrived home from work to find The Floozy with two policemen banging on the front door and their grandmother hiding in the broom cupboard under the stairs.

'She needs locking up!' The Floozy shouted at their

grandfather as they all burst into the hall where Lydia was standing with her arms around Val. Through the open door, Lydia could see that a small crowd of neighbours had gathered outside to watch. 'She's barmy!' The Floozy continued to yell. 'Off her blooming rocker! I'm telling yer, she's not right in t'head.'

'Thank you, madam, we'll take it from here,' one of the policemen said.

'Yer must be joking! I'm sticking round to make sure justice is done. She's made my life a living hell with her obscene letters she's been shoving through my letterbox these last weeks. Not to mention the rubbish she keeps tipping over the fence into my garden. Give me a bleeding straitjacket and I'll put her in it myself! And while yer're about it, why don't you check out them kiddies? If she hasn't turned them into fruitcakes as nutty as she is, they're certainly not being treated right. Especially the older one. Some days I've heard her being shouted at so loud I can hardly hear my telly.'

Eventually The Floozy was convinced that she had done all she could to help, and it was just the two policemen and their grandfather left to try and coax his wife out of the broom cupboard.

'Lydia,' barked their grandfather, 'take your sister up to your bedroom.'

As soon as they were upstairs, Lydia made Valerie sit on her bed. 'Stay here, Val,' she whispered, 'while I go and find out what's going on.'

Standing at the top of the stairs, safely out of sight, Lydia held her breath and listened. One of the policemen was talking. 'I'm sorry about this, sir, but you're going to have to get your wife out of the cupboard. We need to talk to her.'

'Can't I just go next door and make an apology?'

'No, sir. Allegations have been made and we need to speak to your wife.'

'I'm not sure if you're aware of this, but that woman next door is a woman of ... of dubious morals. I wouldn't put it past her to make up those things she said about my wife.'

'We don't think that's the case, sir. Now if you'd kindly—'

'Are you saying the word of my wife, a good Christian woman, counts for nothing against that ... *tart* next door?'

'Let me ask you a question, sir. Do you think it's natural behaviour for a good Christian woman to hide herself in the cupboard under the stairs?'

There was a long silence, a heavy sigh, and then, 'Look, she hasn't been herself for some time. A lot of fuss and bother over a misunderstanding isn't going to help her.'

'I'm afraid you'll have to let us be the judge of what constitutes a misunderstanding. Now, if you could ask her to come out and answer our questions, we can get on.'

Their grandmother never did answer the questions they had for her. Instead, after biting one of the officers, she was bundled kicking and screaming into their police car and driven away. And all with the neighbours looking on. Staring down onto the street from the bedroom window, Lydia swallowed back the worry that had lodged there ever since the police had arrived. What was going to happen to their grandmother? If she went to prison, would that mean Valerie's worst fears would come true? That they would be taken away to live somewhere else.

And would it mean that Lydia would never see Noah again?

The next morning Pastor Digby, Sister Vera and Sister Joan arrived in a flurry of sympathy and scripture to see what could be done to help. With no school – it was Saturday – Lydia and her sister were once more banished to their room. Which meant Lydia took up her listening position at the top of the stairs. She already knew from eavesdropping on her grandfather's telephone calls last night that their grandmother hadn't been taken to the police station.

Shortly after the police car had driven away yesterday, their grandfather had told Lydia that he had to go out. He didn't return until gone ten. He'd spent the next hour on the telephone, his voice low. One of the calls had been with Doctor Bunch. Now, as Lydia listened to the murmur of voices in the front room, it was clear that their grandmother was in a special hospital. *A mental hospital.*

Mad. Her grandmother was mad. Lydia shuddered. It was worse than she thought. And what if madness could be inherited?

That afternoon, while their grandfather went to visit his wife, Sister Lottie came to spend the afternoon with Lydia and Valerie. But if Sister Lottie was her usual chirpy self as they sat in the garden shelling peas together, Valerie was not. It worried Lydia. She had tried her best to coax Val to come and sit with them in the sunshine, but shaking her head, Val had remained at the bedroom window, as though keeping watch for the moment when her precious grandmother would come home. Lydia was so used to worrying about something and keeping it to herself it came as a shock to hear Sister Lottie suddenly say, 'Lydia, what are we going to do about Valerie? I don't believe she's spoken a single word all afternoon.'

'Actually, she hasn't spoken since last night,' Lydia said.

'Really? Oh, dear. Dear, oh dear. That's not good.'

'I don't know whether it's the same thing, and she was only small then, but I remember her doing this when our mother died.'

Sister Lottie stopped what she was doing. 'Yes,' she said thoughtfully. 'Now I recall it, she was very quiet when you first came to live here. She's such a fragile little thing and being so attached to your grandmother, yesterday must have been a terrible shock for her. I suppose all we can do for now is lift her up to the Lord.'

Lydia knew it was wrong and unworthy of her, but she felt a stab of jealousy. She had always viewed Sister Lottie as *her* special friend and she didn't want her feeling too sorry for Valerie. Changing the subject, she said, 'I know what kind of hospital our grandmother's been taken to, but is she very ill? You know, in her head?'

Sister Lottie's face turned red. 'Well, oh dear,' she flustered, 'what with those operations, your grandmother's been through a lot. With something like that, it can make a person's mind think in extraordinary ways. It can happen to us all. Why only the other week I couldn't remember if I'd paid the milkman or not. I got myself into a terrible stew.'

'I bet you didn't call him names or send him nasty notes.'

Sister Lottie's face turned even redder. 'You're such a wise child. Much too clever for a simple old woman like me.'

'Then tell me the truth. Please.'

'I'm not sure I can, other than to say that what's probably happened to your grandmother is that her mind has decided it's had enough to cope with and wants a rest.'

'Will she get better?'

'I'm sure she will. The doctors will take wonderful care of her. She'll be home in no time.'

'I hope you're right, because I think Val is worried that if she doesn't come home, we'll be forced to live somewhere else and she'll never see Grandmother again.'

Sister Lottie patted Lydia's hand. 'Nothing like that's going to happen. You're not going anywhere.'

For Valerie's sake, Lydia hoped Sister Lottie was right.

Chapter Twenty-Eight

Their grandmother eventually came home in time for Harvest Festival, but by January, after she was found roaming the street late at night in her nightdress and being described as a danger to herself and possibly to others as well, she was back in hospital again. It was obvious to Lydia that their grandfather was ashamed of his wife's illness. She'd become known as the local nutter. And just as Lydia had known he would, he took out his frustration on her. If the house wasn't cleaned to his specific requirements he would deliberately mess it up and make her do it all over again. Sometimes, to check if she really had cleaned everywhere, he would hide tin tacks round the house for her to find. If she failed to find them all, she would be made to go without any tea. That was when he was in a good mood. He kept a garden cane handy in the kitchen for when he was in a bad mood.

The person who was suffering most in all of this was poor Valerie. She hadn't spoken properly since the first time their grandmother had been taken away. Everything she said was mouthed or whispered. Sometimes not even that and she would resort to writing instead of speaking. Her teachers said it was a phase she was going through and took the view that rather than upset Valerie further by forcing her to speak, they would patiently wait until she was ready to do so herself. Pastor Digby and the Brothers and Sisters were of the opinion that Val's voice would be returned to her when, and only when, the Lord had decided it was right. After all, who knew what God was trying to tell them through Val's silence?

Lydia wasn't convinced. Not by a long way. But since no one at church ever asked for her opinion, she never gave it. Sister Lottie was the only one to say she thought maybe Valerie should see a doctor, but when she was accused by Pastor Digby and Sister Vera of interfering with God's Great Plan for Valerie, she pressed a handkerchief to her trembling lips and said no more on the matter.

Sister Lottie had also been criticized for having an unmarried man living in her house with her. A foreign man, at that. More than once Lydia heard the Sisters whispering amongst themselves at church about the sins of the flesh and that Italian men were no better than savages when it came to women. 'It's well known they have unnatural passions,' Lydia heard Sister Joan saying to Sister Vera during tea and biscuits. 'They're famous for it. Sister Lottie is making a fool of herself.'

To Lydia's delight, Sister Lottie quietly retaliated by telling the Sisters that Joey was a good and godly man and that he always went to mass twice a week at St Joseph's. She could be surprisingly tough at times, Lydia had learned, yet on other occasions she could be reduced to a tearful child. She was a funny old thing, but Lydia was fiercely fond of her and would for ever be grateful for her help and kindness.

It had been Sister Lottie who had taken Lydia 'women's shopping', as she'd called it, to buy her her first bra. Just as it had been Sister Lottie who'd explained what was what when Lydia had started having stomach cramps.

Lydia hated the way her body had changed. It was like a betrayal. Especially her ever-growing chest. Alfie Stone and Jack Horsley were always ogling at it. Jimmy Fumble had even tried touching her. She'd kicked him hard between the legs – so hard he'd been heard throwing up in the toilets afterwards. Jack and Alfie had kept their distance from then on. Lots of other girls in their class were as big as her, but they all seemed quite happy with how they looked and when they could get away with it, they wore their shirts unbuttoned so low you could actually see their bras. Zoe

Woolf even made a big thing of leaning over her desk so that Mr Taylor, their history teacher and the best-looking teacher in the school, could get an eyeful.

Being a woman wasn't much fun, Lydia had decided. You had to shave your legs and armpits or risk being called a gorilla; you felt like you were dying every month; and the boys suddenly thought you were something to be experimented with. 'Go on, give us a feel,' one of the boys on the school bus had said only yesterday when she'd passed him to get off with Valerie. Donna Jones had been waiting at the bus stop, and if ever Lydia needed proof that being a woman was a bad thing, it was all there in the sight of Donna puffing hard on a cigarette, her massive stomach bulging hideously. Donna was pregnant and now living at Hillside Terrace with her aunt because her mother had kicked her out. Lydia couldn't imagine a girl the same age as her – almost fifteen – expecting a baby. There were all sorts of rumours about who the father was, including one about him being the driver of the rusting Jag Donna had been seen getting in and out of at the school gate at lunchtime.

If everything else around Lydia was changing, at least one thing was as constant as ever: Noah. Unlike the rest of the boys in their class, Noah treated her exactly as he always had. She was no longer taller than him; he'd rocketed in the last year and was now a good five inches taller than her. But like her, he was still thin and gangly and hadn't started to get that broad, chunky look so many of the other boys now had. He'd had another operation on his leg, but it hadn't been the success the doctors had hoped it would be. He still walked with a limp and in his own words would always be a complete tosser at sport.

Lydia was on her way to meet him now. It was a jarringly cold March morning. Newborn lambs were huddling against their mothers for warmth in the shelter of a drystone wall as the wind whipped in from the north, carrying with it the acrid smell of the town. It was a depressing smell, but maybe one that might not be around for too much longer. One of the woollen mills had closed down earlier in the year and there were angry rumours that Marsden's, the biggest producer of worsted cloth in the area, might not make it through the summer. The reports in the local newspaper said Marsden's had borrowed too much money from the bank and couldn't pay back the loans. The owners blamed it on the oil crisis last year, but the workers said it was down to bad management. Either way, it was bad for the town.

Above her, the sky was low and grey and Lydia hoped it wasn't going to snow as she pumped away on the pedals of her father's old bike. It wasn't so difficult for her to ride these days, now that she was so much taller, and since Joey had taken a look at it last autumn before he'd gone home to Italy – as he did every year after the summer was over – it didn't make that awful noise any more. Sister Lottie had received a letter from Joey last week saying that all was well with him and his family in Naples and that he hoped to return to Swallowsdale at the end of April. Lydia looked forward to seeing him and starting up her secret Italian lessons with him again.

So much of her life was wrapped in secrecy. If she didn't protect herself this way, her grandfather would probably ban her from ever leaving the house. Sometimes she thought he was as ill in the head as her grandmother. Particularly when he voiced his disapproval of most of what she was doing at school. 'What's the point in you learning French?' he would say when she was doing her homework. 'It's not like you're ever going to go there, is it?' Chemistry and biology also came in for an equally dismissive blasting. 'Waste of time teaching a girl like you – all you'll amount to is getting yourself pregnant and trapping some fool of a man just as your mother did.'

For someone who was constantly being labelled at home as stupid and lazy, she was doing surprisingly well at school. Along with Noah and Zoe she had been chosen to sit O-levels as well as CSEs. It meant a bigger workload but Mrs Drake, their form teacher, had said she was more than capable of coping with it. Easy for Mrs Drake to say when she didn't have the home life Lydia did!

One more hill to go and she would be there. Climbing over the garden wall was a much quicker route to Noah's house, but she'd had to drop Valerie off at Sister Lottie's beforehand. It had been hard going with Valerie sitting on the crossbar, but thank goodness her sister was still quite small and as light as a feather.

Today was yet another secret Lydia had to keep from her grandfather. He was away on church business – a last-minute arrangement, he'd said at breakfast – and knowing that this was an unexpected opportunity for her to be able to see Noah on a Saturday, she'd asked Sister Lottie if she would have Valerie for a few hours. Lydia wasn't worried that her sister would blab to their grandfather that she'd disappeared off somewhere else. These days Val was very much aware that it was better not to antagonize their grandfather.

It was Noah's fifteenth birthday today and Lydia really hoped that he'd like the presents she'd got him. By saving some of her dinner money every week and doing some odd jobs for Sister Lottie she'd saved enough to buy him a second-hand copy of Alexander Solzhenitsyn's book, *The Cancer Ward*. She'd also bought him a greatcoat in amazingly good condition at a jumble sale for a pound. She used to hate wearing second-hand stuff, but now she loved snooping through the piles of clothes for something out of the ordinary. She wasn't interested in the latest fashions like the rest of the girls at school. She couldn't understand why they all wanted to look the same in their platform shoes, tank tops, tartan flares, and glittery eyeshadow. Noah too had become a fan of jumble sales and they often scanned the local paper together to see when the next one would take place. She especially looked out for large-sized men's collarless shirts and chunky, dark-coloured cardigans that were much too big for her. Her latest bargain was a charcoal-grey beret which she was wearing for the first time. It helped to pin down her unruly curly hair which, now that her grandmother wasn't around to insist on cutting it, had grown down to her shoulders.

It sounded like a party was in full swing when Lydia wheeled the bike round to the back of Upper Swallowsdale House. She took the carrier bag from the basket on the handlebars and knocked on the door. When no one answered it, she banged the knocker even harder. Several minutes passed before the door finally opened and Noah appeared with a loud rush of music behind him. Lydia recognized it as one of Noah's favourite King Crimson albums – *In the Court of the Crimson King*. It was one of Uncle Brad's favourites as well.

'Have you been knocking for long?' he asked above the racket.

'For days,' she said with a smile, as he stood back to let her in.

'Sorry about that. Uncle Brad's just remembered it's my birthday and has decided to throw me a party. He's in one of his wild moods, so watch yourself.'

Lydia was quite used to Uncle Brad's moods, even the wild variety. She used to blush at the outrageous things he said, but now she either ignored him or laughed at him. The one thing you could say about Uncle Brad was that he was never dull.

'We're in the kitchen,' Noah said. She shrugged off her coat and followed behind Noah as he pushed open the door into the kitchen and the source of the loud music: it was so loud the china was rattling on the dresser. A record player and two speakers had been rigged up on one of the counters and Uncle Brad – bare-footed and wearing his hair in a ponytail – was standing on the kitchen table pretending to play an imaginary guitar. 'Hi, Lyddie,' he shouted when he saw her, using the name that Noah always called her by these days. 'It's Noah's birthday! We're having a little celebration.'

'I can see that,' she yelled back, noting the opened bottle of whiskey on the draining board and the ashtray with the smouldering remains of one of Uncle Brad's special hand-rolled cigarettes. She also noticed that the kitchen was its usual disaster zone of mess and muddle. Every inch of space was occupied with books, half-finished paintings, dirty dishes, and electronic gadgets Noah was assembling. It was more of a workshop than a kitchen.

Uncle Brad held out his hands to her. 'Come and play guitar with me.'

'I don't know how,' she shouted.

'There's nothing to it; I'll teach you.'

'Maybe later, after I've given Noah his presents.'

Noah went over to the stereo and turned down the volume. The china stopped rattling but Uncle Brad carried on strumming, his eyes closed, the table creaking ominously.

'What do you want first?' Lydia asked Noah as she tipped the presents out of the large carrier bag.

'I don't mind. You choose.'

She passed him the biggest. 'Happy birthday. I hope you like it.'

He did. She could see it in his face and the eagerness with which he slipped it on and pulled the collar up around his ears. 'What do you think?' he asked, his hands pushed deep into the pockets.

'Um …' She paused uncertainly. The coat was a bit big for him, as she'd thought it would be, but what made her hesitate was how different it made him appear. He suddenly seemed much older. And sort of, well, more handsome and distinctive-looking. Almost a stranger in a funny kind of way. A tall, dark, very good-looking stranger. 'You look very subversive,' she said, at length. 'Like the good Trotskyite Uncle Brad would want you to be.'

'Excellent,' he said. 'Thanks, Lyddie. It's great. Really great.'

She smiled. 'I know. That's why it's called a greatcoat.' She handed him his next present. 'It's not new,' she apologized, 'like the coat.'

'Brilliant!' he said when he'd removed the wrapping paper. 'Just what I wanted.' Knowing that he meant it, she blushed with pride and happiness. But then he did something that made her blush even more: he hugged her tightly. It was the first time he'd ever done anything like it before and by the time she'd decided she quite liked the feel of his arms around her, he'd let go. For a moment neither of them seemed to know what to say next, and just stood there staring at one another. She was just thinking that perhaps he'd regretted what he'd done, when behind them the ominous creaking from the table had turned even more ominous. They both yelled at the same time. '*Jump!*'

But it was too late. The splintering of wood followed by an almighty crash happened before Uncle Brad had an inkling of what was going on. 'Whoa!' he cried out as he hit the floor in a tangle of arms and legs that was the funniest thing Lydia had ever seen.

'Bloody hell!' he let rip while they, hysterical with laughter, pulled him from the wreckage. 'Good thing I didn't have a drink in my hand or I might have spilt it. Hey, nice hat by the way, Lydia. Very groovy.'

When she was back on her bike and heading into town for Sister Lottie's, Lydia was still laughing to herself. It was without doubt the best time she'd had in ages. The highlight of the afternoon, other than Uncle Brad smashing up the kitchen table, had been when he announced that he was going to teach Lydia and Noah to waltz. 'You never know when you might need this particular skill,' he told them as he changed the record on the stereo. Still dressed in his coat, Noah had refused point-blank to take part, but then after Lydia had called him a spoilsport and jammed a saucepan on his head, and then one on herself, they pranced around the kitchen according to Uncle Brad's instructions. She didn't know about their footwork, but the music was amazing. 'It's Russian,' Uncle Brad informed her when she asked him what it was. 'Sviridov.'

'Sure you're not talking about a brand of vodka?' Noah said.

'Philistine!' Uncle Brad roared, turning up the music and

then taking a photograph of them. 'Do try and hold Lyddie properly, Noah,' he continued to instruct impatiently. 'You look like you're terrified to touch her!'

Celebrating birthdays was one of the many things Pastor Digby had ruled out of their lives. According to him, celebrating your birthday was a sin rooted firmly in the mire of personal vanity.

Smiling to herself, Lydia couldn't help but wonder what Pastor Digby and the Brothers and Sisters would have made of the party she'd just been to. But the thought of their reaction soon wiped the smile off her face. If they ever got wind of what went on at Upper Swallowsdale House, what limited freedom she had managed to engineer for herself would be taken from her in an instant.

She was almost at Sister Lottie's when she noticed a car parked on the corner of a narrow side street. It was a car she knew all too well and had her pumping the pedals double fast. But what was her grandfather doing in town? He'd told her he was going to Skipton for the day.

Terrified that her grandfather might get home before her and be suspicious that she'd been up to something, she refused Sister Lottie's offer of a drink and a biscuit and set off with Valerie balanced on the crossbar.

They arrived home to find no car on the drive. Relief flooded through Lydia.

'What's wrong?' Valerie mouthed at her.

'Nothing,' Lydia lied as she opened the garage doors and pushed the bike inside.

Going in the back door, Lydia hurriedly started to peel the potatoes for tea. She'd just got the pan on to boil, when the doorbell rang.

She went to the door, opened it cautiously and peered at the man in the two-inch gap. He certainly wasn't anyone she knew. He had bushy sideburns and an ugly leathery face, and on the ground next to him was a battered suitcase. Maybe he was one of those men who came round with brushes and tins of polish.

'G'day sweetheart,' he said in a voice with a drawling accent she didn't recognize. 'I'm your uncle Leonard. Can I come in?'

Chapter Twenty-Nine

Uncle Leonard turned out to be their grandfather's younger brother, which strictly speaking made him not their uncle, but their *great*-uncle. He said he was happy for Lydia and Val to drop the 'great' and just be their common or garden Uncle Leonard.

According to Sister Lottie, he had been something of a rascal when he was a young man. 'He was very charming and could get away with all sorts,' she'd explained to Lydia. 'There was also a lot of rivalry between the two brothers and it caused, well, let's just say it caused ill-feeling between them.'

Lydia didn't think there was anything charming about the man currently staying with them. He was a big slab of a man with a thick neck, thick hands and a thick voice. For years he'd been living in Australia in a place called Wollongong, which didn't sound like a real place at all. He said he'd emigrated there to make his fortune and told them stories about kangaroos jumping out in front of cars, about koala bears and spiders that were as big as dinner plates and hid beneath the toilet seat. 'Oh, it's a great life,' he boasted, shovelling food into his enormous mouth, then helping himself to more from the dishes on the table.

'Then why have you come back to Swallowsdale?' Lydia's grandfather asked grimly.

'To be with my family, of course, Arthur.'

Lydia didn't believe half of what he said. More than that, he gave her the creeps. There was something in his face. Something sly and dangerous. He looked like trouble.

He reeked of the same aftershave nearly all the boys at school doused themselves in: Brut. In fact the whole house seemed to stink of the stuff; there was no escape from it, other than to go into the garden. But often he was out there, too. Banned from smoking inside, he would stand by the back door puffing away. Afterwards he'd spray his mouth with a minty breath freshener.

Within hours of Uncle Leonard's surprise arrival, it became very clear to Lydia that her grandfather hated having his brother around. Even before Uncle Leonard had unpacked his case and tested the firmness of the bed in the spare room, Lydia overheard her grandfather asking him when he would be leaving.

'I must say, Arthur, I don't call that much of a welcome,' Uncle Leonard had said.

'And I don't call you much of a brother,' came the reply. 'You've got a real nerve showing your face back here.'

'Surely you're not still harping on about the past? I told you, I'm a changed man. I've been reborn in the blood of our dear Lord and Saviour, Jesus Christ.'

'That remains to be seen.'

'I'll prove it to you. Just you see.'

Ten days on and Uncle Leonard didn't seem to be in any hurry to leave. He was still stinking the house out with his revolting aftershave and minty breath. This morning he was coming to church with them. Last week he hadn't got out of bed in time. He'd said the long journey had taken it out of him and he needed to catch up on his sleep. He did a lot of that. He was never up before Lydia and Valerie went to school. Lydia was convinced that he stayed in bed for most of the day. The evenings their grandfather visited his wife in hospital, Leonard would get himself all spruced up after tea and go out. He didn't say where he was going, but Lydia suspected it was to the pub.

At church, the Brothers and Sisters greeted Uncle Leonard politely enough, but not with their usual enthusiasm when anybody new appeared. 'I'm afraid his reputation goes before him,' Sister Lottie whispered to Lydia as they took their seats. 'A lot of people remember why he left Swallowsdale in the first place.'

'What did he do?'

But there was no time for Sister Lottie to say anything more, as Pastor Digby was on his feet, his palms held up before the Lord. It was the signal for them all to do likewise. For some reason Lydia didn't fully understand, she could never find it in herself to come right out and say that she hated going to church. Parts of it she disliked intensely, like the one-eyed, po-faced Pastor Digby for starters and all his silly rules – he'd recently banned them from drinking coffee, saying it was addictive – but when the room was perfectly quiet and everyone was deep in prayer, she felt a strange sense of peace she didn't feel anywhere else. Coming here to this dusty, musty-smelling hall was such a part of her life now, she couldn't really imagine not doing it. Besides, she couldn't bear the thought of disappointing Sister Lottie by not coming.

They were almost at the end of the service when Pastor Digby made his usual announcement that it was Share and Pray time. Lydia hoped that just once, no one would have anything special on their minds that needed praying about. The service was long enough as it was without everybody getting in on the act and wanting, like last week, to pray about the soul of the woman in the dry cleaner's who'd overcharged Brother Derek earlier in the week. A rustle of movement further along the row of seats told Lydia that her wish had not been granted. But when she saw that it was Uncle Leonard who was on his feet with something to say, she sat up straighter, her curiosity sparked. Hello, this should be interesting.

'I'd just like to say what it means for me to be here,' he began. 'As some of you will doubtless remember, I was not a good man in my younger days. Brothers and Sisters, the word sinner doesn't cover what I was then. Let me tell you, I sinned on a scale you can scarcely comprehend. I drank more than was good for me. I drank till I was lying in the gutter in my own vomit. And then I'd drag myself out of the gutter and drink some more.'

Shocked gasps could be heard.

'Yes, good folk, you have every reason to view me with disgust and loathing. But there's worse to come. I went with women. Hundreds of them. As many as I could lay my hands on.'

More gasps.

'And you know what? The devil had me so firmly in his hot sticky grasp I enjoyed every minute of it. It wasn't until I ended up in the barrel of sin, so near the bottom I was covered in the filth of lust and debauchery, that the Lord finally saved me.'

'Praise the Lord,' someone muttered from the back of the hall.

'But what I really want to share with you is something that's been weighing heavily on my heart for so many years. There's this great need in me to share with you exactly what kind of a man my brother is. You see there are things that need to be said, things that—'

'I think you've said enough, Leonard.'

Along with everyone else, Lydia whipped round to look at her grandfather: his face was puce.

'No, Arthur, I haven't. Please let me do this. Because I fear that if I don't, it can't ever be right between us. Only when it's right between us will I know you've forgiven me from the bottom of your heart.'

From the pin-drop silence around her, Lydia didn't doubt that there wasn't a person in the hall who wasn't on the edge of their seat to hear what else Uncle Leonard had to say. She saw her grandfather look to Pastor Digby for back-up, but Pastor Digby raised a hand and shook his head. 'Go on, Leonard,' he said. 'The Lord is listening. Put your confession before Him.'

He's as nosy as the rest of us, thought Lydia, trying not to smirk.

'Thank you, Pastor Digby. This is difficult for me. Very difficult. But the reason I'm here is not just to seek my brother's forgiveness but to open your eyes to show you how my brother—'

'This is intolerable! I won't stand for it!'

Doing exactly that, Lydia's grandfather jumped to his feet. He looked like he was about to explode.

'Sit down, please, Brother Arthur.'

'No! I shan't sit here and listen to this rubbish.' He jabbed a finger in the air at Uncle Leonard. 'You're no different from how you always were. After all these years, you still want to make me look bad. To humiliate me in front of my friends. You're no more filled with the spirit than I'm John the Baptist!'

Next to her, Valerie lowered her head and leaned into Lydia. Lydia reached for her hand and squeezed it. Please God, she silently prayed, don't let anyone make us leave the room. Not when it's getting so interesting.

But interesting wasn't the word for what happened next. Uncle Leonard began to cry. 'I knew it,' he wailed, his enormous hands raking through his greasy, dandruffy hair. 'I knew it wouldn't be possible to put the past to rest and be truly forgiven by my own flesh and blood.'

'Don't listen to him! He's a charlatan. A crook and a cheat. He's doing what he always did, weaving a web of lies to take you all in. He's capable of anything. Believe me when I say the devil has many cunning disguises, and this is one of them!'

'Please, Brother Arthur,' Pastor Digby said sternly. 'Sit down. It's our duty at all times to dig out the sin within ourselves and so I suggest we put this into the Lord's hands.' He swivelled his beady eye round to Uncle Leonard. 'Only when the demons have been fully seen off will the Lamb of God reside in our hearts.' The beady eye was back on Lydia's grandfather now. 'There's clearly some devilry at work here and I feel God calling me to exorcise it.'

A small part of Lydia almost felt sorry for her grandfather as he sank back into his chair, defeated. But the greater part of her was all agog to hear what it was Uncle Leonard was so eager to share with them.

'Like I said, this is difficult for me,' Uncle Leonard began. 'But I know I have to confess all. There can be no hiding from God.' He paused and stared straight at his brother.

Get on with it! Lydia wanted to shout. Just tell us what you did. She suspected he was enjoying himself with everyone hanging on his every word.

'Brother Arthur, I just pray you can find it in your heart to say the words, "I forgive you, Brother Leonard." Would that be too much to ask of you?' When he got no reply, not so much as a glance, he addressed the congregation. 'My brother's a proud man, and who can blame him? For what I did to him was despicable. I expect you all think that the reason I emigrated to Australia was because I stole from my brother. Not once. Not twice. But repeatedly. Small amounts of money at first and then I stole his chequebook and wrote out cheques for myself. I all but cleared out his account. Any other brother would have killed me there and then. But not mine. Not my brother Arthur. He turned the other cheek. Yes, that's what he did. And what did I do in return? Oh, let me tell you, I wanted even more from him. I wanted everything he had. Including his wife. His dear sweet wife.'

The congregation gasped as one.

'And still my brother didn't kill me. Instead, he gave me what little money he had left so that I could make a new and decent life for myself in Australia.' He thumped a fist against his chest. 'All this I did to my own precious brother. Oh, what a miserable wretch am I! But what a fortunate group of people you are, having a saint walking amongst you. A man so good of heart that he let me walk away, even though I'd made unseemly advances towards his wife.' He slumped dramatically to the floor and, down on his knees, he clasped his hands together in prayer.

The reaction to this confession was mixed. Some people tutted, some shook their heads, and some, like Uncle Leonard, got down on their knees and prayed. But Lydia's grandfather remained perfectly still in his seat. His gaze was fixed firmly on Uncle Leonard, and judging from the expression on his face, Lydia didn't think forgiveness was on the cards. But there was something else in his expression that had her wondering. It took her a few minutes to realize what it was: confusion. Why would her grandfather look confused? Unless he was expecting Uncle Leonard to confess to something else.

A few minutes of quiet passed and then Pastor Digby helped Uncle Leonard to his feet. 'I've no time for malingering Christians – those who profess the faith but do nothing to bring others to the Lord. Or those who cannot find it in their heart to forgive. This man has done a brave and virtuous thing here today and it is our duty to take him into our fold and prove to him what our faith really means. Brother Arthur, I invite you to join me here and publicly forgive Brother Leonard.'

'Not bloody likely!'

Chapter Thirty

The Prodigal Son had nothing over the Prodigal Uncle Leonard.

He was now the absolute centre of attention for the Brothers and Sisters in Christ. They couldn't get enough of him and were continually singing his praises. All during Easter week, they'd passed him amongst themselves at hot-pot suppers as a shining example of what the Lord could do for a sinner who had sincerely repented. Even the very worst of sinners. This was what the resurrection was all about: Uncle Leonard had been washed in the blood of Christ. He was truly born again. Hallelujah!

Lydia's grandfather was also coming in for a certain amount of attention. But there wasn't a single voice singing his praises. Pastor Digby was worried about him. As was the rest of the church. They were all busy praying for Brother Arthur.

It was just gone five o'clock in the afternoon and after finishing the ironing, Lydia was now listening to the raised voices behind the closed front room door. Pastor Digby was saying that if her grandfather continued to harden his heart towards Uncle Leonard, he risked letting the devil sneak into his life. 'It's too late for that,' Lydia heard her grandfather say. 'The devil has already wormed his way into my life. He's moved into my spare room and is making fools of the lot of you. I can't believe he's taken you all in.'

'Brother Arthur, I strongly urge you to reconsider your feelings. Search your heart, long and hard, for anything that isn't of our Lord and Saviour. Jealousy is an ugly thing close up. It destroys our walk with God. I say this not just as your spiritual mentor, but as your friend.'

'You know what they say about people who eavesdrop, don't you?'

The question was whispered hoarsely in Lydia's ear. She spun round, swamped by Uncle Leonard's close-up presence and the sickening smell of Brut and breath freshener.

'I wasn't eavesdropping,' she lied.

'Sure you weren't. You just happened to have your ear firmly pressed against the door, checking for the sound of woodworm. So what are they saying in there?'

He was so close to her she could practically count the gingery hairs in his bushy greying sideburns. There were hairs in his enormous nostrils, too. That much he had in common with his brother. 'I don't know,' she lied, moving away fast.

'Were they talking about me?' he asked, following her to the kitchen.

'I told you I don't know.'

He smiled, the leathery skin crinkling around his eyes. 'Don't look so frightened, Lydia,' he said. 'I'm on your side. I know what kind of a man my brother really is. I just want you to know that I'm your friend. If you want me to be, that is. Do you need a friend, Lydia? Someone you can trust?'

She swallowed nervously, but didn't answer him. What could she possibly say? If her grandfather thought for a single second that she had an ally in his brother, he would make life hell for her. Yet, what if Uncle Leonard really did know what his brother was capable of? Wouldn't it be better to have him on her side? Maybe in the short term, but what about when Uncle Leonard left Swallowsdale, as he surely would? 'I'd better make a start on getting tea ready,' she said non-committally.

If he thought she'd snubbed him, he gave no sign of being offended. 'In that case,' he said, 'don't bother making anything for me; I've been invited out to supper again.'

'Lucky you.'

He winked. 'Lucky me, indeed.'

Shortly after Pastor Digby left, Lydia's grandfather came into the kitchen and announced that he would be out for the evening. Excellent, thought Lydia. She and Valerie could have a nice evening together. No grandfather. No Uncle Leonard. The house to themselves. What could be better?

With tea out of the way, Val whispered to Lydia that she was going upstairs to read. Disappointed that her sister didn't want to stay downstairs with her, Lydia decided to leave the washing-up until later. Why not enjoy some time to herself, seeing as it was the last day of the Easter holidays? So whilst it was still light, she went out to the garden and climbed up into the branches of the chestnut tree. She looked out across the moors in the direction of Noah's house. She supposed he'd be home now, back from his holiday down in London with Uncle Brad. London. It was about as foreign to her as Joey's home in Italy. But one day she'd go there. London and Italy. That was a promise. Resting her back against the broad solid trunk of the tree, she played her hands over the large leaves that almost hid her from view. They were still that lovely fresh green colour that you only saw in spring. In the cool evening air, she listened to the birds giving their final burst of busy sing-song before settling down for the night. Then through the chirruping and squawking she became aware of another sound: a car. A car that had stopped nearby. Very nearby. Next she heard the sound of a car door slamming shut.

Remembering the washing-up she hadn't done, she clambered down from the tree and bolted up the garden towards the house, her heart thumping.

But she was too late – her grandfather was already in the kitchen.

'Where have you been?' he demanded.

'I was in the garden,' she said, shutting the back door behind her. She followed the direction of his questioning gaze, to the dishes piled up on the draining board.

'You were in the garden, weren't you?' he said. His tone was slow and menacing and there was a chilling mixture of anger and relish on his face. It made her stomach clench with queasy fear. 'You had better things to do with your time than tidy up, did you?' He took off his jacket and hooked it over a chair.

'I ... I was going to do it when—'

'What?' he interrupted, going over to the door to the hall and closing it. 'Because I wasn't here to keep an eye on you, you were going to do it when you were good and ready? Is that it? Except I came home early and caught you out.' He came and stood directly in front of her.

She pushed up her sleeves to show she was ready to get on with the job now. Right now this very minute, if only he'd get out of the way.

But he made no move to get out of the way, and as if copying her, he began rolling up his own sleeves. She knew what that meant and her stomach clenched even more. 'It makes me wonder what else you get up to while my back is turned,' he said. 'Maybe you haven't been in the garden at all. Maybe you've been somewhere I don't know about.'

'I haven't,' she said, eyeing the cane over by the bin. 'I've been in the garden. And only for a few minutes. Honestly.'

'I don't believe you!' he barked, making her jump. 'I can see it in your face. You're lying.' His eyes blazed and he seemed visibly to swell before her. Then it came: not the cane, but his hand full across her face.

Lydia reeled and nearly lost her balance. She hadn't recovered properly when he came at her again, cracking her on the side of her head. Then the other side too. Dizzy, she could taste blood. She touched her lip; it was split. Shocked, she knew that this was going to be no ordinary beating. The slow, menacing tone he'd used before was gone and he was shouting at her now. Calling her those vile names he always did. She was scum. Worse than scum. She was a whore. She forced her mind to go to that special place where she went when she needed to detach herself from what was happening. She pictured herself being carried away into the night sky by her father; he was taking her somewhere safe.

But the special place wasn't working for her this time. Her grandfather had her by the shoulders and was shaking her with such violence her head flew backwards and forwards. 'If I don't teach you right from wrong,' he yelled at her, 'who will?' He then shoved her from him so forcibly she fell to the floor, the air knocked clean out of her. Just inches from his feet, instinct made her wrap her arms around her head. But that left the rest of her vulnerable. The first kick was aimed at her stomach. The next at her shoulder. This was new. He'd never kicked her before. He really had lost control and she knew she had to do something. She had to get out of here. Keeping her head protected, she twisted round to look over to the back door. To her surprise, it was open and somebody was standing there watching. It was Uncle Leonard.

'Well, well, well, brother dear,' he said, stepping inside. 'So this is how you get your fun these days, is it?'

Immediately her grandfather stopped what he was doing. Relief flooded through Lydia. It was over. She was safe. But the sense of relief was quickly followed by shame. She didn't want to be seen this way, so degraded and humiliated.

'Keep out of this,' her grandfather snarled at his brother. 'It's got nothing to do with you.'

'Is that so? You wouldn't be taking out your frustration on a defenceless young girl because you're too frightened to pick a proper fight with me, would you?'

Faint with pain and fear, and hardly daring to look at her grandfather or uncle, knowing only that the kitchen was suddenly charged with an explosive tension, Lydia dragged herself off the floor. She began to shiver.

'Not everything in this world is about you, Leonard,' her grandfather said. 'I'm teaching her an important lesson. Not to lie to me. You know how I feel about liars and cheats.'

'I know only too well,' said Uncle Leonard with a tight smile. 'You'll be telling me next that she can only be redeemed through true suffering.' He came over to where Lydia was standing. 'Have you lied to your grandfather, Lydia?'

'No,' she replied; her voice was small and pathetic, little more than a strangled croak from the back of her dry throat. She was a cold mess of fear inside. 'No, I haven't.'

'Of course you haven't. You're much too sweet and innocent to do anything like that.' He turned back to his brother. 'You should be ashamed of yourself, Arthur. Now out of my way while I take Lydia upstairs and make sure she's all right. She might need a doctor.'

Panic seized hold of Lydia. Whilst she was grateful for his intervention, she knew that if she accepted any more help from him, it would only make matters worse for her. 'Thank you,' she murmured, already moving towards the door and the safety of the hall and upstairs, 'but I don't need any help. I'm fine.'

Upstairs she found Valerie crying under her bedclothes. 'It's OK, Val,' she assured her. 'It was just some silly disagreement and Grandfather lost his temper like he always does. You're not to worry. Please, Valerie,' she begged, 'please don't cry. You know I hate to see you upset.'

But when Valerie poked her head out from the covers, she took one look at Lydia's face and started sobbing again.

Knowing what her sister was worried about, Lydia spent the next hour comforting her, telling her everything was going to be OK, that nothing was going to change for them. Stability was what her sister needed and it looked like Lydia was the only one who could provide it. With lies and whatever else it took.

Once Valerie was asleep, Lydia quietly got ready for bed. It was a while before she could get comfortable. Shock must have numbed the worst of the pain earlier – now she was conscious of it throughout the whole of her sore, tender body. There wasn't a bit of her that didn't ache. She felt sick and her head wouldn't stop spinning. Maybe Uncle Leonard was right and she did need to see a doctor. She put the thought out of her mind and closed her eyes.

Sleep wouldn't come. Staring at the light cast from the street lamp through the gap in the curtains, she started to worry what she could tell Noah to explain away the bruises. She had used the 'falling down the stairs' excuse too often already. And not just to Noah. Miss Drake had asked her about the livid marks on her legs the last time her grandfather had taken the cane to her. On that occasion she had 'tripped' on the carpet on the stairs.

Downstairs she could hear her grandfather arguing with Uncle Leonard and then the sound of a door slamming. One thing she knew for sure was that after what had just taken place, life was going to get a lot more difficult. If only she'd just done the washing-up when she normally did ... if only she hadn't gone out to the garden. She squeezed her eyes shut and jammed her knuckled fists into her sockets. Why was life so unfair to her? What had she done to deserve it?

The answer came back at her in a flash. *You reap what you sow*. If she hadn't driven her mother to suicide, none of this would be happening. But because of what she'd done, this was her punishment: to be a lightning conductor for bad things. She had no one but herself to blame.

Chapter Thirty-One

As she made him his toast and poured out his tea, Lydia was jumpy around her grandfather the next morning. He hadn't said a word to her. He didn't need to. It was there in the grim set of his face. *Just you wait*, it said. Unable to eat any of her own breakfast, she concentrated on making sure Val ate hers.

In the deathly silence, Lydia could hear movement in the room above them, followed by the sound of heavy foot-steps on the stairs. Then unbelievably, for the first since he'd arrived, Uncle Leonard appeared for breakfast. 'Now that's what I like to see,' he said in a loud, overly cheery voice, 'a happy family sitting round the table together. Room for me?' he said to his brother.

Without answering him, her grandfather threw down his half-eaten toast and marched out of the room. And the house.

Her cereal bowl empty now, Val also left the room and went upstairs to clean her teeth. Keeping an eye on the time, Lydia started clearing away the dishes.

'How are you this morning, Lydia?' Uncle Leonard asked, sitting in his brother's seat. 'Are you sure you're well enough for school?'

'I'm just a bit stiff, that's all.'

'You wouldn't prefer to stay at home?'

Nothing would have suited her more than to hide her-self away in bed for the rest of the week. She didn't know why, but she felt dirty. Dirty all over. Inside and out. No amount of washing would make her feel clean again. 'Best not,' she said. 'I don't like to miss any lessons if I can help it,' she said.

'Good for you. That's the spirit. Any chance of a cuppa?'

She fetched him a mug and poured out the last of the tea from the pot. 'Thanks, sweetheart,' he said, and after taking a noisy slurp, he rested his elbows on the table. 'You know, I meant what I said yesterday. I'm your friend, Lydia. And I'd bet my last dollar or pound that this isn't the first time my brother has hurt you, is it? And that you've never told anyone. Eh?'

Lydia couldn't speak. It was bad enough that he'd witnessed her humiliation, but to talk about it so openly was too much. When she didn't respond, he said, 'You know he's banking on you being too scared to open your mouth. If he was worried that you'd talk to anyone, do you think he'd let you go to school with that face? No. He's done too good a job on you. But like I said, I'm your friend, Lydia, and if you want me to protect you from my brother, you're going to have to trust me. Do you think you can do that?'

Slightly mesmerized, Lydia surprised herself by nodding. Just a small, barely noticeable nod, as though anything more would expose her dirty shame to the world.

Uncle Leonard smiled at her. A big grin of a smile that showed two rows of badly stained teeth. 'Then why don't you stop what you're doing and keep me company while I pack away some breakfast?'

'I'm sorry but I don't have time, the bus leaves in fifteen minutes.'

All the way to school, Lydia kept thinking how badly she'd misjudged Uncle Leonard when he first came to stay with them. He may have done some terrible things in the past, but at least he wasn't cruel and didn't beat people for no real reason. He may not be able to protect her for ever from her grandfather, but the way she felt now, she would take whatever help she could get.

So what if that help sprang from a situation she didn't fully understand? The relationship between her grandfather and Uncle Leonard was a mystery to Lydia. Given that he had publicly refused to forgive his brother, she couldn't work out why her grandfather allowed him to stay.

From what she had pieced together from snippets of overheard conversation, Uncle Leonard had far from made his fortune in Australia as he'd hoped to and had returned to Britain without a bean to his name. Apparently, having allowed Jesus into his life, he'd been overcome with the need for forgiveness from his brother, as well as a desire to see his family again, particularly the two great-nieces he'd never met before but whom he had learned about through an old school pal in Swallowsdale who had recently got in touch with him. Could his return home really be as simple as that? Or was there more to it?

'What the hell happened to you?' Noah asked the second he saw her.

Wishing that just once he wasn't such a good and caring friend, Lydia busied herself with something at the bottom of her bag. 'Oh, you know what I'm like,' she said lightly. 'I'm such a clumsy idiot. Those stairs are going to be the death of me one day.'

When she couldn't convincingly go on rustling around inside her bag any longer, she looked up. Noah was staring at her. He continued to do so for the longest time, his dark, thoughtful eyes searching hers. Then his eyes travelled slowly over her split lip and her swollen jaw. Thank God the rest of the bruises were hidden beneath her clothes. Trying not to squirm, she saw his expression change. There was ... there was anger in his face. Something she had never seen before. She suddenly realized with total certainty that he didn't believe her. That probably he never had. Shocked, she willed him not to say what he had to be thinking. Please, she silently begged him, please allow me to hang on to what's left of my dignity.

When he did speak, he very gently touched her jaw with

his fingers and said, 'It looks painful, Lyddie. Have you seen a doctor?'

His concern made something deep within her ache far more painfully than her bashed ribs did. 'It looks worse than it really is,' she said, turning away and blinking back the tears. 'I'm OK. Really. How was London? Did Uncle Brad take you to the Planetarium as he said he would?'

Everyone else at school had a field day teasing her, wanting to know who she'd got into a scrap with during the Easter holiday. 'You should see the state of the bloke after I'd finished with him,' she bragged to Alfie Stone, 'so you'd better watch yourself.'

How easy it was to tough it out and be full of bravado when you weren't scared of the person.

On her way home, having stayed late for a French conversation class, Lydia was feeling particularly fed up. She had a letter in her bag about a school trip that she knew she would never be allowed to go on. It had been organized some time ago and her grandfather had thrown the original letter straight in the bin, saying it was too expensive. She hadn't given it another thought. But now some extra places had become available and her French teacher had made a point of urging Lydia to take one up.

When she rounded the corner of the back of the house, she found Uncle Leonard sitting in a deckchair in the garden. Her spirits fizzled even lower. She was tired, and wanted only to go in and lie down on her bed for a while. She had a headache and her ribs were sore and tender, as was her jaw.

'Hello,' he said cheerfully. 'How was your day?'

'OK,' she said politely.

'That doesn't sound too good. Any problems I can help you with?'

'I shouldn't think so.'

'Why don't you try me?'

She sighed and went over to him. 'The French department

at school is arranging a trip to Paris at the end of May.'

'So why the glum face?'

'Do you think for one moment my grandfather will let me go?'

He rubbed his chin, then stroked his ridiculous sideburns. 'Mm ... I see what you mean. Well, perhaps I could find a way to convince my brother that you should go. I could play the education angle. No one knows more than me that travel broadens the mind.'

As tempting as his offer was, Lydia decided not to push her luck. Having Uncle Leonard's protection was more important to her than her grandfather's arm being twisted so she could go on some silly French trip. Besides, something told her that it wasn't a good idea to put all her eggs in one basket. Better not leave herself too much in Uncle Leonard's debt. 'No thanks,' she said, 'it's not that big a deal to me.' She turned to go inside.

'Don't rush off,' he said. 'Stay and chat with me while I finish my illicit fag.'

Seeing as there was only a short stub left to his cigarette, she gave in. 'I wouldn't have thought you'd care less about my grandfather's insistence that you smoke outside the house.'

'Are you suggesting a good Christian man like myself would deliberately antagonize my brother?'

'No ... but—'

'It's about respect, Lydia. Whilst I can't respect my brother for what he's done to you, I'm a guest here in his house and as such I have to respect his rules and abide by them.'

Lydia couldn't help but think his answer was about as plausible as his dramatic confession in church. Reminded of his confession, she said, 'Can I ask you something?'

'Ask away.'

'Did you really try it on with my grandmother when you were younger?'

He took a hard puff on his cigarette, inhaled the smoke, then exhaled it through his nose in two long curling ribbons. 'I may have been a bad boy back in those days, but I wasn't desperate. No offence, but your grandmother was no looker.'

'So you didn't?'

'In a drunken moment or two I may have wanted to annoy my brother by making the odd pass at her. But nothing serious took place.'

'Then why did you say you did in church?'

He stubbed out his cigarette on the grass at his feet and tapped his nose. 'That's strictly between me and my dearly beloved brother.'

Chapter Thirty-Two

The day before Lydia's fifteenth birthday, Sister Lottie invited her to tea. It was a special occasion: Joey had just returned to Swallowsdale.

When Lydia saw the dainty crustless sandwiches, the chocolate fingers, the butterfly cakes and a Victoria sponge cake in pride of place in the middle of all the plates, she said, 'This looks wonderful, just like a real birthday party.'

Sister Lottie was immediately all a-flutter. 'Oh, goodness gracious no! Pastor Digby wouldn't approve of that. But if anyone asks, we're celebrating the Lord bringing Joey safely back to us.'

Lydia tried not to smile. She loved it when Sister Lottie got round one of Pastor Digby's silly Thou Shalt Nots.

'I have never understood this strange church of yours,' Joey said, 'so many rules, so many ways to stop you enjoying yourselves.'

'Now, now, Joey,' Sister Lottie said, managing to sound quite stern, something that she was rarely capable of pulling off, 'you Catholics have just as many odd rules.'

Joey laughed, shaking his head of black curly hair. 'Yes, but we ignore almost all of them.'

Sister Lottie tutted and passed him the plate of sandwiches. Watching Joey eat, marvelling at how good his English was now compared to when he first came to Swallowsdale, Lydia thought how happily at home he appeared here in this little house. He was like the son Sister Lottie had never had and it always amused Lydia that she mothered him so lovingly. Joey often spoke about his own mother back in Italy, who had been left to bring up six children single-handedly after her husband died in a gruesome accident with a threshing machine while helping out on a friend's farm. They had been so poor they had regularly gone to bed with only water slopping around in their stomachs. His mother had taught them to imagine the water was a tasty stew of lamb and potatoes. Two of Joey's brothers, like him, had gone in search of work abroad so they could support the family back home – they were now living in America working in the kitchen of a restaurant owned by a cousin.

For all that, Joey was never miserable and not once had Lydia ever heard him complain. He was fiercely proud of his family and utterly devoted to making life easier for them, even if it did mean he had to spend so many months apart from them. He was equally devoted to Sister Lottie, who he claimed was his adopted mother here in England. Continuing to observe him, Lydia listened to the story he was telling about the kind lorry driver who had given him a lift all the way from Dover. He was doing what he always did, punctuating the telling of his tale with wild hand gestures and happy laughter. With his coal-black eyes, straight white teeth, tight jeans and black shirt, he looked impossibly glamorous and Lydia could easily understand why all the women on Hillside Terrace took ages making up their minds when choosing which ice-cream to buy.

The following day it was Lydia's birthday and she was given permission to visit Donna Jones, who had recently come home from hospital with a baby boy. Donna's aunt had put a note through the letterbox asking Lydia to visit her niece that afternoon. Lydia's grandfather had opened and read the note – there was no such thing as privacy in their household – and after a lengthy discussion on the phone with Pastor Digby, who seemed to think the risk of Lydia being tainted and led astray was outweighed by the opportunity of winning a prize sinner for Jesus, Lydia was told she could accept the invitation. She was handed a selection of Pastor Digby's tracts to give to Donna and informed that it was her duty as a believer, and for the sake of the newborn child, to bring Donna to Christ.

Lydia knew Donna would be no more interested in the religious pamphlets than she was in sharing them with her. Anyway, she had plans. As soon as she could get away, she was going to see Noah.

Lydia knocked nervously on Donna's door. The aunt, decked out in pink fluffy mules, a short silky dressing gown and a headdress of Carmen heated rollers, let her in and showed her through to the front room. 'I'll leave you to it,' she said, closing the door after her.

Donna was stretched out on a scabby PVC settee that looked like it was suffering from a bad case of eczema. Donna's feet were resting on a pouffe, with her eyes glued to a colour television. The only television Lydia was familiar with was Noah's TV, a small portable black and white set that had an aerial like a halo sticking out of it. This one was huge. Balanced on Donna's lap was not a baby, as Lydia had expected, but a can of stout. 'Wotcher,' Donna said, briefly flicking her eyes away from the screen, where a man in a hat like a tea cosy was trying to comfort a tearful blonde woman: their faces were a peculiar shade of orange. 'Come in and park yer bum. It's only *Crossroads*. It'll be over in a mo.'

While she waited for the action to come to an end on the television, Lydia lowered herself into a PVC armchair: it made an embarrassing raspberry sound when she put all her weight on it. She glanced around her. There were lots of signs that a baby had recently moved in – a row of cards on the mantelpiece, a pair of woollen mittens on the floor, a half-empty bottle of milk warming in the sun on the windowsill alongside a bottle of Aqua Manda, but no sign of an actual baby.

Although Lydia had known Donna since they were nine years old, she didn't *know* her one little bit. Donna's bullying days may have been left behind at junior school, but

Lydia had never felt inclined to be friends with the girl. She didn't have a clue why she'd been summoned to visit Donna. As far as she was concerned, the sooner this visit was over, the better.

A twangy theme tune started up from the television, signalling the end of the programme. Donna took a swig from the can of stout. 'Switch it off, will yer? Knob's on t'right.'

Lydia did as she was told, and that was when she saw the baby. He was on the floor at the far end of the settee, loosely wrapped in a crocheted blanket inside a plastic laundry basket: it didn't seem much of a start in life for the poor thing.

'He's an ugly little bleeder, in't he?' Donna said.

Lydia was no expert, but he didn't look that bad. Just a bit scrunched up, that was all. Quoting something she'd heard before, she said, 'I expect he'll grow into his looks.'

'Let's hope you're right.'

Sitting back in her chair again, Lydia said, 'What have you called him?'

'Kirk.'

Lydia repeated the name inside her head. Why did it ring a bell? Ah! Captain Kirk from Noah's favourite TV programme, *Star Trek*. Perhaps Donna was a fan too. 'How was it?' she asked. 'You know, the birth?'

'A bloody nightmare from start t'finish. From now on I'm going on t'pill. Come to that, the way my fanny feels I doubt I'll ever want sex again. I'm as big and rattly as a dustbin down there.'

Lydia wished she hadn't asked. She squeezed her knees together. What on earth was she doing here? Why had Donna's aunt put that note through the letterbox?

But Donna had plenty more to say on the subject of giving birth. 'I've got knockers as hard as spuds and me belly's like a wrinkled balloon at the end of a party. I'm a wreck. Fifteen years old and me body's fit only for t' knacker's yard.'

'Has the father been to see you?' Lydia asked, swearing

to herself she would *never* let anyone get her pregnant.

'Has he 'eck as like! Anyway, I don't want him hanging around me. Take it from me, Lydia, you're better off without them. Men! Selfish, useless bastards one and all.' She raised the can to her mouth and tipped her head back. When it was empty, she lobbed it across the room, where it missed the wastepaper bin by a foot and landed on a Bay City Rollers album cover. She belched loudly. 'Midwife says the best way to build my strength up is to drink stout. Makes yer laugh, doesn't it? Seeing as I'm not officially old enough to drink. Funny old world. What've you done to your face?'

It was a week and a half since that awful night in the kitchen and whilst her lip had healed as good as new, her jaw, legs and back were still coloured by faint blossoms of greenish-yellow bruises. She'd be glad when the marks, especially the one on her face, finally disappeared. She was tired of lying to people. Yesterday it had been Sister Lottie and Joey she'd lied to. Now Donna. 'I wasn't looking where I was going,' she said.

'Yer should be more careful. So what've yer got there, then? Sommat for me?'

Time to get the worst over with and then scarper. 'We wondered if you'd like to read these.' Lydia handed over the pamphlets as though they were red hot and about to burst into flames.

Without looking at them, Donna said, 'Who's *we*?'

'Um ... Pastor Digby, the man in charge of the church I go to.'

'I know about that church of yours. Bit bloody barmy if yer don't mind me saying. Why do yer go? Why not have a lie-in on a Sunday morning like most sensible people do?'

It was a question Lydia had never been able to answer properly, even to herself. 'It's something to do,' she said with a shrug. There was also the small matter of what her grandfather would do to her if she did ever refuse to go. 'You don't have to read them if you don't want to.'

Donna briefly looked at the pamphlets in her hand

before tossing them aside. She let out a short, bitter laugh. 'Chance would be a fine thing.'

'Yes, I suppose you are rather busy at the moment, aren't you? What with the baby and everything.'

Donna picked at the flaking settee. 'It's not that,' she said, her voice oddly unsure all of a sudden, 'it's …' But her words trailed off. She pulled back a thin strip of PVC and flicked it away from her. 'Promise yer won't laugh?'

Lydia nodded, despite not knowing what she was agreeing to.

'The thing is, I can't read. I can make out a few words, but not enough to make sense of it all.'

Amazed, Lydia said, 'But however did you manage at school?'

'If yer play up enough the teachers stop bothering yer and yer can get away with murder. I thought I was the mutt's nuts, all that larking about. But now look at me. Stuck here with a baby that resembles a sodding goblin.'

A world without books wouldn't be worth living in for Lydia and before she knew what she was doing, she was offering to teach Donna to read.

Now it was Donna's turn to be amazed. 'Why would yer want to do that?'

'I don't know,' she said, suddenly embarrassed. 'The idea just popped into my head.' As did a long and distant memory of her father sitting on the edge of her bed reading to her when she was little. 'Don't stop,' she used to beg him, even though she was so sleepy she could hardly keep her eyes open. Swallowing back the tender recollection, she said, 'When Kirk's older, it would be good if you could read to him, don't you think?'

Donna looked doubtful. 'Nobody ever read owt to me when I was little.' She reached for a packet of Silk Cut on the pouffe. 'Maybe it's too late for me.'

'Why don't we give it a go? No harm in that, surely?'

'OK. You're on. But no being bossy with me. Or telling anyone. I'll kill yer if you do. And definitely no homework. I ain't got time for that.'

As if to prove her point, a snuffling sound came from the end of the settee, followed swiftly by a loud, demanding cry.

Lydia took it as her cue to leave.

After saying she'd call round in a few days' time, she let herself out and crossed the road to the phone box. For once it wasn't home to a gang of boys making obscene calls.

When her grandfather answered, she crossed her fingers and explained that she'd been invited to stay for tea and that Donna's aunt was going out for the evening and Donna didn't want to be alone with the baby for too long. 'Why are you calling from a public pay phone?' he wanted to know.

'Theirs isn't working. Can I stay, then? Donna wants to know more about the leaflets.'

Grudgingly he agreed, told her not to be too late and rang off.

She then phoned Noah.

To make sure she wasn't spotted by anyone at home looking out from an upstairs window, she had to take a detour, which meant a longer route across the moors to Noah's. She didn't care: it was a beautiful spring afternoon. The day felt newly washed and the air smelled fresh and earthy. The gorse was nearly in flower, with shy glimpses of tiny clusters of yellow just peeping through on the bushes. A perfect day for a birthday, she thought as she picked up pace and headed towards the Dell of the Dead.

Noah now had a blue and white enamelled 'Private – Keep Out' sign on his bedroom door: Uncle Brad had 'stumbled across' it somewhere and had brought it home for Noah.

As she always did, Lydia made herself at home by kicking off her shoes and sitting cross-legged on Noah's bed. She didn't think she would ever tire of his room. Every time she came here there was something new and interesting to get to know. He hated to throw anything away and as a result the room was chock-full of the strangest things. More often than not they were objects he collected to draw – a bird's skull, a fir cone, a pile of smooth pebbles, an old gas mask, a stuffed mynah bird, a one-legged action figure from *The Man From U.N.C.L.E.* There were minutely detailed drawings of some of these things on the walls. There were also things he liked to take apart to see if he could meet the challenge of putting them back together again – a cuckoo clock, a radio, a small steam engine, a Stylophone, a record player.

He was nicknamed The Professor at school, but not unkindly. He had long since earned the respect of everyone in their class because there wasn't anything he couldn't fix with a tube of glue or a soldering iron. He had a nice little sideline going, charging fifty pence a repair. He was the most patient person Lydia knew and would spend hours happily inventing some electronic gadget or other, or piecing together a broken ornament. His latest craze was for three-dimensional wooden puzzles. Lydia regularly confounded him by being able to figure them out faster than him. She didn't know why, but she could always see exactly how the pieces fitted together. It was the same with maths equations or algebra. And French. The tenses and verbs just seemed to make perfect sense to her.

'Happy birthday, Lyddie,' he said after he'd foraged in the wardrobe then closed the door. 'I hope you like what I've got for you.'

She took the two wrapped presents and held them, savouring the moment: they were the only presents she'd received. 'Which one shall I open first?' she asked him.

He joined her on the bed. 'Up to you. You choose.'

She opted for the one that was clearly book-shaped. He'd made such a thorough job with the sticky tape it was impossible not to make a mess of the paper and she reluctantly had to tear it off. 'Oh!' she cried with delight when she saw he'd given her a small hardback of the complete poems of Christina Rossetti. 'You remembered,' she said.

He arched one of his eyebrows. 'Of course I did. What do you take me for?'

She smiled and thought of the day when she was supposedly staying late at school for a netball match. She and Noah had gone into town and spent an hour browsing the shelves in the second-hand bookshop. She had discovered this dusty, faded little gem but had returned it to the shelves as being much too extravagant for her pocket.

She longed to throw herself into reading it, but conscious of the other present on the bed next to her she turned her attention to that instead and made quick work of the wrapping paper.

'It's beautiful,' she gasped, her breath truly taken away. She ran a finger lightly over the tiny pearl and delicate silver chain that nestled in the velvet jewellery box. 'But it must have cost you a fortune.'

'It didn't cost me anything,' he said. 'It belonged to my mother.'

Shocked, she snapped the lid shut. 'But you can't possibly give it to me. It's much too precious.'

'I knew you'd say that, but I want you to have it. I can't think of anyone I'd rather see wearing it.'

'Do you really mean that?'

He frowned. 'Lyddie, why do you always doubt me? If I say something, it's because I mean it.'

Confused, she said, 'But I don't doubt you. You're the one person I've never doubted.'

Just inches away from her, he stared at her steadily, his dark, compelling eyes boring right into her. Right down to the depths of her guilty, secretive soul. The bit of her she never wanted him to know. 'I don't think that's true,' he said softly.

There was a troubled sadness to his voice that made her feel she'd let him down. That he was disappointed in her. Disconcerted as to where he might lead the conversation, she opened the box again and took out the necklace. 'Can you help me put it on, please?'

After a moment's hesitation, he took the necklace from

her and told her to turn round. She lifted up her hair. His hands felt warm and sure on the back of her neck. 'There,' he said, 'why don't you go and look in the mirror and see what you think?'

She jumped off the bed and went and stood in front of the wardrobe. She scrutinized her reflection, wishing she was just a fraction as pretty as the necklace. Or, thinking of the painting Uncle Brad had painted of Noah's mother on her eighteenth birthday, as pretty as the girl who had originally worn it. Why did she have to be so gawky? Why couldn't she have silky straight hair and elegant eyebrows that didn't meet in the middle? 'It's lovely,' she said.

Noah came and stood behind her. Their eyes met briefly in the speckled glass before he lowered his gaze to the pearl at her neck.

Maybe it was because she was staring at his reflection and not directly at him, but Lydia found herself seeing Noah with fresh eyes, just as she had last month when she'd given him that coat for his birthday and had thought how different it made him seem. A tall, dark, very good-looking stranger, she remembered thinking at the time. And here was that stranger again. Except he seemed even more handsome now. The more she looked at his face – a face she had believed to be so completely familiar to her – the more new and unique it became. She tried to make sense of this feeling by studying what she'd always known, but perhaps had never actually seen before: the nose that was straight and neither too big nor too small; the eyebrows – so unlike hers – that were expressive and perfectly arched; the smooth cheekbones that narrowed down to form a perfect triangle with his chin; the hair that was light brown and flecked with shades of gold; and best of all, the dark intelligent eyes.

Dark intelligent eyes that were staring back at her in the mirror.

'What are you thinking?' he asked.

Embarrassed to admit the truth, she said the first thing that came into her head. 'I was thinking how we could be brother and sister,' she said. 'Not in looks. But because we've known one another so long.'

'I suppose we could,' he responded blandly.

Acknowledging that subconsciously she must have been thinking of Uncle Brad's painting of himself and Noah's mother, Lydia said, 'You don't sound very convinced.'

'That's because I'm not.' He put his hands on her shoulders and his expression in the mirror became so intense that she wondered if she'd said something wrong. Something to upset him.

A loud rap at the door had them both jumping.

'Can I come in?' It was Uncle Brad.

'No!' Noah shouted back.

'Come on, Noah, don't be a spoilsport.'

'I've got company.'

'That much I know.'

'Then go away and leave us in peace.'

'But I've got a birthday card for Lydia.'

'You can push it under the door.'

'That's a bit rude, Noah,' Lydia said.

'Is that my sweet Lydia sticking up for me?'

Lydia giggled.

'Ah, message received, loud and clear. You're up to no good in there, aren't you?'

Noah rolled his eyes and ran his hands through his hair so that it was sticking up all over his head. 'Sorry about this. He's probably been drinking.'

Smoothing down his hair for him, Lydia whispered, 'Wouldn't it be easier just to let him in?'

'Not whilst you're wearing that necklace.'

'Then help me take it off.'

'I'll tell him to come back later.'

'But then he really will think we've been up to something.'

'I can hear you whispering in there. Are you making yourselves decent? I hope you're being careful, Noah. If you know what I mean. Nudge, nudge, wink, wink.'

'Go *away*!'

'Hey, no need to blow your cork. I know when to split and leave you crazy cats to enjoy yourselves. Lydia, my sweet, this is for you.' A white envelope appeared under the door.

Listening to his footsteps fading away, Lydia felt doubly bad when she saw that Uncle Brad had gone to the trouble of drawing a card especially for her. It was of a girl who looked remarkably like her and she was shielding her eyes from the glare of the sun, staring into the distance. Inside was written, 'Lucky you, the future is all before you. Make the most of it!'

'He's got a thing about growing old at the moment,' Noah said. 'Worried that time is running out for him. Talking of which, let's make the most of the time you're here and go for a walk before it gets dark.'

While Noah put on his shoes, she fingered the necklace he'd given her and thought of the expression on his face when she'd suggested they could be like brother and sister. Why would that have upset him?

Chapter Thirty-Three

It was dark when Lydia set off on her usual route home across the moors. She hadn't wanted to leave her presents and card behind with Noah, but with no bag in which she could smuggle them safely into the house, she had thought it safer for him to hang on to them for her. She had sensed he had something to say on the matter, but thankfully he didn't. Just as he hadn't commented when she'd told him she definitely wouldn't be going on the school trip to Paris next month, other than to say he hadn't changed his plans either; he was still going away with Uncle Brad for the bank holiday weekend.

More out of curiosity than hope, she'd given her grandfather the letter from school and predictably he'd ripped it in two and said, 'We don't have the money. You're not going.'

'I could get a part-time job and pay for it myself,' she'd suggested. Again, just to see how he'd react.

'I said no. You're not going anywhere and that's an end to it. I'm not having you coming back with your head filled with any foreign nonsense. You've got enough up-pity airs and graces as it is. Time you learned your place, that getting above yourself and flying too high never did anyone any good.'

What a contrast to the encouragement Uncle Brad gave Noah. In his opinion you couldn't fly high enough. 'Look at that Margaret Thatcher,' he'd say, 'bloody awful woman, but nothing's stopped her from being the first woman to lead a British political party. OK, she's only been doing the job for a month, but I'll tell you now, she's damned ambitious. It wouldn't surprise me if we see her running the country one day. God help us if it happens, though. I'll be long gone.'

Uncle Leonard had repeated his offer to help twist his brother's arm in order for her to go to Paris, but Lydia had stood by her original decision not to push her luck. There was enough tension in the house as it was without Uncle Leonard adding to it. Especially as she had the distinct impression that Uncle Leonard was enjoying having his brother where he wanted him: under his thumb. Try as she might, Lydia couldn't allow herself to relax and believe the situation could remain as it was. Always at the back of her mind was the concern that Uncle Leonard's protection would be short-lived. The day would inevitably come when he would want to move on elsewhere. Which meant this period of relative safety was nothing more than the lull before the storm. Everything would go back to how it had been: living in fear and being too ashamed to admit the truth to anyone.

Even though she was confident she wouldn't be seen in the dark, when Lydia climbed over the wall at the end of the garden, she did so as stealthily as she could. After all, she was supposed to have been at Donna's for the evening and the way home from Donna's was straight along the street.

Lydia was just passing her grandfather's shed when she noticed a faint glowing light from inside. Curious, she stopped to peer in through a gap in the manky old curtains at the window. What she saw her had frozen to the spot. Her grandfather was in there and with his trousers undone he was doing that ... that disgusting thing she'd heard the other boys at school boasting about. And he was doing it whilst looking at a magazine like the one Alfie Stone had brought into school once.

Terrified that her presence might be given away by a careless rushed movement, Lydia took a slow, deliberate step back from the shed and promptly knocked over a flowerpot. The noise had her grandfather whirling his head round.

She should have been running. She should have been running like the wind. But she couldn't move. She could hardly draw breath. All she could do was stare back at her grandfather's shocked expression. Anything but look at that revolting *thing* in his hand.

Then in a split second of clear thinking, she knew she could use this to her advantage. Her grandfather knew that he'd been caught doing something he would be deeply ashamed and embarrassed about. It was something he would never want anyone to know about. For once, his shame might be greater than her own.

This is power, she thought. Real power. All she had to do was hold her nerve.

Chapter Thirty-Four

Lydia did hold her nerve. In the shadowy darkness, she lay in wait for her grandfather to emerge from the shed. To stop herself trembling, she concentrated on thinking how much worse this had to be for him. He was the one who should be nervous. Not her.

She watched him lock the shed and as he came up the path and saw her standing there, his eyes were anywhere but on her.

She decided to tackle him with the least important of the three things she wanted him to agree to. 'I want to go on that school trip to Paris,' she said with icy calm. 'Do you think you might like to change your mind about it?'

He pursed his lips and finally met her gaze, regarding her with a look of pure loathing and contempt. All her old fears ran through her and it was all she could do to stop herself from apologizing and running for safety. But she didn't. This was a crucial moment and she mustn't let it slip from her hands. If she did, she would never forgive herself.

'And if I don't let you go?'

'Then I'll have to ask someone at church what it was I saw you doing in your shed.'

'Bitch!' He stepped towards her, his hand raised.

Somehow she managed not to flinch. 'I'd also have to ask about the magazine you were looking at. I'm sure Pastor Digby would have something to say on that particular subject.'

His hand dropped down to his side. 'Hell's too good for you.'

'I'm sure you're right, but after living here I reckon it'll be an improvement. Tomorrow I want my birth certificate so I can organize a passport as soon as possible. You can give it to me at breakfast.'

She took a quick, deep breath. Now for her most important demands.

'Just so that you know, I'll carry on doing a fair share of the household chores, but you are not to be unreasonable about it. There'll be no more hidden tin tacks. No more shouting at me for forgetting something. Lastly, you will never lay another finger on me again. Is that understood? Not ever.'

With that, she walked away, leaving him standing in the dark.

Things are going to be different round here from now on, she told herself when she was back inside the house. This was certainly a birthday she wouldn't forget in a long, long time.

She was up early the next day. Her grandfather must have been up even earlier, because there on the table alongside his finished breakfast was Lydia's requested birth certificate.

The first lesson at school that morning was French and when it was over, Lydia approached Mrs Roberts and asked if it was possible for her name to be added to the school trip. It was! Overjoyed, she rushed to tell Noah.

He didn't ask how she'd won her grandfather round and she certainly wasn't in any hurry to explain it to him. 'That's brilliant,' he said. 'Do you think there'd be a place for me as well?'

'But I thought you weren't going to be around at the end of May?'

He smiled. 'Sudden change of plan.'

'How come?'

'I'd have thought that was obvious,' he said, still smiling. 'I wasn't going to go without you, was I?'

'You mean, you and Uncle Brad weren't ever going away?'

'Nope. So there it is. I lied to you. Call me a devious bastard if you like, but meanwhile, I'm off to find Mrs Roberts.'

After school, letting Val walk home ahead on her own from the bus stop, Lydia called in at the corner shop. Dressed in a pretty rose-pink sari with an Aran cardigan over the top, Mrs Khan was alone and stacking boxes of Ritz crackers onto a shelf near the counter, behind which a paraffin heater was sending heady fumes into the already fuggy air. 'Hello,' she greeted Lydia brightly in her pretty sing-songy voice. 'I'll be with you in a minute. Whilst it's quiet I must just finish doing this.'

Which was all the opening Lydia required. 'Mrs Khan,' she said, 'I don't suppose you need any extra help here, do you?'

Mrs Khan put the last of the boxes onto the shelf. 'Are you looking for a job?'

'Yes. Only part-time, of course. During term time I could work Saturdays and after school, but in the holidays I could work whenever you wanted me to. I can add up really fast. In my head. You can test me if you want.' Lydia crossed her fingers behind her back, praying that Mrs Khan wouldn't hold her grandmother's crazy rudeness against her.

'As a matter of fact, Mr Khan and I were only saying the other day how we could do with an extra pair of hands. You see, I'm going to have a baby and there'll be days when I'll need to take it a little easier in the coming months. But we need someone reliable.'

'I wouldn't ever let you down.'

Mrs Khan's face broke into a smile. 'In that case, when can you start?'

Without worrying what her grandfather would have to say on the matter, Lydia went ahead and arranged to start work after school the next day.

It wasn't often Lydia got the opportunity to thank God for answering any of her prayers, but walking home, she felt that at long last he'd actually been paying attention. So now she had a job and what's more, she was going to Paris. And Noah was coming too! She was so very touched that he'd gone to the trouble of lying about not being able to go on the school trip so that she wouldn't feel left out. She was even more touched that he'd immediately signed up for the last place when he knew she was able to go. Now all she had to do was get the money from her grandfather and arrange her passport. And to think, the furthest she'd ever been from Swallowsdale was Maywood, where she was born.

In the days and weeks that followed, what with dividing her time between working at the corner shop, teaching Donna to read, doing her homework, and keeping an eye on Valerie as well as keeping up with her renegotiated rota of chores, Lydia hardly saw anything of her grandfather. She couldn't be sure, but she had the strong feeling he was avoiding her. Well, good! She wouldn't care if she never set eyes on him again. Sometimes when she thought about what she'd caught him doing that night, her stomach would heave. But one day in church she had very nearly burst out laughing when she imagined leaping to her feet and exposing him for the disgusting pervert he was. 'He looks at porn in his garden shed and plays with himself! What do you think to that?!'

She'd noticed that the padlock on the shed had been changed and the tatty old curtains had been replaced with some thick new ones. Obviously he was still at it in there.

Uncle Leonard had quizzed her one day about the surprising U-turn her grandfather had made regarding Paris and she'd shrugged her shoulders and said, 'Search me what goes through his mind. Perhaps it's your presence here that gave him a change of heart.' She was quite happy to let him take the credit for something he hadn't done. No way was she going to say what had really gone on.

Having been extremely grateful to Uncle Leonard, rather uncharitably she was now wishing that he'd leave

Swallowsdale. She no longer needed his protection. She'd acquired that for herself. Several times he'd referred to himself as her knight in shining armour. He'd wink and call her his little damsel in distress. All of which was enough to make her want to stick her fingers down her throat.

Home from work one Saturday afternoon in May, Mr Khan having given her permission to leave early because it was so quiet, Lydia let herself in at the back door. The house was completely silent. She remembered then that Valerie had been invited to Sister Vera's for tea and that her grandfather wouldn't be home until later. Goodness knows where Uncle Leonard was.

After putting the kettle on for a cup of tea, she went upstairs to change out of her work clothes. She was almost at the top of the stairs when she heard a noise. She stood stock still and cocked her ear. There it was again. Someone was in her bedroom.

Lydia thought of all the precious things she had carefully hidden away, including the necklace Noah had given her, and knew that she wasn't going to let some rotten burglar get away with them. She reached for the heavy brass cross on the small window ledge to her left, took the last few steps as silently as a cat, then launched herself across the landing and into the bedroom, hoping to take the burglar by surprise.

The burglar wasn't the only one to be surprised.

Lydia looked at the groaning body on the floor and couldn't believe who it was. Nor could she believe what he'd been doing: snooping through her things. How dare he!

But looking for what?

A frantic search through her underwear drawer revealed that her wages were gone. All of them. She went back to the body on the floor and gave it a vicious kick.

'Get up, Uncle Leonard,' she said.

He put a hand to the back of his head where she'd clunked him with the cross. 'What the hell did you hit me with?'

'God.'

He squinted up at her. 'Are you mad?'

'Yes. Hopping mad. Now give me back my money or I'll hit you again.'

He got to his feet and sat on the edge of Valerie's bed, still rubbing his head. 'Lydia, I'm shocked. How could you accuse me of stealing from you?'

'I saw what you were doing. You were going through my things.'

'I was looking for something.'

'Liar! Now hand over my money or I'll—'

'Or you'll what?'

Lydia reached for the cross that she'd put on the dressing table. 'Or I'll hit you again. Maybe even kill you.'

Raising himself up from the bed, he shook his head and tutted, as though she'd just said something very tiresome. He came and towered over her. 'Now we both know you're not brave enough to do that. If you couldn't stand up to my brother, you're certainly not capable of killing me just for a few lousy quid. Isn't that the truth?'

She swallowed and gripped the cross tighter, furious that he wasn't taking her seriously. He was treating her like a child. 'So you admit it. You *have* stolen my money.'

'I'm admitting nothing, sweetheart. Now give me that cross before I get angry with you. Which would be a terrible shame when we're such good friends.'

'Perhaps it will be a different story when you tell it to the police, Leonard.'

They both turned. Standing in the doorway was Lydia's grandfather.

'He's stolen my money,' Lydia shouted, 'all of it! I came home early and caught him going through my things.' She was shaking with anger.

Her grandfather stepped into the room. There was an expression of triumph on his face. 'A leopard and his spots, Leonard. I always knew.' He held out his hand. 'Give me Lydia's money. Or I'll call the police.'

'No you won't. One word from me and your whole world will come tumbling down on you.'

'I've had enough of your threats. I want you to pack your things and leave my house. At once.'

'But you know what will happen if you try and make me: I'll have to let Pastor Digby know the real Arthur Turner. The Arthur Turner who takes the punishment of his teenage granddaughter just a bit too seriously.'

'And I'll have to tell him and everyone else at church about you stealing from your own kith and kin. Again. And once I've told them that, and Lydia's backed me up, how long do you think it will be before they see through your born-again claims and refuse to believe a word that comes out of your filthy lying mouth?'

Uncle Leonard smirked. 'Sounds like a stalemate to me. Though personally I think you have more to lose. Your hugely misplaced pillar-of-the-community reputation for one thing. But you know what? I was getting bored staying here anyway. I reckon it's time to ship out and go somewhere where my company will be properly valued and appreciated.' He turned to Lydia. 'I just hope you'll be all right, sweetheart. Remember, I'll always be your knight in shining armour.'

Lydia cringed. 'Just give me my money,' she said, her heart hardened towards him. 'That's all I care about.'

'Oh, Lydia,' he said with a sigh. 'I can't tell you how much that hurts. And after all I've done for you. That's quite a betrayal.' He let his gaze linger on her for a moment longer, then switched his attention back to his brother. 'I have to congratulate you, Arthur. You've manipulated her well. You've really got her well trained. I've read that even the most terrified hostage can become dependent on their captor, no matter how cruel they are.'

'That's enough! Lydia, go downstairs and leave me to sort this out.'

Lydia shot her grandfather a look. 'Don't let him leave with my money.'

'Do as I say. Now go!'

Chapter Thirty-Five

Uncle Leonard was gone within the hour and Lydia's money was safely returned to her. At her grandfather's instruction, she and Val stripped the bed in the spare room, washed the sheets and put them out on the line to catch the last of the evening sun. They also opened the window in the spare room to get rid of the cloying smell of Brut and breath freshener.

At church the following morning, the Brothers and Sisters greeted the news of Uncle Leonard's sudden departure with shock and sadness. They soon changed their stance when they were given the facts: that he'd been caught stealing from Lydia. 'I warned you all about him,' her grandfather told the hushed congregation during Share and Pray time. 'I warned you that he was a pernicious liar, and whilst it grieves me to say it, I think we have to accept there are some people in this world who simply aren't capable of being fully redeemed. The devil had a far stronger hold on my brother than any of us could have known. I just wish you'd listened to me.' He'd looked pointedly at Pastor Digby, then sat down. Apologies were duly made and Lydia's grandfather was once more well and truly back in the fold.

This gave Lydia cause for concern. Her hold over her grandfather might come to an end sooner than she'd hoped. After being proved right over his brother, no one at church would ever doubt him again. If he said Lydia was a liar – just like her great-uncle Leonard – his word would be as good as the word of God. So bang would go her threat to share with Pastor Digby what he got up to in his shed late at night. For the time being, though, the truce remained intact.

With the trip to Paris only a week away, Lydia and Valerie came home from school to find a strange woman in a squashed hat and a raincoat sitting at the table. She seemed hunched with cold, even though it was such a warm day. It was Valerie who was first to recognize who it was. Dropping her satchel to the floor, she flung herself at the woman.

It was four months since they had last seen their grandmother and in the intervening time she looked as if she'd aged by about ten years. Her hair was white all over and she'd lost weight. Beneath her coat, the buttoned collar of her blouse gaped, revealing a scrawny neck like a chicken's. Her hands were knobbly and heavily veined. She looked as brittle as a dried twig. From a chalky-white face, a pair of dull eyes stared at the top of Valerie's head; they didn't seem to be focusing properly. For an awful moment Lydia was worried that her grandmother might not recognize her favourite granddaughter. What would that do to Valerie? Despite repeatedly pleading with their grandfather to take Valerie with him on his hospital visits, he had never allowed her to go, saying it wouldn't be helpful, that maybe it might even be harmful to their grandmother. Now as Lydia watched those unfocusing eyes looking uncertainly at Valerie, she wished he had. Regular contact with her grandmother might have ensured that Valerie wouldn't be forgotten.

But then, as if her brain had just needed time to put two and two together, the arms that had been hanging limply at the old woman's sides came up, wrapped themselves around Valerie and clutched her tightly.

That was when Lydia heard her grandfather coming down the stairs. He came into the kitchen with a lilac cardigan in his hands and seemed surprised to see Lydia and Valerie. 'I didn't know it had got to that time yet,' he muttered, glancing at the clock.

'Why didn't you tell us Grandma was coming home today?' Valerie whispered huskily. Her eyes were shining with tears. 'Is she home for good?'

'Oh, so these days I have to run everything by you, young lady, do I? Now out of the way. Don't go crowding and suffocating your grandmother before she's even got her coat off.'

'Is she home for good?' Valerie repeated insistently.

'How should I know?' he snapped. 'That's for God to decide.' He didn't sound like he was too happy about the situation.

But Valerie, hugging her grandmother again, was delighted. Her happiness made Lydia's throat tighten with love for her.

At school, for those going to Paris, there was only one subject to talk about. The countdown was on. Six days and they'd be crossing the Channel. For most of them it was the first time they would be going abroad. Zoe Woolf had been to Paris before and wasn't slow in showing off her knowledge about the Eiffel Tower or the Champs-Élysées. She took great pleasure in boasting how she'd eaten snails and frogs' legs and how she'd visited a red-light area, where prostitutes sat in shop windows with their legs open. It wasn't long before the boys were all saying that they'd give Mrs Roberts the slip and head straight there.

What came as a revelation was that Noah had also been to Paris before. 'Why didn't you say anything before now?' Lydia asked him when he admitted this would be his second visit.

They'd just bought an ice-cream from Joey's van – which on fine days was always conveniently parked at the gate when school was over – and were on their way into town for a browse round the bookshop and then on to the post office. After Lydia had got her money back from Uncle Leonard, she'd immediately opened a savings account and regularly put her wages into it. 'It hardly counts,' Noah said in answer to her question. 'I was a baby at the time and can't remember a thing about it.'

It was ages since either of them had spoken about their lives before they came to Swallowsdale and it was difficult for Lydia to imagine that Noah had been brought up by anyone other than Uncle Brad. Sometimes it was difficult to remember that she too had had another life before this one. 'Have you done anything else I should know about?' she asked.

'You make it sound like I deliberately keep things from you.'

She licked at the thick coating of strawberry syrup on the cornet Joey had made for her and said, 'Don't you?'

'No more than you.'

She kept quiet. Why had she even broached the subject?

'Well?' he prompted.

'Well, what?'

'Come off it, Lyddie. I'm not stupid.'

Now she knew for sure they were in dangerous territory. She hurriedly stepped off the pavement to cross the road.

She hadn't noticed the car speeding round the corner and she found herself being yanked back onto the pavement. The driver of the car tooted the horn angrily and sped on.

'Look,' Noah said, keeping hold of her arm as they stood on the pavement, 'I know you've always kept stuff from me. I've no idea why, but I just want you to know that if you ever need my help, you've only got to ask for it.' Frowning, he added, 'You must know that I'd do anything for you.'

Oh, God, she thought, suddenly limp with clammy panic. Not kindness and understanding. Anything but that. Yet at the same time, now that she seemed to have a measure of control over her life, she thought what a relief it would be to confide in Noah. Noah, her closest friend. Her greatest ally. The person whom she respected most in the world. The one person whose respect she wanted and valued above all else. She stared into the dark pools of his solemn eyes and felt herself tremble inside as she realized something she had always known but never acknowledged – Noah was so much more than a friend. She suddenly felt a powerful surge of love for him. There were so few people she really cared about, but for Noah she'd willingly give her life.

So why not share with him those things she'd kept hidden?

Don't do it, a low, insistent voice growled in her head. *Don't admit to anything. Do that and he'll see the real Lydia Turner. The grubby, ashamed, frightened Lydia Turner. Didn't he once say that the reason he thought you were so great was because you weren't afraid of anything? If he knows the real disappointing you, he'll treat you differently. And what if he begins to wonder if you deserve what goes on at home?* The voice was right. It was too big a risk. She didn't want Noah to know the truth.

'Noah,' she said, 'I really don't have any idea what you're talking about. You've not been at your uncle's marijuana, have you?'

The frown deepened and he shook his head. Very slowly, he let go of her arm. He spread his hands. 'Sometimes I just don't understand you. Or even feel that I know the first thing about you.'

Once more, just as she had on her birthday, she saw that she'd disappointed him. Except this time it was far worse. The pain in his kind, sensitive face was too much for her. It tore at her heart. How could she be so cruel to him? 'I'm sorry,' was all she could say.

'So am I, Lyddie. More than you'll ever know.'

After tea that evening, Lydia went to see Donna under the guise of trying to win her soul for Jesus by teaching her to read.

Captain Kirk, as Lydia secretly called Donna's baby, was no longer the easy-going baby he'd been when Lydia had first visited. Their lessons were frequently interrupted by his ear-splitting demands to be fed, winded or changed. Donna was not always in the right mood to deal with him and often Lydia would try to soothe the squawking, fractious child. She was reminded of when Valerie had been a baby.

She and Donna had formed an unlikely friendship, given the way they had got to know each other all those years ago in the playground. Lydia supposed the poor girl was desperate for friends. She certainly seemed to be short on them these days. From the moment she'd dropped out of school her so-called friends had dumped her. Maybe they were frightened of catching a baby themselves.

Donna had no qualms about dishing the dirt to Lydia about her family: how her father had walked out years ago and how ever since her mother had had a succession of horrible boyfriends. One of them had broken her mother's nose in a fight over whose turn it was to pay for a drink. Another had been to prison for stealing cars. The most recent boyfriend had been responsible for making Donna's mother kick her out. He worked shifts at Ravencroft's mill and had said he didn't want a baby disturbing his sleep.

'God, this is hard!' Donna exclaimed. 'You don't know how lucky yer are.' She was standing at the open bedroom window trying to read one of Valerie's old Bible story books. She tossed the book onto the floor, lit up a cigarette and inhaled deeply.

'How come I'm so lucky?' Lydia asked.

'Yer might be a bit on the plain side, but you've got brains. And that's gotta be worth more than looks alone.'

Lydia smiled. 'I suppose there's a compliment tucked away in there somewhere.'

Now that Lydia had got Captain Kirk off to sleep, she laid him carefully in his plastic laundry basket and covered him with the blanket. Another couple of weeks and he'd be too big for the basket. She hoped Donna had got something else planned for him. Picking up the discarded book, she joined Donna at the window where she was looking down onto the rubbish tip of a garden – Donna's aunt was to gardening what Donna was to tact.

'Which bit were you struggling with?' Lydia asked Donna patiently, opening the book at the first page.

Donna waved it aside. 'All of it. Mind if I give yer a word of advice?'

'It's not like you to ask my permission. You usually just go right ahead and inform me that I should do something about my hair, my clothes, oh, and let's not forget my eyebrows.'

Donna cast her damning gaze over Lydia's latest eclectic mix of jumble-sale bargains – a man's collarless shirt belted at the waist over a long tiered skirt – and said, 'Yer'll be calling that clobber yer student look, I s'pose.'

'It's the "I don't give a damn" look. So what's this advice you've got for me?'

Donna took a long hard puff on her cigarette, her lips compressed tightly. After she'd exhaled two rings of smoke into the air, she said, 'I bumped into Alfie Stone the other day and he said that Zoe Woolf is after your Noah. Yer wanna watch that girl. She's trouble with a capital T in my opinion.'

Chapter Thirty-Six

It was generally accepted that Zoe Woolf was gorgeous and that she could have any bloke she fancied. All the boys had a thing for her and like any girl as stunning as she was, it was understood that she could keep her admirers dangling for as long as she wanted and never be called a tease. So far she'd been out with three boys in the year above them but never with anyone her own age.

So why had she suddenly decided Noah was of interest to her? Why not any of the other boys in their year? There were plenty to choose from.

Pastor Digby was constantly warning them that jealousy was one of the widest gateways to hell, and in the blink of an eye, Lydia was consumed by it. She could feel it raging through her body like molten lava. Trying hard to conceal her reaction to Donna's 'word of advice', she said, 'Donna, I don't know why you refer to him as being *my* Noah.'

Donna snorted. 'Yeah, and pull t'other one while you're about it! The two of yer have always been inseparable. You're like cheese on toast, salt and pepper, egg and chips, Tom and—'

'Yes, I get the picture,' Lydia cut her off impatiently, 'but we're just friends. Mates. Pals.' She wasn't going to say anything about the real extent of her feelings for Noah. Donna wouldn't understand anyway.

'And t'rest,' Donna said scornfully. 'So have yer done it with him yet?'

'Done what?'

Donna rolled her eyes. 'Sex. Yer know, had it off with Noah.'

Lydia's cheeks flamed. 'Certainly not!'

'Hey, keep your hair on. No need to go getting your knickers in t'twist. I'm only asking.'

'Well stop asking!'

'Is it that church of yours that's stopping yer?'

'I said stop it.'

'Bloody hell, girl, you're a bit uptight about it all, ain't you?'

'A shame *you* weren't before you went and got yourself pregnant.'

Stubbing out her cigarette on the windowsill outside, Donna pursed her lips tightly shut.

Mortified, Lydia said, 'I'm sorry, I shouldn't have said that.'

'But yer did. Yer bloody well did.'

'I didn't mean it. I know you love Kirk and wouldn't be without him.'

'Yeah, well, maybe that's t'trouble. Maybe I don't love him and maybe I could live without him. Ever thought of that?'

Lydia walked home in a miserable mood. What was wrong with her great big gob today? First she'd upset Noah, now Donna. What kind of friend was she?

But more important than that, what was she going to do about Zoe? Her best hope was that Alfie had got it wrong. On the basis that most days he couldn't be trusted to find the end of his own nose, how could he be trusted to know what was going on around him? It was always possible that he was mixing Noah up with someone else at school.

But that was pointless wishful thinking on Lydia's part. There was no mistaking Noah for anyone else. For a start he was the only boy in the school who walked with a limp. He was also the only one had had an encyclopaedic knowledge of every *Monty Python* sketch and knew *all* the lyrics to *Dark Side of the Moon*. In Lydia's view – now that she'd woken up to it – he was also easily the best-looking boy at school. No one else had eyes like his. Or eyebrows that could arch the way his did. He had features that were sharp and clean, not like Jack or Alfie's doughy faces with their bristly top lips and spotty chins. And unlike a lot of the other boys in their year, he didn't have a muscly athletic build that the girls would whistle at during games. Instead, he had a strong, almost secret, inner strength to him. As well as an air of mystery. Other than when he was alone with her, Noah never spoke about his home life. He was a very private person.

Lydia slowed her pace and registered that everything she had listed about Noah marked him out from the competition and would attract any number of girls. There was no doubt about it: Noah Solomon was number one fanciable stuff. Of course Zoe would be interested in him. It would be a miracle if she wasn't. But how had Lydia missed what was going on? Was it a new thing, Zoe making a play for Noah, or had it been a long-term thing?

And why should it matter? Why should she feel like a knife had been plunged into her chest and was being slowly twisted round, at the thought of Zoe with Noah? Of Zoe flicking her impossibly straight shiny blonde hair and kissing Noah. Of Zoe—

She called a halt to any other tormenting images.

But was Noah attracted to Zoe?

Lydia had never seen him ogling Zoe in the way the other boys did, but then she'd been so wrapped up in what was happening at home recently, she probably wouldn't have noticed a spaceship crammed full with one-eyed Martians landing in Swallowsdale.

She recalled her conversation with Noah this afternoon and silently groaned. Completely out of the blue, he'd offered to help her and she'd shoved his kindness right back in his face. If she'd wanted to push him into the arms of another girl, she could not have done a better job.

Donna had been right to say that Noah was Lydia's. He *did* belong to her. And not just as a friend. Her mouth went dry and her heart pounded as she thought what that really meant. Very tentatively, she pictured him leaning in close and kissing her. Suddenly light-headed, she had to catch her breath.

She had no idea if he would find the thought of kissing her utterly repellent or not, but one thing she did know, she now had to find that out. But would it mean having to fight off Zoe? So what if it did? She would do whatever it took.

But how? What did she have to offer Noah that Zoe didn't have? Or perhaps, hadn't already offered?

Exactly, whispered the voice inside Lydia's head. *How can you hope to compete with a perfect girl like that? A perfectly beautiful girl who's led a perfectly beautiful life with no shameful secrets.*

Lydia stamped on the voice hard. Noah was hers. Not Zoe's. And with a flash of inspiration, she knew how she would fight for Noah. Or rather she knew *where* she'd fight for him. Paris. Mrs Roberts had described it as the most romantic city in the world. Lydia would get Noah alone there and Paris would work its magic on him. That would show Zoe!

For the remaining days at school, she watched Zoe like a hawk. Sure enough, the girl was all over Noah: one minute she was asking his opinion on something and the next she was offering to lend him some record or other. It was all Lydia could do not to confront Zoe there and then. But with steely determination she forced herself to wait for her moment of triumph in Paris. Love would win out!

Meanwhile, she became so jittery, she was tempted to knock back some of her grandmother's tablets, the ones that kept the old woman so sleepy she could hardly keep awake. There was something innocent and child-like about her now. Compared to the phases when she'd been scarily aggressive, seeing her this docile was quite unnerving. Outside of school hours, Valerie was constantly by her side, helping her with the simplest of tasks, such as making a cup of tea or bringing in the washing. Her devotion was humbling. The Sisters were frequent visitors again and had roped their grandmother into helping with a tapestry they were making for church. Lydia often found her sister secretly redoing her grandmother's clumsy stitch work.

The good news, though, was that Valerie's voice had almost returned to normal. It was still a little harsh and husky at times – like a gate gone rusty from not being used – but for the most part, it was just as Lydia remembered it. Or as Sister Lottie described it a lot more poetically, it was as joyful and sweet as the sound of summer birdsong.

On Saturday morning, with only two days to go until the coach would take them down to Dover to catch the overnight ferry for Dieppe, Lydia woke with what felt like a prickly golf ball stuck in her throat. She was hot, too. Very hot. She went to the bathroom and pressed a cold flannel to her face. Bliss. She did this several times and convinced herself that nothing was the matter with her. So long as she didn't swallow, the prickly golf ball wasn't a problem. And so long as she didn't wear too many clothes, the scorching heat rising off her wouldn't be a problem either.

She was wrong.

Mrs Khan took one look at her when she arrived for work and sent her home. 'You're ill, Lydia. You should be in bed.'

'No really, I'm fine,' she said through teeth that were beginning to chatter – the hot sweats had been replaced with goosebump shivers that ran bone-deep.

Mrs Khan was having none of it. 'I don't want you here giving me and my unborn baby your germs.' More kindly, she added, 'Go home and rest, Lydia, or you won't be well enough to go to Paris on Monday.'

Nothing could have galvanized her more. It was unthinkable that she would miss out on the trip. By the time she had staggered home, the hot sweats had returned and the prickly golf ball was bigger and more painful. Sister Lottie's Morris Minor was parked outside the house and Lydia could have wept with relief. Sister Lottie would know what was wrong with her and know exactly how to cure her.

Her grandmother didn't even bother to look up from the cooking apples she was peeling with Valerie when Lydia walked into the kitchen. But Sister Lottie took one look at her, put down the bag of brown sugar she was tipping into a mixing bowl and said, 'Dear child, whatever is the matter with you? You don't look at all well.'

'I don't know what's wrong with me. My throat hurts and I'm hot one minute and freezing cold the next. Mrs Khan sent me home.'

'Quite right too. Let's get you off to bed and call for Doctor Bunch.'

'Doctor Bunch?' repeated her grandmother, dropping the apple in her hand.

'Not for you, Grandma,' Valerie said. 'For Lydia. She's got a cold.'

'It feels more than a cold,' Lydia said miserably. She was near to tears she felt so ill. She could feel Paris drifting out of her reach.

In the end, to save time Sister Lottie drove Lydia to Doctor Bunch's surgery. Within minutes of seeing him she was diagnosed as having acute tonsillitis. Antibiotics were prescribed. As was plenty of fluids and bed rest. 'Will I be well enough to go to Paris on Monday?' she croaked.

Through the smeary lenses of his spectacles, Doctor Bunch looked at her as if she were mad. Her heart sank. She wouldn't be going to Paris. She cried all the way home but couldn't tell Sister Lottie why.

She slept intermittently for most of the day, thrashing around in a tangled mess of dank bedclothes. Her dreams were nightmarish and fever-fuelled, and held her in an iron grip that dragged her back in time, then forward. She dreamt of Diane Dixon. Diane was telling Lydia that she needed to have her tonsils out just as she had. The girl then offered to do the operation for her so Lydia could go to Paris. She tipped her head back so that Diane could perform the operation only to then find that it was a ventriloquist's dummy about to do it. The dummy had a menacingly evil look in its eyes as it waved a pair of huge scissors dripping in blood at her. Next she dreamt of Zoe. Zoe was with Noah at the top of the Eiffel Tower. They were holding hands and she was wearing the necklace Noah had given Lydia. Lydia was there in the dream too and she was sneaking up behind Zoe to push her over the edge of the barrier. Except she had got it wrong and it was Noah falling to his death. She tried to reach him, stretching as far as she dared. 'Noah!' she called out as he grew smaller and smaller until he was nothing but a speck in the distance. 'Noah, I'm sorry. Please forgive me.'

She woke with a jolt and found that it was dark. She still felt awful. Her throat was raw and burning and her body was covered in sweat. She turned her face into the pillow to muffle the sound of her choking sobs. 'Oh, Noah,' she wept.

Chapter Thirty-Seven

Lydia could not have prayed harder for a miracle cure, but by the Bank Holiday Monday afternoon, when she should have been arriving at school with her packed case, passport and French francs, all she had the strength for was to sit up in bed for a few minutes or stagger to the toilet. Admittedly her temperature had gone down and the golf ball was less prickly, but her throat still hurt like mad when she swallowed. She could not have felt more sorry for herself. She pictured everyone on the coach larking about and driving Mrs Roberts round the bend, along with the other teachers who'd been roped in for the trip. It wasn't fair. Why had God done this to her? Didn't he understand what was at stake here?

It wasn't until this morning that they had been able to get in touch with school to say that she couldn't go. On her way back from the toilet, hovering at the top of the stairs, Lydia had listened to her grandfather telling the headmistress that she was ill and that he would be expecting a full refund. From the way the conversation went, Lydia could only assume that the headmistress didn't think this would be possible. Her grandfather was in a foul temper from then on.

The most important person whom Lydia wanted to know that she was ill was Noah, but she couldn't bring herself to ask her grandfather to phone him. Not in his current mood, anyway. Arouse his suspicions that she had a friend she really cared about, a boy at that, and he'd probably send for Pastor Digby to fire off twenty rounds of scripture from the hip and then exorcize her. There was no chance to ask Val to make the call either. With it being half-term, she was downstairs practically glued to their grandmother's side. At one point, when Lydia had been having another of her hallucinogenic dreams, she'd dreamt she had climbed over the garden wall and gone to Noah to tell him that she wouldn't be going to Paris with him after all. She dreamt that he'd hugged her and kissed her on the forehead. 'In that case I won't go either,' he'd said. The dream had felt so real that when she woke, she could have sworn it had really happened.

Even now she could feel the touch of Noah's lips on her forehead and the comfort of his arms around her. She stared up at the ceiling, following the cracks with her eyes as they travelled like veins from one side of the room to the other, and tried not to let herself hope that any minute Noah would appear. That he'd throw a handful of pebbles at her window and call up to her that he wasn't going to Paris without her.

What an idiot she was to give in to such ridiculously romantic nonsense. Noah was going to Paris without her and that was all there was to it.

Yet no matter how true she knew this to be, she couldn't stop herself constantly glancing at the alarm clock on her bedside table. It was four thirty-nine: he'd know by now that she wasn't coming, probably would have checked with Mrs Roberts. Perhaps he'd try to slip away before the coach set off and telephone her, even though he'd promised never to do that. But this was an emergency and he'd call, if only to say how sorry he was that she couldn't come and that he would miss her. Yes, that at least would make her feel a little better, would make the next few days almost bearable.

The cracks in the ceiling began to blur and, exhausted from the effort of so much wishful thinking, Lydia closed her eyes and waited for the sound of the telephone to ring down in the hall. She wanted to die.

It was seven o'clock in the evening and after waking from a deep sleep and yet another dream that had her wondering what was real and what wasn't, she learned from Valerie that she and their grandparents had been to a meeting at Pastor Digby's house that afternoon. 'But that means no one was here to answer the phone while I was asleep,' Lydia croaked, sounding eerily like Val used to.

Her sister looked at her, confused. 'If it's important they'll try again later.'

No they won't! Lydia wanted to scream. They'll be on a ferry crossing the Channel and heading to God knows what in Paris.

In the days that followed, Lydia didn't know who she hated more: Zoe or herself. She hated herself for making such a mess of things, and she hated Zoe for all the obvious reasons – for being so pretty, for being so perfect, but most of all for setting her sights on Noah.

For a while Lydia even hated Noah. How could he have gone to Paris without her? But her anger with Noah only made her hate herself more. Noah wasn't to blame. It was her. Her track record for messing things up spoke for itself and this one was entirely down to her.

She deliberately punished herself by imagining Zoe and Noah together.

Alone.

Always alone.

To Lydia's knowledge Noah had never kissed a girl before, just as she had never kissed a boy before, but Zoe was much more experienced and would probably enjoy teaching Noah all she knew. There was a rumour at school that she was an expert French-kisser.

The thought of Zoe's perfect little tongue exploring Noah's mouth had Lydia thinking of Pastor Digby and all his warnings about the perils that awaited the ungodly in hell. The stupid man didn't have a clue what he was talking about. Lydia was already there and it was a hundred times worse than anything he'd ever described.

On Friday morning, the day that the French party was due back, Lydia was well enough to go to work. The Khans were glad because Mr Khan needed to drive his wife to the hospital for her antenatal appointment after lunch, so for most of the afternoon Lydia was on her own listening to Radio One. She was restocking the confectionery display on the counter when the door jangled and in came Donna: Captain Kirk had been parked outside in his pram, next to the Spastic Society's collection box.

'What the sweet Fanny Adams are yer doing here?' Donna asked, her overly plucked eyebrows raised and nearly making contact with her streaked hairline. 'I thought yer were in Paris?'

'I couldn't go. I've been stuck in bed all week with tonsillitis.'

'You poor miserable bugger.'

'Yeah, that about describes it.'

'Hang on a tick. Didn't yer say Zoe Woolf was going on that trip?'

'Please, don't remind me.'

'Bleeding hell! Her and Noah without yer to put a spanner in t'works. No wonder you've a face on yer like a wet weekend in Blackpool. Oh, turn t'radio up, I like this one.'

How fitting, Lydia thought as her friend started singing along to the Bay City Rollers' 'Bye Bye Baby'. 'Thanks, Donna,' she said. 'Can I get you anything or did you just come in to make me feel worse than I already do?'

'Packet of Silk Cut and a box of matches, since you mention it. So what're yer gonna do?'

'Absolutely nothing. Besides, it's probably too late.'

'Come on, girl, I never had yer down as a loser. Thought yer had more fight in yer than that. Stop feeling so sorry for yerself.'

Donna was right. But how to go about it? Nothing Lydia had learned in life had prepared her for this moment. How did you fight for someone whom you now realized you couldn't live without?

The answer, she decided, was to be completely honest with Noah. She would open her heart to him. If he wasn't interested, then at least she could comfort herself by knowing she'd tried.

When the Khans arrived back from the hospital they said she could call it a day. But she didn't go home. Instead, guessing that Noah should be home any minute, she headed for the Dell of the Dead and then on to Upper Swallowsdale House. She was halfway up the garden when she heard the sound of a car pulling onto the gravelled drive. Her heart hammering, she approached the house cautiously and peered round the corner, expecting to see Noah getting out of Uncle Brad's wine-coloured Capri.

What she saw was Noah getting out of an orange Volvo estate car. Lydia recognized not only the car, but also the blonde girl sitting in the passenger seat who was waving madly at Noah as he hoisted his rucksack on his shoulder and patted his jeans pocket for his door key. Just as the car was driving off, Lydia saw that she'd been spotted. At first Zoe merely looked surprised, but then leaning out of the window, she waved back at Noah and pointed in Lydia's direction. '*Bonne chance!*' she shouted.

Lydia wanted to run and hide. Oh, the humiliation! The complete and utter shame of it. Caught like a no-good peeping Tom.

'Lyddie?' Noah had come round to where she was standing like a fool, wishing the ground would open up beneath her feet.

She mustered what little dignity she still had. 'Hi,' she said. 'Thought I'd be here to welcome you home. Doesn't look like you need it, though.'

He threw down his rucksack, and the next thing she knew he had his arms around her and was squeezing her tight.

She wanted to hug him back, but she couldn't. The best she could do was stand stiffly in his embrace and say, 'Did you have a nice time in Paris? You and Zoe?'

He loosened his arms and stepped away from her. 'Why do you ask about Zoe?'

'Because ... because she fancies you and you fancy her. Don't you? Please don't lie to me.'

'Is that what you really think?'

'Well of course you fancy her! What boy doesn't? She's beautiful. She's clever. *And* she knows how to French-kiss.'

He raised an eyebrow. 'That's news to me.'

'I expect you've got that to look forward to then.'

He shrugged. 'I doubt that very much. Can I ask you something?'

'If you want.'

'Do you ...' He cleared his throat and swallowed, suddenly looking anxious. 'Do you fancy me? And is that what this is all about? You being angry and everything?'

Courage, she willed herself. Courage. She looked him squarely in the eye. 'Yes,' she said. 'Yes I do.'

He shook his head, and then he smiled. 'Thank God for that!'

Her cheeks tingling with embarrassment, Lydia said, 'I don't think there's anything to smile about. In fact—'

'Come here, you!' And once again he had her in his arms. 'Lydia Turner, can it be officially put on record that you fancy me and I fancy you?' He tilted her chin up with his hand. 'I'd also like it to be officially recorded that I'm going to kiss you now.'

He did and it was far better than any of her tentative imaginings. His mouth was warm and smooth against hers and she could have gone on kissing him for the rest of time, had she not thought of Zoe. She pulled back from him sharply. 'Did Zoe teach you that?'

'I think you and I need a little talk. Let's go inside.'

'What about Uncle Brad?'

'He's down in London. That's why Zoe's dad gave me a lift home.'

*

They sat at the kitchen table – a new and sturdier version of the one that was destroyed in the dancing-on-the-table incident. It was littered with signs that Uncle Brad had either left in a hurry or, more likely, had forgotten to clear up after his last meal. After Noah had pushed aside the festering remains of a pork pie, along with a mouldy loaf of bread and a piece of dried-out Cheddar cheese, he said, 'You think Zoe and I did stuff together in Paris, don't you?'

'Didn't you?'

'What made you think I would?'

'Alfie told Donna that Zoe had a thing about you, and Donna thought I should know.'

'And it didn't cross your mind to ask me what *I* thought?'

When she didn't say anything, he leaned towards her. 'Look, and this is the truth, OK? God knows why, but Zoe did try flirting with me, and I told her straight that she was wasting her time. I explained that there was only one girl I was interested in and it wasn't her.'

Lydia was incredulous. 'You turned down Zoe? Zoe Woolf? *The* Zoe Woolf? I bet that made her angry.'

'Not really. She guessed who I was talking about and wanted to know why I hadn't got things sorted between us.'

Us, repeated Lydia even more incredulously to herself. 'What did you tell her?'

'I said the trouble was that the girl in question wasn't interested in me. That she always made it very clear we were only friends. Or worse, as she told me on her birthday, brother and sister.'

Lydia gasped. 'You mean ... back then you felt ... but why didn't you say something?'

'I was about to, but my uncle's immaculate timing put the kibosh on my carefully planned speech.'

'Which was?'

He smiled. 'Painfully embarrassing, with hindsight. Uncle Brad did me a favour.'

'I wish I'd known how you felt.'

'Look at it from my point of view. Every time I tried to get closer to you, you pushed me away. Like that day the other week in town when I said I knew you kept things from me.'

She turned from him. 'I'm sorry about that. I was very rude to you.'

'You have to understand, Lyddie, I care about you.' He touched her hand. 'Is that so very difficult for you?'

She returned her gaze to his. 'Maybe not.'

'So can I kiss you again?'

'You might catch my germs.'

'Too late to worry about that.' He lightly brushed her lips with his. She shivered. He kissed her again and she pressed her mouth closer to his. She closed her eyes, lost in the sweet wonder of how magical something as simple as a kiss could make her feel.

'I thought it was supposed to be all bumping noses and clashing teeth,' Noah said when they finally pulled apart.

'I'd heard that it was like having your face wiped with a wet dishcloth.'

'In that case, we're either doing it wrong, or we must be naturals.'

'My stomach felt like it was turning inside out.'

'Mine too. Any butterflies?'

'Masses.'

'I know I'm not supposed to admit to this, being a bloke and all, but kissing you is bloody amazing. You're amazing, too.'

She smiled shyly. 'Why didn't you ring me before you set off for Dover?'

'As soon as Mrs Roberts told me you were ill I nipped off to use the call box by the Co-op. But there was no answer. I tried again the next night from Paris and got your grandfather. I'm sorry, but knowing how much you don't want him to know about me, I lost my nerve when I heard his voice. Did you mind very much that I went without you?'

'Yes,' she said. 'But only because I was convinced you would come back as Zoe's new boyfriend.'

'I knew I shouldn't have gone. The thing was, I had about ten minutes to decide what to do. In the end I reasoned that I wouldn't be able to see you if I stayed, so I might just as well go and bring you back something.' Smiling, he got to his feet.

'You got me a present?'

'Of course.' He pulled out a sweater from his rucksack and unearthed a squashed paper bag. 'It's nothing special. Just a book of postcards to show you what you missed, and a bar of pink and white nougat.'

But to Lydia they were the most special presents in the world.

Chapter Thirty-Eight

A year to the day, they celebrated their first anniversary of being girlfriend and boyfriend by taking a picnic up to the beck near Noah's house to revise for their French oral exam. They'd been there for an hour and all Noah had said so far in French, in what Lydia called his beret-wearing-striped-jersey accent, was *Je t'aime*, Lyddie. *Je t'aime. Je t'aime.*

Lydia could not believe it was possible for two people to be as close as she and Noah were. She loved him and he loved her. It was how it was always meant to be. It was perfect.

Except it wasn't. There was a shadowy darkness creeping ever nearer. A darkness that Lydia knew only too well would eventually eclipse their love for each other. If only she could go on forever keeping Noah at a distance, everything would be all right.

At the age of sixteen, she was embarrassingly ignorant about sex and was convinced that Noah knew far more about it than she did. Certainly he couldn't know less! It stood to reason that Uncle Brad would be a huge potential source of information on the subject, particularly when he was drunk. There was never any actual evidence of Uncle Brad having a sex life, unless the many framed and un-framed nudes cluttering the house represented notches on his belt, but Noah said the reason his uncle was in London so frequently was because he had a woman down there.

Most of what Lydia understood about sex – or thought she understood – was based on biology lessons, listening to Pastor Digby's dire warnings at church and Donna's grubbily explicit tales of her own sexual encounters. Captain Kirk was now a chubby-faced toddler with a baby brother or sister on the way. Donna had confessed to Lydia that she had lost her head in an alleyway on a drunken night out to a club in Bradford. 'Only me bleeding self to blame,' she told Lydia. 'Yer'd think I'd have learnt me lesson, wouldn't yer?'

In Lydia's head sex was to be avoided at all costs, for the following reasons. A) It was dangerous and likely to end in pregnancy, thereby killing all chances of a decent future. B) It was shameful and her grandfather would kill her if he found out. And C) It was wrong. It was a sin. Wasn't it?

But somewhere deeply lodged in the pit of her stomach, where her desire for Noah curled like a wily snake, the message was very different. With guilty greed she wanted him to touch her in those places that in her head were barred with Private No Entry signs and double padlocked for good measure. When they lay together on his bed, their kissing left her breathless, trembling and dizzy, her insides melting, the world forgotten. Lydia and Noah. Noah and Lydia. That was all that mattered. Why worry about the consequences? Remove the No Entry signs, turn the key in the padlock.

But always, just as one of Noah's hands would slowly creep down from her shoulder to slip under her clothes to touch her breast, she would be jolted into a state of rigid panic. She knew that Noah had sensed early on the change in her whenever he tried to touch her and in turn he was always cautious just where he allowed his hands to wander. While his sensitivity reassured and relaxed her, it was still months before she felt comfortable enough to let him touch her bare skin. It wasn't that she didn't trust him. Oh, no, it was Lydia Turner she didn't trust.

Lydia Turner and that wily snake intent on trouble. Give in to it, and who knew what trouble lay ahead for her?

Yet their days together weren't all about sex, or, more precisely, her avoidance of it. Often they would lie on his bed or on the soft leafy ground in the Dell of the Dead, reading to each other. Some days it was the poems of Blake, John Donne and Shakespeare's sonnets in which they lost themselves. Other days they'd go for something amusing like *The Wind in the Willows* or *Three Men in a Boat*, a copy of which Uncle Brad had given Lydia on her sixteenth birthday. 'No library should be without it,' he'd claimed. 'It's essential reading.' These were some of the most intimate moments she and Noah spent together. Probably because she didn't feel threatened and on her guard.

Now as they lay on their backs beside the beck in the warm sunshine, they each had a leg in the air at a ninety-degree angle. In Noah's case, it was his good leg. It was a regular game they played, seeing who could hold the position the longest. Noah was wearing his faithful old black and white baseball boots with the fraying laces and his drainpipe jeans and Lydia had on a new pair of red clogs. The only contact was between their hands. They'd been going for a long time, had reached that crucial point when it felt as if the very last few drops of blood were draining out of their legs; it was when they had to hold their breath and focus hard. Lydia was always tempted to close her eyes, but do that and the game was lost because her leg would simultaneously drop a couple of inches. There was another reason why it was important to keep her eyes open. Noah, as she'd discovered, wasn't above cheating. She'd caught him out once and had never let him forget it. 'Cheat!' she'd exploded, jumping on him. 'Cheat, cheat, *cheat*!'

'It's only a game, Lyddie,' he'd laughed.

'But a game I won fairly and squarely. Admit it!'

'Never!'

There was a friendly competitiveness between them in most things they did. They were fairly evenly matched: one week she would come top in a subject, another week he would. The two subjects they couldn't compete in were French and art. Lydia knew when she was flogging a dead horse and had dropped art as soon as the opportunity arose – she was keen not to have a single blemish on her school reports, which repeatedly glowed with As. French was her best subject and she planned to do it at A-level, along with English and maths, but Noah struggled with it, and since it was a compulsory subject, he had no choice but to grit his teeth and do the best he could. There had been no embarrassment on his part when he asked for Lydia's help, which only proved just how close they were. He'd been surprised, though, when she'd admitted to him that when they'd been at junior school together she had aspired to be as clever as him, understanding even then that it was a better way to be. He'd laughed, saying that as far as he'd been concerned it had always been him trying to keep up with her.

Noticing a slight waver in Noah's leg, Lydia knew she was on the home straight. She inhaled one last time, slowly and carefully. It was all in the breathing. All in the focus. Just keep a single goal in mind and anything was possible. This was the philosophy by which she now lived. Her goal was to do as well as she could at school, go on to the local sixth-form college, and then hopefully make it to university to study French and Italian. Noah still hadn't made up his mind whether to study engineering or art.

Predictably Lydia's grandfather had already informed her that he wouldn't be throwing good money after bad on her; if she wanted to go and live in a world of sex and drugs – which was how he viewed university – she would have to pay for it herself. Luckily there were grants available. Noah and Uncle Brad seemed to think she would qualify for one; she just hoped they were right. But there was a lot of hard work to be done before she needed to worry about that. Meanwhile they had their CSEs to get through, followed by just as many O-levels. She, Noah and Zoe, and a handful of others from their year group had been selected to do the two sets of exams. Since January they'd been having extra lessons after school to prepare for them and that would continue right up until the exams were finally over in June. It was hard grind but worth every minute if it meant Lydia would escape Swallowsdale and her grandparents.

With a thud, the heel of Noah's baseball boot hit the grass. 'You win,' he groaned, clutching his stomach muscles. He rolled onto his side and she slowly lowered her leg and turned to him, her face triumphant. 'You're getting too good at this,' he said.

'Just a case of mind over matter.'

He plucked a long stalk of grass and stroked her cheek with it. 'Tell me what you were thinking all that time.'

'The usual: escaping Swallowsdale. What were you thinking of?'

He ran the stalk of grass over her lips. 'The usual: you.'

'It didn't help, did it?' she teased. 'It didn't keep you focused.'

'True,' he said. But he didn't smile as she expected him to. Something was wrong. She had a feeling she knew what it was.

Anxious, she sat up. 'Do you want something to eat?'

He stayed where he was, on his side. 'No. I want to talk to you.'

'One doesn't rule out the other, you know.'

He touched her wrist. 'Is it me, Lyddie? Am I doing something wrong with you? Tell me if I am. Please.'

She wished that she didn't have a clue what he was talking about, but she knew all too well what was on his mind. It was a measure of how much she loved and respected him that she didn't pretend otherwise. 'No, it's not you, Noah, it's me.'

He sat up and wrapped his arm around her shoulder. 'You know I'd never do anything to hurt you.'

'I know that.'

'Are you worried about getting pregnant? Is that the problem?'

She seized on this and nodded. 'It would ruin everything.

Bang would go my chance of doing A-levels or going to university. It wouldn't make any difference to you, but I'd be stuck here in Swallowsdale like Donna. That's if my grandfather hadn't killed me first. Which, thinking about it, would be the better option by far.'

He squeezed her shoulder. 'Don't *ever* say that. Not even as a joke. But what if I promised you I'd always be careful? That we'd only do it with a—'

She cut him off. 'Donna says they're not always a hundred per cent safe.'

'Not in Donna's hands at any rate,' he said tightly. After a moment's silence, he said, 'Look, we don't have to go all the way if you don't want to. There are other things we can do.'

Lydia's anxiety deepened. Why was it so important? Why couldn't they stay as they were? Just kissing. Just stroking and holding each other. 'What other things?' she asked nervously.

'Well, you know; *other* things.'

She sensed that he was getting impatient with her. 'Tell me, then. Seeing as you're the expert,' she added snippily, not caring now if she seemed naive or stupid.

He swallowed. 'Well ... I ... I could—' He cleared his throat. 'I could give you an orgasm and then you could do the same for me.'

'How?'

He took a breath as if launching himself into an answer, but then seemed to change his mind. 'How do *you* think it might happen?'

She shrugged. 'I've never done it before, so how would I know?'

'Nor have I, but I've a pretty good idea what goes on.'

'Excellent. So tell me how we go about it.' Her tone was even snippier.

He whipped his arm away from her, staring straight ahead. 'God, Lyddie, are you being deliberately difficult? Or just trying to make me look a fool?'

Burning with shame and humiliation, she jumped to

her feet and walked down to the edge of the beck. She'd always known it would come to this. She'd been a fool to hope for anything else. She plonked herself down and scooped up a handful of stones and began hurling them into the gushing water one by one.

Plop! Pastor Digby was right.

Plop! Sex was a curse.

Plop! It really did ruin everything.

Out of stones, she bent her head and buried her face in her hands, wretched with loss. She'd lost Noah now, for sure. Aware of movement beside her, she turned to see him sitting next to her.

Hugging his knees to his chest, he suddenly looked so young and vulnerable. His hair was choppy and all messed up from his hands raking through it. She longed to reach out and smooth it back into place as she often did. To smooth everything back to how it used to be between them. 'I'm sorry,' he said, 'that was a class one pratty thing for me to say. Just call me a pillock.'

She snatched at the grass around her. 'I can't help being the way I am, Noah. You'd be better off with another girl-friend. A more experienced girl who knows what's what and doesn't ask such daft questions.'

'If it's all the same to you I'd rather rip out my eyes and feed them to the crows than be with another girl.'

'So what do we do next?'

'I learn to control my feelings for you.'

She looked at him. 'What do you mean?'

'It means when I kiss you I have to think of something other than how much I love you.'

'Will that work?'

'Search me, because what I feel for you is like nuclear energy. But I don't want to do anything that might result in losing you, Lyddie.'

'What about doing those other things you mentioned? Why don't you explain them to me?'

He smiled and gave her one of his long, thoughtful stares. 'We're sixteen – there's plenty of time for all that later. How about we get our exams over and done with and then talk about it?'

She blinked back tears, wishing she could be the girl he wanted her to be. 'I don't deserve you.'

'Rubbish. You deserve someone far better than me.' He reached for her hand. 'No worrying. You promise? Not when this is such an important time for us.'

She nodded and to make him think that everything really was OK between them, she wagged a finger at him and said, 'In that case, *mon ami*, give me the imperfect tense of *avoir*.'

'*Merde!*' he shouted, tipping back his head and laughing. 'Anything but that!'

After several attempts, he finally got it right and they rolled back onto the grass and once again found themselves gazing up at the sky.

But for all Noah's caring consideration, Lydia knew that what he'd given her amounted to nothing more than a stay of execution. This painful scene would come round again. Just as humiliating. Just as shameful. And what would she do or say then? To lose Noah was unthinkable. But the other option seemed infinitely worse.

Chapter Thirty-Nine

Lydia had never known a summer to pass as quickly as this one. Nor had she known one to be as hot. Joey was permanently running short of ice-cream and ice lollies and joked that if the heatwave continued he'd be able to return to Italy and never work again.

With what seemed like lightning speed, the homemade calendar stuck on the wall above Lydia's bed gained a big red cross in each box for each exam completed, until finally it was all over and she could throw the calendar in the bin. In truth, the exams had been a much-needed distraction from what really worried her – what lay ahead for her and Noah.

Prayers are always answered, just not how we imagine them to be, was something Sister Lottie would often say, so when, after their last exam, Noah grumbled to Lydia that Uncle Brad was taking him away for the rest of the summer, Lydia breathed a quiet guilty sigh of relief. 'You'll have a great time,' she told him. 'It'll be fantastic.'

'No it won't,' he said miserably. 'I'd much rather be here with you. This will be the longest we've ever been apart.'

Being so geographically apart was not a concept either of them was used to and despite the initial rush of relief, Lydia soon realized she hated Noah being thousands of miles away from her. Letters written on flimsy airmail paper from far-flung places such as Caracas, Nicaragua and Guatemala – sent to Donna's house – had her reaching for her school atlas and measuring the distance growing between them.

As the weeks flew by and she began to anticipate Noah's

return, Lydia pictured a very different boyfriend from the one she had kissed goodbye. This one would be tanned and well travelled, his horizons transformed beyond her comprehension. He would be so drastically changed he would view her through new eyes and would inevitably kick off his feelings for her like a shabby old pair of shoes that no longer fitted.

She comforted herself by thinking that they would at least always be friends and this would let her off the hook from the threat of taking 'things' any further.

Sex may have been a silent worry for Lydia, but it was a subject that was referred to with irritating regularity by Donna, and as Lydia knelt on the dry scrubby grass and leaned over the side of the paddling pool to play with Captain Kirk, Donna let out a loud sigh and cursed whoever it had been who'd got her in the mess she was in. It was a habitual complaint and, as ever, Lydia had to bite her tongue from reminding Donna that she should have been more careful and not allowed herself to be led into that dingy alleyway to have her back pressed against the rough brick wall and her skirt hitched up around her hips. But instead of preaching, as Donna would accuse her of doing, she turned to look at her friend who was fidgeting in a deckchair trying to get comfortable. 'Is the baby moving?' she asked.

'Moving! It's like a bleeding octopus doing the twist in there. I'll be glad when it's out and I can get some peace and quiet.' Donna stroked her enormous bare belly that was baking like a swelling loaf in the hot August sun; her belly button resembled a monstrous currant stuck in the middle of it.

'Bleeding octopus,' echoed Captain Kirk with a toothy grin while handing Lydia the watering can to fill again. Lydia had given up reproving the boy; his limited speech was peppered with as many colourful obscenities as his mother's. She submerged the watering can in the pool to fill it then passed it to him to water the pretend flowers she'd just planted.

'Oh, leave him be,' Donna said bad-temperedly, throwing down the magazine she'd been flicking through – she was an avid reader of women's magazines now that she could read. 'Come and keep me company.'

'I'd better not. It's not safe to leave Kirk on his own in the paddling pool,' Lydia said, trying not to sound as if she knew better than Donna when it came to looking after her son.

Donna puffed out her cheeks. 'Honestly, yer spend more time with that little bugger than yer do with me.'

'That's because I'm always babysitting him.'

'Hey snidey gob, a girl's gotta go out now and then. I can't sit here all day. Where's the fun and excitement in that? It's all right for you: in two years' time yer'll be beggaring off and I'll still be here changing shitty nappies.'

'You could change things if you really wanted to.'

'Oh, don't start banging on about that again. I know what I've done, I've made me bed and now I have to sodding well lie in it.' She sighed. 'If I could just find meself a decent bloke, all my troubles would be over.'

'You could try looking for a bloke who wants more than just sex from you.'

Donna gave her one of her withering looks. 'Until yer've tried it, keep your holier-than-thou opinions to yourself. The way you're carrying on, you're going to end up the oldest virgin in Swallowsdale.'

A nudge at Lydia's elbow told her that Captain Kirk needed a refill of his watering can. She obliged only to be further harangued by Donna. 'I can't believe you and Noah still haven't done it. He's not queer, is he? You know, a screaming great bender? A poof? Playing for the other side?'

Captain Kirk rose up out of the water on his chubby legs and proudly peed into the pool. 'Poof, poof, poof,' he chanted as the stream of wee arced gracefully through the air.

Donna laughed throatily. 'Dirty little beggar.'

Lydia whipped her hand out of the water. 'I don't know

why you should think that of Noah, just because he hasn't forced me to have sex with him.'

'Who said owt about him forcing yer?' Donna snatched up the magazine and began fanning herself with it. 'Strikes me that you're scared of sex. Yer should just get on with it and discover how great it can be. Just bear in mind that the first time is always a disappointment. It'll be over in a matter of seconds. Noah won't have a clue what he's doing and you'll feel like a huge branding iron has been shoved up between your legs.'

And that's supposed to encourage me to have sex, Lydia thought minutes later when she was joining the end of the queue outside Donna's house to buy them ice-creams from Joey's van.

The Floozy was at the front of the queue. She was taking for ever. As usual. When at last it was Lydia's turn, Joey mopped his forehead with a handkerchief from his apron pocket. 'You are not working today?' he asked.

'Not this afternoon. I'm doing the late shift in the shop this evening.'

'And your exam results? When do you receive them?'

'The day after tomorrow. By the way, I did that Italian homework you set me.'

'*Brava!* You are my best student.'

Lydia laughed. 'I'm your *only* student, Joey.'

He laughed too. 'I run a very exclusive school.'

Their lessons were held once a week at Sister Lottie's and although both Joey and Lydia had tried to encourage Sister Lottie to take part, she always declined, saying that God had not given her the gift of learning another language. Joey's English was almost perfect these days and he gave Sister Lottie all the credit. 'She should have been a teacher,' he once said to Lydia. 'She is so patient. A true sainted lady.'

Lydia had often thought that Sister Lottie had thrown away her life on caring for her sick mother when she was younger. But it was only recently that she had learned that Sister Lottie's father had done a runner when she was little and that she had left school before her fifteenth birthday because her mother insisted she would be of more use to God working in one of the mills than sitting idly in a classroom. What fascinated Lydia was that when Sister Lottie was nineteen she had become engaged to a man who worked in the accounts department where she worked, but within days of the engagement her mother was bedridden with a mystery illness and claimed she couldn't manage without her only daughter. For the next twenty-five years Sister Lottie worked at the mill and cared for her mother. There was no time for marriage. Not surprisingly, her fiancé had married someone else and moved away.

Sister Lottie never spoke ill of her dead mother, but Lydia couldn't imagine there hadn't been moments when she hadn't resented the woman who had denied her the chance she should have had.

No one was ever going to do that to Lydia. There would be no lost opportunities for her.

For all Lydia's mental tough-talking and plans for the future, she was not without her Achilles heel.

Valerie was ten now and as different from other ten-year-old girls as it was possible to be. She wasn't at all shy around anyone from church, but outside of church it was a different matter. Often she wouldn't speak, not even to Joey. Selectively mute, she would use her lovely waist-length blonde hair as a curtain to hide behind. She had made no real friends at school and refused to go some days. Whenever school queried her absences, their grandmother – who for ages now had been going through a phase of behaving normally, well, normal for her – would say that she was giving Valerie lessons at home of a much higher standard than her teachers were currently providing. These lessons, as far as Lydia could see, were nothing more than hours spent poring over a Bible preparing for the Second Coming.

One such lesson, even though it was the school holidays, was in progress right now when Lydia let herself in at the back door. She knew better than to interrupt, so tiptoed upstairs to change her clothes – Captain Kirk had managed to stain her T-shirt with his orange lolly while pretending it was a rocket.

With the bedroom door closed, Lydia did a quick check of the room. Ever since Uncle Leonard had rifled through her things, she was paranoid about anyone else tampering with her belongings. Last week, when she had made the same routine check, she had accidentally knocked a pencil off the dressing table and, retrieving it from under Valerie's bed, she had discovered, next to a long-since-discarded Belinda Bell, a small case she didn't recognize. Intrigued, she'd slid it out from under the bed and opened it: it was packed with a Bible, a set of neatly folded clothes and a toothbrush still in its wrapper. When she later asked Valerie why she had a packed overnight case hidden under the bed, her sister had said it was perfectly obvious what it was for and that if Lydia had any sense she'd have one too for when Judgement Day came.

Lydia was horrified: Valerie was ready and waiting for when she would be saved and taken up to heaven with the rest of God's chosen people! There was no talking her out of it, either. Valerie was convinced she had to be prepared for the awesome Day of Judgement. That meant having a packed case like Grandma had and keeping away from the ungodly in case she got mixed up with them and the Lamb of God overlooked her when the time came.

Lydia had tried explaining that generations of Christians all over the world had been anticipating the end of the world for nearly 2,000 years and to her knowledge no one else had put together an overnight bag like Val had.

'How do you know that?' Valerie had asked.

Floundering for a logical answer, Lydia had replied, 'Show me where in the Bible it tells us to pack clothes and a toothbrush. Give me an exact scripture reference.'

'It tells us hundreds of times to be ready,' Valerie replied patiently.

'*Spiritually* ready, maybe, but not a packed suitcase!'

'Oh, Lydia,' her sister said with a long sigh. 'I wish you wouldn't be so doubting and stubborn. Can't you see what your wilful self is doing to you? Why don't you let me pray for you? Here, give me your hands.'

Too stunned to object, Lydia listened to her sister imploring God to show mercy on her immortal soul. 'Help Lydia to see that your way is the only way, Father,' Val prayed, 'that Jesus has the power to save her if only she'd turn to him and repent of her sins. I don't want to be separated from my sister when the Day of Judgement comes, so please, Lord, help me to put Lydia on the path of righteousness before it's too late. Amen.'

That was what upset Lydia most: Val's genuine belief, coupled with her genuine need to keep her wayward sister from going to hell. It made her feel horribly unworthy. And guilty. Valerie was her responsibility and for a long time now she had neglected her. What with studying for her exams, working for the Khans, babysitting for them as well as Donna, not to mention doing her chores at home and fitting in the odd visit to Noah, she had given poor Valerie nothing of her time. And because of that, she had allowed her to be brainwashed by their grandmother. What kind of sister did that?

A self-absorbed sister who had only one thought in her big, fat, selfish head: escape.

Lydia hardly dared process the thought, but she knew the reality of the situation was that no matter how much she loved Valerie – and more importantly, no matter how much she reminded herself of the promise she had made their mother – she would have to leave Val behind one day. What choice did she have? She couldn't very well take Valerie to university with her, could she? When the sly voice of her conscience told her she shouldn't go to university, that her place was here in Swallowsdale with Valerie, she would drown out the voice with that of her father saying how proud of her achievements he was and that he only wanted the best for her.

But if Lydia had trouble sleeping at night because of the

guilty turmoil she was experiencing, it was a mystery to her how Val managed to get a wink of sleep if she really believed the end of the world was as imminent as she thought it was.

Lydia's own idea of God went through many different shades of belief and disbelief. Some days she was happy to believe there was a God who worked tirelessly in the background of their lives. Other days she thought it was all mumbo-jumbo. Then there were the days when she wanted to give God a ruddy great piece of her mind for making such a mess of things.

Yet strangely, she couldn't ever really dismiss God out of hand. Not the God that she knew Sister Lottie believed in: the God of love who sacrificed his only son for the sake of mankind. If forgiveness was the cornerstone of their faith, then love and sacrifice were the next crucially important building bricks. Sister Lottie claimed that putting others before yourself was what it was all about.

If that was true, then there was no hope for Lydia. All she ever thought about was herself.

Chapter Forty

On the bus after going into town on an errand for her grandmother – she needed some wax circles for the strawberry jam she wanted to make with Valerie – Lydia decided to call in and see Donna before going home. It would have to be a quick visit; she didn't want to get her grandmother all stewed up by keeping her waiting.

Lydia still thought of her grandmother as the crazy, dangerously out of control woman who'd ended up in hospital for so long and she treated her with kid gloves. That bizarre period in their lives was never mentioned or referred to and it amazed Lydia that someone could be so ill like that and then apparently so completely back to normal. Though presumably the tablets her grandmother still took were partly responsible for that. Yet what wasn't quite so 'back to normal' was the relationship between her grandparents. They were still not sharing a bedroom, and now and then, when their grandmother had had a bad day – a tired, fretful, weepy day – Lydia saw the simmering resentment in her grandfather's face. He'd grit his teeth and clench his fists. She'd heard him shouting at his wife, telling her that she was no use to him, that she should pull herself together, or else. Or else what? Have her carted off to hospital again? Where she would no longer be an inconvenience to him?

But whatever was going on between the two of them, Lydia was determined to stay out of it. The more she could blend into the background the better, as far as she was concerned. And just as her grandfather hadn't resumed sleeping in the same room as his wife, nor had he reverted to bullying Lydia. She didn't think for a minute that it was because of the threat she had once made about his secret hobby in the shed. It seemed more as if he'd become indifferent to her. He was still as irrationally strict as ever, but mercifully they were both out of the house so frequently their paths seldom crossed. She'd like to think he'd had a fit of conscience and regretted what he'd done to her, but like the leopard he'd accused his brother of being, she knew better than to believe he could change his spots entirely.

Off the bus now, Lydia walked the short distance to her friend's house. When she'd seen her yesterday, Donna had been feeling really down. She'd been complaining about everything – the heat, the wasps, the boredom, her swollen ankles, Kirk's refusal to eat anything other than Smash and ketchup, and the fact that her aunt had gone on holiday without her.

Lydia knocked at the door. Knocked again, and then assuming that Donna and Kirk were probably in the garden, she went round to the back of the house. Donna's usual deckchair was empty and floating face down in the paddling pool was a naked Action Man: there was no sign of either Donna or Captain Kirk. Seeing that the back door was ajar, she went inside. 'Donna?' she called out. 'It's me, Lydia.'

Silence.

She went through to the hall and called again to Donna. This time there was a sound from upstairs. Reminded of the day she'd found Uncle Leonard stealing from her, she hoped she hadn't stumbled across a more dangerous and menacing burglar. When Captain Kirk appeared at the top of the stairs, his nappy hanging off him and trailing the floor, her heart stopped pounding so frantically. 'Hello, Kirk,' she said. 'Where's your mum?'

He raised himself onto his toes and pointed vaguely behind him with a pair of kitchen scissors. 'Bed,' he said.

Lydia climbed the stairs. Donna in bed at midday

was not that unusual. Occasionally, when her aunt was at work, she didn't get up till lunchtime and left Kirk to amuse himself. Lydia didn't like to think how her friend was going to cope when the new baby arrived.

'Crying,' Kirk said. 'In there.' He pointed to Donna's bedroom door, which was closed, as were all the others, making the small space feel dark and poky. Lydia noticed that lying amongst the piles of washed clothes and nappies was a telephone lying upside down on the floor with a short stump of cord. Frowning, she asked Kirk to give her the scissors.

She had just slipped them into her pocket when a loud groan, followed by a blood-curdling scream had her hair standing on end.

Lydia didn't wait. She burst into Donna's bedroom, terrified at what she might find.

Donna was lying on her back in nothing but a long T-shirt, her knees bent, sweat pouring off her, her face twisted into a grimace so hideous that it made her almost unrecognizable.

'Thank God you're here,' Donna gasped. 'The baby's coming.'

Lydia froze. 'But it can't be ... you've got more than a month to go.'

The ugly grimace faded from Donna's face and her body went limp. 'Are yer gonna argue with me or do sommat to help?' she snapped.

Never had Lydia felt so helpless or ignorant. Help? How? 'Tell me what to do,' she pleaded.

'Ring for an ambulance. I tried explaining to Kirk how to ring 999 but the silly bugger probably hasn't done it.'

Lydia pictured the telephone out on the landing with its severed cord. Very calmly she said, 'Listen, Donna, I don't think the phone is working. I'll go next door and ask to use theirs.'

Donna's eyes rolled back and she started panting hard. Her face suddenly took on the ugly grimace again and she let out an animal-like scream. Lydia went to her. It scared her to see her friend in so much pain. Kirk came and stood at the side of the bed as well.

'Contractions,' panted Donna. 'They're coming fast. Don't leave me. *Please*.'

'But I need to call for an ambulance,' Lydia reasoned.

Donna clutched at her hand. 'It's too late. I told yer it's ... it's coming.' As if to prove the point, she screamed again, squeezed her eyes shut and crushed Lydia's hand so hard Lydia thought she could feel every bone being crunched to powder. She wanted to let out a cry herself, but in the face of Donna's terrible pain, she didn't dare.

When Donna went quiet and limp again, Lydia stirred herself into action. 'Kirk,' she said, 'I want you to be really helpful. Can you go to the bathroom and bring me all the towels you can find?'

'Yer'll be telling him to bring hot water next,' quipped Donna as she wiped the sweat from her forehead and Kirk scuttled off.

Knowing she had no choice but to take charge, Lydia said, 'Donna, the only one of us who's done this before is you. Now tell me what I have to do.'

'Just catch the little bleeder when it pops out. Which I think ...' Her face contorted violently. 'Is about now. Yer'd better get down t'other end, because I'm about to push it out.'

Lydia did as she was told and just as Kirk came back into the room with a bundle of towels dragging on the floor, something dark and bloody began to appear. Lydia's stomach heaved. Oh, God, what was she supposed to do? Catch it as Donna had said? Her friend was really screaming now, one long, terrifying scream after another. Frightened, Kirk began to howl as well and threw himself under the bed. This is madness, Lydia thought. I'm sixteen years old. I can't deliver a baby!

Suddenly the decision was taken out of her hands. The baby was delivering itself. The crown of a small black-haired head had appeared, followed by a bit more. And a bit more. But then it seemed to get stuck. Something was wrong. 'Stop pushing!' Lydia yelled. She moved in close and saw that there was what looked like a blue and bloody coil wrapped around the baby's neck. It didn't look right. She got to work and carefully unwound the soft, warm, gooey scarf. 'OK,' she said breathlessly, 'push!'

Donna did and in one almighty fluid bloody movement the baby slithered out.

It was only when Donna had stopped screaming that Lydia realized the baby wasn't moving.

Chapter Forty-One

Doctor Bunch said she was a heroine – that if it hadn't been for her quick thinking, the baby girl would most certainly have died. The local paper had picked up the story and plastered right across the front page was a picture of Lydia holding the baby with Donna sitting up in bed beside her. 'Anyone would think you were the mother from looking at that,' Donna had said. 'And just look at the bleeding state of me! They could have waited until I'd got my roots done.'

Donna hadn't been quite so off-hand and cocky at the time, when Lydia had put her mouth to the baby's blue lips, desperately hoping that she could fill its tiny lungs with oxygen. She'd had no idea if she was doing it the right way, but some kind of reflex guided her actions. Donna was crying by then, making a low moaning sound and Kirk was still hiding under the bed, but Lydia didn't waste her breath telling her friend everything was going to be all right, she just kept blowing steady little puffs of air into the baby's mouth. Until suddenly, amazingly, the scrawny little ribcage had quivered and then it had heaved and shuddered.

The next moment the room was filled with the sound of bawling. Lydia couldn't believe that such a deafening racket could come from something that had been totally lifeless a few seconds ago. With fists clenched and punching the air angrily, her stick-thin legs pumping like pistons, Donna's daughter was really kicking up a storm. Wondering what she should do about the cord, Lydia remembered the scissors she'd taken from Kirk. She pulled them out from her pocket and, praying she was doing the right thing, she cut through the cord. When blood began spurting everywhere she grabbed a rubber band from the dressing table and fumbled wildly to tie it around the slippery cord. Miraculously, the flow of blood slowed, then stopped. Lydia wrapped the baby in one of the towels Kirk had brought her and gave the screaming, wriggling bundle to Donna. 'She's just like her mother,' Lydia said, 'a right shirty piece of work.'

Once both Donna and the baby were calm and Kirk had come out from hiding, Lydia had gone next door to call for an ambulance. The neighbour, an elderly woman with a pair of purring cats weaving in and out of her slippered feet and a hearing aid in one ear, said, 'I thought I heard sommat going on through the wall, but I thought it was the radio or the telly on extra loud.'

It was at the hospital, when mother and daughter had been thoroughly checked over, that Donna announced that she was naming her daughter after Lydia. 'You're not going soft on me?' Lydia asked her friend, trying not to show how touched she was.

'Bloody hell! I name me baby after yer and that's the nicest thing yer can say? There are plenty other names out there I could choose from, yer know.'

Wiping her eyes with the backs of her hands Lydia said, 'Yeah, but none of them as special as mine.'

'Give over, yer daft bitch. Any more crying like that and yer'll have me at it too.'

For days afterwards, Lydia couldn't go anywhere without people stopping to congratulate her for what she'd done. Everyone who came into the shop wanted to hear the story, but Lydia couldn't bring herself to give them the details. It had been bad enough actually being there at the time without having to relive it. She'd been having a recurring nightmare in which it was she who was in labour and screaming like a banshee because the baby wouldn't come out. She didn't think she could ever put herself through the ordeal of what supposedly came naturally to every other woman on the planet. How could all that pain and blood be natural?

Lydia had often heard Pastor Digby say that the pain of childbirth was God's way of punishing Eve for her disobedience, but until now she hadn't given it much thought. Having witnessed what she had, Lydia couldn't believe God could be so vindictive.

Usually of little interest to anyone at church, Lydia was embarrassed to be called to the front of the congregation the following Sunday. Pastor Digby then proceeded to lay his hands on her head so he could praise God for having channelled a miracle through one of his flock. Lydia wasn't sure if Pastor Digby meant a member of God's flock or his own personal fan club. 'You must thank the Lord for choosing you,' he instructed her when he allowed her to stand up. 'God picked you out specially that day in the hour of your friend's great need. Perhaps he's calling you to pursue a nursing career.'

When she shook her head and said she thought she would make a terrible nurse, he bore down on her with his swivelling eye. 'Helping others is what we're called to do, Lydia. Never forget that. We're not here on this earth to self-serve.'

Publicly Lydia's grandparents said how proud they were of her, but in private her grandfather told her not to let it go to her head. 'Don't be getting above yourself, girl,' he warned her. 'All you did was save a bastard child from going where by rights it should have gone: straight to hell.'

By the time Noah was due home from his travels with Uncle Brad, Lydia's skirmish with local fame was old news and everyone had gone back to complaining about the weather: how sweltering it was and would it ever rain? Even Mrs Khan, who previously had said she didn't think she would ever get used to the cold British weather, had stopped wearing her thick woolly cardies. There were some places in the country where water was being rationed and you weren't allowed to wash your car or use a hose. But business was booming so well for Joey, he'd bought himself a second-hand car.

The last letter Lydia had received from Noah was from Lima in Peru, to let her know he'd be back late at night, the day before the O-level results would be announced. Right at the end of his letter he'd written: 'I can't wait to see you! Meet me in the Dell of the Dead at 10.00 and we'll go into school together for our results.' The row of slightly smudged kisses made Lydia smile.

The hot August sun blazed down on Lydia's shoulders as she set off to meet Noah. She was so excited about seeing him again, she wanted to run all the way to the Dell of the Dead, but not wanting to greet him red-faced, breathless and sweating, she settled for a steady pace instead.

She was wearing a new outfit in honour of his return – a layered skirt that swished and rustled with each step and a black halter-neck top that her grandparents would most definitely not approve of. Stuffed into her bag was the cardigan she'd been wearing when she left the house. She'd done her hair differently, too. Tied it up on top of her head with a few bits hanging down, just to soften the look. Just to make Noah think she was worth coming back for. As eager to see him as she was, she was still anxious that his feelings for her might have changed. That was why she had made more of an effort with her appearance. Taking Donna's advice for once, she had actually bought some lip gloss as well as going to the excruciating trouble of plucking her eyebrows. Donna had wanted to do it for her, but fearing she would end up with a copy-cat set of spider legs stretched across her forehead like her friend had, Lydia had refused her offer and locked herself in the bathroom two nights ago. She now had neatly arched brows that no longer met in the middle. The difference it made to her face was extraordinary.

Stepping into the welcome dappled shade of the dell and listening to the sound of a woodpecker thrumming in the distance, Lydia felt her heartbeat quicken. A glance at her watch told her she was two minutes early. Would Noah be here already? Would there be any awkwardness between them? Or had he slept in after all that travelling and forgotten about meeting her?

She pressed on, deeper into the heart of the dell, then veering to the right to the semicircle of fallen trees that was their official meeting place. What they called their special place.

And there he was, sitting on the trunk of the largest of the toppled trees. The second he saw her, his face broke into a smile and he got to his feet. He came towards her, arms outstretched. She melted into his embrace and when they kissed she wondered why she'd been so stupid to doubt him. He held her tightly and she pressed herself closer still to his firm, warm body. Clasping her hands around his neck, she rested her cheek against his and breathed in the familiar smell of him: toothpaste, soap and a tantalizing hint of sweat. 'You're the same,' she whispered. 'Exactly the same.'

He tilted his head back so that he could look into her eyes. 'You're not. You're even more beautiful than I remembered you.' He frowned. 'You've done something to your face. Something different. What is it?'

She blushed. 'One of Donna's hot beauty tips: I plucked my eyebrows.'

He smiled, dipped his head and kissed her again, slowly and deeply. Her love for him made her heart ache and she felt consumed with a dreamy contentedness. Then suddenly, for the first time ever, Lydia felt her body respond to his in a way it had never done before. There was no fear or guilt bound up in her desire for him. No reluctance to let him touch her and hold her. This is what wanting another person is all about, she thought. It was a revelation. A true awakening. But just as she thought this, Noah arched his body away from her.

'What's wrong?' she asked.

His eyes were dark and wide. He swallowed. 'Nothing. Just a bit of a problem going on down ...'

She lowered her gaze and realized what he was referring to. Whereas previously she would have been instantly on her guard, now she smiled, pulled him back into her arms and pressed herself hard against him. He kissed her neck, first one side, then the other. When his hand covered her breast through the thin cotton of her top and held it gently, she felt her insides dissolve. His lips moved lightly over her skin, and he murmured her name. 'Did you miss me?' he asked, drawing away and looking into her eyes.

'Every day. I never want us to be apart again.'

'Me neither. All I could think about during the long flight home was you. But I was afraid. Afraid you might have changed your mind about me.'

'Never. I love you even more.'

'Really? Because before I went away I thought ... I thought maybe you were getting fed up with me. You didn't seem that bothered about me going.'

She should have known he'd be sensitive to any change in the way she treated him. Unable to lie to him, she said, 'It was knowing how much you wanted to ... to have sex. I knew that once our exams were over I'd have to face it. And then when you announced you would be away for the whole of the summer I ...' She paused, blushing guiltily. 'I'm sorry, but I felt relieved.'

He stepped back, putting a small but meaningful distance between them. 'My God, Lyddie, I'd never make you do something you don't want to do. Surely you know that? I'm not some kind of monster.'

'I didn't ever think you were. But I feel differently now. Seeing you again ... well, I'm not scared any more.' She closed the gap between them and kissed him, badly wanting him to know that she meant it.

He held her in his arms and stroked her hair. They didn't speak. Lydia felt safe and cocooned, as though the world beyond the dell didn't exist. Their love was all that mattered.

'Uncle Brad goes down to London at the weekend,' Noah said eventually. 'We'd have the house all to ourselves. How does that sound?'

She pressed herself closer still to him. 'Perfect,' she murmured.

'And remember,' he said. 'I'll always love you and take care of you. No matter what. Don't ever forget that.'

With so few of them having taken any O-levels, there wasn't much of a crowd at school to collect the exam results. It was very different from when the CSE results had been announced. That day the place had been packed. 'Nine grade ones,' Zoe had said gleefully after she'd opened her envelope. 'Mind you, they hardly count really; it's the O-level results that are important.' She'd then pestered Lydia to open her envelope and say how she'd done.

'I'm waiting for when Noah gets back,' Lydia had explained. 'We made a deal to open them together.'

'Yeah, but a little peek wouldn't hurt, would it? I mean, you wouldn't have to tell him, would you?'

But Lydia had stuck to her guns and changed the subject. Apart from the deal she had with Noah, she knew that deep down Zoe wanted to know if she had done better than her. 'So how was your holiday?' Lydia had asked. 'I can't remember where you were going.'

Disappointment had momentarily wrong-footed Zoe, but she soon got over it. All credit to her; she wasn't a girl who harboured a grudge. Not even over Noah.

Zoe arrived soon after Lydia and Noah.

'Hiya!' she greeted them as they waited for the deputy head to hand out the all-important envelopes. 'How was your summer, Noah?'

'Pretty good.'

'And the best bit?'

He laughed, glanced quickly at Lydia and squeezed her hand that had been tucked inside his all the way to school. 'Coming back was easily the best bit.'

Zoe rolled her eyes. 'Honestly, you two!'

Listening with only half an ear to Zoe telling Noah about a great idea she had for a gang of them to go camping together next summer, Lydia stole a moment to observe Noah. Since leaving the Dell of the Dead, they'd been so busy talking – mostly about Noah's holiday – she hadn't actually checked to see if there really was anything different about him. His hair was longer and messier and he was more tanned, but essentially he was the same. She wondered if he had any idea just how good-looking he was. Probably not. And maybe that was part of his attraction. There had never been anything remotely showy about him; he'd never needed to prove himself. Just as she'd once envied him his cleverness, Lydia also envied the comfortable ease he had when he was around other people, and how they naturally warmed to him.

She thought back to when they'd been in the dell and the way her body had reacted when they'd kissed and touched. Just the memory of it caused her mouth to go dry and her stomach to somersault. She replayed the memory again. And again.

'You OK, Lydia?'

Shaken out of her reverie, her cheeks blazing, Lydia snapped to attention. 'Sorry, Zoe, what were you saying?'

'I was just telling Noah about you delivering Donna's baby, that you made the front page of the paper.'

Before she was able to respond, Mr Johnson appeared in the corridor. 'Right, folks, gather round. Time to put you out of your misery. Good luck.' He passed round the envelopes. As already agreed, Lydia and Noah went outside to sit on the tennis court to open theirs. But first they had their CSE results to read. 'I have a confession,' Lydia said when they'd both ripped open the envelopes. 'The results were in the paper and Donna blabbed them out to me. I should never have taught her to read.'

'It doesn't matter,' he said. After a hurried look at his piece of paper, he asked, 'How did you do?'

'Nine grade ones.'

'Snap!' He leaned over and kissed her. 'Now the other ones.'

They were both quiet for a moment.

Lydia was the first to speak. 'Happy with yours?'

'All As except for French. I got a B for that.' He grinned. 'I blame my private tutor. She kept distracting me. How about you? No, let me guess. Straight As. Am I right?'

She nodded. 'You don't mind?'

'Mind what? That I'm in love with the smartest girl in the entire school and that she's smart enough to be in love with me? A local hero into the bargain!'

His words wrapped around her as tightly as his arms. She basked in his praise – and the knowledge that now they really were on their way to escaping Swallowsdale.

One day, she vowed, she would really make something of herself. That would show her grandfather. How was that for getting above herself?

Chapter Forty-Two

With Donna's words echoing in her head as she emerged from the cool shade of the Dell of the Dead – *the first time is always the worst* – Lydia's step faltered. What if it really did hurt and she couldn't go through with it? Or worse, what if she survived it only to get pregnant?

Noah had promised he would never do anything to hurt her, just as he'd sworn he would always be careful. 'The last thing I want is to get you pregnant,' he'd repeatedly assured her. 'It would be a disaster for us both.' She took comfort in the knowledge that he was as paranoid as she was.

Since the birth of her daughter, Donna had vowed she would spend the rest of her life living like a nun, if only because she couldn't be trusted to remember to take the pill every day. Lydia reckoned she wouldn't have the same problem, but what she couldn't bring herself to do was ask Doctor Bunch if she could go on the pill. The thought of him questioning her reasons for wanting to use *any* form of contraception was too mortifying for words. She just knew he would sit there peering at her through his spectacles making her feel dirty and shameful.

But it wasn't shameful what she and Noah were about to do. Nor was it something dirty, as no doubt Pastor Digby would describe it. Anyway, what would Pastor Digby know about sex? He'd probably never done it in his life. Or known what it was like to kiss someone and know that they loved you as much as you loved them. That was the trouble with her grandparents and everyone at church; they went on and on about the right way to live, but had any of them *really* lived?

She pressed on up the hill, the hot sun shining down on her. Overhead, a pair of buzzards circled gracefully, climbing higher and higher in the cloudless sky, their melancholy mewing call the only sound in the still air. She decided that when the moment came, if it did hurt, she would think only of Noah and that this was the sacrifice she was making for him. Wasn't the Bible always talking about sacrificial love?

Why, she wondered crossly, was she thinking of the Bible at a time like this?

Because a small, niggling part of her could not be entirely convinced that what she was about to do was not a sin. She had only to think of the mess Donna had made of her life by not following the supposed rules, to know that she, too, could so easily be punished for throwing caution to the wind.

Enough! she told herself. No more doubts! No more worries! Instead, concentrate on that morning in the dell when everything changed. Yes, that she could do. How could she ever forget the intensity of her feelings when in an instant she had wanted to give herself to Noah? The whole of her. All her reserve gone.

Noah was waiting for her at the end of his garden. He helped her over the wall and kissed her, a light, tantalizing brush of his lips against hers. Then a kiss with more force. His hair was damp and he smelled as if he was fresh out of the bath.

'I can't remember the last time I was this nervous,' he confessed with a fleeting smile when he led her inside the house.

'Me too,' she said.

He turned to face her. 'You're sure you want to do this?'

She swallowed. 'Why, have you changed your mind?'

He took her hands in his. 'No. I just don't want to let you down. What if—'

'I've already played the "what if" game all the way here,' she interrupted him.

'I just don't want anything to change between us. I'm worried we'll do this and everything will be spoilt. You might end up hating me. I'd rather be dead than make that happen.'

'I could never hate you. Not in a million years.' Relieved that it wasn't only her who was plagued with nerves, she added, 'Come on, let's go upstairs. Let's pretend it's just an ordinary day and I've come to see you as usual.'

They lay on the bed as they had countless times before, listening to music, going through Noah's holiday snaps, laughing at how ridiculous Uncle Brad looked riding a donkey, and making plans for when they moved on to sixth-form college in a little over a week's time.

Relaxed and happy, Lydia raised herself onto an elbow and studied Noah, who now had his hands clasped behind his head. His eyes were closed; they were perfectly still, not a flicker. She loved the calm, unhurried pace of him. She let her gaze wander to the curved arches of his eyebrows, then to his cheekbones and his clean-shaven chin, and then to the soft underside of his arms where blue veins snaked beneath the surface of his skin. With his arms raised, his T-shirt had ridden up and she could see the flatness of his stomach. On an impulse she leaned over and planted a light kiss just above the waistband of his jeans. She felt his muscles tense. She did it again and then slowly moved up to kiss him on the mouth. He kissed her back and sweeping her hair away from her face with his hands, he held her face. Their eyes locked and all at once Lydia knew that it was going to be all right.

Chapter Forty-Three

In the following year, a month after her seventeenth birthday, Uncle Brad reminded Lydia of something he'd said to her a long time ago.

She and Noah were making themselves some toast before settling at the kitchen table to do their maths homework together, when Uncle Brad burst in on them. 'Lydia!' he roared so loudly she dropped the knife in her hand. 'Just the girl I've been thinking about all afternoon!'

'Oh, yes?' Noah said, looking and sounding dubious.

'Not like that, you mucky-minded scoundrel!' Uncle Brad remonstrated. Wearing odd shoes – one a battered cowboy boot, the other a black slip-on moccasin – and walking with a comical lopsided gait, he came over to where Lydia was now rinsing the knife under the tap at the sink. Without warning, he grabbed hold of her chin, twisted her head to the right towards the light coming in from the window and then to the left. His hands stank of linseed oil and were dusty with dried-on paint. She laughed when he stroked her nose. 'Perfect,' he declared, prodding a cheekbone with his thumb. 'Absolutely perfect. Come with me. There isn't a moment to be lost. Didn't I promise you I'd paint you one day?' He lunged for her hand and would have swept her out of the kitchen if Noah hadn't intervened.

'All well and good, Uncle B, but here on planet earth, Lyddie and I have homework to do.'

Uncle Brad stared at Noah, bewildered. 'Homework?' he repeated. 'But ... but the light. It's just right.' He appealed to Lydia. 'Lydia, tell him. The light. It's perfect.'

'How long will it take?' she asked, feeling sorry for the

poor man. He looked like a distressed child who had been told by the grown-ups to leave the room.

He shrugged, his hands extended. 'How the hell do I know? It takes as long as it takes. I'm an artist, not a car mechanic!'

Noah shook his head. 'Another time, Uncle B. Our homework has to be handed in tomorrow.'

Uncle Brad took a second or two to think about this. Then: 'Tomorrow!' he cried, leaping on the word as though it was the answer to everything. 'You'll pose for me tomorrow. There, it's decided.'

'You could try actually asking Lydia if she wants to pose for you,' Noah intervened again. 'And you better not have any ideas about asking her to take any clothes off. No nudes. OK?'

'Oh, Lydia, Lydia, he's such a pedant these days. To say nothing of his prudish, high-minded morals. I don't know where he gets them from.'

'Certainly not from you,' muttered Noah, going over to the toaster.

Still addressing Lydia, Uncle Brad said, 'His mother would turn in her grave to know he's grown into such a bourgeois.'

'What kind of picture did you want to paint of me?' Lydia asked. She couldn't pretend she wasn't just a teensy bit flattered that Uncle Brad was so keen to paint her.

'A brilliant one!' he responded without a trace of modesty. 'Maybe my best yet!'

Lydia had heard this kind of talk from Uncle Brad many times over the years. She knew that he spent his every waking moment in pursuit of what he called the ultimate artistic high. His pictures these days tended to be enormous stormy landscapes with paint layered so thick in places it looked like it had been shovelled on with a garden trowel. The last portrait she could remember him doing was one of Noah and that was last year. It was Lydia's favourite picture in the house and was hung in the hall beneath Adolf the Stag.

'You don't have to sit for him if you don't want to,' Noah said when they had decamped upstairs to his bedroom to do their homework, whilst Uncle Brad commandeered the kitchen to make a start on cooking one of his ferociously hot curries. Tapping a pencil against his teeth, Noah added, 'If you're not comfortable with the idea, I'll just tell him you're too busy and can't spare the time.'

'I am busy, but so long as it doesn't take for ever, I don't mind doing it. I'm sort of curious, if I'm honest.'

Noah twirled the pencil, flipped it in the air and caught it deftly. 'And if *I'm* honest, I'm jealous. I hate the thought of my uncle doing something that I've wanted to do for ages now.'

'But you're always sketching me.'

He tossed her words aside with a wave of his hand, a dismissive gesture amusingly reminiscent of his uncle. 'They're just sketches. I've had something special in mind to do for some time.'

'Oh?'

'I want to draw you properly, but in a way you might not be happy about. I've tried doing it from memory but it just won't work. I can't do you justice.'

Lydia pushed aside her textbook. Applied maths would have to wait. She gave him her full attention. 'Exactly how do you want to draw me?'

He fiddled with the pencil some more and said just one word: 'Naked.'

When she didn't say anything, he said, 'No one else would ever see the picture. It would be for me. For us.' He paused and let out his breath. 'You hate the idea, don't you? I should never have said anything.'

'I don't hate the idea, it's just ... well, you know, a surprise. How would you feel if it was the other way round and I wanted you to pose for me without any clothes on?'

A ghost of a smile flickered across his face. 'I'd hate it. I'm hardly Mr Universe, am I?'

She smiled too. 'And I'm hardly Miss World.'

'You don't see yourself the way I see you.' He moved away from where he was sitting at his desk and joined her on the bed. He kissed her and when she kissed him back, long and deeply, it was only a matter of seconds before Lydia felt her body go weak then spring to life as a bolt of electric desire ripped through her. She knew, though, that they couldn't take things any further. They had a rule: never do more than kiss when Uncle Brad was around. They always locked the door, but neither of them wanted to risk Uncle Brad hearing what they were up to. Noah said his uncle probably wouldn't give a tinker's cuss what they did, but they stuck to the rule all the same. And anyway, it was so much better when the house was empty. They didn't have to worry about the sound of Noah's ancient bed creaking and squeaking, or the noise either of them made when that wonderfully delicious moment overtook them both.

They had learned a lot about their bodies since that very first time. To Lydia's great relief it hadn't hurt anywhere near as much as she had dreaded. Noah had been as gentle and careful with her as he'd promised he would be, and although he'd been embarrassed that it had been over so fast, the next day when they lay on their sides in bed together, their bodies a perfect fit, Lydia revelled in the extraordinary and totally unexpected beauty of what they were doing. How could it ever be considered a sin when it felt like the most loving thing you could do?

It was several weeks later, when Uncle Brad was away in London, that she experienced her first orgasm. She had cried when it had happened, with surprise and disbelief as much as anything. Noah was concerned that he'd hurt her, but when she'd described the amazing feelings that had flooded through her, he'd admitted with a smile to sneaking a look at one of his uncle's books and trying on her what he'd read.

Whilst babysitting for Donna, she had secretly started to read her friend's magazines, especially the problems pages. Orgasms were every woman's dream, she'd discovered, yet it wasn't every man who was able to work out how to make it happen. Lucky her, she thought smugly.

The following Saturday after she'd finished work, with Noah's blessing – he was out having a driving lesson – Lydia sat in Uncle Brad's studio modelling for him. She had her hands crossed on her lap, her mouth shut, her breath held, her face pointed towards the window and the soft afternoon light, just as she'd been instructed.

'No, no, *NO!*' Uncle Brad yelled at her. 'Who is this preposterously prim-faced girl I see before me? Where's Lydia? Where's the Lydia I've watched grow from being an awkward, shy child into the beautiful, confident young woman I know?'

Letting out her breath, Lydia flushed. 'I was only doing what you told me to do.'

'Lies. Lies. And damned lies! Did I say anything about looking like a constipated racoon holding its breath? Relax, Lydia. I said *RELAX!*'

'I would if you stopped shouting at me,' she said, flustered.

'Shouting? You call this shouting? Why, this is the gentle murmuring of a—'

'Psychopathic tyrant?' she suggested.

He laughed and she laughed too.

'That's more like it, my girl. Now put your elbow on the arm of the chair, rest your chin on the heel of your palm and stare out of the window. I want you to think of Noah.'

'Why?'

'Because you love him, my sweet, and he loves you. Now get a move on. Elbow up, and think those delectable thoughts of love.'

The session lasted a lifetime, although in real time it was only an hour. 'I feel so stiff,' she complained when he said he'd finished for the day. He immediately covered the easel with a dirty old bit of cloth so she couldn't see what he'd done. 'Same time next week,' he said.

It was an order.

They went through the same process again the following Saturday, Uncle Brad shouting his head off at her until she'd adopted the correct relaxed pose. How he expected her to relax when he was so rude, she didn't know, but the moment he ordered her to think of Noah, it worked. While he was painting, Uncle Brad spent a good deal of the time muttering and cursing to himself. She was just thinking that he was oblivious to her as a person and was treating her as an object – like an apple in a still life – when he said, 'Does Noah ever talk to you about his parents?'

Surprised at the question, she turned to answer him, but was immediately yelled at. She adopted the correct position again.

'Well, does he?'

'Hardly ever,' she replied.

'More to the right. Chin up. That's better. Why do you think that is?'

'Because they died so long ago?'

'Are you asking me or telling me?'

'I'm giving you an educated guess.'

He cursed and dabbed viciously at the canvas. A few minutes passed. 'What about you?' he demanded. 'Your parents died more or less the same time; do you talk to Noah about them?'

'Not really.'

'What does *not really* mean?'

'When we first got to know each other at primary school we swapped stories; it was what we had in common. It's what made us friends, I suppose. But now we don't need to do that.'

'You now have each other in common; is that what you're saying?'

'Yes.'

'Mmm ... So way back in the beginning, when you were swapping life histories, did he tell you about his leg?'

'His leg?'

'Don't be obtuse, Lydia. His useless smashed-to-pieces leg. Did he ever tell you about the accident?'

As extraordinary as it was, Noah had never told Lydia how he'd wound up with a limp. More extraordinary perhaps was that she had never asked him for an explanation. She had vaguely assumed it was something he'd been born with, like Lisa Fortune and her artificial hand. 'No,' she answered Uncle Brad. Intrigued, she said, 'Are you going to tell me about it, then?'

'Time's up.'

In the week that followed she could so easily have asked Noah about the 'accident' that Uncle Brad had referred to, but instinct stopped her. If it was something Noah had wanted to share with her, he would have done so by now.

But that didn't stop her wanting to prompt Uncle Brad to pick up where he'd left off when, once again, she was settled into the required position.

The May afternoon light was bright and glittery and a breeze was shaking the last of the blossom from the cherry tree outside Uncle Brad's studio. Lydia watched the petals fall and disappear into the long, unkempt grass. In a nearby patch of earth, a blackbird was tugging at a worm, stretching it like a grubby piece of elastic, until finally it was pulled free from the soil. If this was a cartoon, Lydia thought, the bird would have fallen back onto its feathered behind and the worm would have made a top-speed escape. As it was, the worm stood no chance and because Lydia couldn't turn away or close her eyes, she was forced to watch its grisly demise. For a distraction, she said, 'So tell me how Noah got his bad leg. Was it a car accident?' She winced as she asked the question – right now, Noah was out on his penultimate driving lesson before his test. Her heart skittered at the thought of him coming to any harm.

'No, not a car accident,' Uncle Brad answered her.

'What then?' she asked when several minutes of silence had passed.

'It was an accident that should never have happened. His mother blamed herself. She never got over the guilt.'

Lydia thought of the ugly two-headed portrait upstairs of Noah's mother and felt a stab of hatred. 'She did it deliberately?'

'Of course not! Ingrid would never have wilfully laid a hand on anyone, let alone her own son.'

'What did she do? And how old was Noah at the time?'

'He was five. Nearly six. His father was away on business – he did that a lot. Stephen never grasped how lonely Ingrid became. She was a gregarious girl. She needed company. Lots of it.'

'She had Noah for company,' Lydia interjected.

'He was a child, Lydia.' Uncle Brad's voice was sharp. 'Ingrid needed the stimulating company that only another adult can give.'

Donna's own claim of needing company chimed in Lydia's ears. 'Go on,' she urged.

'Ingrid decided to throw a party. Like the ones we used to have in the old days, before she married Stephen. What you need to know is that Stephen was a good man, but not a charismatic man. He was devoted to Ingrid, but devotion isn't always enough. Anyway, in Stephen's absence, she invited the old crowd from our time at college. They were a pretty wild bunch.'

'Were you there?' Lydia interrupted.

'No. I couldn't make it.' He seemed to think about this for a while, before saying, 'I've often wondered if things might have turned out differently if I had.'

'How do you know what went on in that case, if you weren't there?'

'Ingrid told me later. She poured it all out to me, based on what she knew personally and from what Noah and some of the guests had told her.' He fell silent again. Minutes later, he cursed loudly. 'Damn you, Lydia, I've lost my thread. Where was I?'

'They were a pretty wild bunch.'

'Oh, yes, that's right. Well, the party was in full swing when Noah woke up wanting a drink. It's not difficult to imagine him coming to the top of the stairs, calling for his mother and getting no response. What would any child do in those circumstances? He went downstairs to the kitchen to help himself to a glass of milk from the fridge. The place was crowded with people who all made a big fuss of him. He was on his way back upstairs when he noticed some plates of chocolate cake. When no one was looking, he stuffed his dressing gown pockets full, and went back upstairs to enjoy his illicit feast.'

'Where was his mother when all this was going on?'

'That's irrelevant. Now stop interrupting. What Noah didn't know was that the cakes he ate weren't ordinary cakes. They were jam-packed with LSD.'

'No!'

'God knows how much of the stuff he ate, but the effect it had on him was disastrous. He must have been literally out of his mind, because he ... he opened his bedroom window and for whatever reason – perhaps he thought he could fly, or was being chased by something – he jumped. He wasn't found until the next morning. Ingrid thought he was dead at first. It was a miracle that he was alive and that his only injury was—'

Lydia couldn't sit still any longer. She was consumed with fury for the uncaring, irresponsible mother who should never have allowed such a terrible thing to happen to her child. She jumped up from the chair. 'Your sister was a monster! She should have gone to prison for what she did!'

There were tears in Uncle Brad's eyes. 'Worse, Lydia. She went to hell. She was never the same again.'

'Good! It's where she deserves to be.'

'Perhaps you're right,' he murmured, wiping his eyes with the backs of his hands. 'But it doesn't make me miss her any less. She wasn't only my twin sister; she was my best friend. You have no idea what it feels like to watch someone you love disintegrate before your eyes. She began having a series of meaningless affairs, shoving them in Stephen's face to force him into punishing her for what she'd done to Noah. She was hell-bent on a course of self-destruction, pure and simple. And then one day, she told Stephen she was leaving him for some new man she'd taken up with. That was when she finally got her wish. Stephen took her by the throat and killed her. He strangled the very last breath out of her. Do you have any idea what that did to me? Knowing that I, who loved her more than anyone, didn't save her from herself? There isn't a day when I don't think I should have tried harder.' He flung down his paintbrush and reached for the cloth to cover the easel.

Seeing the wretched torment etched on Uncle Brad's face, Lydia could feel his guilt as tangibly as her own regarding her mother's death.

'Why have you told me all this?' she said.

'Because Noah heard and saw things a young boy should never see. He was at an extremely impressionable age. I want to know how much of this he's carrying around inside him. I thought if anyone would know, it would be you.'

'You could have just come right out and asked me yourself, Uncle Brad.'

They both turned to see Noah standing in the doorway of the studio.

Chapter Forty-Four

It wasn't until Tuesday the following week, when it was half-term, that Lydia saw Noah again. She had hurriedly made herself scarce on Saturday afternoon when Noah had walked in on that terrible conversation, deciding that whatever was said next was strictly between him and his uncle.

She was working at the shop, and while the Khans were at the wholesalers and there was a lull in customers, she was lugging crates of Coca-Cola out from the stockroom to go on the shelves. She'd just emptied the last of the crates when she noticed a red sports car pull up. The hood was folded back and Noah was waving at her from the driver's seat. He was alone. Which meant only one thing. She rushed outside to congratulate him.

'I thought I'd blown it,' he said, getting out of the car and hugging her. 'I did a lousy three-point turn and my hill start could have been better. Are you working tomorrow?'

'No. I've got the day off.'

'Excellent! Fancy a trip somewhere?'

The car had been a present from Uncle Brad for Noah on his seventeenth birthday and Noah had done all his lessons in it. It was years old, but Lydia knew it was his pride and joy. He spent hours washing and polishing it as well as messing about under the bonnet. It was a Sunbeam Alpine, almost identical to the model Uncle Brad had owned more than a decade ago, before Lydia and Noah had even met. Noah couldn't drive a car with a manual transmission

– because of his leg – and Uncle Brad had secretly phoned round hundreds of garages and private dealers until he'd tracked one down in the right condition with an automatic gearbox. What really mattered to Noah, so he told Lydia, was that for the first time in his life he was truly independent; he could get around without relying on anyone else for lifts.

He never complained about not being able to walk that far or ride a bike any real distance, but Lydia knew it bothered him. She knew also that if he did push himself too much, the pain in his knee and ankle could be excruciating. She'd once seen him turn white with pain and actually be sick after he'd missed his footing. What went through his head when that happened? Did he blame his mother? Did he hate her for what had happened to him?

She waited for Noah to come and pick her up at the end of her road, where she hoped certain prying eyes wouldn't see her. More out of habit than anything else.

Her grandfather had retired from working for the council, yet he rarely seemed to be at home. 'Church matters' kept him busy most days and evenings. When he was at home he bossed them all about as usual – including their grandmother – but Lydia sensed his heart, ironically, wasn't in it. He was merely going through the motions of being a tyrant. Time was he'd have raised merry hell if the tea wasn't ready on time or cooked to his exact liking. Nowadays, he seldom shared a meal with them and showed not the slightest interest in what was going on. If it wasn't for the painful memories Lydia had of all those times when he'd lashed out at her – the cane was still there in the kitchen – she might have taken advantage of his apparent apathy and stayed out later and more often. She might even have asked to be allowed to go to an occasional disco in town. Or a concert like the ones Zoe was always going to. As it was, she counted her blessings that life was so much easier for her. She wasn't greedy. She had as much freedom as she needed these days. No point in pushing her luck.

Lydia couldn't be sure, but she had a feeling that her grandfather stayed out as often as he did because his wife had started behaving oddly again. She was hoarding tins of food in the airing cupboard, refusing to answer the telephone and hiding from anyone who came to the door. The only time she left the house was to go to church. She would scuttle to the car, paranoid that there was someone watching her. Her mood swings were increasing, too. She cried more and seemed restless and agitated. She wasn't sleeping properly, either and would visibly shake and cower if her husband lost his temper and shouted at her. He locked her in the bedroom one day, shouted that he wouldn't let her out until he was satisfied she would behave.

More recently Lydia had heard the old woman downstairs in the kitchen, in the middle of the night, reading aloud from the Bible. For the last two nights, Valerie had been down there with her. It was obvious to Lydia that their grandmother should see Doctor Bunch. So why didn't their grandfather get on and arrange it? Perhaps he simply didn't care. Or worse, was he cruelly waiting for his wife to go completely mad again so that he could be conveniently rid of her like before?

When Noah's red car came into sight, Lydia forgot all about her grandparents and wondered whether it would be Noah or her who would raise the subject of the conversation he'd overheard her having with Uncle Brad.

Noah had always been good at surprising her, and he did so again today.

'I want to see where you lived before you came to Swallowsdale,' he said after she'd stowed a picnic of crusty rolls, a packet of sliced processed cheese, two bags of crisps and several cans of Seven-Up into the boot of the car.

She sat in the front passenger seat, dumbfounded. 'Why?'

He smiled enigmatically. 'It's that kind of a day. A day for getting to know each other even better.'

'But I've never been back to Maywood. I ... it sounds silly, but I don't know the way.'

He reached behind him. 'No problem. I have a map. And it's not that far. I've already checked.'

'You're serious about this, aren't you?'

'Yes.' He hesitated. 'Unless you'd rather not because it would stir up too many bad memories.'

She regarded him levelly. 'Maybe it's time,' she said. 'For both of us.'

He kissed her cheek. 'That's exactly what I thought.'

Lydia couldn't remember much about the journey she and her sister had made from Maywood to Swallowsdale all those years ago, other than the car being hot and stuffy and her falling asleep with Val on her lap.

This time, as map reader, there was no falling asleep. Nor was there any conversation about why they were really making this trip. That would come later, they had both agreed. And with the hood back, the warm May sun shining down on them and the wind tugging at Lydia's hair, they drove out of Swallowsdale and followed the road as it dipped and climbed and twisted across the moors towards Cheshire.

And the past.

It was market day in Maywood and the narrow streets were busy with shoppers. 'Recognize anything?' Noah asked as he negotiated the traffic.

'Sort of. But it doesn't feel real. It's like a dream. Like I've been here before but in my sleep.'

'I'll drive around a bit. Shout if you see something that you want to stop and look at properly.'

Five minutes later she did exactly that.

'What is it?' Noah asked when he'd brought the car to a halt and reversed a few yards at her request.

Lydia couldn't speak. She just stared at the shop window. It hadn't changed. The toys had, of course, but the way they were crammed into the small space, each toy and board game jostling for position, took her right back to when she'd longed for that awful ventriloquist's dummy. She could see herself standing in front of the window, scheming like mad to get that most prized of possessions for her birthday. She remembered the dummy staring back at her as if it would make everything right in her world. She'd wanted it as a friend, she now understood. Something to fill the gap her father had left behind.

'If you take my father's death out of the equation, this is where it all started,' Lydia said, her voice almost inaudible. She felt Noah's hand on hers.

'Do you want to go inside?'

'No. This is enough.' She told him the story. How she'd pushed her mother to the limit because she'd wanted something so badly. He made no comment, just kept hold of her hand.

'I know where I want to go next,' she said resolutely, after they'd sat in silence for a while.

'To the church where your parents are buried?' Noah asked.

'No. Somewhere that means more to me.' She studied the map, then pointed to where she wanted Noah to drive.

It took a few attempts to find the right road, but gradually the houses and buildings thinned and the pavements were replaced with hedgerows and grass verges sprinkled with daisies and dandelions. Lydia wasn't sure she would find what she was looking for; this was navigation by some mysterious instinct, a memory so deeply buried inside her she couldn't believe it would work.

'Slow down!' she said, snapping forward in her seat. 'Here. Pull over, if you can.'

The road was narrow and Noah had to park the car right up against the hedgerow; Lydia had to clamber over his seat to get out. At her suggestion, they took the picnic with them. 'You'll think it's a weird place to eat lunch,' she told him, 'but as you said earlier, it's that kind of a day.'

She led the way and after they'd pushed through the

hawthorn hedge, she said, 'Do you mind if I go on ahead on my own? I need a few minutes alone.'

'I'll wait here. Give me a wave when you're ready.'

When she'd made it down to the level area of long grass, Lydia looked back up at Noah and, remembering how she'd struggled down the steep slope with Valerie in the pushchair that night, she hoped that he wouldn't find it too difficult. Just as her mother had done, she inspected the grass for a likely place to sit down. Having found a suitable spot, she hugged her knees tightly, closed her eyes and tried to picture her mother. Not the anxious, worn-down woman she had become after Dad had died, but the woman who had loved to get dressed up and who smiled when Dad put his arm around her waist and told her how pretty she was and that he was the proudest man in all the world to have such a beautiful wife and two lovely daughters. The image of a delicate exotic bird flew into Lydia's mind. A bird that simply wasn't strong enough to cope with the worst that life could throw at it. Tears filled her eyes. She tried to picture her father, but his face wouldn't come to her. What came to her instead were those words Lydia had drifted away to on that shattering night: *Tell it to the skies, Lydia ... Tell it to the skies ...*

Was that the answer? If she could say the words out loud, here in this place, would it be over? Would it untie the knot of her guilt? Would she stop hating herself for what she'd done?

Only one way to find out. She took a deep breath, opened her eyes, tipped her head back and stared up at a large drifting cloud. 'I haven't forgotten you,' she said softly. 'I still love you both.' And to her mother, with more strength to her voice, she said, 'Please forgive me, Mum. Forgive me for what I did to you. I'm so very sorry. I never meant to hurt you. Please believe me.'

She began to cry. Quietly at first, but then she bowed her head and wept so hard she felt like she was choking on her sobs. As she struggled to breathe, the tears kept coming. It was what she had never allowed herself to do before now: to grieve for her parents. The wrenching pain was unbearable. It was shredding her heart, tearing her apart. Never had she felt so desolate or alone.

But suddenly she wasn't alone. Noah was there. He had her in his arms. She was shaking but he held her to him. Tightly. Protectively. Unable to speak, she clung to him, pressing her face to his shoulder.

He stroked her hair and soothed her. 'I'm sorry,' he said. 'I'm so sorry. I shouldn't have brought you here. I'll take you home right away. Forgive me, please, Lyddie.' His words were a poignantly haunting echo of her own just minutes earlier and made her cry even harder.

But they didn't go home right away. Once Lydia had recovered, they sat staring down at the railway track. 'This is where she did it,' Lydia said. 'While Valerie and I slept here on the bank, she threw herself under a train. But then you'd probably worked that out for yourself.'

He nodded. 'Are you sure you want to stay?'

'I'm fine.'

'You're not, you know. And you won't be until you stop blaming yourself. It wasn't your fault your mother killed herself. Any more than it was my fault what my parents did to each other.'

Surprised at his words, she said, 'Surely you never blamed yourself for their deaths?'

'I used to. I used to think that if I hadn't eaten that cake, they'd still be alive. Then I decided that I'd probably drive myself mad if I kept thinking that way. I only had to look at my uncle to see what guilt could do to a person.'

She turned and gazed into his eyes. 'Can I ask you about that night and your accident?'

'Not much to tell. It was an accident that could have happened to any family where cakes laced with LSD are served at a party.'

'Did you hate your mother for what happened to you?'

'For a while, yes. I hated everything about her. Her selfishness. Her ineffectualness. The way she treated my father. But then I understood that she hated herself enough for the two of us. Now I feel sorry for her.'

'What happened immediately afterwards, when you were taken to hospital?'

'Most of it I can't remember. I was quite ill. Children aren't meant to consume that much LSD. The upside, I suppose, was that I didn't feel the pain when I fell.'

'Do you remember jumping from the window?'

'Only vaguely. Or maybe I kid myself I do.'

'Were the police brought into it? You know, there being drugs involved.'

'I don't know how, but that side of things was magically hushed up.'

'And your leg, how bad was it?'

'Smashed to pieces; it took the full brunt of my fall. It was touch and go whether they were going to amputate it.'

Lydia flinched. 'Why did you never tell me this before now?'

'Same reason you've never told me your grandparents use you as a punchbag. You feel useless, worthless. Almost deserving of what they dish out.'

She caught her breath, shocked. Shocked that he'd broken the unspoken rule between them and had come right out with what he'd said, but equally aghast that he'd described exactly how she felt. Shaken, she said, 'You always knew, didn't you?'

'Yeah, me the genius.' He shook his head. 'Trust me, it wasn't difficult, Lyddie. I can't tell you how many times I've wanted to come to your house and beat the hell out of your grandparents. It is both of them hurting you, isn't it?'

Embarrassed, she lowered her head, letting his question hang there between them while she summoned the courage to be honest with him. 'Just my grandfather,' she murmured eventually.

'But your grandmother lets it go on? She's never tried to stop him?'

'I think she's as scared of him as I am.'

'He probably gets off on scaring people. His type do. Does he hit Valerie?'

Lydia looked up sharply. 'He wouldn't dare. My grandmother wouldn't stand for it. Nor would I.'

'That time you came into school with a cut lip and a swollen jaw, that wasn't an accident, was it?'

For all of a split second, out of habit, still wanting to conceal the ugly truth, Lydia considered lying, but she couldn't bring herself to do it. Why bother? Noah had known the real her for a long time. 'No,' she said. 'My grandfather lost control that time.'

'For any special reason?'

Knowing how petty the reason sounded, she felt the last of her pride and dignity being demolished. 'I hadn't done the washing-up when I should have.'

Noah clenched his jaw. 'Bastard! Complete and utter bastard!'

'He hasn't touched me in ages,' she said quickly, wanting to mollify Noah. 'It's almost as if I don't exist to him any more.'

'Good. And it had better stay that way. Because if anything like that happens again, I swear I'll kill your grandfather. That's a promise.'

She saw the intense, fierce conviction in his eyes and felt her heart miss a beat.

Chapter Forty-Five

During that summer term at college, everything in Zoe's world was either a-*maaz*ing, *grrr*eat or phe-*nommm*inal. Lydia and Noah's daily walk with her down to the sandwich shop, where a group of lower-sixth formers congregated at lunchtime, wouldn't be complete unless they had these over-used, over-stretched adjectives thrown at them at least half a dozen times.

Zoe now had jet-black hair, a stud in her nose, and a boyfriend at Exeter University. Rick was an a-*maaz*ing guy, as she never tired of telling them, and was a *grrr*eat guitarist with his own punk band. According to Zoe, the band was so shocking and outrageous they made the Sex Pistols look like founding members of the Val Doonican fan club. They had a string of gigs lined up for the summer in Devon and Cornwall and just as soon as term ended, Zoe was joining the band in Devon. They'd be sleeping on the beach at night. If they slept at all. It was going to be phe-*nommm*inal, the perfect antidote to the Queen's Jubilee and all those stupid street parties.

So much for a gang of them going camping together as Zoe had suggested last year. The casual abandonment of that original plan had come as a relief to Lydia. Asking her grandfather for permission to go would have been more trouble than it was worth. She'd had enough trouble from him when she'd worn her Doc Martens for the first time in the house. He'd snapped and snarled at her like the ferocious Rottweiler that had moved in at number twenty-five and had banned her from wearing them to church. He probably thought she was going to give the Sisters and

Brothers a good kicking and rob them of their pensions, or make off with the collection plate.

In another Rottweiler moment, after a spate of increasingly weird behaviour from their grandmother, he blamed Lydia for her illness, saying that until she had come to live with them – before the strain of having evil under their roof had become too much for her – his wife had been perfectly well.

Finally he got round to sending for Doctor Bunch and some new pills were prescribed. Initially they seemed to do the trick, but then, having grown used to their grandmother being too scared to leave the house, they started suddenly having to watch her all the time in case she slipped out and made a nuisance of herself with the neighbours. Embarrassingly, she had become convinced that God was calling her to root out the ungodly living on Hillside Terrace.

'But what if she really is under God's orders?' Noah had once asked Lydia when she was sharing with him her grandmother's latest escapade, that of shouting scripture through a neighbour's letterbox late at night, urging the neighbour to give up his life of sin and turn to Christ.

'That's not funny, Noah.'

'I'm just playing devil's advocate,' he'd replied. 'What if everyone had dismissed Christ as being clinically insane?'

'There's no mention in the Bible about him going round shouting through letterboxes under cover of darkness, so I'll stick my neck out and say you're barking up the wrong tree. As well as sounding like Val.'

Eleven years old now, an age when she should be much more aware of what was real and not real, Valerie still badly wanted to believe their grandmother's behaviour was rational. It was as if she saw herself as a devoted disciple, and that scared Lydia more than anything their grandmother got up to.

These thoughts came back to haunt Lydia about a fortnight later at two o'clock in the morning, when she discovered her grandmother kneeling on the kitchen floor hacking off her hair with a pair of blunt scissors.

The following night in bed, Lydia was jolted awake by being shaken. She opened her eyes half expecting to discover she was about to die in an earthquake. Instead, perhaps far worse, she saw her grandfather standing over her.

'Get up!' he ordered, at the same time switching on her bedside lamp.

Blinking in the sudden burst of light, she grabbed hold of the bedclothes and held them tightly against her. 'What's wrong?' she asked.

He pointed to Val's bed. It was empty, neatly made as if it hadn't been slept in. 'They've disappeared,' he said. 'I've checked the whole house.'

'They?' she repeated, groggy with sleep.

'Your grandmother and Valerie.'

All grogginess suddenly gone, Lydia leapt out of bed. Down on her hands and knees, she peered under Val's bed.

'Are you mad?' her grandfather exploded. 'You think they're both hiding under there?'

Lydia got to her feet. 'Did you know Grandmother and Val have both had cases packed since last year for when the time came to be taken up to heaven? Val had hers hidden under her bed: it's gone.'

Hardly ever was her grandfather stuck for words, but in this instance he was. He shook his head in disbelief.

'We should go and look for them,' Lydia said, reaching for her jeans and T-shirt, sensing that it would have to be her who took the initiative. With her sister's safety uppermost in her mind, and knowing that their grandmother had been acting even more erratically of late, she added, 'If we can't find Grandmother and Val, we'll have to call the police.'

The police found them several miles away, out on the moors. The scene they later described to Lydia and her grandfather was a chilling one.

Wearing only slippers and her nightdress, Valerie had been found sleeping in the shelter of a drystone wall, while their grandmother, also in only her nightdress, had been down on her knees, praying. It had been her wailed entreaties to God that she and Val be spared Armageddon that had led the two police officers to them. They probably knew her as 'Mrs Turner, that barmy old bat' and though they had tried to handle her respectfully she was having none of it and had whipped out a carving knife from her case.

From then on, they'd had no choice but to treat her as armed and dangerous and had forced her to the ground, her arms cuffed behind her back. They radioed for help, and it was only then that they registered something was wrong with Valerie. She wasn't sleeping peacefully as they'd thought, but was out cold: she'd been drugged. For what purpose, no one liked to say.

Which left Lydia to dwell on the inconceivable. Had Grandma drugged Valerie with her own medication – medication that she had been secretly hoarding in the suitcase – with a view to making some kind of obscene sacrifice? Why else had she packed that knife?

Inevitably the local press got wind of the story. Lydia was glad. It meant that her grandfather could no longer turn a blind eye to what had been going on, or ignore the harm it had done to Valerie.

Valerie was now signed up for weekly sessions with a child psychologist. Lydia had no idea what went on during these visits because, once again, her sister had given up talking altogether. Her loss of voice was officially put down to her suffering from psychological trauma – as if they couldn't work that out for themselves. The Brothers and Sisters rallied, especially Sister Lottie, but to all intents and purposes Val had shut down. She wouldn't go to school – with only a week left of term, no one thought this mattered – but then nor would she venture outside to the garden, let alone leave the house. Which included not going to church. And since they couldn't leave her on her own, Lydia stayed at home, too.

Meanwhile, their grandmother had been admitted to the psychiatric ward where she had been before. There was talk of her being schizophrenic, of her actions being a response to voices in her head. A month after she'd been taken to hospital, nobody was talking about when she might return home.

'It all stems back to that operation she had,' Sister Lottie said, her voice so hushed Lydia could hardly hear her. 'Your grandmother was never the same after that.'

Lydia grabbed hold of this thought. It was the operation that had caused her grandmother's madness. It wasn't some strange gene that she or Val could inherit. But what if Sister Lottie was wrong? No, she told herself. She must put the fear right out of her head. Anyway, there was a greater fear she had.

'Do you think she would have ... you know, actually hurt Valerie?' Lydia's gaze flickered to the ceiling, where above them Valerie was in the bedroom.

Sister Lottie finished pouring herself a cup of tea and carefully put the stainless steel pot down. She straightened the crocheted tea cosy, then added a spoonful of sugar to her cup. 'I can't let myself think that, Lydia dear. Irene loved Valerie so much. And still does. Why, that child is the apple of her eye.'

'Abraham loved his son Isaac, but look at what he was prepared to do.'

'But God stopped him, didn't he?'

'Grandfather says I'm to blame for Grandmother's illness. He says there wasn't anything wrong with her until I showed up.'

Sister Lottie stirred her tea slowly. 'Your grandfather's been under a lot of strain these last few years and is bound to say things he'll later regret. Try not to hold it against him. Anyway, didn't I just say it was that operation your grandmother had that did the damage?'

'You always think so well of people, don't you?'

Sister Lottie blushed. 'Not always.'

'I don't believe you. Who have you ever thought badly of?'

The blush deepened. 'I haven't always seen eye to eye with some of the Brothers and Sisters. I didn't really approve of the way Pastor John was treated. He should have been given a chance to repent. You probably don't remember him, do you? That business happened so long ago. Poor man.'

'No, I do remember him.' And seeing as it was confession time, Lydia said, 'The first time I met Pastor John I stole a book from him. A dictionary.'

Sister Lottie smiled. 'I watched you do it.'

'You did? Why didn't you say anything?'

'You'd just lost your mother. And your father before that. What was a sneaked dictionary compared to what you must have been going through?'

Tears welled up in Lydia's eyes. 'You've always been so kind to me, like a guardian angel. You were my first real friend here.'

The teacup wobbled in the saucer in Sister Lottie's hand, and the old lady pressed her white plimsolled feet together. 'You were kind to me, too,' she said softly. 'You took me just as I was, with all my many faults. Which is something some of the Brothers and Sisters have never managed to do. Oh, yes, I know they call me dotty old Lottie behind my back, and perhaps I am dotty. But that's the way the Lord made me, a simple woman. As Brothers and Sisters in Christ, one of the things we're called to do on this earth is not to judge others. It's not our job.'

'I don't think I'll ever be as good as you. I have terrible thoughts about some people. Really bad thoughts.'

Sister Lottie reached across the table and patted Lydia's hand. 'You're still so very young and with so much to learn.'

'Do you ever regret not getting married and having a family of your own?'

'Sometimes, yes. But then I think how blessed I've been

to have you and Valerie in my life. And of course, there's Joey too. He's been like a son to me.'

'He's very fond of you.'

'And I of him. I shall miss the dear boy when he stops coming to work here in Swallowsdale.'

Lydia sat up straight. 'He's not coming back after this summer?'

'Oh, I don't know about that. But one day he won't return. He'll find a lovely wife in Italy and want to settle down with her there and have a family. It's inevitable.'

'A summer without Joey doesn't seem possible. It just wouldn't be the same.'

Sister Lottie topped up their teacups. 'You'll be leaving soon as well. Off to university. I shall be so proud of you. Didn't I always say you were as smart as paint? Lydia? Whatever is the matter? You suddenly look so serious. Have I said something out of turn?'

Lydia took a deep breath. 'You might just as well know; I won't be applying to university for next year.'

'What?'

'How can I? I have to stay and take care of Valerie. I can't possibly leave her here on her own with our grandfather. It wouldn't be right.'

Chapter Forty-Six

Sister Lottie wasn't the only one to be horrified by Lydia's decision.

Joey spent the rest of the summer being furious with her. In September, when he was packing up his things into the boot of his rusting old car – which didn't look like it would make it to the end of the road, never mind all the way down to Dover through France and Switzerland before finally arriving in his village near Naples – he had stopped what he was doing and told her he would never speak to her again if she didn't change her mind.

'I'll just have to take that risk,' she'd said, tired of everyone telling her what she should do.

Exasperated, he'd thrown his hands in the air. '*Mamma mia!* You have the expression of a stubborn, stupid mule on your face! What is more, you are acting like one!'

It was all very well, Joey going on like this, along with anyone else who wanted to throw in their tuppence worth, but what they refused to see was that this wasn't about her, it was about Valerie. Lydia's duty was to take care of her sister, because their grandfather, for all his outwards displays of piety, didn't give a fig about her or Val. They could both drop down dead tomorrow and he'd feel nothing but relief finally to be rid of them both.

Not so long ago their grandfather would not have delayed Lydia's leaving for university; moreover he would probably have gladly waved her goodbye. But now everything was different. She had heard Doctor Bunch telling him that he doubted their grandmother would ever fully recover from her most recent and dramatic breakdown. Which meant two things: their grandmother would probably never come home again and their grandfather, as galling as it must be to him to admit, needed Lydia's help with Valerie.

Uncle Brad had been as furious with her as Joey. 'You stupid little idiot!' he'd roared at her. 'Don't you dare come near me with that holy "I have to do the right thing" crap! You're throwing your life away. Don't you understand that?'

'Did you think you were throwing away your life when you stepped in to bring up Noah?'

'That was completely different,' he'd yelled, stomping off to his studio. He'd reappeared five minutes later brandishing the portrait he'd painted of her and announced he'd be selling it at his next exhibition. He'd said he couldn't bear to lay eyes on it knowing that she could be such a bloody useless fool.

Whilst she was hurt by Uncle Brad's condemnation, it was nothing like the sick, empty loneliness Noah's silence invoked. She longed for him to voice his feelings, but all she got from him was an anxious permanently preoccupied look.

The teachers pitched in, but only fleetingly. What could they say, anyway? Other than tactfully murmur about her taking up a university place as a mature student in years to come.

The person who wouldn't let up, though, was Donna. Every time Lydia saw her, Donna would remind her what a mistake she was making. She was doing it now as they sat with the children watching television. 'OK, so tell me what's the one thing yer've dreamt of doing ever since yer came to live in this dump of a place?'

'Change the record, why don't you?' Lydia answered her. 'I've heard it all before and there's nothing you can say to make me change my mind.'

'Like fu—'

'Don't swear in front of the children,' Lydia interrupted, just as Kirk leapt up from the shag pile rug and reached for the money box on top of the telly.

'I'll do as I piggin' well please. This is *my* house, in case it had slipped yer memory.'

It was ironic that as Lydia's life was becoming horribly tangled, Donna's was straightening out nicely. Donna had recently moved out of her aunt's place and was now happily installed in her very own council house. She'd got herself a part-time job in the evenings, stacking shelves at the new supermarket that had opened in town. Noah also worked there, along with Alfie Stone, and sometimes they all stacked shelves together. Occasionally Noah worked on the delicatessen counter on a Saturday, when he had to wear a paper hat with the words 'A Taste of the Continent' printed on it. He had to slice exotic cold meats like peppered salami and hand out samples of Polish sausages. Lydia had bought some once, as well as a round of Camembert in a sort of flimsy wooden case, and had taken it home only to have her grandfather condemn it as foreign muck.

While Donna was doing her shelf-stacking shift, Lydia babysat Captain Kirk, now two and a half, and Lydia Junior, who was thirteen months. If their grandfather was out for the evening, as he so often was, Valerie would come with Lydia. She was wary of Donna – but then who wasn't? – and occupied herself by playing with the children, patiently building towers of wooden blocks for them to knock down. Happy now to leave the house, she was once again attending church. She'd even made the transition to big school and had progressed to speaking in a whispered gruff voice, which fascinated Kirk and Lydia Junior. This evening she was having supper with Sister Vera and Sister Joan.

'Yer know what really bugs me,' Donna said after lighting up a cigarette, 'is that I really believed in yer. I really thought yer knew what yer were about. Idiot that I was, I actually respected and admired yer. Christ on a bike, I thought I wanted to *be* yer at one stage!'

Once again Kirk was on his feet and rattling the money under his mother's nose.

'Give over, Kirky, I didn't swear.'

Sharing a smile with Kirk, Lydia said, 'Blasphemy incurs a fine as well.'

'I'll have to write yer an IOU, Kirky,' Donna said. She then pointed a finger at Lydia. 'Kitchen. Now. We need to have a private conversation.'

Out in the kitchen, Donna began slamming cupboard doors as she made them some coffee.

'You'll have the council round here if you carry on like that,' Lydia commented. 'This being council property.'

Donna thumped the jar of Maxwell House down on the counter. 'Like I give a damn! Now shut up and listen to me for once. Think about what I just said. I believed in yer. It was *you* who taught me to read. *You* who got me to be a better mum. Not some do-gooding, arsed-faced teacher, or some tosspot of a social worker. And that takes something rare and special. You're by far the cleverest person I know, so why the hell do yer want to chuck it all away?'

'I'm not chucking it away; I'm just putting it to a different use.'

'And then what? Yer'll stay at home until Val's eighteen, then what happens?'

'Valerie will go to university and I'll—'

As if she hadn't spoken, Donna stabbed a teaspoon in the air just inches from Lydia's face. 'I'll tell yer what happens. Val's going nowhere when she hits eighteen. After everything that nutty grandmother of yours has put the girl through, she's going nowhere but Swallowsdale for the rest of her life.'

'Well, if that's true, there's even more reason for me to stick around and make sure that doesn't happen.'

The teaspoon nearly made contact with Lydia's nose. 'It's too late!' Donna snapped. Then less angrily, she said, 'Look, Lydia, I know yer love yer sister and want the best for her but the way I see it, she'd be better off being looked after by that church of yours. She's one of them, isn't she? In a way you never were and never will be. Didn't yer once tell me she was never happier than when she was at church?'

Feeling less sure of herself now, Lydia said, 'What you're saying is out of the question. I couldn't abandon her to them.'

'It wouldn't be abandoning her. Your mate Sister Lottie would be there for her. I can always keep an eye on her too. After all, she knows me well enough now. And the kids. And it's not as if yer'd be going to a university on t'other side of the world. Yer'll have holidays and weekends to come home and make sure she's OK.'

Donna's words should have gone in one ear and straight out the other. But they didn't. For days afterwards, they lingered inside Lydia's head, whispering to her that maybe, just maybe, with Sister Lottie's help, it could work. But it was a lot to ask of Sister Lottie. And what about the guilt Lydia would always carry round with her, knowing that she had put her own needs above those of Valerie?

The one person in all of this whose opinion Lydia hadn't asked, was the most important person: Valerie.

Four months had passed since Valerie had gone out that night with their grandmother thinking that they were both about to be snatched up to heaven, their souls to be for ever saved. No one, least of all the child psychologist – whom Valerie no longer visited – had managed to get her to speak about that night. Doctor Bunch said she had probably blocked it out of her memory, like the time Lydia had woken up in hospital and hadn't been able to remember how she'd got there. Except, of course, she had remembered in the end. So maybe Valerie was keeping quiet in just the same way Lydia had.

What she did talk about now was that God spoke to her and that she had visions. Mystical visions. They came to her quite regularly, she said. Her claims made a shiver run up Lydia's spine. God only knew what the child psychologist would have made of it. Sharing her concerns with Sister Lottie, they decided to hope for the best and put it down as a brief phase of attention-seeking by showing off a very special imaginary friend. Although Sister Lottie was quick to point out to Lydia, there was nothing imaginary about God. And while they also both felt that Val was too old to have an imaginary friend, given the circumstances they didn't think it was that surprising she would want the comfort of one.

Valerie may not have made any real friends at school, but she did have a tentative friendship of sorts at church. A new family had joined them – Brother Gordon and his wife, Sister Prue. They had a son called Brian. Brian was two years older than Valerie and never went anywhere without a droopy-eared rabbit made out of patchwork fabric. He'd latched onto Valerie right at the outset. They always sat together and he trailed round after her when tea and biscuits were being served, his clumsy lumbering body towering above her. Sometimes he got a bit excitable and knocked things over and Valerie would shush him with a single look and a finger pressed to her lips. It was clear to everyone at church that he worshipped the ground Valerie walked on.

'But I want you to know that if you're not happy with what I've suggested, I won't go to university,' Lydia said. 'I'll stay here and take care of you. I'll do whatever you want me to do.'

It was Saturday afternoon and Lydia and Valerie were walking back from the bus stop, having been into town to buy Valerie her first bra. She had grown dramatically this year and Lydia had already given her the 'talk' about what to do when her periods started.

'Of course you must go, Lydia,' Val replied gruffly. 'How could you even think of not going?'

'But I hate the idea of leaving you here alone with our grandfather.'

'But I won't be alone. Grandma will come home soon. And anyway, I don't think your presence here helps.'

Lydia slowed her step. She let the remark about their grandmother go and said, 'Who or what aren't I help-ing?'

'Please don't be cross, but I'm sure I could take better care of our grandfather if you weren't here. You do seem to have a habit of upsetting him.'

Lydia hung onto her jaw. 'Shouldn't it be *him* taking care of *you*?'

'I'm not a child, Lydia. I really wish you'd stop treating me as one.'

'You're not yet twelve,' Lydia pressed.

'Age is unimportant. It's what the Lord wants of me that counts.'

'And what exactly does the Lord want of you?' Lydia hardly dared think.

'To serve him in all ways. It's time for me to "put childish ways behind me", one Corinthians chapter thirteen, verse eleven. I know you mean well, but you've wrapped me in cotton wool for long enough. I have to learn to stand on my own two feet.'

Every one of Val's responses should have made Lydia feel happier about leaving her, but this irritating I'm-a-big-girl-now routine made her want to scream with frustration. 'It's not as if I'll be leaving home permanently,' she said as calmly as she could. 'I'll be backwards and forwards all the time.' She attempted a light laugh. 'You'll be sick of the sight of me.'

Valerie didn't say anything, she just carried on walking, her eyes straight ahead, her chin up as rain began to fall. She didn't even flinch when the Rottweiler bared its teeth and hurled itself at the gate of number twenty-five.

Feeling hurt and confused, Lydia tried one more time to elicit an emotion from her sister that she felt was genuine and not some evangelical cliché. 'Will you miss me?' she asked.

'Don't be silly, of course I'll miss you. You're my sister. And I'll pray every day for you not to come to any harm. Now let's not talk about it any more. When the time comes, you're going away to university and that's an end to it.'

Chapter Forty-Seven

It was the night before Lydia's first A-level exam when she had a massive shock. In the big scheme of disasters that had so far dotted her life, it was actually pretty small potatoes, but it was still nasty and unwelcome. It came just when she least needed anything to distract her. Ever since both she and Noah had received conditional offers from Oxford University, her every waking thought had been focused on achieving the required grades. Grades that would set her free! Amen and hallelujah with bells on to that!

Their grandfather was out and Valerie had gone to answer the door – Lydia was at the kitchen table trying to cram her head with some last-minute quotes from *Hamlet* – and from the second she heard the hearty greeting Valerie received, she was on her feet. Three years had passed, but she would know that voice anywhere. The last they'd heard, he'd returned to Australia, so what was he doing here? And how did he have the nerve to come back? Heaven only knew what their grandfather would say.

For some inexplicable reason Valerie was welcoming him in. There was cheek-turning and then there was sheer bloody madness!

Lydia went out to the hall. A chilly wind was gusting in through the open door. 'Great-Uncle Leonard,' she said.

She was greeted with a loud wolf-whistle. 'Well, if it ain't my damsel of a grand-niece! Just look at you! Quite the sight for sore eyes. You must be eighteen now; am I right?'

'What brings you to Swallowsdale?' she replied coldly. 'We're hardly on your doorstep, are we?'

'Now if you don't mind me saying, that doesn't sound too friendly. But I can understand your animosity. I was just telling your sweet little sis that the Lord has dragged me here by the scruff of my neck. I told him, "Lord, I can't go back there. I made a terrible mistake during my last stay. I'll go anywhere you want, just not Swallowsdale." You know what he said to me?'

'Surprise me.'

'He said, "Leonard, you may be the blackest of my sheep, but take my word for it: them folk are the only people who can save you. Your salvation depends on them forgiving you."'

'I seem to remember you saying something similar once before.'

'Indeed I did. And I'm ashamed to say I screwed up my chance then.' He laughed. 'But what can I say? God seems intent on saving me.'

And before Lydia could say anything else, Uncle Leonard had deftly closed the door behind him and was shoving his scruffy suitcase towards the bottom step of the stairs, messing up the rug and nearly knocking over the telephone table. He reeked of aftershave. Not Brut, as before. But something just as strong and overpowering.

While Uncle Leonard was upstairs relieving himself in the bathroom – the embarrassingly loud Niagara Falls sound of him suggesting he hadn't done so since he was last here – Lydia was in the kitchen with her sister. 'Val,' she said, 'it's very important that you listen to me. That man is not to be trusted. He lies and steals and he doesn't care who he does it to.'

Her sister stared at her blankly. 'We can't turn him away. That would be wrong. If God has told Uncle Leonard to come here then I'm sure Pastor Digby would say it's our duty to help him.'

Above their heads, Niagara Falls was coming to a trickling stop-start finish. 'Pastor Digby won't want to help him, I guarantee it,' Lydia said.

But Valerie stared serenely back at Lydia. 'He will when I tell him about a vision I had some weeks ago.'

Lydia tried not to overreact. She was tired of her sister's supposed gift of prophecy and had listened patiently to many of these so-called visions. They ranged from simple pronouncements such as God loving everyone, or Valerie foretelling that someone was going to receive good or bad news in the coming days, to more complicated and ambitious predictions to do with angels and plagues and golden cups. The latter Lydia invariably put down to Val's imagination working overtime after Pastor Digby had read from Revelation in church.

'So what was this dream about?' she asked her sister.

Valerie frowned. 'I've told you before; it's a vision, not a dream. God showed me a man knocking on our door, asking to take shelter from the storm that was on its way.'

There'll be a storm all right, thought Lydia, just as heavy footsteps thudded across the landing. But the knocking on the door vision wasn't new. Valerie had described similar scenes before. They were nothing more than dreams influenced by basic New Testament teaching – don't turn anyone away because it could be Christ disguised in filthy tramp's rags on your doorstep.

Uncle Leonard was halfway down the stairs when Lydia heard the sound of their grandfather putting his key in the front door lock.

From the kitchen doorway, she saw it all: the challenging look on Uncle Leonard's face as he continued slowly down the stairs, and the expression of shock and hatred on the other man's face. If looks could kill, Uncle Leonard would be lucky to see the night through.

Their grandfather carefully shut the door. He uttered just three words. 'Lydia. Valerie. Upstairs.'

Some masochistic desire to stick around to watch the fireworks made Lydia say, 'But I was revising.'

'Then do it upstairs!' When neither she nor Valerie had moved so much as an eyelash, he roared at them. '*NOW!*'

*

In the morning, just as soon as she'd finished her breakfast, Lydia was summoned to the front room. Doubtless her grandfather wanted to confide in her so they could devise a way between them to get rid of the sly, deceitful man who, even now, was hogging the bathroom when she needed to brush her teeth before catching the bus for college.

She could not have been more wrong.

'My brother will be staying with us for a while,' her grandfather said, his back to Lydia as he stood looking out onto the front garden, the wind and rain lashing the window as they had done for most of the night. He turned round. 'I expect you to welcome him into our home and treat him with respect. Do you understand?'

Lydia's jaw dropped.

Chapter Forty-Eight

For years now Lydia had had the Brothers and Sisters down as a fickle and naive lot, and so it really should not have come as a surprise when they were once again taken in by Uncle Leonard's claims that without their help and forgiveness he was sunk.

Their forgiveness of him – self-acknowledged and hopeless sinner as he was – was to be decided during an emergency meeting of the most senior members of the church and was being held at number thirty-three Hillside Terrace, exactly twenty-four hours after his arrival. Apparently Uncle Leonard had gone to Pastor Digby earlier in the day and thrown himself on the man's mercy. As a consequence, here they all were, crammed into the front room.

Everyone had had something to say, including Valerie. She had asked to be allowed to give her own personal testimony in support of Uncle Leonard. His return to Swallowsdale had been foretold in a vision God had personally given her, she explained, up on her feet. With her gruff voice strained to its limits, she went into considerable detail about her mystical vision, embroidering her tale with all sorts of extras that interestingly she hadn't given Lydia last night. The whole thing stank of theatrics. Val was enjoying herself just a little too much – her pretty face was utterly animated, her eyes were wide and glittering, her cheeks flushed. But then Val revealed her trump card, and she did it with such a beatific flourish, you'd have thought she'd just turned water into wine. 'God told me that after Uncle Leonard's return,' she paused for dramatic effect, her eyes wider still, her hands extended, 'a terrible storm would follow in his footsteps.' A gasp went round the room. A storm! And what had happened that very night? While Uncle Leonard had been snoring his head off in the spare room, thunder had cracked and boomed overhead and a deluge of rain had poured from the heavens. Such a torrent, in fact, that part of the church's corrugated roof had given way and water had poured in, taking out the electrics.

How could the assembled gathering not fall for it?

But equally so, how could Lydia's grandfather just sit there and not say anything? Surely he didn't believe any of this ridiculous hokum? Why had he even let the wretched man stay the night in his house?

As the final clincher, just in case there were any doubters lurking amongst the group, Uncle Leonard got to his feet and offered to put his building skills to use free of charge – oh, that was big of him! – by repairing the church roof. 'I sure as heck have no idea what the Lord wants from me, but whilst I'm here, I might just as well try to do something useful,' he said.

'In the light of what we've been told by Sister Valerie,' Pastor Digby said, also rising to his feet, 'I think it would be a good idea if you stepped outside for a while so we can come to a decision.'

Uncle Leonard wasn't the only one to be banished from the room: Lydia and Sister Lottie were asked to go and make some tea. Interestingly, Valerie was allowed to stay. Perhaps they wanted to be held in rapture by her story all over again?

'I do hope we haven't been too hasty in all of this,' Sister Lottie whispered later when she and Lydia were washing up and Uncle Leonard's readmittance into the fold had been confirmed.

Lydia was surprised to hear Sister Lottie, of all people, question what was going on. She was always so generous in wanting to find the best in another person. Her goodwill was endless. 'Why do you say that?' Lydia asked her.

With her head bent over the saucer she was drying so intently, the old lady said, 'False prophets can be very convincing, not to say appealing and ...' Her words trailed off.

Lydia saw why. Val was standing in the doorway. Standing tall and straight-backed, she looked immensely pleased with herself. 'Christ had no time for doubters and gossipers,' she said primly.

Uncle Leonard was behind her. He was smiling directly at Lydia, as if to say, there's not a damn thing you can do to get rid of me. I'm here for as long as I want to be. He even had the cheek to wink at her. She could have punched his ugly face into a bloodied pulp.

As disturbing as this thought was, it was nothing compared to the sight of his proprietorial hand placed on Val's shoulder. He certainly knew which side his bread was buttered. Valerie had stuck up for him in a way he could never have foreseen, so now, all of a sudden, she was his new best friend.

Noah had once said that he didn't understand the first thing about her, when he'd tried to coax out of Lydia what was being done to her at home and she'd refused his offer of help. But since that day last summer when he'd driven her to Maywood and she'd shared with him what she'd hidden for so long, he'd not only made her promise that she would never lie to him again, even by omission, but had apologized for not understanding sooner the reasons for her secrecy. He'd also made her promise that she would never blame herself again for her mother's death. Some days she managed to convince herself that this was true, but then other days the guilt would creep up on her, tap her on the shoulder and say, 'Hi, remember me?' Keeping relentlessly busy was the answer, she'd found. Leave herself with no time to dwell on those old memories and she was able to put them out of her mind.

Revising for her exams was perfect for blocking out anything she didn't want to be reminded of, and today, with her final exam tomorrow morning, she was in the garden stretched out on her front on an old towel, leaning on her elbows while eating an ice-cream she'd bought from Joey. Discreetly positioned so no prying neighbours could see her over the fence, she was enjoying the warm sun on her back.

She'd just eaten the last mouthful of the ice-cream when a shadow fell across the page of her *Wuthering Heights* study notes. She scrambled to an upright position and grabbed for her top which she'd removed, sure in the knowledge that she had the house and garden to herself for the afternoon – Grandfather was visiting Grandmother, Val was at school, and Uncle Leonard was supposed to be fixing the church roof. He was not supposed to be here, catching her sunbathing while she was half undressed!

But she wasn't quick enough. Smiling, Uncle Leonard dangled her top in front of her. Embarrassed, she stood up to take it from him, but he snatched it away. 'What will you give me in return for it, my little damsel in distress?' he asked.

Embarrassment now turning to anger, she covered herself with the towel, securing it firmly under her arm. She glared at him. 'I'm not your little damsel,' she said.

'Oh, don't be like that. Not after everything I did for you. Here, take it.'

Once again she put her hand out for her top, but just as he'd done before, he flicked it out of her reach. She was close enough to him now to be aware of the cloying smell of his aftershave. And to know that he'd been drinking. He stank of another hard day at the pub.

'Just give it to me,' she said.

'Say please.'

'*Please*,' she said through gritted teeth. But she didn't move her hand. She didn't trust him. She could see he was just going to make her look stupid again.

Grinning, he said, 'Go on. It's yours. Take it.'

Her annoyance growing, she did as he said, only to find herself suddenly caught in his strong grip. Startled, she let out a cry of alarm. 'That's better,' he said, both of his hands around her now. 'Doesn't that feel nice and cosy?'

'Let go of me,' she gasped.

'Don't be like that. I just want us to be friends. Special friends. Is that too much to ask?'

'Friends don't steal from each other.'

'Everyone else has forgiven me; why can't you?'

'Because I don't trust you. Now let go of me!' She tried again to wriggle out of his revolting hands.

But he just laughed and increased his hold on her. 'A little recognition for when I came to your rescue is what I'm after, Lydia. I reckon you owe me something by way of thanks, don't you?' He trailed a finger along her bare shoulder, stopping at her bra strap. 'How about a kiss? For starters. If you know what I mean.'

In a state of shock and panic, she tried to shove him away. But it was no good. He was so much bigger and stronger than she was. She started to shout at him, hoping one of the neighbours would hear.

He clamped a hand over her mouth. 'Not so loud, my little damsel. We don't want to disturb anyone, do we? And really, you know, you shouldn't go parading your half-naked body round the place without expecting trouble. You have only yourself to blame. But then you know that deep down, don't you?' He then slowly removed his hand from her mouth, and before she was able to draw breath, he slammed his rough, dry lips against hers, and jabbed his fat tongue around inside her mouth. His rank, boozy tobacco breath made her want to gag and she willed herself to be sick over him. She fought to break free, but his enormous hands were holding her fast, digging into her skin. When he started rubbing himself against her and pushed one of his hands under the towel and between her legs, anger turned to paralysing fear. What if he raped her? The house was empty. They were alone. How could she stop him?

Then as suddenly as he'd grabbed her, he let her go. 'That's just a taste of what's to come,' he said. 'Because I'll tell you this: before I leave Swallowsdale, you're going to pay me back what you owe me. It's my right. My reward. And who knows, you might even enjoy it.'

'I'll kill you before that happens! I swear it.'

He laughed. 'Such tough, brave words from you. But then I've seen you in the woods, Lydia. You're not the innocent girl you make out to be, are you? I've followed you several times now and got a right old eyeful of you and that crippled boyfriend of yours. Oh, don't look so outraged. You put on a nice little show, the pair of you. Really turned up the voltage for me.'

'I'm going to tell my grandfather what you've just done to me,' she hissed, shaking with murderous hatred.

'Tell him whatever you like. It won't make a jot of difference. Haven't you figured it out yet?'

'Figured what out?'

'That it's me who's in charge now. I'm the one calling the shots. Your grandfather will do whatever I ask him to. If I asked him to strip you naked and deliver you to my room, he'd do it. Why do you think he changed his mind about me staying here again?'

'I don't know. Just as I don't understand why you came back in the first place.'

An evil smile oozed across his bloated, leathery face. 'I've always believed a good con is worth trying more than once. You see, a little birdie told me what your grandfather's been up to. He's a very wicked man, you know. Much worse than me. There he is, pretending to be oh-so-good and virtuous, when all the time he's hiding a dark and dirty secret. But that's fine by me because it gives me a nice bit of financial leverage. And that's very handy since I'm down on my luck again.'

The penny dropped for Lydia. 'You've got something on my grandfather? You're blackmailing him?'

'As surely as God made little green apples. It's something he would never want anyone to know about. While his loopy old wife's locked up making raffia baskets, he's at it like a rutting ram, and all the while pretending to those crackpots at that church of yours that he's whiter than white.'

'He's having an *affair*?' Lydia's voice was nearly as shrill as the blackbird that was innocently singing its heart out in the tree next to them. 'An *affair*?' she repeated. 'I don't believe it.'

'As true as I'm standing here. Been at it for years. If it isn't true, my sweet, voluptuous Lydia, why has he allowed me to move back in? Eh?'

'Why didn't you expose him when you were here three years ago?'

'Because all I had on him then was that he'd been unfaithful to Irene when they were first married. He was terrified I was going to spill the beans on him, but then you went and spoilt everything by siding with him. My word against the two of you … I knew the odds were stacked against me.'

'And now?'

'Now's different.' He tapped his nose. 'I've got all the information I need to keep my brother just where I want him.'

'So why did you go through with that fiasco of seeking forgiveness from Pastor Digby and the others?'

'In my experience, a little extra insurance never hurt anyone. That, and I can't help myself. They're so naive. So easy to manipulate.'

'You're pure evil, aren't you?'

'If that's the case,' he said with a wink, 'you'd better watch yourself.'

The more Lydia thought about it that night in bed, the more she knew it had to be true. Of course her grandfather had been having an affair. Why else would he be spending so much time away from the house? Why else would he flatly refuse to take Val with him when he claimed to be visiting their grandmother? She recalled a day a long, long time ago when she was cycling home with Val and she'd seen his car parked in town when he was supposed to be away somewhere. Had he been carrying on then with someone? Was it the same woman now, all these years on? If so, who? Someone from church? Surely not. She ran through the list of Sisters in the congregation and couldn't for the life of her imagine any of them in bed with her grandfather. For that matter, she couldn't imagine her grandfather in bed with anyone other than her grandmother, and then it was only to fall asleep. Wasn't he too old for sex?

Not if his brother was anything to go by.

She shuddered. After what Uncle Leonard had done to her in the garden that afternoon, she'd waited for him to go out again, then locked herself in the bathroom for an hour. She'd scrubbed every inch of her body in the bath and brushed her teeth until her gums bled. But nothing could take away the sense of violation she felt. She felt dirty, inside and out. And ashamed that somehow she'd allowed the situation to happen. Never again would she sunbathe in the garden like that.

But what if he tried it again? What if he really meant to make her pay him back as he'd said? To claim his reward? Oh, God, and to think she'd trusted him once.

She would have to be vigilant. She would make sure she was never alone in the house with him, either. She would arm herself with Val at all times. He would never dare try anything with Val around.

What was almost as sickening as what he'd done to her that afternoon was knowing that he had spied on her and Noah in their special place in the dell. They had always been careful, but she supposed they'd got away with it for so long, they had grown complacent and assumed they had the place to themselves.

Despite her promise not to keep anything from Noah, Lydia had no intention of telling him what Uncle Leonard had said and done to her. She knew he would go ballistic. But the following day at college, when they'd finished their very last exam and he leaned over in his car to kiss her, she recoiled from him. She hadn't meant to. Her body had simply reacted of its own accord.

As usual, whenever she did something he didn't fully understand, Noah didn't comment on it straight away, just gave her a quick puzzled glance which left her feeling worthless and guilty. He raised the matter later, though, when he'd driven them to his house and they were sitting at the wooden table in the shade of the cherry tree where he was slicing an apple with his Swiss Army knife. Anxious to put his mind at rest, needing him to know that it was nothing he had done to upset her, she reluctantly told him everything. She instantly felt better for sharing it with him.

But not for long. Noah was very still. His face had turned dark with anger. When he spoke, his voice was so low she had to lean forward to hear him. 'I don't want you going back there, Lyddie,' he said. 'Stay the night here with me. Where I'll know you'll be safe.'

'I can't do that, Noah.'

'I don't see why not. You're eighteen. You can do what you want.'

'Thanks, but I'll be fine. So long as I stay on my guard.'

Noah gripped the penknife in his hand and drove the point of it viciously hard into the surface of the table. 'You make sure you do. But I'm telling you now, if he touches you, or threatens you again, I'll go after him. I'll push this knife straight through his ribs and out the other side.' Again his voice was low and tightly controlled.

'Sorry to disappoint you, but if anyone's going to stick a knife in him, it'll be me.'

'I'm serious, Lyddie.'

She walked home, full of regret now that she'd told Noah what she had. She should have lied, made up some story to fob him off. She had never seen him stay angry for so long. They should have been celebrating the end of their exams, but instead, Noah was morose and locked deep in his own thoughts. It was all her fault. Her and her great big mouth. When would she ever learn?

As she climbed over the wall at the end of the garden and wondered what awaited her at home, she considered the possibility of counter-blackmailing her grandfather by insisting that if he didn't get rid of his brother, she would tell everyone at church about the affair he was having. Which, apart from putting her grandfather between a rock and a hard place, did raise an interesting question: whose will would he bend to?

While scraping the potatoes for tea, Lydia listened out for Uncle Leonard's movements upstairs. She knew he was up there, but whatever he was doing, he was very quiet. As was Val. Maybe she was having another of her so-called mystical visions. Immediately Lydia was cross with herself for having such a mean-spirited thought. For all she knew, Val might well turn out to be some kind of modern-day prophet. She smiled at the thought, picturing pilgrims from all over the world visiting number thirty-three Hillside Terrace in search of enlightenment.

She had almost finished the potatoes when the telephone rang. If her grandfather was in the house she wouldn't dream of 'being too big for her boots' and answering the phone, but since he was 'visiting their grandmother' she wiped her hands and went out to the hall.

'Is Mr Turner there, please?' asked a woman with a crisp, well-ironed voice.

'No, I'm sorry, he's out at the moment.' Busy rutting like a ram, she was tempted to add. 'Can I pass on a message for him? I'm his granddaughter.'

'Well, it's a bit awkward, really.' The crisp voice wasn't so crisp now. Lydia wondered fleetingly if this was the object of all the secret rutting. 'But I suppose it will have to do. My name's Mrs Vickers and I'm calling from the hospital. The thing is, his wife has disappeared. We can't find her anywhere.'

The sound of a door opening upstairs momentarily

distracted Lydia and out of the corner of her eye she saw Uncle Leonard crossing the landing to the bathroom. 'We wondered,' continued Mrs Vickers, whose voice had now lost all its professional poise, 'well, to be honest, we're hoping that she might, like a homing pigeon, find her way back to you. If she does, we'd be grateful if you could telephone us right away. Meanwhile, I'm afraid we're going to have to call the police to help us find her. She could be anywhere.'

Within seconds of ending the conversation, Lydia's first thought was how to keep the news from her sister. Val would worry herself sick if she thought their grandmother was wandering the streets, lost and confused. A ring at the doorbell made her jump. For a split second she wondered if their grandmother had found her way home already.

But it wasn't their grandmother: it was Joey. At once Lydia could see something was wrong; he looked so unhappy. 'I didn't want to leave without saying goodbye, Lydia,' he said. 'I wanted to wish you well for when you go to university.'

'Goodbye? But where are you going?'

'I'm going home. I heard today that my mother is very ill. It is not good news. She has had an attack of the head, no, I mean, of the heart. Forgive me; I am so upset, my English is all over the place.'

'Oh, Joey, I'm so sorry. When are you leaving?'

'Tomorrow. Early.' He almost smiled. Just a small flicker. 'But not before breakfast. I do not think the good Sister Lottie will allow me to leave without something to eat before my long journey.'

'Do you think you'll be back next year?'

He shrugged. '*Chi sa?* Who knows? If my poor *mama* dies, then I will have to stay and look after the rest of the family.'

The thought that she might never see Joey again filled Lydia with such sadness, she put her arms around him. 'If you don't come back I'll come and visit you in Italy one day. That's a promise.'

They were just pulling apart when Lydia heard a roar and saw Noah's red sports car hurtling at top speed down the road. Just inches from Joey's rusting old Ford, he swerved to a stop, tyres squealing. Slamming the car door shut, he made his way up the garden path. She could see he had something on his mind. He was so agitated he didn't even acknowledge Joey. 'Lyddie,' he said, 'I want to speak to that bastard uncle of yours. I can't stop thinking about what he said he'd do to you.'

Joey frowned anxiously. 'Would you like me to stay, Lydia?'

'Um ... it's OK, Joey. You go. I can sort this out.'

Noah swung round and faced Joey. 'That's just the point: she can't sort it out. He's threatened to rape her. I mean, he's her great-uncle, for God's sake! What kind of a sick pervert is he? And what kind of a boyfriend would I be to stand by and let that happen?'

Lydia put a hand out to Noah to try and shush him; his raised voice was attracting curious neighbours out on the street. But Noah wasn't having it. 'Please, Lyddie, you've been through enough. I won't let you suffer again at the hands of this twisted family of yours.'

'Is this true?' Joey asked. 'Has this man touched you? Your uncle Leonard?'

'Hello, hello, hel*lo*. What's going on here, then? Do my ears deceive me, or do I hear my name being taken in vain?'

Ambling nonchalantly down the stairs was Uncle Leonard. Noah took one look at him and hurled himself over the doorstep. 'You! I want a word with you. And then I'm going to fucking kill you!'

Chapter Forty-Nine

Noah's fist slammed straight into Uncle Leonard's face.

Rocking back on his heels, Uncle Leonard put a hand to his mouth, saw that he was bleeding and then glared at Noah. There was a furious glint in his eye. 'You're gonna bloody well pay for that, sonny.'

'Oh, yeah?' yelled Noah. 'Well, so are you for touching Lydia.' He raised his fist again, but Uncle Leonard was ready for him this time and moved fast. He blocked Noah's arm, then aimed a vicious kick at his leg. His bad leg. Noah crumpled and dropped to the floor. He clutched his ankle and groaned.

'Boys still wet behind the ears shouldn't take on grown men,' Uncle Leonard said dismissively, as if he'd done nothing more than swat an annoying fly out of his way.

A surge of savage rage filled Lydia and she took a swing at him herself. To her amazement, she landed a punch smack on his nose and felt something squish beneath her knuckles. Blood gushed. It was such a satisfying sight, that and the look of astonishment on his face, that she experienced a heady rush to hit him again. She flexed her arm, all set to unleash another punch, but Joey stepped in and took hold of her elbow. '*Basta*,' he said, quietly. 'Enough.' He pointed to the top of the stairs where Valerie was staring down at them. She looked petrified. 'This is not good for her to see.'

Joey was right. And ignoring Uncle Leonard's shout for someone to give him a handkerchief – blood was pouring from his nose and dripping onto his clothes – Lydia bent down to help Noah to his feet.

She'd just got him upright when her grandfather appeared at the door. He took in the scene with a look of icy disapproval. 'What the hell's going on here?' he demanded.

'Try asking your brother,' Lydia flung back at him.

Noah was all for having it out there and then, with both men, but Lydia pleaded with him not to. 'Please,' she begged, dragging him outside with Joey's help. 'It's better that you go.'

'But I can't leave you here like this,' he said, struggling hard to break free and go back inside the house.

'If you stay, you'll only make things worse,' Lydia said firmly. 'I don't want Valerie getting any more upset. Please, just leave everything to me.'

His anger was still palpable, but she could see she'd left him no choice and reluctantly he let her steer him to his car. 'I'll never forgive myself if anything happens to you. Ring me if you need me. Promise?'

'I promise. But only if you promise to calm down and stop worrying.' Remembering that his uncle was away until tomorrow, she added, 'When the dust's settled here, I'll come and see you later tonight. OK?'

He opened the car door and got in. 'No, I've got a better idea; I'll meet you halfway. In the dell. Midnight. That way we'll know we've got the place to ourselves.'

'Will your leg be all right?'

He nodded and reached up to kiss her, his hand on the nape of her neck. 'Take care,' he said. She kissed him back. But only briefly. She was conscious that they still had an audience.

He started the engine, reversed away from Joey's car, then pulled out. 'I'll be waiting for you!' he called to her as he drove off.

She waved at him, then turned to Joey. He looked serious. 'There is real evil in there, Lydia,' he said, glancing back at the house. 'I don't feel happy returning to Italy knowing what I now know. Like Noah, I too do not want to leave you here.'

'But you have to go, Joey. Your mother needs you. Besides, I've a feeling everything's going to be different from now on.'

He looked doubtful. 'I could finish off what Noah started,' he said.

She smiled. 'It was you who stopped it in the first place.'

He didn't return her smile. Instead he hugged her and said, 'Promise me you will look after yourself.'

I've been looking after myself since for ever, she thought, waving him goodbye.

Ignoring the handful of neighbours who were still hanging around in case there was anything else worthwhile seeing, she edged her way around them and found herself face to face with Uncle Leonard, who was standing by the gate. How long had he been standing there with a handkerchief pressed to his nose? 'Perhaps you should get yourself off to the doctor and have that looked at,' she said, barging past him.

'Don't think I won't get my own back,' he snarled.

'My, what a big man you are. Threatening girls and kicking boys wet behind the ears. What's your problem? Got a small willy?'

Inside the house, her grandfather was waiting for her in the front room. 'I'd like an explanation,' he said.

'As I said earlier, why don't you ask your brother for one?' responded Lydia. 'When you've done that, tell him to push off out of Swallowsdale for good.'

Nostrils flaring, he stared at her, then at Uncle Leonard, who'd come in behind her. She tried not to feel as if she was caught between the two of them.

'Just what gives you the right to tell me what to do?' her grandfather said, plumping up his chest to assume his usual air of authority.

She took a step towards him, reminded of that very first time she had stood in this room and cowered beneath his scrutinizing gaze. But that was then. This was now. Never had she felt more sure of herself.

'Your reign of terror is over, Grandfather,' she said. 'You can stick your pompous, self-righteous, holier-than-thou act where the sun doesn't shine. I know about your affair. I also know about your brother blackmailing you. But, and here's the dilemma for you, if you don't agree to get rid of him by this time tomorrow, I will tell everyone, and I mean *everyone*, about your sordid double life. Oh, and you might like to know, the hospital telephoned earlier to say Grandmother's disappeared. They haven't a clue where she is and were calling the police to look for her. But then I suppose it would be wonderful news for you if she were to be found dead in a ditch somewhere. How convenient that would be for you.'

The powerful energy that had fuelled her words in the front room soon fizzled away to nothing, and by the time Lydia reached the top of the stairs she felt emotionally and physically drained.

She tapped on the bedroom door – something she and Valerie always did now as a mark of respect for each other's privacy – and went inside. But Valerie wasn't there.

Nor was she in the bathroom.

Where had she gone? And when? Lydia stood on the landing, concerned. What if her sister had overheard what Lydia had just said about their grandmother? *Wonderful news … Dead in a ditch …* Lydia cursed herself. Why couldn't she ever think before she spoke?

Lydia had good cause to be concerned about her sister. She reappeared in time for tea – it was only the two of them eating, thank goodness – but Val refused to say where she'd been. In fact, she refused to speak at all. Not even a whisper. Nor would she write anything down as she'd done before when she'd been upset. All Lydia could assume was that after overhearing her conversation with their grandfather, Valerie had irrationally rushed straight out to look for her precious grandmother. Lydia tried her best to reassure her by saying there wasn't anything to worry about, that by the morning everything would have been sorted out. But it made no difference to her. Valerie just sat there at the table, glassy-eyed and silent. She was unreachable.

They went to bed early. Lydia didn't want to be downstairs when either her grandfather or Uncle Leonard returned home. Her grandfather had been out all evening, having driven off shortly after she'd given him her ultimatum. Minutes later, Uncle Leonard had left the house, too.

Lydia's plan was that she would snatch an hour or two of sleep, and then when the house was perfectly quiet, she would go and see Noah.

But she ended up sleeping the sleep of the dead. Mid-dream, she woke with a start. It was the kind of start that made her think something – a footstep perhaps – had woken her.

She checked the luminous hands on her alarm clock and saw to her dismay that it was ten minutes past one. Poor Noah, he would have been waiting all this time for her. Worse, he was probably worrying himself sick, imagining that something terrible had happened to her.

After listening for the tell-tale steady breathing sound that told her Valerie was fast asleep, she pushed back the bed covers. From the floor, she picked up her shoes and carefully folded clothes, and quietly padded out of the room downstairs to the kitchen. There, she hurriedly got dressed and turned the key in the back door.

The moon was full and bright and the sky so clear and spangled with stars, she had no trouble making her way to the dell. Once there, following the well-trodden familiar route through the trees, her eyes rapidly adjusting to the change in darkness, she could hear the rustling sound of animal life in the distance. Hearing a noise nearby, off to her right, she turned and saw a pair of unblinking eyes staring back at her. A fox. A second later and it was gone.

She pressed on. A little further and she would be at the

halfway point. From there it was only a short distance to her and Noah's special place. A place now that would be for ever tainted by the knowledge that Uncle Leonard had spied on their every intimate gesture. She would never feel comfortable there again.

It was always possible that Noah had given up waiting for her and gone home, but somehow she doubted it. He was too tenacious for that. She had never known him to go back on his word. She hoped he'd fallen asleep in that case. At least then he wouldn't have been worrying about her.

She allowed herself a small smile when, in the shadowy darkness, she saw a pair of legs sticking out from behind one of the fallen trees. How well she knew Noah! And by the looks of how still he was, he hadn't been able to stay awake whilst he waited for her.

Moving as silently as she could, she inched her way forward, deciding to creep up on him and wake him with a kiss. Sleeping Beauty role reversal, she would tease him. Then she would lie down beside him and they would spend the rest of the night here wrapped in each other's arms to keep warm. It would be their first whole night together and they'd wake in the morning to the sound of birdsong.

It was the smell that alerted her. The sickly smell of aftershave that made her realize it wasn't Noah sleeping against the fallen tree. Shock wrenched a startled cry from her lips and she stepped back clumsily, her only thought to run. And fast. If he caught up with her, alone here in the dell, God only knows what he would do to her. But she'd only taken a few steps when she missed her footing and tumbled headlong over a tree root. Again she let out a cry, louder this time because her fear had turned to wild panic. Scrabbling to get up, her hands clawing at the dry, dusty ground, she was near to tears, terrified that he would come after her.

Once she was back on her feet, a slither of logic

penetrated her brain: with all the noise she'd made, why hadn't he woken and come after her?

And something else. If he'd been sleeping, why hadn't he been snoring? He *always* snored. Just like the revolting pig he was.

Her heart thudding against her ribcage, she summoned all her courage and retraced the steps she'd taken. She was almost back where she'd been before, when she froze. What if he was playing a game with her? Was he drawing her near, biding his time before pouncing on her?

To the left of her, she saw a handy-sized branch. It looked solid, like it could do some damage. 'I know you're there,' she said, gripping the branch with both hands and lifting it, ready to take aim. If she had to, she'd take his head clean off. 'So why don't you just stop messing about?'

When he didn't answer her, she took another step forward. And another. Until finally she was level with not just his legs, but the whole of him.

The first thing she saw was that his head was tilted to one side and his eyes were wide open; they were staring straight at her. Then she saw the blood. It was on the side of his head. The front of his shirt was also soaked in it. Bending down, she could see holes in his blood-soaked shirt. He'd been stabbed. Several times.

There was no doubt in her mind that he was dead.

Chapter Fifty

The enormity of what Noah had done was coming at Lydia in ever-growing waves of horror.

Initially she had been calm, focusing only on what had to be done. But now, the next morning, in the cold light of day – oh, how apt that phrase was – the reality of Noah's actions was hitting her with all the force of an atom bomb.

Noah had killed Uncle Leonard. He had said he would. And he had. He really had.

And yes, she too had threatened to kill the vile man. In the dell last night, when she thought she might have to protect herself against him, she had picked up that branch with the full intention of knocking his head off. But would she really have gone through with it? Wasn't it just something you said in the heat of the moment?

She began to shake uncontrollably, her stomach pitching and heaving. She clamped a trembling hand over her mouth, but it was no good. She went round to the back of the garage, bent over into the bushes and retched until she thought her stomach was going to turn itself inside out.

Exhausted, she leaned against the wall of the garage and closed her eyes, dizzy with the storm that was raging inside her head.

Murder. If caught, Noah would go to prison. He would stay there for the rest of his life, all because of her. He had done this dreadful thing for her sake. Because he loved her.

But how had he thought he would get away with it? He hadn't thought, had he? That was the whole trouble. He had acted on impulse to protect her.

Noah may not have been thinking straight last night, but Lydia had more than made up for that oversight on his part. She had done nothing but look at the situation from every possible angle, trying to work out the best way she could save Noah from going to prison. She had immediately dismissed the two of them running away together. Where would they go? What would they do? The police would find them within days; two young people on the run were much more conspicuous than only one. And if that happened, if they were caught, Noah would confess to killing Uncle Leonard and then that would be it. He'd be locked away for ever. His life finished. Her life over, too.

She just couldn't let Noah suffer for something he'd done out of love for her. The awful truth in all of this was that it was her fault. Everything always came back to her. Whatever she touched, she destroyed. Her mother was dead because of her. Valerie wasn't the happy carefree child she should be because Lydia hadn't taken good enough care of her. And now, because of her, Noah had killed a man. She could not, *would not*, let him be punished for it.

It was this thought that was the driving force behind her actions now; it was all she had to give her the courage to go through with what she had instigated whilst in the dell. There was no other way. The evidence against Noah was enough to condemn him in an instant. How soon would it be before those neighbours came forward and told the police they had witnessed a fight only yesterday afternoon, that they had even heard Noah shouting at Uncle Leonard that he was going to kill him? Her grandfather, too, would be quick to corroborate their claims, saying he'd come home to find a violent young man sprawled on his hall floor. He would do it if only to spite Lydia.

Tears slid down her cheeks. Why did Noah have to love her so much?

Once again, she pieced together what had happened, seeing the events all too clearly in her mind's eye. In the aftermath of the fight, Uncle Leonard had overheard the two of them arranging to meet in the dell – why else had he been hanging around by the gate, if not to eavesdrop? – and had consequently decided to go there and spy on them. Or just cause trouble. Noah, having got to their special place on time, had then come across Uncle Leonard. There had been words between them. More taunts and insults from Uncle Leonard. Probably still feeling humiliated by that vicious kick to his leg, Noah would have picked up a heavy branch, just as Lydia had, and hit Uncle Leonard with it. The blow would have knocked him unconscious, giving Noah the perfect opportunity to take out his penknife and ...

Unable to carry on, Lydia squeezed her eyes shut. Shaking again, she didn't think she would ever forget the sight of all that blood.

Hearing a car approach, she pressed herself against the wall of the garage and watched it rumble out of sight down the cobbled single-track road. Was this what the rest of her life would be like? Always watching over her shoulder? Always wondering if someone was coming for her?

Even if it was, she had no choice but to do everything she could to trick the police into looking the other way. They had to be so convinced that she was the one who had killed Uncle Leonard, they wouldn't consider Noah as a possible suspect.

The first part of her plan had been to plant the right kind of evidence on Uncle Leonard's body. Taking one of those hateful hands of his, she had raked his nails across her arm, pushing them painfully hard into her skin. Next she had pulled out some strands of her hair – nobody could ever confuse her long wavy hair with Noah's – and then she had kicked up the leaves around the body trying to ensure that only her footprints would be discernible. She didn't know how soon it would be before the body would be discovered, but knowing that few people walked through the dell, she hoped to be long gone when it was.

She had then thought about going on to Upper

Swallowsdale House to tell Noah what she'd set in motion. She'd soon changed her mind. Noah would try and stop her by saying it was too big a risk. Instead, exhausted and numb with shock, she had stumbled home, but not to sleep. Sitting at the kitchen table, she had written two letters – one to Sister Lottie and one to Noah – and then going upstairs, taking care not to wake Valerie, she had quietly packed a rucksack, carefully stowing inside it her passport and birth certificate and those few precious things she just couldn't leave behind. Fully dressed, just as dawn was breaking, she had finally gone to bed.

She'd woken up later than she'd intended. Valerie was already out of bed and, judging from the sound of running water, was having a bath. Her grandfather was nowhere to be seen.

The hardest part was leaving without saying goodbye to Valerie, but she just couldn't risk it. One look at her sister and her resolve would have faltered. Shouldering her rucksack, she had shut the back door after her, caught the bus into town and gone straight to the post office. From there she had hidden at the back of Sister Lottie's garage to wait for the one person on whom she was pinning all her hopes.

If Joey did refuse to take her to Italy with him, it wouldn't be the end of the world. Hadn't that happened already? No, she had a plan B to fall back on if need be.

Now, as she patiently waited for Joey to appear, she felt her stomach churn again. Could she really go through with this? Could she really bear to be separated from Noah?

She took a deep breath, played her fingers over the marks she had made on her arm with Uncle Leonard's nails, and shuddered. Yes, she could. If it meant saving Noah from going to prison, then she could. Hadn't they both always promised they would do anything for each other? Was she about to prove that the promise had meant nothing? Just empty words that had tripped off her tongue? It would be a sacrifice, like no sacrifice she had ever thought she would have to make, but do it she would.

Besides, it wouldn't be for ever. Somehow they would find a way to be together again. They just had to be patient. So long as Noah did exactly as she had instructed in the letter she had just posted to him, everything would work out in the end.

Now

Chapter Fifty-One

Lydia's head was zinging. She and Fabio had drunk so many cups of espresso during the telling of her story, she didn't think she would sleep for a week. If it wasn't for her ankle, she would be pacing up and down. As it was, she had to stay frustratingly still and wait for Fabio to ask her the inevitable question. As well as all the others that would follow.

'So what happened next, *cara*? Did Joey bring you here to Italy?'

She nodded. 'It was easy to convince him to take me with him. I told him that I had killed Uncle Leonard, that he had followed me to the dell in the middle of the night and attacked me while I was waiting for Noah. Don't forget, I had those marks on my arm to back up my story.' She paused, remembering the look of explosive anger on Joey's face and how good he'd been to her. 'I've always felt guilty about that lie to Joey,' she continued, 'but I'm afraid I was prepared to do anything to protect Noah.'

'You had no difficulty getting away from England?'

'None at all. My original idea depended upon slipping away before the body was discovered and leaving the country on the ferry for France quite legally, but Joey wouldn't have it. Despite the awful risk he was taking, he was adamant that he would smuggle me across the Channel in the boot of his car. I was totally against it. If we were caught it would have put him in danger of going to prison as well. He argued that it would be better that no one knew that I had left England on the same day as

363

him. Better that people thought I was hiding somewhere in England.'

'But surely, once the body was found, with the evidence you had placed, the police would have put two and two together and concluded that chances were you had left with Joey?'

'That's exactly what did happen. The British police got in touch with the Italian authorities and two officers from the local *questura* turned up to question Joey in his village. He told them he didn't have a clue where I was, and that he certainly hadn't brought me to Italy.'

'Did they search the house?'

'Yes, in a rather desultory fashion. They really couldn't have cared less, so Joey told me later. I wasn't there, of course. When we arrived in Italy, the first thing he did was to take me to friends of his who lived in Naples. He said Naples was so big and busy no one would find me there; it would be the classic needle in a haystack scenario. Moreover, with my dark hair I'd blend in easily; no one would look twice at me. To earn my keep, I immediately started work, washing dishes in a restaurant. I learned to speak Italian pretty fast, I can tell you.'

'*Dio mio!* You were eighteen years old, Lydia. Anything could have happened to you there. Imagine Chiara at that age and her doing something similar.'

Lydia sighed. 'I know, Fabio. But don't you remember when you were eighteen? You think you're invincible and have all the answers. Bear in mind just how determined I was to keep Noah safe. I was prepared to do anything for him.'

'You did, *cara*. From what you tell me, I'm only too surprised you didn't hand yourself over to the police and confess that you were the murderer.'

'There wouldn't have been any point in doing that. Noah would have immediately told them the truth, that I was trying to protect him. It was my greatest fear all along that he would feel the need to confess.'

'Would you really have gone to prison for him?'

'If I'd had to, yes. But given what kind of a man Uncle Leonard was, I was banking on a jury having some sympathy for me. That they would see me as a distraught young girl trying to defend herself, and as a result I'd be given a lesser sentence. Noah, on the other hand, would have been found guilty of murder.'

'It was an enormous risk.'

'I know, but I was hoping it would never come to that. Everything hung on my escape to Italy. Once I arrived I knew I could disappear for as long as it was necessary and then eventually, when it was safe, Noah would come to me. I thought we'd find a way to be together. Somehow. Somewhere.' She shook her head. 'I know from the expression on your face, Fabio, exactly what you're thinking. As plans go, it sounds wobbly and ill-conceived. But that's with the benefit of hindsight and objective thinking. I was eighteen. Incredibly naive. And very frightened. It made perfect sense to me at the time.'

'Actually you're wrong,' Fabio said. 'I was thinking that Noah is not coming out of this well. He murders a man, you make sure the finger is pointed at you, and he makes no effort to find you and thank you? Where has he been all this time? What has he been doing? Murdering other people?'

'Oh Fabio, you sound so cross.'

'I am! You sacrificed so much for his sake. Why didn't he look for you? A better man would have searched the entire earth until he found the girl he truly loved.'

'You think I never once thought that myself? Believe me, there were many times when I lay in bed at night crying myself to sleep that Noah could have let me down. I couldn't believe it. Not Noah. Then, when at last I had no choice but to accept he'd betrayed me, hurt turned to anger. Then bitterness.'

She fell silent and looked down at her hands; they were balled into ugly, tight fists on her lap. Even now, the pain of Noah's betrayal had the power to hurt her. Relaxing her hands, she cleared her throat. 'You sidetracked me, Fabio.

What I was going on to explain was that the morning I left Swallowsdale, after I'd drawn out all my savings from my post office account, I posted two letters, one to Noah and one to Sister Lottie.'

'Yes, I remember you saying that. Do you want another drink, by the way?'

'No more coffee for me, but a small glass of Vin Santo would be nice.'

While Fabio crossed the room to the console table behind the sofa where she kept a collection of decanters and bottles on a silver tray, Lydia thought of the letter she had written to Sister Lottie. It had been no more than a few lines to put the woman's mind at rest, explaining that after the pressure of all the exams she needed to get away from Swallowsdale for a while. The last thing Lydia had wanted was Sister Lottie worrying about her, imagining that she had been abducted and insisting the police search high and low for her. Lydia had had no such fear that her grandfather would instigate a search. But whether or not her letter would have put the old woman's mind totally at rest, Lydia didn't know. Probably not. Especially after Joey had admitted that when he'd reluctantly left Lydia standing on the pavement of Hillside Terrace, he'd driven straight to Sister Lottie's and shared with her his concerns about the kind of man Uncle Leonard really was. The news had come as a terrible shock to her, so Joey had explained to Lydia, and she'd promised him faithfully that she would do something about it. Whatever it was Sister Lottie had planned to do, Lydia would never know.

The letter she had written to Noah had been harder to write and she had worded it as carefully as she could in case it got into the wrong hands. She had prayed that he would read between the lines and understand the real message she was giving him. She'd told him that he wasn't to worry, she had it all worked out. All he had to do was trust her and everything would be OK. She'd stressed the importance of him keeping quiet and not trying to find her. She'd also stressed just how much she loved him and that she always would.

When Fabio was back sitting next to her on the sofa, Lydia took up the story once more and explained about the letters. 'I didn't dare write again to Noah, or Sister Lottie, once I was out of the country because I was certain the police would be watching their mail, just waiting for a letter from Italy to arrive and confirm their suspicions. But when Christmas came round, Joey wrote to Sister Lottie as he would normally, except this time he wrote to say he wouldn't be returning to Swallowsdale in the summer because he and two cousins were opening a restaurant in Sorrento. Two months later, his card was returned to him with a solicitor's letter informing him that Sister Lottie was dead and that she'd left him a small amount of money in her will. She'd had a massive stroke and never recovered. I was devastated. I'd known her since I was nine and loved her like—' Lydia's voice broke off abruptly. She put down her glass and tried to compose herself. 'Sister Lottie was always so kind to me.' Her voice wavered again and she covered her mouth with her hand.

Fabio put his arm around her.

'I feel so silly,' Lydia said, trying to make light of it, 'getting so upset after all these years. But she was such a sweet innocent woman who never did a bad thing in her life. By most people's standards she was probably a bit daft, but I loved her. I loved her so much and never got the chance to say goodbye. Or thank her for everything she did for me. I've always regretted that.'

One of the things Lydia loved about Fabio was that he always managed to say and do the right thing. For now he understood that silence was what she needed and so in the welcome quiet, she rested her head companionably against his shoulder. Moments passed. On the canal below, a motorboat was puttering past and someone nearby was closing their shutters for the night. Then Fabio pressed Lydia's forgotten glass of Vin Santo into her hand. 'Here's to Sister Lottie,' he said, touching his glass against hers.

Lydia echoed his words. 'Sister Lottie.'

'And what of Noah?' he asked after she'd taken a restorative sip and was in control of her emotions again.

'I didn't dare risk sending a letter to him in Swallowsdale, so I took a gamble and sent one to Oxford, to the college he'd applied to, not knowing for sure whether he'd got in or not. I gave him an address he could reply to in Naples. I waited weeks for a reply. Then months. Nothing came. By now a year had gone by since I'd left. I tried ringing the house in Swallowsdale, and I knew I had the right number, but it was as if the line was dead. There was no ringing tone at all.'

'Weren't you tempted to go back to England to see him?'

'Only about a hundred times a day, but I was convinced I would be picked up the minute I set foot on British soil.'

'You could have slipped in the same way you left.'

'I've always believed that one shouldn't push one's luck, not when it's such a finite commodity. I'd got away with illegally leaving the country; I certainly wasn't going to try sneaking back in illegally. No, what I did next was to ask a couple of British tourists to post a letter for me when they got back. A letter to Noah in Swallowsdale with a British postmark would be safe enough, I thought. I gave them the money for the postage, but I'll never know if they posted it for me or not. Three months later when I hadn't received a reply, I tried it again with another couple from London, but still nothing. I tried phoning as well, but drew the same blank as before.'

'Why didn't you write to Donna? Didn't you trust her?'

'I thought about it, but she was always so careless about things. What if she now had a boyfriend and he got hold of the letter? I even considered writing to Valerie, if only to let her know I was safe, but decided against it. If my sister believed I was a murderer, heaven only knew how she would react to a letter from me.'

Letting out his breath, Fabio said, 'So in the end, you

did what anyone would have done in the circumstances: you gave up?'

Lydia nodded. 'Yes, I did. I had no way of getting in touch with Noah. And I suppose it was then that the anger crept in and I began to think that if Noah really wanted to get in touch with me he would have. He could have made the same leap the police did and suspected I'd come to Italy with Joey. He could have found out Joey's address from Sister Lottie, before she died, and written to him. He could have tried. It seemed so—'

'Ungrateful of him, after everything you had done?'

'Yes. Exactly. I had to accept that he'd probably weighed up the pros and cons and decided that for us to be together he would have to give up his place at university and everything else he'd planned on doing. Put simply, it was too big a sacrifice for him. He'd had a lucky escape and wanted to put it behind him and move on afresh.'

'Maybe he did write to Joey, and Joey, thinking he was protecting you, didn't pass on that letter?'

'Never. Joey knew my feelings for Noah.'

'But he also believed you were guilty of murder and could go to prison if anyone found out where you were. Perhaps he trusted you, but not Noah?'

Lydia frowned. 'In all these years, I hadn't ever thought of that. How strange.'

They both drained their glasses. 'Another?' asked Fabio.

'Not for me. You go ahead, though.'

'No, I'll pass, thanks.' He leaned back on the sofa, crossed one leg over the other and played absently with a shoelace. But then his expression became serious. He uncrossed his legs. 'Something's just hit me,' he said, looking directly at her. 'You could still be found guilty of a murder you never committed.'

Lydia slowly nodded. 'Now that is a thought that's occurred to me often over the years.'

'How can you be so calm about it?'

'I've had years to come to terms with it. I soon learned

to stop jumping out of my skin whenever there was a knock at the door.'

'But you yourself just said that luck is finite. What if it runs out for you? What then? What if the past does catch up with you?'

'Who knows what I'll do,' she said, suddenly bone-weary, despite the caffeine zapping through her bloodstream. She looked at the photographs still laid out on the table and felt the past drawing and repelling her with equal force.

'I won't let anything bad happen to you, Lydia,' Fabio said. 'I made a promise to Marcello and I intend to keep it.'

'Now you're just being melodramatic.'

At the sound of a key unlocking the front door, and voices – happy laughing voices so at odds with their solemnity – Lydia and Fabio looked at each other.

'You have to tell him you knew his father,' Fabio said as Lydia quickly gathered up the photographs. 'I won't leave until you do.'

'And I suppose you'll then want me casually to drop into the conversation, oh, and by the way, Ishmael, did you know your father's a murderer?'

'Now who's being melodramatic?'

Chapter Fifty-Two

Lydia was spared from having her hand forced by Fabio there and then because Ishmael didn't come in with Chiara; he had merely been doing the gentlemanly thing and seeing Chiara safely home. But when Fabio was putting on his coat to leave and Chiara was conveniently out of earshot, he made Lydia promise that in the next twenty-four hours she would tell Chiara what she'd shared with him.

After a night of predictably restless sleep, Lydia woke the following morning feeling heavy-headed and anxious. Putting on her dressing gown, she slowly made her way to the kitchen. Her mood wasn't helped by having to rely on a crutch again. She found Chiara making breakfast, humming along to the radio, her head and shoulders moving in time to the music, an aura of happiness bouncing off her like sunlight on a spring day.

'I thought I'd cook something special for us tonight,' Chiara said when she saw her. 'If it's OK with you, I'd like to invite Ishmael to join us. Are you all right, Lydia? You don't look so good. Is your ankle very bad again? Uncle Fabio told me about you and the stepladder. Honestly, what on earth did you think you were doing?'

'Heavens! You're chirrupy this morning. Can I have a cup of tea before I submit myself to any further questions? Do you mind if we don't have the radio on?'

Chiara was all smiles. 'Of course. Sorry. Sit down and I'll make you some breakfast. What would you like? Some fruit?'

'Just tea, please.'

Humming to herself again, Chiara finished putting her breakfast together and finally sat down. 'So what do you think about Ishmael joining us for dinner tonight? I thought I'd make your favourite *spaghetti con le vongole*. We could invite Uncle Fabio and Paolo.' Her face dropped. Always an intuitive child, she said, 'What's wrong?'

'Nothing's wrong. Why would you think that?'

'There is something; I can see it in your face. You're worried about something. Is it me? Have I done something to upset you? Have I been too bossy about making you stay away from work?'

Lydia smiled. 'No, Chiara, it's nothing to do with work or you bossing me about. But that will have to stop, you know.'

Dipping a spoon into her pot of yogurt, Chiara smiled, too. 'You're the boss.' Then more seriously, clearly not prepared to let the matter drop, she said, 'So what is worrying you?'

Stalling for time and hoping against all the odds that the answer to her question might let her off the hook, Lydia poked at the slice of lemon floating on the surface of her tea. 'Just how fond of Ishmael are you?' she asked. If there was a chance of Chiara and Ishmael's relationship fizzling out any time soon, then Lydia would never need to take things further. Everything could go back to how it was.

'What does that have to do with anything?' Chiara asked warily.

More than you can imagine, Lydia thought. 'Please, just answer the question. I know it's early days and you really hardly know each other, but do you think it's serious between the two of you?'

Chiara put down her yogurt. 'Yes,' she said. 'Very serious. I've never felt this way about anyone before.' She smiled and relaxed a little. 'We both feel like we've always known each other. It's quite extraordinary.'

'In that case, I have to tell you that I'm one hundred per cent sure I knew his father.'

'Really?' Chiara leaned forward, her elbows resting on

the table. 'How amazing. But how can you be so sure?'

It was time to bring out the photographic evidence. 'In my bedside table drawer, there's an envelope with some photos inside. Could you get them for me, please? When you see them, you'll understand my reaction last night.'

As soon as Chiara had the photographs in her hands, she let out a whistle. 'Now I see why you were acting so strangely. It really could be Ishmael, couldn't it?'

'I didn't tell you before, but Ishmael's the reason I hurt my ankle. I saw him in the crowd and was so stunned I lost my footing.'

'Tell me about the man he looks like.'

'We met at school when we were nine years old. We became inseparable. Like brother and sister. But that changed when we were older ... when we were teenagers ... then our relationship became ... became something else.' Lydia stumbled clumsily over her words. How could she possibly describe what she and Noah had meant to each other in so few inadequate words?

Chiara came to her rescue. Her eyes shining, her expression animated, she said, 'Did you fall in love? Were you lovers?'

Lydia nodded. 'We thought nothing in the world would ever part us.'

'But that's so fantastic!' Chiara cried, her whole demeanour that of a girl newly in love and wanting everyone else to be in love, too. 'How wonderful. If it's true, of course, and Ishmael really is the son of this man you knew.' She looked again at the photograph of Noah on his own. 'But it has to be true. It can't be a coincidence. What a fabulously romantic story!'

Romantic was not the word Lydia could bring herself to use. 'It's not as straightforward as you think, Chiara. There's more to it than that. Ishmael's father and I haven't seen one another since we were eighteen.'

'Why? Did you have a row and a huge falling-out?'

'No. We never argued, we—'

'You're not ... you're not going to tell me Ishmael is—'

Chiara's eyes were wide now. 'He's not your son, is he? A love child you had to give away because you were too young to keep him? Not that that would make any difference to Ishmael and me. It's not as if you and I are blood related.'

Lydia swallowed back the sting of Chiara's remark. She knew Chiara didn't intend any offence, yet nonetheless she couldn't help but feel like she'd only ever been a caretaker mother. But for Chiara to blurt out such a comment meant that the connection she and Ishmael had was real. Lydia knew she hadn't imagined the closeness between them when she'd watched them leaving the apartment together last night. 'No, Chiara,' Lydia said calmly, glad that there was at least one concern she could put to rest, 'Ishmael is definitely not my son. He wasn't a love child I had to give away.'

'So why do you look so miserable? I'd have thought this was something to make you happy. We explain everything to Ishmael and he'll put you in touch with your long-lost love. What could be more exciting and romantic?'

Lydia was about to suggest that Ishmael's mother may have something less enthusiastic to say on the matter, when Chiara's mobile trilled inside her handbag on the other side of the kitchen. She went to it.

'It's a text from Ishmael,' she said, her lovely face blushing with a happy smile. Back at the table, still smiling, she glanced at her watch. 'Hey, I must dash! I want to get to work early so I can leave early this afternoon to shop for tonight's meal. I'll give Fabio and Paolo a call. I can't wait to tell Ishmael everything.' She drained her coffee cup in a single gulp, then kissed Lydia on the cheek. 'I'll ring you during the day.'

Would there have been any point in making Chiara promise not to say anything to Ishmael? Lydia asked herself when once again she was listening to the sound of Chiara's departing footsteps on the stairs.

No. Why not sit back now and see what happened next?

It seemed she was at the centre of a situation over which she had no control.

For the rest of the day, Lydia was on tenterhooks. She was dreading the evening ahead. She couldn't imagine how she would survive the small talk she would have to endure with Noah's son. There would be endless cross-referencing while all the time Fabio would be wanting to chip in impatiently and say, '*Sì sì*, that's all very well, but what about Uncle Leonard?'

A little after lunchtime, while she was testing her ankle to see if she could walk without the aid of her crutch – and finding to her annoyance that she couldn't – the phone rang: it was Chiara. 'I've just been talking with Ishmael and there's been a change of plan for this evening,' she said. 'Ishmael and I are going out for dinner instead. You're not disappointed, are you?'

'Not at all,' Lydia replied, although perversely she was. 'Did you say anything to him about me knowing his father?'

'No, I'm saving it for when we're alone. Anyway, I can't chat for long, I've got someone to show round an apartment in ten minutes. Don't wait up for me tonight.'

'Won't you be back to change for dinner?'

'No, Ishmael's meeting me straight from work. *Ciao, ciao*.'

The rest of the day stretched out long and tediously for Lydia. She tried ringing round a few friends, but no one was at home. They were all out Christmas shopping, she supposed.

After a brief, unintentional nap – not surprising really, considering the bad night she'd had – she woke to find the apartment in darkness. It was nearly six o'clock. Now she had only the evening to get through.

Up on her feet, she negotiated her way round the room carefully, switching on lamps then going over to the windows to draw the curtains. Since Marcello had died, seldom did she close the shutters as well. She didn't like to shut out too much of the world.

Desperate for some kind of company, she flicked through the TV channels for something to while away the time until she went to bed. Nothing. She then resorted to the phone once more and tapped in Fabio and Paolo's number. Irritatingly, all she got was their voicemail. She tutted. Why was everyone busy except her?

When the front door bell rang, she could have whooped with delight. Saved! Company! And not just any old company – it was probably Fabio here to check up on the promise he'd forced her to make. More fool him. She would hold him captive now for the rest of the evening. Better still, maybe he'd brought Paolo with him.

She went out to the hall, registering that either the main door downstairs had been left open, or one of her neighbours must have let Fabio in. Leaning on her crutch, she turned the lock and pulled open the door.

For an eternity they both stared at each other. It couldn't be. It wasn't possible. Her brain was playing games with her. If she closed the door and opened it again, he would be gone. A figment of her imagination.

'Lyddie,' he said.

She swallowed. 'Noah.'

Chapter Fifty-Three

'Is this when I faint?' she asked.

'I was wondering the same thing myself.'

'In that case you'd better come in.'

He stepped inside and at once she noticed his limp was more pronounced than she remembered and that he carried an elegant silver-topped walking cane. She closed the door and again they stood and stared at each other.

'Snap,' he said, indicating her crutch with his cane.

'I fell,' she said. 'I wasn't looking where I was going.'

'The way I heard it, my son is to blame. I hope you've taken him to task.'

She blinked, then shook her head as if it would make everything clearer. 'I'm sorry,' she said. 'I can't take this in. I need to sit down. Then you have to explain what's going on. How, after all these years, you appear from nowhere on my doorstep.'

He followed her through to the sitting room. She pointed to a chair, but he said, 'If you don't mind, I'd prefer to move around.' He made it sound like he preferred to be a moving target rather than a sitting one.

'At least take off your scarf and coat.'

When he'd removed his coat she could see he still had the same slim build that would compel every Italian *mama* to feed him up. She took his things from him and laid them over the back of a chair, noting that the black woollen coat was beautifully made. Cashmere. Expensive. A far cry from the stiff-as-cardboard jumble sale greatcoat she'd once bought him.

She sat down and tried to pull herself together. If

377

anything, the shock of seeing him was gaining momentum. 'Twenty-eight years,' she managed to say, 'and you look the same. Different. But the same. If that makes any sense.'

'And you've proved my uncle's prediction absolutely right. You're even more beautiful.'

'Uncle Brad,' she repeated in a small, dazed voice. 'How is he?'

'Living in the south of France with the latest love of his life and still behaving disgracefully. He knocks out an occasional painting when the mood takes him, which isn't very often. He's seventy-two now. Can you believe it?'

'I can believe that more than I can believe I'm looking at you right now.'

Noah prodded at the rug with his cane. 'Nice segue. I suppose it's time to ditch the small talk, isn't it?' He moved stiffly over to one of the windows, then turned to face her. 'Ishmael called me this morning. He told me about a girl he'd met here called Chiara and that her English stepmother was called Lydia. He then asked me if I'd known a Lydia when I was a child, because apparently this Lydia said she'd grown up with a boy called Noah Solomon. I didn't doubt for a second who he was talking about. I'm sorry, but from that moment on, only an apocalypse would have stopped me from coming straight here. Once I knew there was a flight I could get on, I rang Ishmael to meet me at this end. He did, along with your stepdaughter. Don't be cross, but Chiara was the one who suggested I surprise you like this. I wanted to ring you, to give you time to prepare yourself, but Chiara wouldn't hear of it.' He smiled ruefully and went and stood in front of the fireplace. 'She seemed to think it would be more romantic this way.'

'You'll have to excuse her. Her head's full of romantic nonsense just now.'

'If I'm honest, I was frightened that if I did call you first, you might disappear before I got here.'

'Why would I do that?'

'Because ...' He shrugged, and ran a hand through his

hair, oblivious to the fact that it was now all messed up. 'Because I can't believe that after all this time, it could really happen. That we'd be in the same room again.'

He looks so young still, Lydia found herself thinking. And just as handsome. Her hands began to itch to smooth out his ruffled hair and she was reminded of all the times in that other life when she had done exactly that.

'What?' he said.

'Sorry?'

'You're looking at me strangely.'

She relaxed a tiny bit and smiled. 'Take a look in the mirror behind you.'

He spun round and looked at his reflection in the mirror above the mantelpiece. 'Ah, I see what you mean.' He did the necessary and faced her again. 'I think it's fair to say I haven't improved much. I'm about as sartorially aware as a chipmunk.' He raised his walking cane. 'Ishmael bought this for me with the idea it would help to sharpen up my act. He calls it my Jack the Ripper accessory, and then has the nerve to accuse me of having a sick sense of humour.'

'You always had your own look,' she said, taking in the white T-shirt beneath the grey V-neck sweater, and the black jeans rumpled at the knees.

'So did you.'

'Have we reverted to small talk again?'

'It's bound to happen.'

'Perhaps a drink will help.' She levered herself up from the sofa. 'Wine? Or something with more kick?'

'Actually, I don't drink these days.'

'Oh?'

'I had a problem with it for a time.'

'When?'

'When you left Swallowsdale. Or more precisely, when I was finally discharged from hospital.'

They were sitting at the kitchen table now, two omelettes in front of them, as well as a bowl of salad and a bottle of Pellegrino.

Whilst Lydia had prepared their meal, she had asked Noah to stay in the sitting room and listen to some music. She had needed time alone to try and gather her thoughts and steady her nerves. Even without his presence in the kitchen, she had still been a mess. Twice she'd nearly taken the end off a finger when she was slicing the tomatoes. The second time she'd cursed loudly and dropped the knife with a clatter. 'Everything all right?' he'd asked, coming into the kitchen.

'It's nothing,' she'd said, flustered. 'I was being careless.'

'Let me see.'

Embarrassed, she'd held out her hand. 'It's nothing,' she repeated, despite the evidence to the contrary. Blood had already dripped onto her bandaged ankle.

He ripped off a square of kitchen roll, folded it in half and in half again, then wrapped it tightly around her finger. 'Where do you keep the plasters?'

'In the drawer behind you.'

As he bent over her hand to apply the plaster, Lydia had to hold her breath. It was the smell and touch of him. It suddenly made him more real to her. This was no dream. He was really here.

When he'd dealt with her finger, he stooped to pick up the knife she'd dropped. He handed it to her and for a moment, their eyes met. Was he, like her, remembering that night in the dell?

Neither of them said anything. He left her to get their meal ready and only reappeared when she called him.

Sitting opposite him now she was reacquainting herself with his face. She knew a lot of men who, by their mid-forties, had grown paunchy with age and good living; they had developed jowls and lost the distinctive sharpness of their youthful looks. Everything became a little blurred and faded. But not Noah. He had somehow defied the passing of years. There were lines at the corners of his eyes, and a smattering of grey hairs, but if anything, his features were sharper and more defined. His eyebrows were just as expressive, still perfectly arched, giving him that slightly puzzled expression. Life had not been too harsh for him, she concluded. He looked well. But then she remembered what he'd said earlier, about alcohol having been a problem for him for a time, and that he'd been in hospital.

'How's the finger?' he asked, interrupting her thoughts.

'It's OK,' she lied. It was actually throbbing quite painfully, but there were more important matters to discuss. 'Tell me about the drinking. What made you start? You'd always been so anti. You used to say you hated what it did to your uncle.'

He put down his knife and fork and flung himself back in the chair. 'What a sanctimonious prig I was.'

'You were never that.'

'Oh, yes I was. Uncle Brad drank and used drugs because he needed to escape. Turned out, when push came to shove, that was what I needed to do as well.'

It made sense to Lydia. He'd murdered someone – why wouldn't he want to escape the guilt of what he'd done by drowning his sorrows in the bottom of a glass? But it was much too soon to voice such an opinion. Though how they were ever going to discuss what he'd done that night, she didn't know. Would he expect her to say 'thank you' after all these years? *Thank you, Noah, for wanting to protect me by killing Uncle Leonard. Thank you for screwing up the rest of our lives.*

There it was again. The bitter pain of his betrayal.

'You mentioned you'd been in hospital,' she said, reining in her hostility. 'What was that for?'

He opened his mouth to say something, but then frowned and massaged his temple. 'Sorry to change the subject, but do you have any paracetamol?' he asked.

She went to the same drawer where she kept the plasters, and handed him a packet. He popped two out and downed them with a gulp of water, his head tipped back. At the sight of the smooth, pale skin at his throat, she felt a strong compulsion to put her arms around him.

Stunned that she could feel anything like that for him

still, she sat down quickly, hoping he hadn't noticed, and resumed eating. Noah didn't. He rested his elbows on the table, steepled his hands together, his long slender fingers neatly entwined, and said, 'I'll explain about my stay in hospital later. If you remember I was always a tedious pedant. I haven't changed, so I'll stick to the chronological order of events, if that's OK with you. I spent the journey here trying to remember exactly how things happened.'

If she hadn't known where the conversation would lead them, she would have smiled at his description of himself. 'Nothing wrong in being a stickler for detail,' she said lightly. 'Go on.'

'It all started that awful afternoon when I'd tried to take your uncle on and then your grandfather appeared and you insisted I went home. God, if I'd known what was to follow, I'd never have listened to you. I would have stayed and ...' He paused, breathed in deeply and exhaled with a weary sigh. 'Sorry, no point in stating the obvious, is there? Anyway, I reluctantly drove home, and when I got there I was all over the place. I couldn't stop think-ing how I'd never forgive myself if that man did anything else to you. I wanted to get in my car again and drive straight back to you. But instead, and this was when I made the biggest and worst mistake of my entire life, I decided that what I needed was something to calm me down. A glass or two of whatever my uncle currently had stocked in the house. Just something to take the edge off things.'

The corners of his mouth curved into an expression of scathing self-reproach. 'It certainly did that,' he said. Suddenly fidgety, he covered his face, then rubbed his chin. 'My memory's a bit hazy on some of the details of what happened next,' he continued, 'but I do remember that once I'd started, knowing that my uncle wasn't due back from London until the following day, I decided that what I really needed was total oblivion. So I set to with a vengeance. I was on a mission to drink myself into as deep a comatose state as I could. Anything that would take away the shame of not being able to protect you in the way I'd wanted to. For having failed you so spectacularly. You know, I hadn't appreciated until then just what a proud idiot I was. At some point during all the drinking, I decided I wanted to listen to a record that was in my room. I remember very clearly staggering to the top of the stairs and feeling ridiculously infallible when I got there. I was capable of anything, I thought. Now I could really take on that scumbag and prove myself to the girl I loved.' He paused again and took a long drink from his glass of water.

Lydia felt sick. She wanted to hear the rest of what he had to say, but at the same time she didn't. To hear Noah confess to what he'd done that night was too much.

'So there I was,' Noah went on, 'at the top of the stairs, when I remembered I was supposed to be meeting you in the dell. I had no idea what time it was and as I moved my arm to look at my watch, I somehow lost my balance. The next memory I have is waking up in hospital with Uncle Brad dozing in a chair by the side of my bed. Turned out he'd had a lousy time in London and came home a day early. He rolled up just after eleven o'clock and found me lying unconscious at the bottom of the stairs. Apparently I was lucky not to have broken my neck. As it was, and it was sod's law of course, I'd shattered my already wrecked leg and was on traction for several months afterwards. I've got these metal pins now. Lyddie? You're staring at me again. What is it?'

'But what about—' Lydia stopped herself short. What if he was demonstrating a classic example of selective memory? Was he in denial? Had his brain conveniently put a block on that gruesome part of the night?

'Lyddie,' he repeated. 'What is it? Tell me.'

'But that can't be right. You went to the dell at midnight. Just as we'd arranged.'

An expression of sad regret passed across his face. 'I only wish I had.'

'But you went,' she asserted. 'You went there to meet me at *midnight*.'

He shook his head slowly. 'I didn't. I couldn't have found my way to the back door, never mind to the dell. As I just said, Uncle Brad found me unconscious at the bottom of the stairs a little after eleven.'

'But that's not possible. You were *there*.' Lydia's voice was rising with impatience. How dare he sit here twenty-eight years later and rewrite history!

Once more he shook his head. 'I can't tell you how many times I wished I had gone to meet you. If only I hadn't got drunk, everything would have been so different. That bastard wouldn't have attacked you and you wouldn't have needed to—'

'Needed to do what?' she said when he left the words hanging.

He met her gaze. 'Defend yourself, Lyddie. I just wish you hadn't run off like that without me. I would have gone with you. I'd have done anything you asked. *Anything*.'

Lydia felt like she was drowning in a sea of confusion. None of this was making sense. 'But I didn't do it, Noah. *You* did it. You just don't remember.' She could feel herself shaking. '*You* killed my uncle. Not me.'

He looked baffled. 'But when the police questioned me in hospital, they said they were looking for you. They said there was evidence. It was in the papers.'

Exasperated, Lydia banged her hand down on the table. 'This is how it happened! OK? I overslept. I got to the dell much later than we'd arranged. I found the body. I then put the evidence there to make the police think I had done it.'

'Why? Why would you do that?'

'So they wouldn't think you did it, of course! I covered up for you.'

'But I keep telling you, I didn't do it.' He raked his hands through his hair. 'I couldn't have done it. I swear it.'

'But if you didn't do it, and I know I certainly didn't, who the hell did?'

*

Their omelettes practically untouched, they moved back into the sitting room. Lydia was shivering. 'Here, let me put this around you,' Noah said.

She gratefully accepted the offer of his coat. He sat next to her on the sofa, took her hands in his and rubbed them gently as if to warm them. 'I'm not cold,' she said. 'It's shock.'

'I know,' he said. 'But this gives me something to do while I try and make sense of what you've just told me.'

'I can't believe it,' Lydia murmured. 'I just can't believe it. All this time, you thought *I* had killed Uncle Leonard.'

'I thought it from the minute I read of the murder in the local paper when I was in hospital. That and your letter, which Uncle Brad eventually brought in for me. He'd forgotten all about the mail piling up at the house and when he got around to bringing me your letter, the local paper was rife with the story of your uncle's body found in the dell and that you were missing and the police wanted to talk to you to help them, as they put it, with their inquiries. He must have recognized your writing and had his suspicions because when he gave me the letter, he said, "Better not let anyone else read it. Keep it hidden. Better still, throw it away afterwards."'

'Do you think he'd steamed it open and read it for himself?'

'Not a hope. Uncle Brad is many things, but he's not a sneak. Do you want to know how I got rid of it?'

She nodded.

'I ate it.'

In spite of everything – in spite of feeling she was hopelessly adrift, that a lifetime of belief had just been swept away – Lydia laughed.

'How else was I to destroy what the police might have thought was important evidence, when I was stuck in bed?'

'So you read the letter and thought what?'

'Relief, initially. It explained why your grandfather had

told Uncle Brad he didn't know where you were when I got him to ring you to tell you I was stuck in hospital. I'd been worried sick something had happened to you. Then it hit me. You were in big trouble. You'd as good as admitted to killing your uncle. You said you had everything all worked out, that I had to keep quiet and trust you. And most importantly, I wasn't to try and look for you.'

'No! That wasn't what I meant. What I was trying to say, without coming right out with it in case someone else read the letter, was that I knew what you'd done and why and that I had it all under control. That so long as you didn't say or do anything, the police would think I did it and you'd be safe. I was protecting you.'

'What would you have done if the police had found you?'

'That was my Plan B. I would have stuck to the story that Uncle Leonard had attacked me and it had been self-defence.'

'Oh, God, Lyddie. You were prepared to do that for me?'

'Without a second thought.' *Would you have done the same for me?* was on the tip of her tongue, but she didn't dare ask him.

He lowered his head and pressed the palms of his hands against his eyes. 'Sorry,' he said, when he looked up. 'I can't seem to shift this headache. Could I have some more water, please?'

She fetched his glass from the kitchen and handed it to him. 'Why didn't you answer any of my letters?' she asked.

'What letters?'

'The ones I sent to Swallowsdale. And the one I sent to the college in Oxford you'd been offered a place at.'

'I never made it to Oxford. I was discharged from hospital at the end of the summer and that's when I hit the booze. I blamed myself for everything. I should have been able to prevent what had happened. Every day I didn't hear from you was another day I blamed and tormented myself some more and drank some more. By the time I was supposed to take up my place at Oxford I was completely off the rails. The only way I could function was to hit the vodka bottle when I got up in the morning, although it was usually afternoon by the time I surfaced, and then it was a full-time job keeping the levels topped up throughout the rest of the day.'

'Didn't Uncle Brad step in?'

'He tried for a bit, but he was busy down in London. Then one day he announced that he was madly in love with a poet from Cork and he was selling the house and we were moving to Ireland. I think he had some half-cocked notion that the change of scene would do me good. The last thing I wanted was to leave Swallowsdale. I was desperately hanging onto the hope that you might come back. But my uncle insisted. So off we went. Needless to say, he didn't stay madly in love for long, and for about a year we were constantly on the move, going from one place to another. We were like gypsies.'

'Well, that explains why you never got any of my letters.'

'Uncle Brad had organized for our mail to be forwarded, but since we never stopped anywhere very long, there was little chance of it ever catching up with us.'

'I used to hope you'd guess exactly what I'd done and come and find me.'

'I'm sorry, but I was too mired in my own misery to figure out anything useful. I'd even started to think that you were dead. That was when I wished I was dead too. Then occasionally I had drunken moments of bravado when I imagined tracking you down, but then I would sober up and remember your letter. Your instructions were very explicit. I was terrified of doing the wrong thing and leading the police to you.'

'Can you remember when Uncle Leonard's body was discovered?'

'Not exactly. But it must have been nearly a fortnight after you'd disappeared. Shortly afterwards two policemen came to visit me in hospital. They kept saying how important it was that they found you. They claimed they had compelling evidence that you'd been in some sort of a struggle with your uncle in the dell before he died. I had no idea what evidence they were talking about, but I did my best to convince them they'd got it wrong. I lied and said that, yes, you had been in a struggle with your uncle, but it had taken place that afternoon when I'd turned up at your house, and that was why I'd threatened to kill him, just as your neighbours had told the police. With no one to dispute what I'd said, I just hoped I'd given them something that might help to put you in the clear, or at least distract them. What sort of evidence had you left for the police to find?'

'My skin under Uncle Leonard's nails and some strands of hair. Did it say in the paper who found the body?'

Noah took hold of her hands again, as though she needed to be prepared for yet another shock. 'Yes,' he said. 'It was your sister.'

Chapter Fifty-Four

Valerie. She would be forty now. A grown woman. Married? With children? Still having mystical visions? Lydia had no idea. Yet for peace of mind, and to assuage her guilt for having abandoned Valerie in the way she had, Lydia had to believe that against all the odds, her sister had gone on to live a happy and fulfilling life. The guilt ran deep, though. Not only had she chosen Noah over and above her sister's needs, Lydia had never once in all the years that followed tried to make contact with Valerie. Selfishly, for self-preservation, she had needed to cut the tie. To look back would have given her hope for something that could never be. False hope, as she'd learned, was too costly. It was better to start afresh. To be someone new.

But now Lydia had the added guilt of knowing that her twelve-year-old sister had been the one to discover Uncle Leonard's decomposing body. What further harm could that have done to the poor girl's already fragile state of mind?

'It's not your fault, Lyddie,' Noah said, still holding her hands. She hadn't said a word, hadn't voiced what was in her head, yet he had known what her reaction would be.

'I think I'd like to be alone now,' she said.

He didn't argue with her, merely hauled himself to his feet. 'Of course,' he said.

Grateful for his understanding, she passed him his coat. 'Presumably you're staying with Ishmael?'

'Yes.'

'Will you be able to find your way to the apartment? Venice is a very disorientating place.'

'Not unlike the past,' he said. 'But don't worry. I'll be fine. I have a map.'

At the front door, she watched him doing the buttons up on his coat and suddenly thought of something. 'Have you ever been to Venice before?' she asked.

He shook his head. 'No. It's my first time.'

She allowed herself a secret smile of satisfaction. 'I thought so.'

'Why?'

'I would have known. That's all.'

His gaze held hers and he put a hand out to her arm. 'Can I come back tomorrow? There's still so much more we have to say.'

'Of course. And I'm sorry I'm kicking you out now. It's just that I don't think I'm capable of another coherent thought tonight.'

He increased the pressure on her arm and dipped his head, just the merest hint of movement as if he was going to kiss her, but then he drew back. 'Good night, Lyddie,' he said. 'Sleep well.'

'I doubt I will.'

'Me neither.'

She stood at the window, holding the curtain to one side as she watched him appear on the *fondamenta* below. Again he must have known what she would do and standing in the glow of the street lamp, pausing to tighten his scarf around his neck and to turn up his collar against the cold, he raised his gaze and saw her. He acknowledged her with a small smile and went on his way.

She stayed watching him until he'd vanished out of sight. A profound sense of loss came over her and she felt compelled to open the window and call after him. What if he disappeared in the night and she never saw him again?

She went straight to bed with the intention of pretending she was asleep when Chiara came home. She wasn't capable of dealing with the level of interrogation Chiara would want to pursue. It could keep until morning.

*

As it turned out, she didn't need to fake sleep. She was dead to the world until she became conscious of someone moving around in her room. She heard the swish of curtains being parted, followed by sunlight pouring in. 'I've brought you a cup of tea,' said Chiara.

'What time is it?' Lydia asked with a groggy groan. She felt like she'd been drugged.

'It's half past nine.'

Lydia roused herself into a sitting position. 'But it can't be. I can't have slept so long.' Bleary-eyed, she checked her alarm clock; sure enough it was nine thirty.

'I looked in on you when I got home last night,' Chiara said, settling herself on the bed, 'and you were fast asleep. I must say, I was very disappointed. I was looking forward to a chat.'

'I bet you were.'

Chiara smiled. 'Well? How did it go?'

'For a start you've been a very devious girl, haven't you? You told several whopping great lies yesterday; all that stuff about there being a change of plan. What an understatement! Presumably you and Ishmael cooked the whole thing up between you. It was probably you who let Noah in downstairs, wasn't it?'

'Guilty of every accusation. You're not cross, are you?'

'Not exactly. But it was a huge shock.'

'A good one?'

Lydia sipped her tea thoughtfully. 'I don't know yet.'

'He seemed lovely. A bit serious, maybe, but very handsome. Ishmael really is the spitting image of him, isn't he?'

'No doubt about that.' Then registering Chiara wasn't dressed, Lydia said, 'Shouldn't you be getting ready for work?'

'It's Saturday. Which means I'm going to sit here on your bed until you've told me everything about last night.'

'No! ... You thought he was a murderer all these years! ... You ran away! ... You left everything for him! ... You put yourself at risk of being sent to prison! ... *No!*'

Jumping up and down, twirling round on the spot, and flinging her arms in the air, Chiara was a whirlwind of typically over-the-top Italian reaction to Lydia's story. She finally came to rest and perched on the edge of the bed, and spoke the first calm, reasoned words since Lydia had started speaking. 'Did my father know any of this?' she asked.

'No. But I think he always knew deep down that there was something I was hiding from him. And it's important that you know I never actually lied to your father. He just never asked the kind of questions that would have forced me to lie to him.'

Chiara's face was pensive. 'Which suggests that he did suspect something, but loved you so much he didn't want to ruin things. He accepted you as he saw you.'

Lydia nodded sadly. 'He was a wonderful man who always tried to take others at face value.'

'Uncle Fabio says he was one of the most honourable men he knew.'

'Your uncle's right. Maybe that was what I was attracted to in the first place. Perhaps I was hoping his decency would rub off on me.'

Chiara frowned. 'Why would you, of all people, think that?'

'Because in the early days, long before I came to Venice, the thing I hated most about myself was the lie I was living, not being able to be honest and be the real me.'

'I don't understand.'

'By coming to live in Italy I had to lose my true identity. I'd been living illegally in the country for nearly two years when Joey decided it was time to get my paperwork in order. So, through a friend of a friend in Naples where, as we both know, just about anything can be arranged, a new passport was organized for me, as well as all the other official documents I needed in order to stay in the country legally.'

'Is Lydia your real name?'

'Oh, yes, I kept that, but on my passport it's my middle

name. Before I married Marcello, I was officially Teresa Lydia Jones. If ever I had to explain this to anyone, your father included, I said that I preferred to use my middle name.'

Suddenly concerned by what Chiara might be thinking, Lydia said, 'Are you very shocked by what I've told you? Do you feel I've conned you in some way? That I'm not the woman you thought I was?'

Chiara smiled. 'Not at all. You've been a fantastic mother and friend to me. Nothing could ever change that.'

With tears in her eyes, Lydia leaned forward and hugged Chiara. 'I couldn't bear to lose your love and respect,' she said. 'Or your friendship.'

After telephoning ahead, Noah and Ishmael arrived together just before midday. Seeing the two of them standing side by side, Lydia was rendered speechless. For longer than was polite, she openly stared at them. 'Now I know what it feels like to be a museum exhibit,' Ishmael joked.

Leaving Ishmael and Chiara to chat, Noah came over to where Lydia was standing at the window. 'How are you feeling?' he asked.

'I'm OK, thank you. How about you? Did you sleep?'

'Not a wink. I kept thinking that if I did sleep I'd wake up and find yesterday was a dream and that you were still lost to me.'

'I thought the same when I watched you walk away last night.'

He was standing very close to her. Mixed in with the light scent of his aftershave, she could smell the tangy, crisp winter air on his coat. It made her long to be outside.

'I hope you don't mind,' he said, 'but I've told Ishmael everything.'

'Chiara also knows the whole story now.'

At the sound of their names being mentioned, Chiara and Ishmael glanced over at them. Chiara said, 'What do you want to do about lunch, Lydia? Shall I cook us something?'

Seized with the desire to be anywhere but stuck indoors, Lydia said, 'Why don't you two do your own thing? Seeing as it's the first fine day we've had in ages, it's time for me to tackle the stairs. I'll go stir-crazy if I don't have some fresh air and a change of scene. I promise I'll take it steadily,' she added when she saw the warning expression on Chiara's face. 'Noah will help me, won't you?'

Noah was complicit, and with a hand placed at her elbow, he helped Lydia make her escape. It took them for ever to cover the short distance down to the Zattere, and once there Lydia sank gratefully into a chair at one of the open-air cafés. With their chairs facing the bright December sun, sunglasses firmly in place, Noah said, 'You haven't changed at all, have you? You're as single-minded and determined as ever.'

'I'll probably end up paying for it later when my ankle swells to the size of a football, but for now, this is blissful. You're not too cold, are you?'

'Not at all.' He looked around them. 'It's a popular place, by the looks of things.'

Most of the clientele were smartly dressed Italians; many of the women were wearing full-length fur coats. Her voice low, Lydia said, 'It's a bit of a tourist catch, but on a day like today I don't care. I love to do all the things the snobby purists say you're not supposed to do in Venice.' Seeing a waiter approaching and thinking of what Noah had told her last night, she said, 'Do you mind if I have a glass of Prosecco?'

'Please, go ahead. Have whatever you want. I'll have some hot chocolate.'

Their drinks ordered and delivered to the table, the conversation went the only way it could, with Lydia recounting her life in Naples. 'I then moved to Sorrento, where Joey had opened a restaurant with some cousins,' she explained. 'I worked for him for about three years, then decided it was time to go my own way. I went to Positano, where I got a job working in a hotel and taught

English as a sideline. Before long I was teaching English full-time.'

'God only knows you must have had so many regrets, effectively living in exile as you were, and I don't mean to sound insensitive, but did you particularly regret missing out on university? It was such an important goal for you.'

'I never allowed myself to go down that road. I channelled all my energy into sustaining the new life I was creating for myself.'

'And Joey? Are you still in touch with him?'

'Not as much as either of us would like, what with all our commitments, but yes, we talk on the phone now and then. He's married with five children and a grandchild on the way. He owns three restaurants now. I don't suppose you even knew the reason why he had to rush back to Italy so suddenly.'

Noah shook his head.

'His mother had had a heart attack and he dropped everything to get home to her. She not only survived, but is still alive and looking forward to being a great-grandmother.'

An elderly couple with a small dog dressed in a tartan overcoat came and sat at the table nearest to them. When they were settled, Noah said, 'So if it hadn't been for Joey's mother, you wouldn't be here in Italy, would you?'

Lydia stared up at the faultless blue sky; it seemed wonderfully infinite and crystalline, Venetian through and through. This place was so very much home to her. 'Who knows where I would have gone if it hadn't been for Joey's mother,' she said thoughtfully.

'And Positano? How long did you stay there?'

'Oh, for years. Long enough to put down some tentative roots.'

'A man?'

She nodded, aware that Noah was staring hard into his empty cup.

'Did you marry him?'

'He asked me, but that was my cue to start running.

Until I met Chiara's father I'd been happy to keep things on a fairly superficial level.'

'Did you leave Positano to come here to Venice?' Through his sunglasses, Noah's gaze was now back on hers.

'No, I went to Sardinia, followed by a brief spell in Rome and then I came here. I've always found work easy to find, whether it's been teaching English, reception work, working as a guide, or doing translation. I've enjoyed the variety. I particularly enjoy what I'm doing now. Chiara's father and I started the agency together.' She turned to look out across the glittering water towards the church of the Redentore where every July she and Marcello used to light a candle along with all their friends and family. 'We were a good team,' she said wistfully. 'He died of a heart attack four years ago. I still miss him.'

'I'm sorry,' Noah said. 'I'm truly sorry that you found happiness, only to have it snatched away.'

Her eyes still on the church across the water, she said, 'Sometimes I think he made me happier than I deserved.'

'That sounds like you're being too hard on yourself.'

'I'm afraid it's true. I never really gave Marcello the whole of me. I always held something back.' She slowly turned and looked straight at Noah. 'I did it once before, handed my heart over, and look where it got me.'

For a few moments, Noah considered the paper serviette in his hands, folded it carefully, then laid it aside on the table. 'How different it could all have been, Lyddie. If only—'

She raised her hand to stop him, suddenly finding it too painful to think what might have been. 'Please, don't say it. Instead, fill me in on what you've done with your life. And your wife. What does she think about you coming here to Venice without her?'

'I don't have a wife.'

'Yes you do, Ishmael's mother.'

'She's my *ex*-wife, Lyddie. We divorced six years ago.'

'Oh. And you haven't remarried?'

He stared at her steadily, her face reflected in his sunglasses. 'No,' he said. 'I've been extremely wary about making another mistake. I married Ishmael's mother for all the wrong reasons. I wasn't a good husband to her. I wasn't a terrible husband, just not a very good one.'

'For ages after I left Swallowsdale I used to have this recurring dream that I would come back to England and discover that you'd just got married.'

'To anyone in particular?'

Lydia chewed on her lip and watched a *vaporetto* pull away from the nearby landing stage. What if by saying the name she made it true? Don't be ridiculous, she told herself. And so what if Noah had found solace in her arms? 'It was someone from school,' she said. 'Maybe you don't remember her. Her name was Zoe Woolf.'

Noah pushed his cup to one side and leaning in close, removed first his sunglasses, then Lydia's. 'I think that would be a coincidence too far, don't you?' He put his hand to her cheek, and kept it there. 'For all these years, I've felt your presence in my subconscious. Sometimes it was in my dreams. Sometimes it was when I heard a song from when we were growing up. And sometimes it was in the fleeting glance of a stranger or a gesture. I tried to forget you. I tried so hard. But you were always there, giving me hope that one day I would be able to do this.' His hand moved to her chin, tilted her mouth towards his, and very tenderly, he kissed her on the lips.

It was as if they'd never spent a day apart.

Chapter Fifty-Five

They ordered something to eat, neither of them caring what it was. It was merely fuel. Something to occupy them through the awkward pauses.

'Why didn't you try to find me?' Lydia asked. 'Not straight away, but later, when maybe you thought it would be safe to do so?'

'Initially I didn't want to do anything that would put you in danger. Then when I reasoned you'd got on with your life without me, that that was probably how you wanted it, I did something careless and in an instant the rest of my life was set on a course that couldn't include you.'

'What did you do?'

'I got a girl pregnant. I met Jane in London while I was kidding myself I could hack it as an art student. She thought she could save me from myself. For a while I almost believed she could. We married within a month of her discovering she was pregnant. The combination of us both being Catholic, no matter how vaguely so on my part, together with my need to be a better person, to get something right just once in my life, meant there was no question of her having an abortion. And, of course, things were different then. Abortion and single-parent families still carried a stigma. Marriage was the answer.'

'You must have had some moments of happiness or you wouldn't have stayed together as long as you did.'

'Jane gave me stability, so yes, therefore a degree of happiness. But it was Ishmael who really made it worthwhile. I wasn't prepared for that. He was born a week before my twenty-first birthday and he just blew me away. I couldn't get over how this small scrap of life was totally dependent on his mother and father, when we were barely out of our own childhood. I was staggered by the effect he had on me. It made me understand I couldn't go on wallowing in self-pity; I had to pull myself together and shape up. I had to make it work. I couldn't let anyone else down. Which meant no more booze.' He paused for a few moments. 'And no more thoughts of you,' he added, his voice tight.

He turned from her and as he stared out across the water, Lydia could see the haunting sorrow and deep regret in his eyes. All at once, he seemed weighed down by it. Her heart went out to him. He had suffered as much as she had. He hadn't forgotten or abandoned her as she'd believed. The realization sent a whoosh of longing and desire straight through her. It made her want to hold him close to her, to breathe in the smell of him. She wanted to kiss him as he'd kissed her earlier and feel her heart beat a little faster again. Was it really possible that time had done nothing to diminish the powerful effect he had on her? While he continued to be lost in his own thoughts, she allowed herself the indulgence of studying him, absorbing the way his eyes crinkled at the corners, the way the line of his mouth curved, and the firm smoothness of his jaw. She wondered what it would be like to make love with him after all these years. Would he still be as tender and loving as he had once been? Would their bodies fit together as well?

He suddenly turned and looked at her. Alarmed that he might not have lost his talent for reading her mind, she said, 'When I met Ishmael for the first time, he joked that his father had been responsible for his fine Old Testament name. He attributed it to you having a weird sense of humour.'

'He tells everyone that.'

'You're very close, aren't you? You could almost be brothers.'

'I've been lucky in that respect. Did you never want children?'

'For years I had a real aversion to the idea, and then

when I met Marcello I thought a child between us would make everything perfect. But for whatever reason, it didn't happen.'

'But at least you have Chiara.'

'Yes, Chiara has given real meaning to my life. She was only nine when I met her and still missing her mother, who hadn't long since died. She reminded me of myself at that age. I wanted to wrap her in cotton wool and keep her safe from the world. Her father had decided that learning English might work as a distraction for her, something to keep her occupied. That's how I met Marcello: he responded to one of my adverts.'

'And now Ishmael and Chiara have met. What do you make of it?'

'I don't know what it is about the Solomon men,' Lydia said with a smile, 'but Ishmael seems to have swept Chiara off her feet. I've never seen her like this before.'

'The same goes for Ishmael. They've fallen for each other in a big way, haven't they?'

'They're so young, though.'

'Not that young.'

'You sound as if you want to encourage their relationship.'

'I do. For the simple and very selfish reason that if they get seriously involved, you and I will have the perfect excuse to keep seeing each other.'

'Do we need an excuse?'

'I thought maybe you might want one.'

'Oh, Noah, how could you think that?'

He reached for her hand. 'The truth is I'm scared. Scared how unreal sitting here with you feels. It seems too good to be true.'

They paid the bill and left. The moment they were out of the sun, the coldness of the day hit them and by the time they made it back to the apartment – there was no sign of Chiara and Ishmael – they were grateful to be in the warm.

'It's a beautiful apartment,' Noah said, looking appreciatively around him. 'The proportions are grand without being at all ostentatious.'

'Thank you. You're probably thinking that it's a far cry from Hillside Terrace, aren't you?'

'Just a touch.' He went over to take a closer look at the furthest wall, which was covered in silk damask. 'Not old, I presume,' he said, a statement rather than a question. Taking out a pair of glasses, he traced a finger over the Venetian red fabric. 'It's in too good a condition. Polyester in the mix, I'd guess.'

She laughed and sat down so she could rest her ankle. 'You're right on both counts. I bought it locally here in Venice and it's a fraction of the price of the genuine article, but allegedly it'll last longer. You sound like an expert on the subject.'

'I have my moments,' he said with a smile, switching his attention to one of Lydia's favourite watercolours: a picture of San Giorgio at dusk. She watched him appraising the painting as he leaned on his cane. She could see from his expression that he liked and approved of it.

'What kind of house do you live in?' she asked. 'For that matter, where do you live and what do you do for a living?'

He put away his glasses and went over to the window. He seemed to be restless and in a prowling sort of mood. 'Now we really are indulging in small talk, aren't we?' he said.

'I'm sorry. There's so much I know about you, but so much I don't. There's this huge gap I need to fill.'

'OK then, here goes. I live in a Northamptonshire village in a house I had built for me three years ago. Work-wise, I run a textile company making soft furnishing fabrics. We've recently bought a small Italian company near Padua that specializes in a particular finish we want to start using. Which is why Ishmael is here in Venice studying at the language school. He works for me, or as he likes to say, he's my heir apparent, and is going to be based in Padua for the foreseeable future. You look surprised.'

'I am. I never pictured you in a suit-and-tie kind of job. How did you get into the world of textiles?'

'Blame Uncle Brad; he was the one who encouraged me to have an interest in drawing in the first place. Anyway, when Jane and I got married and I left art school, I dabbled in a bit of graphic design and then my uncle got me a job doing textile design work for an old friend of his. Next thing I knew, I discovered I had a talent for it and started doing stuff on the side that I could easily sell. By the time I was Ishmael's age, I'd set up my own company and had a dozen people working for me. Now we have almost a hundred.'

'Impressive. Do you still do any of the creative work?'

'It's pretty much all I do. Some years ago, I lost my appetite for what I see as the more tedious aspects of running a business, and now have an excellent team to take care of that side of things. I'm in the fortunate position of looking forward to taking more of a back seat before too long.'

'Did your work ever bring you to Italy?'

'There were, and still are, the trade fairs in Milan and Bologna, but since that was always Jane's forte, I opted out of them after a couple of years, happy to leave it to her.'

'Jane worked with you?'

'She still does. She runs the company with me. And that's another reason why we didn't rush into a divorce. What was the point when we were spending every day working together? It would have been different had we been at one another's throats, but we weren't.'

Lydia felt an unexpected twang of jealousy. 'A real family affair, then?'

Noah frowned and walked stiffly across the room. He sat on the sofa next to her. 'It's the way it turned out. Didn't you have the same situation here when Marcello was alive? Except for you it was different: you loved each other. Jane and I have an excellent working relationship, but as to the other, there's been nothing but friendship between us for years. She remarried eighteen months ago and is happier now than I ever made her.'

Lydia closed her eyes, a surge of reddening shame flushing her face. 'I'm sorry,' she said, her head lowered as she fiddled with the plaster Noah had applied to her finger the previous night. 'I don't know where that came from. I suddenly felt so jealous. Ignore me. I'm just being irrational.'

Putting a hand to her back and working his palm up and down her spine, he said, 'You sound perfectly rational to me.'

Rational or nor, there was one thing Lydia couldn't let go of: the thought that Noah hadn't tried to find her. 'Those times you went to Milan and Bologna,' she said, 'didn't you ever think that I might be in Italy? You must have suspected that this was where I'd run to with Joey.'

Noah's hand came to a stop in the small of her back. He sat very still for a long time, staring ahead of him. Then switching his gaze back to her, his voice low, he said, 'Every place I ever went to, I thought you could be there, Lyddie. When I was living in London, I became convinced you'd deliberately disappeared the same day as Joey to make the police think you'd gone to Italy, whereas really you hadn't left the country at all. The more I thought this, the more I believed you'd gone where every runner-away goes: London. I nearly drove myself crazy imagining that you could be living just around the corner from me. I used to go through the phone book picking out numbers with the name of Turner and ring them. Which was absurd. If you were trying to keep your identity secret, you'd hardly advertise your whereabouts in the telephone directory, would you?' His hand moved to her shoulder. 'I'm sorry, but for the sake of my marriage, and Ishmael, I had to let it go. I had to believe that wherever you were, you were happy.'

The light was beginning to fade when Noah raised the subject that had been eclipsed by everything else they had needed to ask each other.

'Lyddie,' he said. 'You realize, don't you, that you have to come back to England with me? We have to find out who really did kill your uncle. If you don't, people will always think you did it. You have to clear your name. You can't live the rest of your life with this hanging over you.'

It was exactly what Lydia had dreaded Noah saying. She didn't want to go back to Swallowsdale. Not when she was frightened she might never return home to Venice.

Chapter Fifty-Six

Two days later, it was all arranged and Lydia was boarding a BA flight for Heathrow. She was fraught with nerves. She had never been at ease on planes, something Marcello hadn't ever understood the few times they had flown together. But then he hadn't known the cause of her anxiety, had just assumed she nursed the perfectly conventional fear of their plane crashing. How could he have known that the sight of a customs official, his or her hand outstretched for her passport, gave Lydia far more anxiety than the thought of a mid-air explosion.

Staring at the tarmac as she strapped herself into her seat, Lydia wondered if it wasn't too late to change her mind. Why couldn't she just take her chances and live out the rest of her life in Venice never knowing who had killed Uncle Leonard? After all this time, did it matter?

When she had aired these thoughts over dinner last night with Fabio and Paolo, she had been met with the same argument that Noah had given her: that she had to clear her name. Whilst they'd all been in agreement on this point, Fabio had added a word of caution and made Noah promise that he would take good care of Lydia while they were away. But how would Noah be able to do that if the police discovered she had entered the country? Whilst he seemed to think the case would be so long dead and buried that she could walk into the police station in Swallowsdale and no one would bat an eyelid, she was not so sure. Nor was she convinced by his reassurance that her passport wouldn't set off any alarm bells. 'You've taken out Italian citizenship, you have an Italian passport, and your married name is Tomasi. What possible reason would there be for anyone to suspect you of committing a crime in England that happened so many years ago?' was Noah's reasoning. He was one hundred and ten per cent sure that she was safe.

But as the thrust from the aeroplane's engine kicked in and she saw the tarmac rushing away from beneath her, Lydia felt anything but safe. She wished she had never given in to Noah and the rest of them. Now she had proved that she could move around relatively painlessly and without the aid of a crutch, Fabio and Paolo had invited them all to dinner last night. Lydia hadn't been fooled. She had known that Fabio wanted to meet Noah, to check him out. 'And your opinion of Noah?' she had asked him discreetly in Italian when he had been helping her into her coat at the end of the evening. 'I like him, Lydia,' he'd whispered, 'and his son. But please, be careful. You broke your heart over him once before. I don't want to see you hurt again.'

There was no question of Lydia falling in love all over again with Noah. It just wasn't possible, for the simple reason that she had never stopped loving him. She may have succeeded in blocking him out for most of her adult life, but the connection was still there. If anything, the magnetism was even stronger.

The plane was levelling out now with Venice and the lagoon no longer within sight. Its absence tugged at Lydia's heart. Would she ever see it again? Why was she risking everything? As if seeking assurance, she glanced at Noah.

'You OK?' he asked.

'No,' she said. 'I'm terrified.'

He put his hand on her wrist and stroked it lovingly. 'We're in this together. Don't forget that.'

Once they were off the plane, Noah held her hand all the way to passport control. 'Nothing's going to happen,' he whispered in her ear when it was finally her turn to step forward. Sure enough, she and her passport were given no more than a cursory glance and she was waved through.

Their luggage retrieved from the carousel, they took the route signposted 'Nothing to Declare' and emerged into the arrivals hall. An enormous Christmas tree dominated the crowded space. Her nerves all jagged, feeling like a child, Lydia wanted to feel the security of Noah's hand again, but he was pushing the trolley with their luggage on it.

'So far so good,' he said when they had stowed their luggage into the boot of a sleek, silver Mercedes sports car. 'Now all we have to do is negotiate the horrors of the M25.'

When on the mainland, away from Venice, Lydia was quite used to Italian drivers and their love of speed – she was no slouch herself – but the second Noah had negotiated their way out of the confines of the airport, he put his foot down in a way that would have put any one of them to shame. But not once did he frighten her. He drove confidently, never carelessly, his eyes on the road at all times.

'Nice car,' she remarked.

'Thanks. Cars are a weakness of mine I'm afraid, and this is definitely the kind of car a boy can get himself into trouble with.'

Relaxing a little, Lydia smiled. 'Go on, I know you're itching to: give me the specification. What model and what size engine?'

His eyes lit up. 'It's the SL600 with a V12 biturbo 5.5 litre engine that can zap to sixty in 4.5 seconds. I had to wait nearly ten months for it.'

She laughed. 'I loved the car Uncle Brad bought you for your seventeenth birthday. What happened to it?'

'I crashed it. I was very drunk at the time.'

It was dark when Noah eventually brought the car to a stop on a gravelled drive in front of a pillared porch. From what Lydia could see of the house, it looked gracious and individual. Not unlike its owner.

Inside, Noah dumped their luggage in the hallway,

flicked on lights and dealt with an alarm system. 'Sorry it's not very warm,' he apologized. 'I left the heating ticking over on its lowest setting. I'll go and give the boiler a talking to.'

She followed him into a large L-shaped kitchen and while he disappeared through another door, she scanned her surroundings, curious to observe Noah as an adult in his natural habitat. He was meticulously tidy, was her first observation as she took in the uncluttered granite surfaces. How different it was from Uncle Brad's messy workshop of a kitchen at Upper Swallowsdale House. The decor was unfussy, cool and neutral. Nothing jarred. There was an island unit in the middle of the room with a discreet flat-screen television built into the cream-coloured units directly opposite: Lydia imagined Noah eating his supper here whilst watching the evening news. Next to a stainless steel range-style cooker was a shelf of cookery books and a set of professional kitchen knives. He was a cook of some merit, perhaps? On a shelf above the cookery books was a framed photograph of a young Ishmael, ten or eleven years old. It could so easily have been a picture of Noah at that age.

'That's the heating booted up,' Noah said, coming back into the kitchen. 'Coffee?'

'Please.'

She watched him put the kettle on and then go over to an eye-level fridge. 'Excellent,' he said. 'Not only do we have milk, but something to eat for tonight. Shepherd's pie. What would I do without Mrs Massey?'

'And who might she be?'

'My housekeeper. She comes in three times a week and is a godsend. I called her yesterday to ask if she could get some food in for us. Stupidly, I forgot to ask her to turn up the heating, though.'

Mrs Massey had also been asked to prepare the largest of the guest rooms and when Noah took Lydia upstairs they found a vase of prettily arranged flowers on the dressing table and clean towels hanging on the rail in the en suite bathroom.

'It's a big house just for one,' Lydia commented when they were back out on the spacious landing and she was admiring the dramatic vaulted ceiling.

His hands resting on the oak balustrade, looking down onto the hall with its pale oak floor, Noah said, 'What can I say? I like some space around me.'

'You must have found Venice very cramped. Some people find it claustrophobic and never take to the place.'

'I didn't feel that at all. Quite the reverse in fact. Come with me: there's something I want to show you. But you have to promise you won't freak out when you see it.'

'Why did you think I'd freak out?' Lydia asked, after he'd pushed open the door into his bedroom and they'd gone inside. On the wall opposite his bed, above a chest of drawers, was the portrait Uncle Brad had painted of Lydia shortly after her seventeenth birthday.

'I was worried you might think me a bit weird for still having it,' he said, 'especially as it's hanging in my bedroom. And before you ask, no, I didn't have it on show when I was married. It was carefully stored away then.'

'When did it see the light of day again?'

'When I came to live here. Mrs Massey is the only person who's seen it. No one else ever comes into my room.'

Lydia stepped in closer to get a better look at her seventeen-year-old self. How young she looked. And how serious and melancholy. Was that how Uncle Brad had seen her? She wondered how he would paint her now. Would he exaggerate the lines around her eyes, add in the grey hairs her hairdresser so artfully disguised for her, so as to show the real her? To reveal the life she'd led? 'At the time I was never really sure if Uncle Brad was any good as a painter,' she said, stepping back from the oil painting and her lost youth, 'but now I can see he was more than good. He had a deft touch. No wonder he was always down in London with some exhibition or other.' She suddenly laughed. 'I remember the very first time I came to your house and seeing all the candles, I thought you were so poor you couldn't afford electricity.'

Noah came and stood behind her. 'I could never tire of looking at that face,' he said. She felt his hand on her shoulder, then her hair being lifted to one side so that he could kiss the nape of her neck. She melted at his touch and wanted to turn round and kiss him, but she knew if she did that, with the bed so conveniently positioned there would be only one outcome. Were they really ready for that? She thought of the guest room Noah had had made up for her. Was that good manners on his part, or an indicator of his reluctance to take that step?

After they'd eaten and tidied everything away, with an early start planned for the morning, they both agreed that an early night would be sensible.

'You're sure you've got everything you need?' Noah asked her on the landing outside her room.

'You've asked me that twice already.'

He smiled, embarrassed. 'I know. I guess I'm just putting off the moment.'

'What moment?'

'The moment when I ask you what I really want to ask you.'

'Which is?'

'Can we dispense with the guest room sham? I thought it was the right thing to do but I can't go through with it. I can't lie in the room next door to you knowing that you're sleeping just yards away from me. I want you in my bed tonight. I want to make love to you. I want to wake up in the morning with you in my arms.'

She leaned towards him. 'I'd like that, too.'

Noah held her in his arms, kissing her, touching her lightly. 'I've missed you so much,' he breathed heavily.

She stroked his face and stared deep into his dark, familiar eyes. 'I've missed you for a lifetime.'

He led her to the bed and started kissing her again, his

hands fumbling with the buttons on her top. 'God, I'm suddenly so nervous,' he said. 'I'm like a teenager again.'

'Me too,' she admitted, and suddenly shy, she took hold of his hands. 'Noah, you realize, don't you, that it won't be the same between us? I'm ... I'm older.'

He raised a questioning eyebrow. 'And your point?'

'I don't look how I used to.'

He smiled, peeled off his T-shirt and threw it on the floor. 'Thank God for that. Because neither do I.' He kissed her again. 'Don't worry,' he whispered, 'it'll be fine.' He went back to the buttons on her top, slipped it off, then reached round to unhook her bra.

'Don't say I didn't warn you,' she said, half joking, half serious.

He silenced her with another long, tender kiss, then lay her down on the bed. His lips moved to her neck and then her throat, tracking a slow path to her breasts. Her head spun.

When they were both fully undressed Lydia pressed her hands flat against his chest, then rested her ear against him. 'I used to love doing this,' she murmured, 'listening to your heart.'

'Your body hasn't changed at all,' he said, taking the whole of her in. 'You still look eighteen.' There was an expression of wonder on his face.

'It's the light in here,' she said. 'It would flatter a rhinoceros.'

'Hey, here's the deal. While you get on with disagreeing with everything I say, I'll apply myself to the business of making love to you. How does that sound?'

Lydia laughed and then gasped when he gently placed his hand between her legs. She wrapped her arms around him. His touch was slick and dexterous, and when he slid down the length of her and she felt the warmth of his mouth on her, her body responded in a way it hadn't done in years. She closed her eyes and gave in to the quivering, intense pleasure.

He took his time, keeping her on the brink until finally

the growing tingling tremors exploded into an orgasm suffused with so much love she could hardly breathe. The release was immense, almost spiritual. When she was still, he lay beside her, crushed her to him.

When at last she could find the words to speak, she said, 'I see you're still a natural genius for conjuring up an orgasm.'

'It helps to be with the right woman,' he said quietly, raising himself up onto an elbow. He stared at her intensely, his eyes dark and penetrating. He stroked her cheek. 'It always felt right with you. It still does.'

Lydia turned her face into the palm of his hand and kissed it. 'I used to dream of us being together again like this. In bed. I always woke up crying. I had to teach myself never to think of you. It was the hardest thing I ever did.'

'I'm sorry,' he said. 'Sorry for all the wasted years.' His voice was thick.

'So am I.' She ran a hand along the length of his long, lean body. In the soft light cast from the lamp behind him, she could see the myriad scars on his badly damaged leg. He saw what she was looking at and reached for the duvet to cover it. She stopped him. 'Please don't,' she said. 'It's a part of you.' She tipped him onto his back and kissed him lightly on the mouth, no more than a teasing whisper of a kiss. His lips parted and she traced them with her tongue. He shivered and opened his mouth wider, wanting more of her, one of his hands on the back of her head pulling her down to him. She resisted with a smile. 'I think you'll find I'm calling the shots on this one,' she said.

He gave her his best Question Mark Face.

Laughing, she hooked a leg over his hips and sat up astride him, her back straight. 'That car of yours, how long did you say it took to get to sixty miles an hour?'

He groaned. 'Be gentle with me, Lyddie. It's been a while.'

Chapter Fifty-Seven

The following morning, a light dusting of snow had turned Noah's garden into a magical winter wonderland. In the dark, Lydia hadn't noticed the formal box hedging or the stone urns that lined the gravel drive. In the distance, beyond the spire of a church, and behind a swell of gently sweeping hills, a ball of shimmering gold light was climbing the pale sky. It was a stunningly beautiful day. With their breath forming in the cold air, they packed their luggage into the boot of the car and hurriedly got in.

At the end of the driveway Lydia turned to take one last look at the house, as though committing it to memory.

'Don't worry,' Noah said. 'I promise you'll see it again.'

Their destination was Swallowsdale. Noah had everything planned, right down to where they would be staying and what their first move would be. Before leaving Venice he'd booked them into the Oak Manor Court Hotel, which was to be their first port of call. Lydia had imagined they would then go to the library in Swallowsdale and spend hours poring over microfilm, reading up on newspaper reports of the murder. But apparently not. Noah said they would nose around first, then check out the library.

They were on the motorway when Noah pressed a button and music filled the car. She didn't recognize it, but then she was more familiar with Italian bands and singers. 'What are we listening to?' she asked.

'It's Thom Yorke's album, *The Eraser*.'

At her blank expression, he said, 'Radiohead?'

'That rings a bell,' she said vaguely.

'Don't tell me we've hit our first cultural divide.'

She smiled and stared out of the window, taking in the landscape. England, twenty-eight years on. She had some catching up to do.

The Oak Manor Court Hotel, with views across a scrubby golf course to the west, and Swallowsdale and the moors to the east, proudly boasted its three-star status with a sign that was hanging off a rusting hinged bracket. It creaked and grated as it swung in the raw, blustery wind that welcomed them with a stinging slap in the face when they stepped out of the car. There was no snow to soften the bleak landscape and it was hard to imagine anywhere more isolated or depressingly remote.

'It's life, Jim, but not as we know it,' Noah murmured as they stood in the small reception area waiting for someone to appear behind the desk. Above their heads, Christmas music tinkled away from a speaker that, like the sign outside, had a perilous tilt to it. Over by the window, an artificial Christmas tree was festooned with decorations and flashing lights. 'I know what you're thinking,' Noah said, 'but believe me, this was the best on offer at such short notice. What's the betting Basil Fawlty's lurking here somewhere?'

'You always did watch too much television,' Lydia said. 'Why don't we ring the bell?' On the desk next to a miniature Christmas tree was a small brass bell. She gave it a light tap and straight away a voice called out, 'Be with you in a jiffy.'

Within seconds the half-glazed door behind the desk opened and a sturdily built woman pulling off a pair of rubber gloves greeted them. 'Sorry about that,' she said, 'plumbing trouble. Right then. Checking in? Or just here for morning coffee?'

'Checking in,' Noah said. 'Mr and Mrs Solomon. We have a reservation.'

The woman consulted something out of sight to Lydia

and Noah and said, 'Ah, yes, here we are.' Still struggling to get one of the gloves off, she pushed a piece of paper towards them. 'If you could just fill out your name and address and car registration then I'll show you to your room. Would you like a wake-up call and a newspaper in the morning?'

'Darling?'

Lydia hesitated, then shook her head.

Putting on his glasses, Noah completed the form and passed it back to the woman. 'Righty ho,' she said, 'that's the formalities dealt with. Now I'll show you upstairs.' She lifted up part of the desk top and came round to join them. When she saw Noah's cane, she said, 'The stairs won't be a problem for you, will they?'

Noah assured her they wouldn't, but even so, she insisted on carrying their luggage. 'I've put you in the Hardcastle Suite,' she said. 'It has the best views and a lovely big jacuzzi bath. I've got you down for three nights. Are you here on holiday?'

'Sort of,' Noah said. 'A trip down memory lane you could say. I used to live in the area.'

'That's nice.'

'How about you?' Noah asked. 'Are you local?'

'Me? No. My husband and I bought this place ten years ago after running a pub in Coventry. We fancied a change. And we certainly got that.'

At the top of the stairs, while the woman unlocked the panelled door to the Hardcastle Suite, Noah exchanged a look with Lydia. She knew what he was thinking: at least there was no danger of the owners of the hotel recognizing her.

They were shown the room with such zeal and attention to detail – everything was superior or deluxe – it was as if they were potential buyers. Alone at last, they both sat on the edge of the four-poster bed. Its flimsy, repro structure creaked ominously. They looked at each other and laughed. 'Sex is definitely off the agenda,' Lydia said. 'Not unless we want to entertain the other guests.'

'There's always the jacuzzi bath to frolic in,' Noah suggested, 'though God knows what deluxe horrors that may have in store for us. More seriously, you don't mind that I booked us in as being married, do you? Only I thought it would be simpler that way. I'd hate for you to think I was being presumptuous when I booked the room back in Venice. Separate rooms, or twin beds, especially twin beds, would have provoked more questions.'

'Of course I don't mind. Although you took me by surprise with that "darling" business.'

'I took myself by surprise.' He smiled. 'Shall we put the superior tea and coffee-making facilities to the test and discuss what we're going to do next, *darling*?'

It wasn't in Lydia's nature to let someone else make so many decisions on her behalf, but she had sensed since leaving Venice that finding out the truth about Uncle Leonard's death was something Noah needed to do. Knowing that she had sacrificed so much for him – even mistakenly so – he probably saw this as his way to try and make amends. Yet for all that, it was difficult for her to take a back seat. As an adult she had always been in control of her life, and rightly or wrongly she had a tendency to make snap decisions – more often than not, snap unilateral decisions. It was a lifetime's habit based on a need to defend and protect not just herself but those she loved.

A shame she had got it so colossally wrong that night in the dell.

They drove the short distance to Swallowsdale, stopping first in Upper Swallowsdale. The engine idling, they stared up at Uncle Brad's old house. White PVC-framed windows had been installed, along with a satellite dish. A handmade poster was tied to the gate; it was advertising a fundraising mince pie and mulled wine do for the local Conservative party.

'Uncle Brad would die on the spot,' Lydia said.

'Wouldn't he just?' Noah agreed, his foot already tweaking the engine. 'Seen enough?'

'Yes.'

'Swallowsdale town centre, here we come. Unless you want to go to Hillside Terrace first?'

She shook her head. 'Let's save that till last.'

In the gloomy half-light, the town was nothing like they remembered. The shabby parade of flat-roofed shops along the main street had gone. As had the scruffy old barber's on the corner opposite the bank. Where was the post office? And the dry cleaner's and the old bookshop? And how about the supermarket where Noah had worked?

The whole place had been transformed beyond recollection. There was now a pedestrianized area where the main street had once been, and as they moved amongst the crowds of Christmas shoppers, they could hear piped carols in the cold afternoon air. There were ye olde street lamps and matching rubbish bins and tea shops galore. There were antique shops aplenty, and a store selling expensive leisurewear and walking boots. Where their favourite second-hand bookshop had been was an Italian restaurant called *Il Trattoria*, complete with red and white chequered table cloths and lots of fake hams and salami hanging from hooks above the bar. Next door to it was a shop claiming to be selling vintage clothing. 'Looks just like the stuff we used to buy from jumble sales,' Lydia said, standing at the window.

'I hate to be the bearer of bad tidings, Lyddie, but those clothes count as genuine vintage these days.'

She gave him a playful punch. 'And you can keep the ageist comments to yourself. It all looks so much more prosperous than I remember it.'

They went in search of the Church of The Brothers and Sisters in Christ. But it was gone – all trace of it. In its place was a public convenience, complete with a ramp and a pay-on-entry turnstile. The irony was just too fitting to be funny. 'Pastor Digby and his ilk flushed away for all eternity,' Lydia remarked, feeling sadder than she might have expected.

They'd missed out on lunch, but didn't dare risk one of the gentrified tea shops for something to eat. Lydia was paranoid about staying still for too long and being recognized – even with her hat and sunglasses on, and a scarf wrapped high around her neck. They risked a sandwich shop, joined the queue inside and scanned the extensive menu options. Behind them the entire wall was a mirror, probably there to make the shop feel bigger and airier.

'Who's next, then?'

Noah nudged Lydia. 'We are,' he said to a man behind the counter, who had a striped apron tied around his waist. His hair was very short and gelled to form little peaks at the front. 'I'll have a bacon and avocado baguette, please,' Noah said. He turned to Lydia. Lydia dithered. 'Um ... oh, the same for me, please.'

'That'll be five pounds ninety, please.'

They were the only ones in the shop now, and whilst the man made their baguettes for them, Noah glanced at Lydia and frowned. 'What's wrong?' he whispered.

Lydia tipped her head towards the man. 'He reminds me of someone,' she whispered back.

'Who?'

'I don't know. But I want to get out of here. Now.'

'You go on ahead to the car.' He pulled his keys out of his coat pocket and gave them to her. 'I'll catch you up.'

She had been sitting in the car for almost ten minutes, wondering if she had let her paranoia get the better of her, when Noah appeared. He got into the driver's seat beside her. He looked pleased with himself. 'You were right to think there was something familiar about that guy. Remember Donna Jones?'

Lydia nodded. 'Of course. It was her surname I used for my new identity.'

'Well, that was none other than her son, Kirk.'

While Noah explained how he'd got chatting to the sandwich man – after all, they were here to dig up whatever information they could – Lydia did the maths. 'That

418

makes him thirty-one. I can't believe it! Captain Kirk, thirty-one. It's not possible.'

'Never mind how old Captain Kirk is,' Noah said, 'he told me his mother still lives in Swallowsdale. Now pass me that phone book I pinched from the hotel.'

'I knew my hunch to come here and nose around would pay off,' Noah said when they were negotiating the road system of a smart housing estate. The houses all had the sharp-edged look of having only been in existence for a short time.

They'd found Donna's entry in the phone book under her married name – which Kirk had supplied when Noah had said he'd been at school with Donna and was visiting the area to look up a few old friends – and the plan was for Noah to park the car some distance from Donna's house, leaving Lydia in it while he went and chatted with Donna about the 'old days'. It was inevitable that the conversation would innocently lead to Lydia and the murder of her great-uncle.

It seemed a foolproof plan. All along Noah had been convinced that they'd be better off showing up in Swallowsdale and running into people from the past to get what he called an 'on the ground' perspective about the murder. 'Donna is perfect,' he said now to Lydia as they turned into a road signposted as Lark's Close. 'She's bound to have an opinion, and who knows, she might just know something important.'

Lydia said nothing. She couldn't believe it could be as simple as that.

With Donna's house located – it was a large detached property with a double garage and a BMW on the drive – Noah drove back out of Lark's Close and into an adjoining road. 'Right,' he said with a determined expression. 'I could be a while.'

She watched him walk stiffly away in the fading light.

No clock-watching, she told herself, when after only a few minutes had passed she found she couldn't stop looking at her watch. Noah had left the keys in the ignition to switch the engine on if she got too cold. Another five minutes and she might have to do exactly that.

To distract herself, she counted the number of houses with lights shaped as icicles attached to them. From there she progressed to counting the illuminated bulbs on the Christmas tree in the garden next to her. Bored of that, she decided to call Chiara and bring her up to date. But all she got was the engaged tone ringing in her ear.

She put her mobile away in her bag, leaned her head back against the headrest and relaxed into the soft, comfortable leather seat. She let her thoughts drift. Swallowsdale. She was really here. Against all the odds and every fiercely made vow, she had actually returned. And to find a killer, of all things. Or at least, discover who the killer had been. It was possible that the person who had brought an end to Uncle Leonard's life was also dead now. Who knows, the two men might even be buried side by side. How they would have hated the idea of that!

Ruling out some random nutter roaming the dell that night, the most obvious suspect was her grandfather. With the most to gain by Uncle Leonard's death, he was certainly not lacking a motive. She and Noah had checked the phone book for an A. Turner and had drawn a blank. If her grandfather was still alive – he'd have to be in his nineties now – he was no longer living at number thirty-three Hillside Terrace. Or if he was, his name had been removed from the listing. The prospect of going to the house to find out filled Lydia with dread. She'd told Noah she wanted to leave driving there until last, and she meant it.

Cold now, she reached across to the driver's seat and turned the key in the ignition to activate the car heater. She put her gloves on and closed her eyes, pondering what Donna's reaction would be to Noah turning up unexpectedly on her doorstep. Immediately, she thought of her own reaction when Noah had appeared on her doorstep in Venice. Shock. Disbelief. Anger even. But most of all, the sure knowledge that nothing was ever going to be the same again.

Late last night, Noah had confessed to her that after he'd left her apartment that first night in Venice, he'd lain awake in bed thinking how badly he'd wanted to take her in his arms. How he'd wanted to kiss her. He'd wanted to turn her face up to his and kiss her mouth. All that, the first night.

A tap on the car window made her jump. She looked up to see Noah. He opened the door and leaned in. 'I think you'd better come in and hear what Donna's just told me.'

Chapter Fifty-Eight

'Friggin' hell!' Donna roared at the top of her voice. 'Just look what the bloody cat finally dragged in! Who'd have thought it?'

Lydia hugged her old friend, genuinely delighted to see her again. 'And who'd have thought you'd turn into such a shy, retiring little thing?'

Donna laughed. 'Like that was ever gonna happen! Now come in out of the cold and sit down and let me get a proper look at you. Hey, Noah, how about some tea while us girls do some catching up here? You'll find everything you need in all the obvious places. Oh, and there are some mince pies in the tin on the draining board. Chop, chop!' she added with a mischievous wink.

When they were alone, Lydia said, 'You look well, Donna. Really well.'

'I am. A little fatter than I'd like, but I blame that on good living and giving up the fags. But look at you! Quite the classy tart in your finery. You finally got around to doing sommat about your appalling dress sense, then? Just wait till I tell Alfie you were here. You remember Alfie, don't you?'

'Of course. Kirk's grown, hasn't he?'

'Yeah, just a bit. Noah said you'd run into him in town. He's married with a kid of his own now. I'm a grandmother. How about that?'

'Congratulations. And Lydia Junior?'

Donna pointed to a large framed photograph on the mantelpiece. 'See for yourself.'

Lydia went to have a look at it, along with all the

other pictures that were partially hidden behind a row of Christmas cards. 'She's the smart one,' Donna said. 'Took after you, I reckon. You must have whispered sommat in her ear when you delivered her. She's a teacher. Lives in Birmingham with her boyfriend who's a solicitor.'

'You must be so proud of them both. Did you have any more children?'

'Are you crazy? No, I kept my knickers firmly on and my powder dry after Lydia. I then had the sense to channel my energies into a different direction. I went back to school. Just as you used to nag me! I got myself all educated up and started my own little business. You've caught me on a rare afternoon when I'm home early. I now run a flooring company. Floors Direct, it's called. Doesn't sound very exciting, I know, but I built it up from nowt, and what with everyone currently mad for laminate and wood flooring, business has been booming a treat these last few years. My only disappointment is that Kirk refused to come and work with me like Alfie did a few years back. He's a stubborn whatsit and wants to do his own thing.'

'Good for him,' Lydia said. 'And especially good for you.' Then looking around the spacious sitting room with its cream carpet and oyster-coloured leather three-piece suite and large plasma screen television she said, 'I don't see any wood flooring here.'

'Not on your life! I'm a carpet girl through and through. When I'm not in the kitchen and bathroom, I like a nice bit of wool under my feet. You can't beat it in my opinion.'

Lydia laughed. 'So when did you and Alfie get together?' She picked up a photograph of Donna and Alfie on their wedding day. Donna was sporting a blonde perm of monumental proportions; Alfie's hair looked suspiciously like it had had the same treatment. Donna's hair now was chestnut brown and styled into a softly layered bob that suited her perfectly. As did the silvery-grey roll-necked sweater.

'We started dating about two years after you slung your hook,' Donna said, 'and without so much as a by your leave on your part, I might add.'

Lydia put the photograph back in its place. 'I'm sorry I left without saying goodbye. I had to.'

'So you should be. I was furious with you, but once all that stuff about your uncle hit the papers, it made sense. Later, though, when the truth came out, I thought, right, now she can come—'

'Truth?' Lydia interrupted, leaping on the word. 'You know what happened?'

'Of course. But we'll get to that in a moment. First off, where the hell have you been all this time?'

'Italy.'

Just then, Noah came in unsteadily with a tray of mugs and a plate of mince pies. Donna jumped up from her armchair and took it from him. She placed it on the glass coffee table in front of the sofa. 'Have you got to the point and told her yet, Donna?' he asked.

'Give us a moment to catch up, won't you?' Donna handed Lydia one of the mugs of tea. 'I don't remember him being this bossy and impatient. You want to watch that.'

Amused, Lydia sat down. 'I'll do my best,' she said. How good it was to see Donna again. Time and prosperity may have changed her – certainly her language and broad accent had mellowed – but essentially she was still the same.

'Right then,' Donna said when they were all settled, 'now it's your turn to bring me up to date. Let me guess, you two are married? And I wouldn't blame you if you were, Lydia. Apart from that chronic impatience of his, he's turned out to be quite a looker, hasn't he? Kept himself in good shape as well. If I didn't have Alfie, I might be tempted myself.'

'Donna!' Noah remonstrated, his face a picture of embarrassment. 'Please, just tell Lydia what you told me.'

'Well,' Donna began, 'you can imagine what a big deal it was when the papers got hold of the story of some bloke who'd been murdered in Swallowsdale, right here on our doorstep. Within no time everyone had a theory about who could have done it. Most folks thought Joey, the ice-cream man, had done it, being foreign and all, and what with him leaving when he did, so sudden-like. Then once it became known you were missing, people said it had been a double murder, that Joey had killed your great-uncle, then killed you and hidden your body. Or carted it off to Italy with him.' Donna laughed. 'I can't tell you how many people went round saying they'd always known Joey had a look about him, that he was a mass murderer just waiting for the right moment to strike.'

'What did you think?' Lydia asked while Donna drew breath and sipped on her tea.

'Me? Oh, I was having no truck with all that nonsense. I reckoned you'd done the old pervert in good and proper. Don't look so shocked. I might have done it myself given half a chance.'

A cold unease crept over Lydia. 'Why do you call him an old pervert?' she asked.

'Because that's what he was. I knew he must have tried sommat on with you.'

'Why would you think that?'

Donna rolled her eyes. 'We girls know these things. Now will you stop interrupting me and let me get on with being the centre of attention? Now then, where was I?'

'The pervert,' prompted Noah.

'That's right, the old perv. Yeah, well, the disgusting tosser tried it on with me. He came to my house one day asking if I wanted any odd jobs doing and when I said he could have a go at sorting out the washer on the kitchen tap, he said he hadn't been thinking of that kind of job. I told him I'd hack his dick off and throw it to the dogs if he came near me again. Next time I saw him he tried to get a cop of my jing-jang when I was on my way home from work one night and I gave him a right mouthful.'

'Why didn't you ever tell me this?'

'Come off it! No girl wants to admit that some horny old perv has tried it on with her. Different story if it's some drop-dead gorgeous guy. Then we're practically shouting

425

from the rooftops about it. Anyway, the point is, when he was found dead and you were missing, I put two and two together, just as the police did. Next thing we knew from reading the papers was that you were wanted for questioning in connection with the murder. We were all questioned, those who knew you. 'Course, I never said anything. It was never actually printed in the papers, but it got out somehow, as these things do, that there was evidence to put you at the scene of the crime. Well, it was a done deal as far as we were all concerned. But then, and I can't be sure exactly when, but let's say it was some months later, it was in the paper that the murderer had been found. As far as I know, no arrest was actually made, but the police had a confession and the case was closed. End of story.'

'Who was it, Donna? Who confessed?'

'Your grandmother. Crazy as crazy, she stuck a knife in the old devil and then for some reason started bragging about it when everything had gone quiet. She told the police God had made her do it.'

Lydia was stunned into silence. She couldn't believe it. Her grandmother? The night she'd run off from the hospital? It certainly fitted. 'But what about the evidence the police found that made them think it was me?' she asked Donna. 'How did the police think that had got there?'

'They went along with the theory that that fitted in with the fight you'd had earlier with your uncle.'

'Did it come out why my grandmother did it?' Lydia asked.

'Look, and no disrespect, but your grandmother was a complete psycho, capable of doing anything and for any reason. It's a wonder she didn't kill us all! The way the story went, she got lost on the moors, found herself in the dell with your uncle and God spoke to her. He told her that she was his avenging angel and had to kill your uncle. You can't help but think that it was the one good thing she ever did in her life.'

'What happened to her?'

'The case never went to trial because she was considered unfit to plead. Instead she was moved to a secure psychiatric hospital to live out the rest of her life. Her death was reported in the papers three years later, a week after Alfie and I got back from our honeymoon.'

Whilst Lydia was still trying to absorb everything Donna had told her, Noah said, 'Is Lydia's grandfather still alive, Donna?'

'No. He snuffed it a long time back. Before that, he remarried when his batty old wife died, though. To the woman he'd—'

'My sister,' Lydia said abruptly, cutting Donna off midsentence. 'Valerie. Do you know what happened to her, where she is and what she's doing?'

'I can't swear to what she's doing now, but back then, when that cranky old church of yours closed down, she moved away and became a nun. And let's face it, there's not a soul alive who could be surprised by that.'

Over dinner in a half-empty dining room at the Oak Manor Court Hotel, accompanied by a CD of schmaltzy Christmas songs, Lydia and Noah were discussing what their next move would be.

'If only Sister Lottie was alive, she'd be able to help us,' Lydia said. 'She would have known where Valerie had gone.' Finding Valerie had now become Lydia's number one priority.

'Donna was pretty sure it was a convent in Staffordshire. Is it too much to hope convents are listed online or in the phone book?'

'After our run of luck today, I could believe anything. How are you feeling, by the way? Any better?' When Noah had been driving them back from Donna's, he had complained of a headache.

'Not really,' he said. 'I'll take some more paracetamol when we go to bed.'

'Are you prone to headaches now? You never used to be.'

'No more than anyone else. I probably just need to get my eyes tested again.'

A waiter brought them their main course, and after he'd left, just as Johnny Mathis started singing 'When a Child is Born', Noah lifted his glass of water and said, 'I think we should celebrate the fact that we cracked the case within a few hours of arriving in Swallowsdale and, more importantly, you're now officially off the UK's most wanted list.'

'No disagreement there.'

They clinked glasses.

'If you don't mind me saying, you don't look too thrilled by our day's work.'

Lydia lowered her glass. 'That's because I feel as if I've been incredibly stupid all this time. All those measures I took to keep myself safe, and you safe, they were for nothing. My whole life has been a mockery. A ridiculous illusion. A cheap joke.'

'Don't be so hard on yourself. What you're feeling is perfectly understandable. It's difficult to change the way you've always thought about things. For so long you've believed something to be true and now you're finding it's turned on its head. It'll take a while to come to terms with it.'

'I suppose it's true for you as well. All these years, you thought I was a murderer.'

He stared at her intensely, his eyes dark and luminous in the flickering light from the candle between them. 'I never thought of it quite like that. I pictured a frightened eighteen-year-old girl trying to protect herself. Did you view me as a cold, calculating murderer?'

'No. Never.' She picked up her knife and fork, but then sighed wearily. 'I'm being morose and ruining the evening, acting like a real killjoy. I'm sorry. God, this beef is tough! Have you tried it yet?'

Noah cut a small piece off his steak and chewed on it. And chewed. 'You're right. It's awful.'

They ate as much as they could and lied politely to the

waiter when he came to clear their plates away. 'We had too much to eat at lunch,' Noah said with an apologetic shake of his head.

They ordered coffee and, serenaded by Bing Crosby singing 'White Christmas', Noah leaned forward, his elbows on the table. 'Tomorrow we try to find your sister. OK?'

Lydia leaned forward as well, pushed the candle out of the way and kissed him. 'Yes, Sherlock.'

Up in their room whilst they were getting ready for bed, Lydia's mobile rang. It was Donna.

'I've just remembered something that might help you find your sister,' she said. 'Do you remember Lisa Fortune? She was the girl at school with the artificial hand.'

'Yes, I used to have nightmares about her.'

'Really?'

'I'll tell you why another time.'

'Well, I often see her at Weight Watchers, and blame it on all the excitement of seeing you again, but I clean forgot that she joined that church of yours. She got really involved with it, too, and despite the age gap became quite pally with your sister. I've just been on the phone with her. Have you got a pen and a bit of paper handy? You might want to write this down.'

The weather was even colder the next morning. It was raining, too. It was a real misery of a day, not helped by the restless night they'd passed.

Everything had been fine until they'd got into bed and realized just how creaky the wretched thing was. Spreading the duvet on the carpet, they'd made love as discreetly as they could, given that the floorboards were almost as indiscreet as the four-poster bed. For sleeping purposes, they'd risked the bed, but if it wasn't that that had disturbed them every time one of them moved, it was the sound of the wind rumbling down the chimney or rattling the not-so-deluxe windows in their rotting frames. The headache that Noah had complained of earlier also kept him awake. It was made worse by lying down, so he'd snatched what little sleep he could by sleeping upright.

They were the only people in the dining room for breakfast, which suited them fine. They were served by the same waiter as the previous night. He was probably the only waiter the hotel had.

By the time they drove into Swallowsdale, the rain had turned to sleet. They were early enough to beat the traffic and managed to park directly outside the chemist. Noah was in and out within minutes. He passed a paper bag to Lydia. 'The pharmacist thought I might have a migraine,' he said, starting the engine.

Their next stop was to fill up with petrol and to buy a bottle of water. Whilst still on the forecourt, Noah swallowed two of the tablets and chased them down with a gulp of water. 'Soon be as right as rain,' he said with a half-smile, driving out of the petrol station and into the wintry sleet that was coming down harder and faster. 'Which way for Sister Lottie's house? I hope you can remember, because I can't.'

'Left,' Lydia said, the instruction surfacing from her unconscious mind without hesitation. 'And then right into Cuckoo Lane.'

But Sister Lottie's house was no more. Where once her little house had formed part of a row of terraced houses, there was now a video rental shop with a large car park to one side. Noah turned off the road and pulled onto the car park.

'It's all so depressing,' Lydia said, staring at where her dear old friend used to live. 'So much change.'

'Would you like to try and find where she's buried?'

Her throat painfully bunched up, Lydia shook her head. After a few minutes had passed, she said, 'I was so close to her, yet I could never be completely honest with her. I never once told her what my grandparents were really like. It would have upset her too much. I wanted to protect the belief she had that we lived in a beautiful world, where nobody meant any real harm. She accepted that people made mistakes, but she didn't believe they could ever be cruel and wicked to the core. "No one is beyond redemption," she used to say. I've always wondered about that.'

'You wouldn't be the first. Do you want to go on to Hillside Terrace now?'

She shook her head again. 'No. I've had enough of Swallowsdale. Why don't we cut short our stay here? Let's drive back to the hotel for our stuff and then head for Staffordshire to find Valerie.'

According to Donna, Valerie had entered the convent when she was eighteen and the last time Lisa Fortune had been in touch with her was ten years ago. The sensible thing to do would be to ring the convent, to establish whether Valerie was indeed still there, but – call it instinct – Lydia knew that she was.

The child in her wanted to arrive unannounced and surprise her sister.

Chapter Fifty-Nine

Lydia had been expecting the convent to be a gloomy, forbidding place in a remote location, heavily gated to keep out the rest of the world, and to keep the nuns inside from escaping.

But no, here they were looking up at an impressive Victorian house at the end of a quiet residential road. It was an affluent neighbourhood with substantial houses well set back from the road. Discreetly tucked behind tidy hedges and high walls, they had enormous plots of land all to themselves.

There was a gate to the Order of St Agnes, but unlike the one of Lydia's imagination it was wide open and welcoming. The front garden was immaculate, mostly laid out with well-established rhododendrons and conifers. They parked alongside a filthy white Transit van on the tarmac drive. Someone had written in the grime on the back of it, *I'm a dirty slag!*.

Out of the car, Lydia slipped her hand through Noah's and they approached the house. Either side of an imposing front door there were two stained-glass windows. One portrayed a spindly-legged lamb and the other, the Tree of Life. On closer inspection, Lydia could see some gardening implements propped against the tree: a hoe, a rake and a spade.

There was a polished brass ship's bell hanging from a wall bracket. Lydia gave it a polite ring and tried to quell the hostility that had been rising within her during the journey from Swallowsdale. No matter what had brought her sister here when she was eighteen years old, Lydia didn't feel it was right that Val had wasted the best years of her life in a place like this, shut off from the rest of the world, a virtual prisoner.

'I think you might have to give it a bit more welly than that,' Noah said, indicating the bell.

Lydia expended some of her anger and gave the short piecc of rope a vicious tug.

Shortly afterwards, the door was opened to them by a woman dressed in a black, full-length habit. Only her ageing bespectacled face and hands were visible. It wasn't Valerie, was Lydia's first thought. As briefly as she could, she explained why they were here. With a nod of her head, the other woman invited them inside. Her habit swishing and her shoes squeaking on the polished wooden floor, she showed them into a room across a spacious hall with a wide staircase leading off from it. 'Please help yourselves to coffee,' she said, indicating a surprisingly high-tech piece of equipment on an oak sideboard. 'Just press the appropriate button, and Bob's your uncle.'

When the door closed silently behind her, Noah approached the coffee machine and Lydia read the plaque on the wall next to a painting of the convent's namesake. 'Listen to this,' Lydia said. 'It says here Saint Agnes is the patron saint of betrothed couples, gardeners and virgins.'

'That's a relief,' Noah said. 'Imagine if she'd been the patron saint of lost causes. It wouldn't have felt like a good omen, would it?'

'Not funny,' Lydia said. 'Anyway, you're the Catholic: you should know all this stuff.' She continued reading from the plaque. 'Since the sixth century, because Agnes's name is so like the Latin name for lamb, the lamb has been her emblem.'

'Hence the stained-glass window at the front door. Coffee's up.'

Lydia took the small china cup from him and sat down. 'But gardeners. That's a funny thing to be a saint of, isn't it?' She took a cautious sip of the hot coffee. 'What if visitors aren't allowed?' she said anxiously.

'Drink your coffee and stop worrying. We know visitors are allowed because we were invited in as visitors and we're sitting in what feels suspiciously like a visitors' lounge. I could be wrong, of course.'

What they thought would be a ten-minute wait turned into twenty, then thirty, then forty minutes. Almost an hour later the nun they had seen earlier reappeared and said that Mother Superior would see them now.

Mother Francis Ann was a real cold fish. She had the word 'BOSS' chiselled deep into her icy, detached demeanour. With her wimple framing her perfectly oval face, she sat behind her desk and listened impassively to what Lydia had to say, her sharp grey eyes fixed on her at all times. Lydia put her at about sixty. There was an underlying air of the imperious headmistress about her. Perhaps running a convent wasn't that different from being in charge of a school? Her office, if that was what it was called, was sparsely furnished with a desk, four chairs and two book-cases. The wood was all shining with the kind of lustre that came with constant polishing. Pride of place above the fireplace was an oil painting of the Christ child in his mother's arms.

'I wonder you didn't think to telephone ahead,' the woman said when Lydia had finished speaking. 'You might have saved yourself the trouble of a long journey, as well as a great deal of disappointment.'

Lydia's heart sank. Valerie wasn't here after all. So much for her instinct.

'But as it is,' Old Frosty Knickers continued, her tone as impassive as her manner, 'your journey has not been in vain. I've spoken to Sister Valerie Michael and she says she'll see you.'

And the point of this interview? Lydia wanted to ask. But what did the process matter, when the end result was seeing Valerie again? Suddenly filled with heart-skipping excitement, Lydia couldn't believe it was really going to happen.

The woman rose from her chair, smoothed down her habit and straightened the crucifix hanging around her neck. There was something so controlled and sure about her; she didn't look like she'd ever experienced a moment's doubt or fluster. It riled Lydia. Made her want to shake the woman out of her trouble-free complacency and explain to her just how tough the real world was.

'I don't know if you know anything about us,' Mother Francis Ann said, as Lydia and Noah joined her at the door, 'but we're an Anglican order and we don't isolate ourselves from the rest of the world; we do a lot of work in the wider community. Having said that, we do have a few contemplatives who have taken the decision never to step beyond our walls here. Sister Valerie Michael is one such contemplative.'

Lydia had already discussed with Noah that she wanted to meet her sister on her own, so he was invited to return to the visitors' lounge to play with the coffee machine again. Lydia was led outside to where a man was at the top of a long ladder fixing a broken window. Presumably he was the owner of the Transit van on the drive. 'Follow the path round to the chapel,' she was instructed, 'then go through the arch in the wall, which will take you into the kitchen garden. You'll find Sister Valerie Michael in the greenhouse.'

They may have left the worst of the weather behind them in Swallowsdale, but the wind was just as bitterly cold here; it whipped at Lydia's face, making her eyes water. She passed several nuns wearing navy-blue fleecy jackets; they were busy raking leaves from the lawn, at the same time doing their best to stop the skirts of their habits from flying up in the wind. An irreverent image of Marilyn Monroe dressed as a nun popped into Lydia's mind. In the kitchen garden, another gang of workers was hard at it, staking and tying what looked like Brussels sprout plants. One of the women acknowledged Lydia with a wave and pointed to the large greenhouse in the distance. Word must have got round.

The door of the greenhouse slid back as Lydia drew near and a nun stood to one side to let her in. Lydia was about to thank her when she realized she was face to face with Valerie.

Seized with a split second of uncertainty, Lydia didn't know what the etiquette was in these situations. Did nuns hug people? She made an instant judgement call. What the hell! Valerie had been her sister long before she ever became a bride of Christ! Bursting with euphoria, she threw her arms wide and embraced Valerie.

But Valerie didn't return the hug. If anything, she stiffened in Lydia's arms and Lydia found herself awkwardly letting go of her. 'Sorry,' she said, embarrassed, 'is that not allowed?'

'Let me close the door,' Valerie said, without answering her question. 'It's cold out there. Please, come and sit down.' She led the way to where two wooden chairs were placed next to a small, ineffectual heater in the aisle of the greenhouse. Lydia made no move to take off her coat. Valerie, she noticed, wasn't wearing anything over her habit. 'How do you do it?' she asked, holding her hands out to the heater. 'Don't you feel the cold?'

'You get used to it. Thermal underwear helps.'

'Oh, this is much too surreal,' Lydia burst out. 'I haven't seen you in twenty-eight years and we're talking about the weather and thermal underwear!'

A flicker of a smile passed across Valerie's face as she straightened her habit around her. Beneath the severity of her clothing, Lydia could discern the pretty child she had once been. If anything, her delicate face was enhanced by the wimple. She looked fragile and vulnerable, much younger than her forty years. And quite beautiful. Presumably her lovely, long, blonde hair was no more, cut short to ward off the threat of vanity. But at least her voice was normal. Thank God she'd lost that ugly rasp of a voice.

'You look well, Valerie,' Lydia said.

Her back ramrod straight and her hands crossed on her

lap, making her seem almost child-like, Valerie said, 'So do you. I knew God would take care of you. I never doubted that one day he would bring you safely back to me and we'd—' Her voice wavered and tears suddenly filled her eyes. 'I just wasn't ever sure how it would make me feel when I saw you again,' she managed to add.

Lydia instantly leaned forward to comfort her but Valerie jerked away. 'Please don't,' she said. 'It's the shock. That's all.' She closed her eyes, clenching her hands tightly together. Feeling shut out, Lydia watched helplessly as her sister struggled to regain her composure. It was painful to see. Eventually Valerie opened her eyes. 'Where have you been all this time?' she asked quite calmly.

Tears filling her own eyes now, Lydia fumbled inside her bag for a tissue. 'Italy,' she said.

'*All* this time?' Valerie's tone had changed. Gone was the poignancy of just moments ago. Now she sounded polite, almost formal, as if they were strangers. She had clearly won the battle over her emotions.

But Lydia was losing her battle fast. This wasn't how she had imagined her reunion with her sister. Where was the spontaneous outpouring of love and joy over finding each other again? 'Yes,' she said, wiping her eyes. 'This is the first time I've been back to England since … since I left Swallowsdale.'

'Really?'

The cold, indifferent way she said the word made Lydia think her sister didn't believe her. It made her worry all the more over Valerie's reaction to what she was about to say next. 'I'm sorry I left without saying goodbye to you,' she said. 'I've never forgiven myself for that.'

'The past is so long ago,' Valerie replied mechanically, without appearing to consider Lydia's words. 'It isn't something we should allow ourselves to dwell on.'

Lydia didn't know whether she admired her sister's extraordinary self-control or was angered by it. Was this what shutting yourself away from the real world taught you? To stamp hard on your emotions and bury them deep? 'I disagree,' she said. 'The past is right here in this greenhouse. It's us, Val. You and me. It's why we haven't seen one another in twenty-eight years. Don't you want to know why I left without saying goodbye? Aren't you curious? Just a little?'

'It's enough that you're here,' Valerie said smoothly. 'That's all that matters to me.'

'Are you saying you've forgiven me?'

'Is that what you came here for?'

Surprised by Valerie's blunt frankness – and the truth of it – Lydia caught her breath. 'I ... I came because you're my sister and I love you.'

'But you also want me to forgive you, don't you?'

'Is that so very bad?'

Valerie stared back at Lydia in silence.

Lydia knew then that she had hurt her sister profoundly. Maybe irrevocably so. It was what she had always feared. Hanging on to that initial display of emotion Valerie had given way to, she said, 'I can't undo what I did, Val, but please, let me try and explain why I did what I did. Will you let me do that?'

'If you think it will help you, yes.'

'I hope it will help us both,' Lydia said, trying not to feel so unnerved or disappointed by her sister's coolness towards her. 'It's important to me that you know that my actions weren't premeditated. I didn't wake up that morning with the intention of hurting you.' Then, in as few words as she could, Lydia outlined the events in the dell and everything that immediately followed.

When she finished, a tiny crease of a frown appeared on Valerie's face, just between her eyebrows. 'But everyone knew straight away Noah couldn't have done it,' she murmured. 'The police had ruled him out because he'd fallen down the stairs and knocked himself unconscious. I don't understand why you went on protecting him.'

'I only discovered very recently about Noah falling down the stairs and ending up in hospital. From Noah himself.'

The frown deepened. 'But why didn't he tell you before?'

'We hadn't seen or spoken to each other until last week. All this time he thought I'd killed Uncle Leonard and I thought he'd done it. And that's why I'm here back in England. I came home to find out who really did kill that dreadful man. Noah and I saw Donna yesterday. Do you remember Donna Jones?'

'Yes.'

'She told me about Grandmother. That it was she who'd killed Uncle Leonard the night she'd escaped from the hospital. Donna said Grandmother confessed to the police that she had been acting according to God's wishes.'

Some of the tension went out of Valerie's body. 'You have to understand, Grandma was very ill,' she said quietly, a small tremor to her voice. 'She didn't know what she was doing. For so long the balance of her mind had been kept stable by the use of drugs. How could she possibly have any control over her actions?'

'I'm not judging her,' Lydia said quickly, sensitive to Valerie's devotion to their grandmother, even now. 'Please don't think that. I decided many years ago that it was probably our grandfather who helped to make her so ill. He was a very cruel man. I can't begin to think what kind of a god he believed in.'

Valerie took a moment to respond. 'You never really did have a faith, did you?'

'Actually, I did. And still do. Just not as clear-cut as yours. I was told that you're a contemplative nun; does that mean you've never left the order since you came here?'

Valerie nodded. 'That's right. And I never will leave it.'

'Don't you ever wonder what's going on out there?' Lydia very nearly said, 'in the real world', but she stopped herself. This place, for Valerie, *was* the real world.

'I have all I need here. This is where I belong.'

Intrigued, Lydia said, 'What do you spend your days doing?'

'Apart from serving God through prayer, we're committed to sharing our love of the Lord with our neighbours. And as well as baking communion wafers and making candles, we grow all our own fruit and vegetables and sell it to a number of local shops. We do the same with the honey we produce. We're not idle here, Lydia, if that's what you're thinking.'

Lydia caught the defensiveness in her sister's voice and changed the subject. 'Donna said that both our grandparents are dead now. Which makes us the end of the line.' She smiled ruefully. 'When we're gone, there'll be no more Turners.'

'I assumed you'd have children.'

'I have a stepdaughter called Chiara. She's beautiful, very clever, and I love her dearly.'

'How old is she?'

'Twenty-four. She was nine when she came into my life.'

'What about her father?'

'He died four years ago.'

'And now Noah has come back into your life?'

'More amazing than that, he has a son more or less the same age as Chiara.' She then told Valerie the full story of how she'd first seen Ishmael on the steps of the Rialto Bridge and everything that had fallen into place since.

Valerie looked thoughtful, and suddenly a lot less tense. 'When God wants something to happen, there's no obstacle that can get in his way,' she said.

'You're right; it does feel like fate.'

Valerie tutted. But she was smiling too, making her face quite radiant. 'Don't you remember what Pastor Digby used to say about fate? He said it was the heathen's way of rejecting God's existence.'

'Maybe I'll concede that one to you and Pastor Digby. But as to the vast majority of that man's teaching, I wouldn't give you tuppence. He was a dangerously malign influence on a lot of vulnerable people and he certainly enjoyed the power of his position.'

The sound of the greenhouse door sliding open had them both turning.

A breathless, red-faced nun burst in. Valerie gave her a disapproving look. 'Sister Peter Margaret,' she said, 'I specifically asked not to be disturbed.'

'Please, it's Mr Solomon. He's not well. We found him on the floor.'

Chapter Sixty

Lydia took back every bad thought she'd had about Mother Francis Ann. The woman's cool efficiency could not be faulted and by the time Lydia was by Noah's side, she had the situation under control. An ambulance had been called for and the two young nuns who had found Noah had been interrogated and sent on their way. After a brief exchange with Lydia, she also made a discreet exit in order to give them some time alone.

Lydia had been warned that Noah was groggy and disorientated, and keeping her voice level, she said, 'They seem to think you had some kind of a seizure, Noah. Have you ever had one before?'

She could see his dazed eyes trying to focus on her, as if he were drunk. 'Where's Lydia?' he murmured.

'I'm here, Noah. Right here with you.' She put her arm around his shoulder. His body was taut.

'Where's Lydia?' he repeated. 'I want Lydia here with me.'

All the way to the hospital in the ambulance, he remained in a weakened state of confusion. He still didn't know who Lydia was, but once he'd been checked over by the paramedic, he was happy for her to hold his hand. He kept murmuring to himself and closing his eyes, but if his eyes were shut for any length of time, because she was terrified what that might mean, Lydia would squeeze his hand to wake him.

He was seen immediately at the hospital. 'Mr Solomon,'

the young doctor said, whilst shining a light into his eyes, 'do you know where you are?'

The doctor's words seemed to bring Noah to his senses and he suddenly looked more alert. He opened his mouth to say something but then hesitated. He glanced uncertainly at Lydia. 'My office?' he said, like a small, anxious boy desperately wanting to give the right answer. Lydia smiled back at him encouragingly.

The doctor put away her torch and came and stood at the end of the bed with Lydia. 'What's wrong with him?' Lydia asked, her voice hushed even though she was sure Noah had no idea he was being talked about. 'It's as if he has amnesia.'

'I'm fairly confident that the loss of memory will pass, as will his general state of disorientation. The real concern is that the discs at the back of his eyes are swollen. It's called papilledema and is caused by a rise in pressure of the cerebrospinal fluid in the skull. I'm going to arrange for a CT scan first thing tomorrow morning.'

Suddenly amnesia was sounding a much better option. Lydia swallowed. 'What do you suppose the scan will show?'

'It's highly likely it will indicate the presence of a brain tumour.'

The world began to slide away from Lydia. 'But not always. Right?' Please God, not always.

'When we factor in what you've told us, the persistent headache, the seizure he experienced earlier, coupled with the subsequent confused and disorientated state, I'm afraid the evidence is stacking up. I think it would be best if he stays here with us tonight so we can keep an eye on him.'

Within the hour Noah had been transferred to a main ward. It was eight o'clock, visiting time, and Lydia was allowed to stay with him. They had the curtains pulled around the bed and Lydia was just pouring a glass of water from the jug on the locker when, in a sleepy faraway voice, Noah said, 'Lyddie, what's going on?'

443

She stopped what she was doing and sat on the bed. 'You know who I am now?'

He frowned. 'Of course I do. But how have we ended up here?' His words were slow and blurred around the edges as if he'd woken from a deep sleep. 'Have we had an accident?' He raked a hand through his hair. 'I feel so tired.'

'What's the last thing you remember?'

He blinked. 'Your sister. We were ... we were somewhere and I was waiting for you. And then ... Oh, God, I remember being scared. I was shaking. I thought I was going to die.' Each tiny fragment of memory seemed to weigh on him as heavy as a great boulder. Lydia could see him exhausting himself with the sheer effort of so much concentration. Her heart ached for him and she desperately wanted to prompt him, but she kept quiet, hoping he'd be able to find his way through the fog. Eventually he looked at her in despair. 'Help me, Lyddie, please. Tell me what's going on.'

Lydia wasn't allowed to stay the night with Noah, and when she took the lift down to the ground floor of the hospital she was tempted to rush back and defy anyone who tried to kick her out. But she knew it was useless. She had to trust what the doctor had said: that Noah was in safe hands.

The lift opened onto the main reception area and she was met by the sound of singing. Carol singers were gathered around a Christmas tree, giving voice to 'Away in a Manger'. It was so reminiscent of school carol services – standing next to Noah and smirking their way through the verses – it made Lydia want to burst into tears. She had nowhere to stay for the night. No transport. And worst of all, so very, very worst of all, maybe no Noah.

Going outside into the dark and the cold, she dug around in her handbag for her mobile to make the all-important call to Chiara, who would then have to explain things to Ishmael.

She woke the next morning feeling stiff and hung-over. Not from alcohol, but from fear. Letting her eyes grow accustomed to the light filtering in through the badly fitting curtains at the window, she lay very still, gathering her senses and willing the tension out of her body. She could hear a television through the wall at her head and voices in the corridor the other side of the door. Signs that for some people this was just another ordinary day. She pushed back the bedclothes and hauled herself off to the bathroom in need of a hot, reinvigorating shower. What she got was little more than a lukewarm trickle. Afterwards, to add insult to injury, she had to put on the same clothes she'd worn yesterday.

A porter at the hospital last night had recommended this soulless hotel because it was within easy walking distance. Its location was pretty much all it had going for it. Downstairs, in the faux Mediterranean dining room where badly painted sunny scenes of al fresco dining adorned the walls, Lydia endured a breakfast of tinned grapefruit and floppy toast whilst watching overweight men gorging themselves on piled-high plates of fried food. Lydia imagined sharing the horribleness of the place with Noah later that morning, joking with him that they would never again bad-mouth the Oak Manor Court Hotel.

She checked out and retraced her steps along the busy road of nose-to-tail traffic to the hospital. She was almost there when her mobile rang. It was Fabio. Without preamble he said that Chiara had told him everything. Above the roar of traffic noise, the sound of his dear voice, so full of love and concern, was too much for her and she thought she might choke with the strain of not giving in to her fears. Throughout the conversation, passers-by threw odd glances in her direction, and it was only when she was saying goodbye to Fabio that she understood why: she had been speaking in Italian. She had forgotten how British people stared at anyone different from themselves.

Passing the locked gate of a church on her left, Lydia

thought of her sister. She couldn't even remember saying goodbye to Valerie yesterday; she had somehow melted away into the background with all the other nuns. Lydia hoped that the next time they met, Valerie's chilly reserve might have thawed. She couldn't hope to be forgiven so soon, but surely now that Valerie knew the truth she would gradually come to accept the sacrifice Lydia had made, and would let go of the hurt she had hung on to all these years. After all, hadn't Lydia done the same with Noah? Hadn't she harboured feelings of hostility and angry resentment towards him when she'd been blinded by misunderstanding?

Noah was definitely in better shape than when she'd left. He was still experiencing a degree of tiredness, causing his movements to appear slow and leaden, but he was mentally alert and fully aware of what was going on. Lydia was given permission to go with him for the CT scan and held his hand when it was confirmed that he did indeed have a tumour. In layman's speak it was situated at the front of his skull, above his left eye and was about the size of a satsuma. The good news was that it was highly probable it wasn't malignant. Even better, it was in an accessible spot where it could be removed. Given the seizure Noah had experienced and the prolonged spell of grogginess he'd undergone, the recommendation was that the tumour should be dealt with sooner rather than later. With his healthcare cover, he was to be referred to a private neurosurgeon near to home in Northamptonshire. He could expect to be admitted for surgery in a couple of days. It was made to sound so commonplace. They could have been sitting in a travel agent's office booking a holiday.

But what about the What Ifs?

This was brain surgery they were discussing, not some trip to the dentist for a filling. Start opening up a person's skull and anything could happen. What if the operation went wrong and Noah ended up in a vegetative state for the rest of his life? Or what if the tumour turned out to be malignant? What would Noah's chances of survival be? And the biggest What If of all: what if Noah was taken away from her? For ever.

Officially discharged from the hospital, they took a taxi back to the convent where they'd left Noah's car. The dirty white van was still there on the drive alongside his Mercedes. The words on the back of it had been wiped off.

Lydia paid the driver and they went and rang the bell. Noah had said he'd wanted to thank Mother Francis Ann for her help yesterday and to apologize for creating such a commotion. And, of course, Lydia wanted to speak to her sister again.

Back into Old Frosty Knickers mode, the woman disregarded Noah's thanks with an airy wave of the hand. Then without another word on the subject, she turned her attention to Lydia. 'While you're talking with Sister Valerie Michael, I'll take Mr Solomon to the chapel to pray with him.'

Lydia might have been less surprised if the woman had offered her a marker pen to scribble a moustache and a pair of glasses on the Madonna and Child painting above the fireplace. However, while she was glad of the opportunity to see Val again, she was less than enthusiastic about letting Noah out of her sight. Those What Ifs were never far from her mind. He was definitely much more his old self, which was what the doctor had said would happen as the day wore on, but what if he had another seizure? As though reading her mind, Noah said, 'I'll be fine, Lyddie. Don't worry.'

To confirm matters, Old Frosty Knickers said, 'I'll send for Sister Valerie Michael. You can talk to her here.'

Left on her own to wait for her sister, Lydia brooded anxiously. Why was Old Frosty Knickers so keen to get Noah alone with her in the chapel? He hadn't mentioned his tumour to the nun – they hadn't even had the chance to discuss it properly themselves yet – but did the woman suspect his life hung in the balance and want to encourage him to put some serious petitioning in before it was too late?

The minutes ticked slowly by whilst Lydia waited patiently for Valerie to appear. She mentally began compiling a list of all the things she needed to ask her sister. For instance, who had their grandfather married after their grandmother had died?

A faint knock at the door, followed by the appearance of a frail, elderly nun interrupted her list-making. 'I'm very sorry, but Sister Valerie Michael says she's unable to see you today. Can I get you a drink instead?'

'And she gave no reason why she couldn't see you?' Noah asked when they were on the road once more. This time, though, it was Lydia at the wheel of the expensive car. Having never driven on the left-hand side of the road before, she was taking it steadily, finding her way cautiously with the powerful engine.

Her gaze glued to the road ahead, she said, 'No reason given at all.'

A mile sped by and Noah said, 'You haven't told me how it went yesterday with your sister. Being the unthinking bugger I am, I rather stole the show on your reunion, didn't I?'

Seething with a potent mix of disappointment and anger that Valerie could have snubbed her so pettily, Lydia said, 'If you don't mind, I don't want to talk about Valerie just now. I'd rather talk about you.' She hated to think this was her sister's way of getting her own back. See, this is how it feels to be tossed aside!

'You sound cross, Lyddie.'

'I am.'

'Then don't be. Especially when you're driving my car.'

She slid him a sideways glance and saw that he was smiling. She smiled back at him.

'That's better,' he said.

Several miles later, after Noah had directed her onto the motorway, she was feeling more confident behind the wheel. 'You haven't told me what you and Mother Superior got up to in the chapel.'

'Funnily enough, she did exactly what she'd offered to do. She prayed for me. And for the coming days.'

'Did you tell her what the doctors had diagnosed?'

'That was the odd thing. It was as if she already knew that it was pretty serious.'

Another silence lapsed between them. Minutes later, when Lydia glanced across at Noah, she saw that his eyelids were closed. She hoped he wouldn't sleep for long; she needed his directions to get home.

From its hands-free cradle on the dashboard, Noah's mobile let out a sudden loud trill. He leaned forward immediately – as if he hadn't been asleep at all – and pressed the answer button. A voice Lydia knew straight away filled the car. It was richer and fuller than when she'd last heard it, but unmistakable all the same.

'Noah, it's me, Brad. Ishmael's been on the blower. What's the latest news? Bearing in mind these doctors don't know their arse from their elbow these days.'

'They certainly know a brain tumour when they see one. I've seen the picture of it myself.'

'I don't believe it!'

'I'm having trouble believing it myself.'

'What's the next step?'

'Surgery. There's talk of an operation the day after tomorrow.'

'Bloody hell! They're not messing about, are they? How do you feel?'

'Like I've been hit with both barrels.'

'Has the C word been mentioned at all?'

'It's not been ruled out. Although they seem to think it's unlikely. They'll know for sure when they open me up.'

'Is Lydia there with you?'

'Yes she is. You can speak to her if you want.'

But Lydia couldn't speak to anyone. She was having

trouble seeing, too; her eyes were brimming with tears. Spotting an exit slip road for a service station, she swerved into the inside lane and shot off the motorway. When it was safe to do so, she brought the car to a stop. She was crying so hard now she was shaking.

'I'll call you back later, Uncle Brad.' Noah ended the call. 'Lyddie?'

'I'm sorry,' she said, her forehead against the top of the steering wheel. 'I just can't bear to hear you talking about it so calmly. You sound so in control, whereas I feel utterly useless. You need me to be strong and supportive, and I'm a pathetic emotional wreck.'

Very gently, he pulled her head away from the steering wheel and turned her to face him. 'I was going to wait until we got home,' he said, 'but I might just as well say it now. I want you to listen very carefully to what I'm about to say and understand that this is what I want. What I *need*. OK, Lyddie?'

She wiped her eyes with her hands. 'I'm listening.'

'We've done exactly what we came here to do. We found out who really did kill your great-uncle Leonard and you now have nothing hanging over you. From here on you're free to get on with the rest of your life and enjoy it to the full. No more guilt. No more regret.' He paused and took a breath. 'I want you to go home to Venice tomorrow.'

'Are you mad? I'm not going anywhere tomorrow unless it's with you.'

He shook his head impatiently, as if he'd explained this several times already. 'Look, the truth is, I don't need you here. I want you to go home. I want you to promise me you'll stay there in Venice and get on with your life and live happily ever after.'

Chapter Sixty-One

Nothing could have more effectively knocked the feebleness out of Lydia. She wiped her eyes again and blew her nose. 'I thought it was me who had the habit of making misguided unilateral decisions,' she said.

He turned away from her and stared straight ahead. 'You don't need to be involved.'

'I am already. So just accept I'm not leaving you. I'm here for the long haul.'

'I mean it, Lyddie. I don't want you around if things get ...' He didn't finish. Lydia waited. 'Sticky,' he said finally.

'I'm not arguing with you, Noah. So you can forget about me going back to Venice. And anyway, who says things are going to get sticky? The doctor says this is a perfectly routine operation with a good rate of success.'

He turned and settled his fractured gaze on hers. Seconds passed before he spoke. 'Then why are you so scared?'

She covered his hand with hers. 'Because I wouldn't be human if I wasn't. I love you, Noah. I don't want anything bad to happen to you. Ever.'

'And I don't want you to see me if it goes wrong and I become some dribbling—'

'Don't say it,' she said, cutting him short. 'We're both stunned and exhausted and latching on to worst-case scenarios. Besides, how would it be if the boot was on the other foot? If it was me facing this?'

Rain began to patter lightly against the windscreen. He breathed in deeply, then exhaled slowly. 'Damn you, Lyddie.' He raised her hand to his lips. 'I'd be there with you every step of the way. As well you know.'

Twisting round in the small space, she took him in her arms and kissed him. 'We've been through too much not to survive this little glitch, Noah.' She kissed him again. 'What's more, we have your birthday to celebrate next year. I want you to be in Venice with me and we'll do something special. Something outrageous.'

'I'm not bungee jumping off the bell tower in St Mark's. Not even for you.'

She smiled. 'Spoilsport.'

Lydia was not the only one who was taking matters into her own hands. They were twenty minutes from home when Ishmael phoned to say that he would be flying over tomorrow. 'Any chance I can persuade you not to?' Noah asked him.

'Absolutely none whatsoever,' came back Ishmael's reply. 'Oh, and I've told Mum. She's going to ring you in the morning.'

When the call was over, Noah said, 'You're all ganging up against me.'

'Are you surprised? My advice is to give in gracefully.'

He put a hand on Lydia's leg and kept it there for the rest of the journey.

It had been a long day and they went to bed early. But neither of them could sleep. Noah's head ached more when he lay down and Lydia's was too full of What Ifs to sleep. 'Only one thing for it,' Noah said, gently easing Lydia onto her back and dispensing with her nightdress. 'Better make hay whilst we can, because after tomorrow who knows when I'll be able to get you in bed again?'

'And don't forget all the years we need to catch up on.'

'Good point,' he said, pushing away the duvet so he could look at her. He placed the palm of his hand on her stomach. 'Do you remember those nude sketches I did of you?'

'You haven't still got them, have you?'

'Of course I have. I could never have parted with them. And before you ask, no one else has ever seen them.'

'Where are they?'

'Hidden at the back of Uncle Brad's portrait of you. I put them there when I resigned myself to the unthinkable: that I was never going to see you again.'

'I kept the few photographs I had of you,' she admitted. 'I hadn't looked at them in years. Not until last week, after meeting Ishmael. Do you still draw?'

'When I have the time. I'd love to draw you again.' He lowered his head and kissed her.

For a brief blissful time they lost themselves in each other, banishing the strain and anxiety of the last twenty-four hours from their minds. Yet there was a poignant, bittersweet intensity to their lovemaking. With every touch, every kiss, was the fear their newfound happiness might be cut short.

They were still in bed when the telephone rang just before nine o'clock the next morning. It was the hospital, to say Noah's operation was booked for the following day.

Not ten minutes later, when they were still in bed, the phone rang again. This time it was Noah's ex-wife, Jane. Lydia left him to take the call in private while she went downstairs to make some breakfast. In response to a call from Noah yesterday, Mrs Massey had once more worked her magic and stocked the fridge for the coming days. A cafetiere of coffee and scrambled eggs on toast seemed a fitting way to start the day.

Lydia put the kettle on first, and while opening the fridge for the eggs, her attention was caught by the framed photograph of Ishmael. As he smiled back at her, she thought how different his childhood must have been from his father's. Did he even know about Noah's parents and the way they died? Or was that something Noah never discussed? Just as she had never shared with Marcello and Chiara the truth of her upbringing, glossing over it with a highly edited version of the truth. Lydia had read about people who became obsessed with their ancestry as a way to affirm who they were themselves, but she had never felt the urge to dig deeper than her own parents. Her mother had been an orphan and Lydia didn't have a clue who her maternal grandparents had been. Nor did she care. She had always been more concerned with the present.

When she had everything on a tray, Lydia carried it upstairs. Noah was still on the phone when she nudged open the door. He beckoned her in when she held back, not wanting to intrude. 'Thanks, Jane,' he said. 'No, I promise I won't worry about work; I know you've got it covered. And yes, I'll get Ishmael to give you a call just as soon as he knows anything. You take care as well. I'll see you soon. Bye.'

'Do you think we ought to take the phone off the hook?' he asked when Lydia put the tray on the end of the bed and passed him his breakfast. 'I'm not sure how convincing I am at reassuring people that everything is going to be fine. Poor Jane was trying her hardest not to sound like she was saying goodbye to me for the last time.'

'You're still very fond of one another, aren't you?' Lydia said, sliding back into bed with him and surprising herself that she didn't feel any jealousy now towards the woman who'd been lucky enough to be married to Noah.

'We may not have been ideally suited as husband and wife, but in other ways we get on extremely well. I told her about you. About *us*.'

'What did she say?'

'She said that it explained everything. She never suspected me of being unfaithful, but she'd always known that there had been someone else. She wished us luck. She meant it, too.'

'I'd like to meet her one day.'

Noah smiled. 'That's what she said about you.'

They showered together, got dressed and decided to go for a walk. They left their mobiles behind, not wanting to be disturbed.

It was a bitterly cold day. The sun was scarcely more than a faint white glow in the grey sky. The fields and hedgerows were still covered in a thick white frost. Puddles were iced over and bare tree branches looked blackened and petrified.

At the end of Noah's drive they took the main road, following it until the cottages and houses – all dressed for Christmas with holly wreaths on their doors and cards at the windows – ran out either side of them. Leaving the road, they slowly meandered their way towards a large oak tree on the crest of a hill.

At the top, they stopped to take in the far-reaching views; the only sound to be heard, other than their breathing, came from the crows cawing loudly from the highest branches of the tree. The landscape was very different from Swallowsdale. There was a beguiling softness to it. No bleakness. No dark stretches of treacherous moorland. Just a satisfying sense of peace.

Noah leaned his cane against the tree and came and stood behind Lydia. He wrapped his arms around her, resting his chin on the top of her head. 'The day seems frozen in time, doesn't it?' he said.

Wishing that it really could always be this moment – the day before Noah's operation when he was still safe – Lydia said, 'You must be very happy living here. It's so beautiful.'

'I'd be happier with you here.'

She pulled his arms more tightly around her.

'I know what you're thinking,' he said. 'You're trying to figure out how we can make it work, aren't you? Well don't. I've got it licked. We divide our time between our respective homes and businesses. I come to you. You come to me. See, it couldn't be easier.'

She turned and faced him. 'Smart-arse Solomon, you always did have all the answers, didn't you?'

Ishmael arrived just as Lydia's mobile rang. She left Noah and his son to talk and went upstairs to take the call.

She was slow to pick up on the voice. 'Valerie?' she said uncertainly.

'Lydia, I want to talk to you again.'

The hurt and anger Lydia had felt before surfaced at once and multiplied. 'Why wouldn't you see me yesterday?'

'I couldn't.'

'Couldn't or wouldn't?'

'Please don't make this any more difficult for me than it already is. Come here tomorrow and I'll explain properly.'

'I'm sorry, I can't. I'm with Noah. He goes into hospital tomorrow morning for an operation and I'm afraid there's nothing on this earth that will tear me away from his side.'

There was a long silence. It went on for so long that Lydia thought the connection had been broken. 'Val?' she said. 'Are you still there?'

'Yes, I'm still here. I was just recalling how you always did choose Noah over me.'

The accusation scythed through Lydia. 'Please don't say that to me. I did everything I could for you, Val. *Everything!*'

'Did you? Did you really?'

Again the scything blow. Whoever came up with the phrase 'the truth always hurts' knew what they were talking about. 'I know you'll never forgive me for leaving you the way I did, but remember, I was eighteen. I did my best. For the rest of my life I'll have to live with the knowledge that it wasn't enough for you.'

Hearing herself pleading with her sister made Lydia even more upset. What she was feeling was too deep for rational argument and so she flung at Valerie her one last desperate attempt to make things right between them. 'If only for everything your faith must mean to you, Valerie, can't you find it in yourself to forgive me?'

When even that failed to elicit a response from her sister, Lydia said, 'If you really want to speak to me, why don't you come and see me here?'

'You know that's not possible.'

'Nothing's impossible, Val. Not if you want it badly enough.'

In the morning, Ishmael drove the three of them to the hospital in his car. They met the surgeon who was going to operate. His manner was confident and reassuring, and he spared no effort in describing what the procedure would be during and after the operation, saying that if everything went according to plan, Noah was looking at approximately five hours on the operating table followed by ten days' recovery in hospital. It was the word 'recovery' that Lydia focused on as she listened to the soothing voice of the surgeon, at the same time sizing up the man's hands – the hands that Noah's life now rested in. Just how capable and experienced were they?

At last it was the moment Lydia had been dreading; she had to say goodbye to Noah. Ishmael had already spent some time alone with his father. Now it was Lydia's turn.

'Just in case you don't recognize me when I see you next, I'll be the one who looks like a boiled egg with the top cracked open,' Noah joked with her.

'Now I know what to buy you for Christmas,' she said. 'A hat.' She bent down and squeezed his hand. 'I'll be waiting for you.'

He beckoned her closer.

She bent down. 'Yes?'

'Closer,' he said. 'There's something important I want to say.'

She did as he said and bent so close that his mouth was brushing against her ear. 'Just in case there's any doubt in your mind,' he whispered, 'I love you, Lyddie. Always have. Always will.'

She forced a smile to her trembling lips. 'I love you too, Noah.'

*

Three hours into the operation, Lydia left Ishmael in the waiting room and took the stairs down to the ground floor. At the bottom of the stairs, she followed the signs. Several corridors later, a set of automatic doors let her into the reception area. The doors hadn't even swished behind her when she spotted two nuns sitting with their backs to her.

She went over and whilst she didn't know the one who was knitting and talking to a young mother with a child in a pushchair, the other nun wasn't a stranger. Sitting rigidly with her hands on her lap, no one could have looked more thoroughly out of place than Valerie. Lydia felt a pang of pity towards her. And empathy. Because ironically they were both experiencing a similar culture clash – after twenty-eight years of living in Italy, Britain was just as alien to Lydia as it must be to Valerie.

She went over and touched her sister lightly on the shoulder.

Valerie visibly started. Seeing the strain in her face, Lydia could see that this visit was costing her dearly. The other nun broke off from her conversation with the young mother, shoved her knitting to one side and introduced herself as Sister Catherine John. She was possibly ten years Valerie's junior and was altogether more relaxed and assured. 'I've travelled down with Sister Valerie Michael,' she explained in a jolly voice. 'We had an excellent journey, didn't we? And met some fascinating people.'

Lydia detected annoyance in Valerie's face. Lydia didn't blame her. Doubtless Sister Catherine John thought she was being a helpful, friendly minder but two seconds in her company and it was obvious to Lydia that she was a stone's throw from patronizing and insulting her nervous charge. Lydia stepped in. 'You're probably desperate for something to eat or drink,' she said to Sister Catherine John. 'There's an excellent coffee bar here on the ground floor.' Lydia had no idea how good or bad the refreshments on offer were – she and Ishmael had been using the vending machine on their floor – but the sooner she got Valerie alone, the better.

'Thank you,' Valerie said, when Lydia was leading the way to where she hoped her sister would feel more at ease. 'Sister Catherine John means well, but she has yet to learn the rich reward of silence.'

'How very tactfully put,' Lydia said with a smile. 'Was your journey very awful?'

'I pretended to sleep for part of it.'

The hospital chapel was empty and with only the simple altar and wooden cross subtly lit from an overhead light, even Lydia felt a soothing calm embrace her when they entered. She felt glad now that Noah had had the presence of mind to give Mother Francis Ann their mobile phone numbers so that Valerie would be able to get in touch at a later date if she so wanted. If he hadn't, she and Valerie wouldn't be here now. The fact that Valerie had made the sacrifice of leaving the convent meant everything to Lydia. It meant her sister must have had a change of heart.

They sat down in the front row of seats and in their different ways offered up an act of prayer. Lydia didn't know what Valerie might be sharing with God, but she was in the mood for some straightforward blackmail: take Noah from me, she warned God, and our relationship will be over. *Finito!*

Valerie lifted her head long after Lydia had finished dishing out her threats, and with both hands holding on to the cross round her neck, she said, 'You were right the other day when you said the past is always with us, that we can't pretend otherwise. It never leaves us, no matter how hard we try to isolate ourselves from it.'

'What made you change your view?'

'You. You stirred up too many memories. Memories I didn't want to relive.'

'I'm sorry.'

'Don't be. I've spent a lifetime being penitent and I'm ashamed to say it hasn't worked entirely.'

Surprised by this admission, but deciding to address it later, Lydia voiced the first of so many questions she had to ask. 'Why did you accuse me on the phone yesterday of not taking care of you?'

'I was suddenly reminded how, as a child, you had what I always wanted, a friend. A real friend.'

'But you gave the impression of not needing one. You had the Brothers and Sisters. And our grandmother. You were close to her in a way I never was. She adored you.'

'You're describing relationships I had with adults. Is that normal for a young girl?'

'I've come to know there's nothing normal in this world, Val. When we were children I thought everyone else was normal except for me.'

'But you had Noah. You could share things with him.'

'I didn't always. For a time there were things I was so deeply ashamed of I hid them even from Noah, because I was convinced I'd lose him if he knew the truth. I've since discovered we all do it. We're all scared and vulnerable. In fact, we're all so abnormal we're completely normal.'

Looking down at her hands, her voice low, Valerie said, 'I tried so hard to be what Grandma wanted me to be. I trusted her and believed everything she ever said. And all the time, she was ill. Deluded.' She raised her eyes and faced Lydia. 'Do you ever worry that we may have inherited that from her? That maybe we could be the same?'

'Schizophrenic, you mean?'

Valerie nodded.

'As an adult I've never considered it. But as a teenager, when we were coping with Grandmother's illness, yes, I did sometimes worry about it. I also had the memory of our mother's behaviour after Dad died. I could see that on both sides of our family there were problems.'

'Don't you worry about it now?'

'No. Do you?'

'Constantly. I've suffered with depression for years. Sometimes I sink so low with it I feel I can't face another day.'

'Oh, Val, I'm so sorry. Is there help available to you? At the convent?'

'I have a spiritual mentor. She's very patient and kind but we both know that our sessions together are never going to heal the sickness that lies at the heart of my problems.'

'Are you honest with her?'

Valerie shook her head.

Very tentatively, Lydia said, 'Could you be honest with me?'

As though she hadn't heard, Valerie said, 'For two nights now, since you came to St Agnes, I've had nightmares. Terrible nightmares. I've been screaming out aloud and walking in my sleep. It hasn't happened in a long time. Mother Francis Ann heard about it yesterday morning and suggested it might be useful for me to speak to you again.' She swallowed. 'Actually, it was more of an order than a suggestion.'

Once again Lydia had to think well of Old Frosty Knickers. Whatever the source of the woman's intuition, Lydia was happy to go along with it. Choosing her words with care, she said, 'In what way did she think a meeting between us would be useful to you, Val?'

An eternity passed before Valerie answered her. 'I can't speak on behalf of Mother Francis Ann,' she began, 'but I've ...' She faltered and squeezed her eyes shut. Then opened them. 'I've reached the conclusion that you're my only hope. You're the only person I can tell this to. And I'm afraid that if I don't, I'll end up just like Grandma.'

Chapter Sixty-Two

The door of the chapel opened, spilling light in as well as a breathless old man. He sat in a chair on the back row of seats, his head bowed, his wheezy, laboured breathing dominating the small space. He didn't stay long. When the door closed after him, Lydia said, 'We could go somewhere else if you'd rather?'

'No, this is fine.'

Before picking up where they'd left off, Lydia had something she needed to say, something that on top of everything else had been bothering her enormously. 'I'm sorry I was so short with you on the telephone yesterday,' she said. 'I was angry with you. Which I know is no excuse. But I was just so upset not to see you again.'

'We do many things through anger,' Valerie said faintly. 'It's a powerful emotion. Possibly the most dangerous weapon anyone can ever be in possession of. Even our Lord wasn't above it.'

Lydia had always thought that episode of Christ's pique – when he turned over the tables in the temple – was every bad-tempered Christian's over-played Get Out of Jail card. She kept this to herself, though.

'I also need to apologize,' Valerie said, 'for being distant with you when you came to see me. I hope that by the end of this conversation you'll understand why I found our meeting so difficult. Not that this one is going to be any easier. Suddenly I don't know where to start.'

'How about those nightmares you mentioned?'

Valerie's hands returned to her cross, her eyes fixed firmly on the altar. She swallowed. 'They're to do with

Uncle Leonard. He wasn't killed by our grandmother as everyone thinks.'

'But she confessed to it,' Lydia said. 'Donna told me it was in the newspapers, and that she was moved to a secure hospital after the police had to accept she was too ill to stand trial.'

'I know all that,' Valerie said, her gaze now coming slowly round to Lydia's. 'Don't forget I was there living and breathing it. I saw how the hospital was only too happy to let our grandmother be moved somewhere else and the whole case hushed up. The last thing they wanted was anyone pointing the finger at them for allowing her to escape in the first place. But I'm telling you, I know who really murdered Uncle Leonard. I've always known. And I can promise you it wasn't our poor sick grand-mother.'

The intensity of Valerie's words carved out a momen-tary silence between them. Lydia's mind raced. If not their grandmother, who? Her grandfather? Of course it had to be him. Just as she'd thought.

'Aren't you going to ask me who it was?' Valerie said.

'It was our grandfather, wasn't it?' Lydia replied.

Valerie sighed and shook her head wearily as if Lydia had just got the simplest of questions wrong. 'No, Lydia, it wasn't our grandfather. It was me. I murdered Uncle Leonard.'

An icy sliver of shock pierced Lydia's heart. She battled it. It couldn't be true. But why would Valerie say it was? Was it possible she was displaying some kind of extreme misplaced devotion for their grandmother? 'But you couldn't have done it,' Lydia reasoned. 'You were a child. You were only twelve years old.'

'I was an angry, confused and very scared child. I was perfectly capable of committing murder.'

Another sliver of shock found its target. Bewildered, Lydia said, 'But why?'

Valerie's gaze, which had been rock solid until now, wavered. 'That afternoon ... Uncle Leonard came into

463

our bedroom, he ... he made me—' She clasped her cross tighter still, her knuckles as white as her face.

Lydia felt the colour drain from her own face. No! He wouldn't have dared. Not Valerie. 'Val,' she said, 'tell me he didn't touch you. Please God, tell me it wasn't that.'

Valerie shuddered. But she didn't speak. Her eyes were wide and Lydia could see the horror and anguish in them.

'Tell me what he did, Val.'

She opened her mouth to speak but no sound came out. Instead her face twisted in a grimace of anguish. Tears spilled down her cheeks. 'I ... I tried to make him stop, but—' Her shoulders heaved. 'But he wouldn't. He kept saying it was in the name of Jesus. He said it was what God wanted for me and I would enjoy it. He said I was special. His special friend.' She began to shake violently, wrapping her arms around her body.

Cold, implacable anger gripped at Lydia's insides. 'Are you saying he raped you?'

Valerie let out a low-pitched groan of immense pain. Tears rushed to Lydia's eyes and she put her arms around Valerie. But Valerie's body was like stone and Lydia could feel her cowering away from her. 'I'm sorry,' she sobbed, gulping for air. 'Even now I can't bear to be touched.'

Lydia let go of her. She frantically hunted through her bag for some tissues, then, risking a hand on her sister's shoulder, she gently dabbed at Valerie's face, wiping away her tears. 'Why didn't you say anything to me?' Lydia asked when at last Valerie seemed able to speak. 'I would have done something. I would have gone to the police. I would have killed him myself!'

'I was in shock. Then immediately after it had happened, Noah appeared at the house and of course all that mattered to you then, was him.'

Lydia froze, remembering with awful clarity the way Uncle Leonard had sauntered down the stairs. She remembered, too, Valerie standing on the landing. At the time she and Joey had thought her sister was alarmed by the commotion going on in the hall, when really ...

when really she'd just been raped by that monster and was traumatized. Another sickening realization hit home. The evil act had taken place when Lydia, she, who had promised their mother she would always look after Valerie, was downstairs in the kitchen getting tea ready, oblivious to what was going on above her head.

'It was while we were washing up after tea that I decided to kill him,' Valerie said quietly. 'It came to me so clearly I was convinced it was the right thing to do. I'd heard Noah shouting on the doorstep that Uncle Leonard had done something to you, too and I knew he had to be stopped. All I had to do was wait for the right moment. It came sooner than I expected. That very night. I couldn't sleep and when I heard footsteps on the stairs, then the sound of the back door being opened, I crept to the bathroom window where I could look out onto the back garden. I saw Uncle Leonard climbing over the garden wall. I didn't bother to get dressed. I went downstairs, grabbed my shoes and anorak and the carving knife from the drawer and followed him.'

'But how did you ever think you would be able to overpower him?' Lydia asked. 'He was such a big man.'

'If you had been in my place, would you have worried about a trivial detail like that? All I could think about was plunging that knife deep into his chest. The very thought of it was hypnotic and it guided me through the darkness as much as the moonlight did. It was as if I was being led. I really had no choice in the matter.'

Lydia watched her sister closely. Watched her lips. Watched her hands. She was very still now. Very calm. Very composed. Unnaturally so. It was as if she had gone into a trance, hypnotized again by the memory of reliving that dreadful night.

'Again luck was with me,' Valerie continued, 'because when he got to the area of fallen trees, he sat down behind one of them, as if he was waiting for someone. It was so much easier than I'd thought it would be. I watched him get comfortable, then silently crept up behind with a thick branch in my hand. I thought if I could stun him first, then I'd stab him. And I did. With both hands, I pushed the knife into his heart as hard as I could. I did it several times. Just to be sure. Just to be sure he'd never come near me ever again. Or you.' She turned to Lydia. 'Are you very shocked by what I've told you?'

Lydia swallowed. 'He deserved it, Val. He really did. What did you do next?'

'I ran home. I washed the knife in the sink, put it back in the drawer and then stuffed my anorak and nightdress under my bed to clean in the morning. I hadn't bargained on there being so much blood. I'd been in bed for no more than a few minutes when I saw you get up in the darkness. I pretended to be asleep. When I heard you go downstairs and open the back door, I went to the bathroom window again and looked down onto the garden. There you were, climbing over the wall. I assumed you were meeting Noah and I thought of going after you and telling you what I'd done. I suddenly wanted your assurance. I needed someone to tell me it wasn't wrong what I'd done. But then I lost my nerve. What if you told me it was wrong? What if you were angry with me?'

'Oh, Val, I would have helped you any way I could. Just as I had thought I was helping Noah.'

'Really?'

Her heart and throat tight with sorrow, Lydia said, 'Of course.' She stretched out a tentative hand to her sister, palm upwards. A moment passed and then Valerie placed her own hand lightly on top of it. With extreme gentleness, Lydia curled her fingers around Valerie's. In a muffled, faltering voice, she said, 'Do you want to carry on talking or have you had enough for now?'

Valerie blinked her eyes rapidly, chasing away more tears. 'I want to tell you everything,' she said. 'That's why I've come here. I'm not leaving until I have. I want to tell you what else I did that was so wicked.'

'Don't ever say that. It wasn't wicked.'

'Hear me out and then you might change your mind.

After I'd watched you climb over the wall, I got back into bed and prayed and prayed that you wouldn't discover the body. The next thing I knew, it was morning and the only thing on my mind was to lock myself in the bathroom and wash myself clean. Over and over. When I finally came out from the bathroom, you were gone. I thought you'd left for work early. I never dreamt it would be so long before I'd see you again.'

'When did our grandfather notice his brother was missing?'

'He didn't start to wonder where either of you were until that evening when I was bringing in the washing. When you still didn't show up at bedtime he became angry, saying you'd catch it from him in the morning. Two days later he spoke to Sister Lottie to see if she knew anything, but she said she hadn't seen you. But at church, she said something odd to me, something that made me think she knew more than she was letting on. She said I wasn't to worry, that she knew with total certainty that God had you tightly in his hand.'

Lydia nodded. 'I sent her a letter saying I needed to get away from Swallowsdale for a while. I asked her not to tell anyone that I'd written to her. She was a surprisingly good keeper of secrets.'

'As far as I know she kept that letter a complete secret. You know she died the same year, don't you?'

Lydia nodded again. 'It was very brave of you, but why did you go back into the dell and then pretend to discover Uncle Leonard's body?'

'Do you remember Brian from church?'

'The lad with the toy rabbit?'

'Yes. While his parents were having a meeting with Pastor Digby and our grandfather at our house, I suggested Brian and I went for a walk. I was sure the police would never suspect me, a twelve-year-old girl, of being the murderer, but just to be on the safe side I'd got it into my head that it might look better if I innocently stumbled across the body when somebody was with me. But it all went wrong. People started saying that you must have killed Uncle Leonard. And that was why you'd disappeared. Then it dawned on me. You'd run away because you thought Noah had killed Uncle Leonard just as he'd threatened to do, and you were protecting him. I couldn't believe the mess I'd made of everything. I didn't know what to do. The last thing I'd wanted was for you to be blamed for something I had done. I wanted to go to the police and tell them the truth, but the thought of explaining why I'd done it made me feel ill. I couldn't do it. I even thought of talking to Noah, but he was in hospital. And to be honest I couldn't bring myself to tell anyone what had happened.' She bowed her head. 'I'm sorry, Lydia. I ruined everything. I ruined your life by turning you into an exile. I never meant to do that. Believe me, please.'

'It was my love for Noah that turned me into an exile,' Lydia said. 'It was my decision entirely.'

'But if I hadn't killed Uncle Leonard you would never have had to make that decision. I committed the very worst crime of all, murder, and didn't confess to it. I deliberately allowed you to be my scapegoat.' Valerie's eyes were brimming with tears and she looked so vulnerable, Lydia glimpsed the frightened little girl who hadn't been able to go anywhere unless she had Belinda Bell in her arms.

'It doesn't matter,' Lydia said. 'None of that matters now. What's important is that you try and put it behind you. It's understandable what you did. You were a child who was raped and struck back in the only way you knew how.'

But Lydia could see Valerie wasn't listening to her. She had let go of Lydia's hand and was rummaging around inside her habit. She drew out a handkerchief and wiped her eyes. After she'd tucked the handkerchief away, she grasped Lydia's hand again. 'I still haven't told you everything,' she said. 'As time went by, I came up with a way to make amends to you. All I needed was to make someone else confess to the crime. That way it would be safe for you to come home and everything would be normal again.'

'And that someone was Grandmother?'

'A month after she'd been found lost and confused wandering the moors for two whole days and nights, I started visiting her. Our grandfather had stopped going to see her, so I went on my own, and very slowly, but very surely, I poisoned what was left of her mind. I used to sit and pray aloud with her. I would pray that God would forgive her for killing Uncle Leonard. Sometimes I prayed that she would free herself fully and confess to the crime, and other times I prayed that God would have mercy on her for having believed she was acting as his avenging angel. Oh, Lydia, what could be more evil and twisted than taking advantage of such a sick mind? But I desperately wanted you to come home. I missed you so much. But you didn't come home. And so it was all for nothing. Grandma died with everyone thinking she was a killer and my guilt and shame grew and grew. I began to hate you. I blamed you for what I did to Grandma. If only you had come back, it would have been worth it.'

What words of comfort could Lydia possibly offer her sister? Other than to say the words she'd been saying nearly all her life. 'I'm sorry, Val. I should have been a better sister to you. I let you down in so many ways.'

'No you didn't. It was me who was at fault. I wasn't an easy sister. I got all the attention from our grandmother and there wasn't any left for you. Only hatred from our grandfather. The worst of it was, I was so desperate to be Grandma's favourite, I couldn't show you how much I loved you. I knew that if I tried to, it would have made her jealous, and that would have made life more difficult for you. Then whenever she was really ill and taken away, a part of me was taken away as well. I wanted to turn to you, but I couldn't; it would have been a betrayal of Grandma's love for me. I convinced myself you didn't really care about me so that I could justify not caring about you. Your love for Noah was all I needed to harden my resolve. And when things just got too difficult for me, it was easier to block everything out and disappear inside myself. Losing my voice was a defence mechanism. Even now I find that difficult to understand.'

'How did you know Noah and I were more than just friends?'

'Don't be cross, but I followed you into the dell once and saw you kissing. I wanted to know where you were going.'

'And those visions you claimed to experience?'

'They felt real at the time, is all I can say. And, of course, I enjoyed the attention everyone gave me because of them.'

Once more they were disturbed by the opening of the door. This time a couple came in; the woman was quietly crying with a tissue pressed to her face. The man looked like he'd been crying too. Their whispered exchange rose and fell. Ten minutes later they left.

The interruption enabled Lydia to steer the conversation in another direction, to fit yet another piece into the puzzle. 'Why did the police never seriously consider our grandfather as a suspect?' she asked.

'He had a good alibi. He didn't come home that night. In fact, he didn't come back until almost lunchtime the next day.'

'Where had he been?'

'With a woman. Not that I was supposed to know that. But I overhead him telling the two police officers who came to the house after Brian and I had supposedly discovered the body in the dell. He'd been having an affair with this woman for some time.'

'Was it anyone we knew?'

Valerie shook her head. 'He used to work with her at the council offices. She was one of the women from the typing pool. The real details of their relationship only came out when Pastor Digby was exposed for stealing money from the new roof fund. To get his own back he went round telling tales about the Brothers' and Sisters' weaknesses and transgressions, including our grandfather's. Apparently Sister Vera suffered from kleptomania, Brother Walter had gambled nearly all his savings away in the betting shop, and Sisters Mildred and Hilda were more than just close friends. I have no idea how he knew all this.'

'Was that why the church folded? Pastor Digby helping himself to money and the aftermath?'

'Yes and no. When he went, there was no one suitable to take his place. People just drifted away. For all his faults, he did have excellent leadership skills. He kept the church together.'

'That's what people said about Hitler and the Third Reich,' Lydia said bitterly.

They fell into a long, reflective silence. Beyond the white-painted walls of the chapel, Lydia was conscious of a distant other world. Here, with Val, she felt locked in the past. It was beginning to stifle her. She would need to escape soon. Perhaps Valerie was experiencing the same sensation. 'How are you feeling?' she asked her sister.

'Numb. And frightened. I'm afraid of the consequences of this conversation. I could go to prison for what I did.'

'By rights Uncle Leonard should have gone to prison for what *he* did.'

Valerie shook her head. 'Please don't say anything about an eye for an eye and a tooth for a tooth. I couldn't bear that.'

'I won't, but you have to start believing that you've been punished enough for what happened that day. You mustn't go on blaming yourself. Not for any of it. As for the consequences of this conversation, I think they'll be positive ones. You don't have to tell anyone else what you've shared with me, but never again will you have to feel that this is something you have to deal with on your own. From now on, I'll always be there for you, Valerie. I mean it.'

'But do you understand now why I behaved the way I did when you came to see me? I knew that if I showed you how genuinely pleased I was to see you I would fall apart. I just didn't think I could risk it. It seemed too painful.'

Again they were interrupted by the door opening and

light flooding in. This time it wasn't a stranger seeking solace in the chapel. It was Ishmael.

He came over, his handsome young face tight with anxiety. 'I'm sorry to disturb you, Lydia,' he said quietly, 'but you said I was to come here if there was any news. I've just heard that Dad's out of surgery.'

AND THEN ...

Chapter Sixty-Three

Lydia sat at the table alone. It was eleven o'clock at night and Caffe Florian was doing good business. Dressed in their smart white jackets and chattering discreetly amongst themselves, the waiters were keeping a casual watch over the tables of customers.

It had been a pleasantly warm March day but now it had turned into a chilly, damp night. An impenetrable mist had started to roll in from the Adriatic and the piazza of San Marco had acquired a melancholy feel that was greatly at odds with what the musicians were playing – 'New York, New York'. It was a perennial favourite with the tourists who flocked here as persistently as the pigeons did.

Lydia had always preferred the piazza at night: fewer tourists, and zero pigeons. After Marcello had died, unable to sleep, she had often come here to the deserted square in the dead of night, wandering through the colonnaded arcades, her footsteps echoing in the haunting emptiness.

She watched the mist continue to roll in; the top of the Campanile had magically vanished, as had two of the domes on the basilica. It was an extraordinary and eerie sight, which she had seen many times before. She touched the pearl hanging from the delicate chain at her neck and wished Noah was here to see it.

More than three months had passed since that day when she had tripped on the steps of the Rialto Bridge. In some ways the time had sped by as fast as a blink of an eye, but in other ways, she felt she had lived an entire lifetime during those few months. It had been a period of great change and adjustment.

Not least of all for Chiara. She and Ishmael were even more in love and with Ishmael now working in Padua they were planning to move in together. Selfishly Lydia was delighted that there was no question of Chiara leaving Venice to be with Ishmael in Padua. Padua was only thirty minutes away on the train, yet Chiara was adamant she wasn't moving to the mainland. Venice was her home, she'd told Ishmael; it was also where the agency was and now that she was easing Lydia's workload, she wanted to remain on its doorstep. She was a girl who knew her own mind and fortunately Ishmael was quite prepared to commute from Venice. They'd found a recently restored apartment to share and Lydia couldn't be happier for Chiara.

Another source of happiness for Lydia was that she and Valerie were in regular touch by letter. All these years on, they were finally getting to know each other properly. Her greatest hope was that Valerie could now find the peace of mind she deserved. Absolution, too. As a result of their correspondence, Lydia had reviewed her opinion of the Order of St Agnes. Gone now was her hostility regarding the closed world Valerie had chosen to live in. Where once Lydia had viewed the convent as little better than a prison depriving her sister of the rich and varied life she was meant to experience, she now understood it had been a place of sanctuary for Valerie, somewhere she had been surrounded by compassion and kindness. Somewhere she felt safe.

The exchange of letters was also enabling them to fill in the gaps in their lives. Lydia now knew that their grandfather had remarried four years after that dreadful night in the dell, a year after their grandmother's death, and the year Valerie turned sixteen. Life at number thirty-three Hillside Terrace changed dramatically when Doris moved in. The house was redecorated from top to bottom, the kitchen was knocked through to the dining room and a breakfast bar installed, the shed in the garden was replaced with a summer house, and part of the lawn was dug up to make room for a pond and a patio of crazy paving. While

Doris was not an unsympathetic woman, she had had no idea how to deal with a sixteen-year-old girl, especially one as complex as Valerie. When Valerie announced on her eighteenth birthday that she was leaving Swallowsdale to join the Order of St Agnes, it had come as a huge relief to all concerned.

Lydia had promised her sister faithfully that the truth about Uncle Leonard's death would always remain their secret. It may have been unfair that their grandmother had died with everyone believing her to be a murderer but then it wasn't fair that poor Valerie had had her innocence so cruelly stolen, or that her life had been blighted as a consequence.

The one person who seemed not to have been affected in any way by what had gone on was their grandfather. Lydia hated that. She hated knowing that he hadn't suffered for what he'd done. She would never know what had made him into the cold-blooded, vicious sadist he'd been, or what had made his brother into an abusive monster who preyed on young girls, but she knew she would never find it within her to forgive them. If there really was such a place as hell – especially the nightmarish place of torment Pastor Digby used to rant about – she hoped they were both there.

The night before his operation, Noah had joked of his preference not to go to hell if anything went wrong. As to be expected, neither of them had been able to sleep. All day Lydia had managed to stop her thoughts from becoming maudlin, but alone in bed with Noah, she couldn't keep up the act any more. 'I know what you're worrying about,' he'd said in the darkness. 'You're wondering, in a worst-case scenario, whether I'm hell or heaven-bound, aren't you?'

'Please don't joke about tomorrow,' she'd said, rolling onto her side to look at him. 'Everyone I've ever really cared about has been taken from me long before they should have.'

Ignoring her, and clasping his hands behind his head,

he'd said, 'I have to say, heaven's my preferred choice. That way I'll get the chance to meet your parents at long last, as well as catch up with mine. And then there's Marcello. I'd give him a high-five and let him know that he had impeccable taste in women. I'd be discreet, of course; I wouldn't—'

She'd silenced him with a kiss. A very long kiss. Anything but listen to him making light of what was so precious to her.

It pained her unbearably to think of that conversation now and she let her thoughts drift to the people whose lives had touched her so deeply, and the link that connected them all – Lydia's mother had been orphaned at a very young age, Lydia and Valerie had lost their parents, as had Noah and Chiara. Was it coincidence they had all been brought together? Or fate? She suddenly smiled to herself, imagining Valerie admonishing her for using the F word.

From high up in the dark, misty sky, the bells in the tower struck the half hour: it was half past eleven. Lydia looked across the piazza, its damp surface gleaming in the bright lights spilling out from the colonnaded arcades. That was when she saw that her wait was over. Spontaneously, her heart beat a little faster and she felt a wave of tender love wash over her. She knew that for as long as she was able to draw breath, the effect that face had on her would never diminish. She put a hand in the air to show where she was and received an acknowledging wave in return.

Even though they'd been apart only briefly, Noah kissed her before pulling out a chair for himself. 'Did you get Uncle Brad safely back to his hotel?' she asked.

'I left him ordering a drink at the bar. He'll be nicely settled in for the night I shouldn't wonder.'

Now that she was no longer alone, a waiter materialized at their table and they ordered two espressos.

Staring up at the partially hidden campanile and basilica, Noah said, 'I've never seen a mist roll in as fast as this.'

'That's Venice for you. Utterly unique.' Suddenly anxious,

Lydia said, 'You *do* like it here, don't you? Truthfully.'

He leaned in close and grazed his lips against her cheek. 'I've told you before: it feels like home.'

It was exactly what she'd said about his house in England. When the medical staff at the hospital had said he was well enough to go home after Christmas, Lydia had stayed with him the whole time, almost afraid to let him out of her sight. She didn't think she would ever forget those agonizing hours while she and Ishmael had waited for him to come round from the operation. Despite the emphatic assurance from the surgeon that there had been no complications throughout the five-hour operation – the tumour had been benign – and that there was no reason to doubt Noah wouldn't make an excellent recovery, she had convinced herself that he would never wake up, or, if he did, he wouldn't be the man he'd once been. Never had she been happier to be proved wrong. And on both points.

It was during Noah's convalescence that she had grown to love his house and the village where he lived. She had felt very much a part of it. As soon as he was strong enough, friends and neighbours began dropping in, and again, Lydia became part of those friendships. Noah's ex-wife, Jane, stopped by regularly, and whilst they initially tiptoed warily around one another, they quickly became firm allies in their determination to get Noah well again, mainly by enforcing as much bed rest on him as they could get away with.

Three weeks after Noah's operation Uncle Brad flew over to England from France. It was an emotional reunion for Lydia. His first words were to tell her and Noah what a pair of bloody fools they'd been for not finding each other before now. He'd then presented Noah with a smart fedora to wear until his hair grew back. Age had not mellowed him in the slightest. If anything, he'd turned into an even more irascible old devil and Lydia loved him for it. Now here he was in Venice, no expense spared, pitching his tent at the Gritti Palace for the weekend. Good for him!

Noah had been staying with Lydia in Venice for the last fortnight. It was the start of things to come. Just as he'd said on that cold winter's day when they'd gone for a walk before his operation, they planned to divide their time between here and England. Noah had already taken steps to hand over more of the day-to-day running of his business and with Chiara proving to be a force to be reckoned with at the agency, they had high hopes of being able to make their slightly unconventional new life work.

Their coffee arrived, and while the waiter placed the tray of drinks on the table, he bent down and whispered in Lydia's ear. '*Grazie*,' she said, glancing over the top of Noah's head towards the musicians. The violinist gave her a questioning look. She nodded.

'Have you and the waiter got something going I should know about?' Noah asked when they were alone. 'If I'm in the way, just say the word.'

She flashed him a smile. 'I have something going with every waiter in Venice; it's how I avoid paying the full price for anything.'

Whilst they drank their coffee, a Sri Lankan teenage boy approached them with a bunch of red roses. They were a sitting target. 'A rose for the pretty lady?' the boy said hopefully to Noah.

Noah reached for his wallet from inside his coat, but then hesitated. 'How much for the whole bunch?' he asked.

The boy looked astonished.

'I'm serious,' Noah said, his wallet in his hand now.

'Twenty euros,' the boy said hurriedly, seeing the unexpected opportunity of an early night.

Noah handed over the money and gave Lydia the flowers. People sitting around them smiled approvingly. 'Cheesy as hell, I know,' he said quietly, 'but if a man can't make romantic gestures in Venice to the woman he loves, where can he?'

She laughed happily and kissed him. 'If you thought

that was corny, just wait and see what I've got in store for you.'

With perfect timing, the musicians came to the end of the number they'd been playing and in the sudden silence, the bells in the campanile pealed the hour. It was midnight. 'Happy birthday,' Lydia said. She pushed back her chair and got to her feet, just as the musicians started playing their next piece. She held out her hand. 'Noah Solomon, may I have the pleasure of this dance?'

Recognition dawned on Noah's face. He looked horrified. He shook his head. 'Lyddie, *no*!'

She grabbed his hands. 'Oh yes!'

'But I can't. Not in front of everyone.'

'Yes, you can. Imagine we're here on our own.'

'But my leg. All I'll manage is a clumsy shuffle.'

'That'll do for me.'

In the space next to their table – the table Lydia had chosen specially when she'd arrived earlier and had made her request to the lead violinist – they held each other closely, their gaze unbroken. They settled into the rhythm, and to the delight of everyone around them, they danced to the waltz from Sviridov's Snow Storm, just as a drunken Uncle Brad had taught them to do on Noah's fifteenth birthday in the kitchen at Upper Swallowsdale House.

'Lyddie?' Noah said.

'You're not going to say you'd rather be bungee jumping off the campanile, are you?'

'No. But I am glad it wasn't a tango Uncle B taught us.'

She smiled. 'I thought you were going to thank me for not forcing you to wear a saucepan on your head.'

He smiled too and she felt him relax against her. 'You know, I think I'd like to do this again sometime,' he said.

'When were you thinking?'

'How about when we get married?'

'I didn't know we were.'

'I thought it was a given.'

'A girl likes to be asked.'

He held her closer, his expression intensely solemn. 'Will you marry me, Lyddie? Marry me so that we can finally be together, man and wife, just as we always should have been.'

'Yes,' she said, almost before he'd finished speaking.

'You might like to think about your answer.'

'I have. Since for ever.' She stopped moving and kissed him.

They were still standing there, wrapped in each other's arms, long after the music had stopped.

Tell it to the Skies

Reading Group Notes

In Brief

Lydia saw him and fell. As simple as that. A face amongst the crowd of tourists around the Rialto Bridge had so caught her attention that she'd turned, captivated, and down she'd gone. The result: a sprained ankle, the promise of crutches, and a growing disbelief in what she'd seen.

Stuck in the apartment, Lydia can't help dwelling on the uneasy feelings the sight of that face caused. Is her world about to come tumbling down? She dreams of a sinking Venice, the water lapping around her as her world disappears. It is, after all, such a fragile world she has created.

Then her step-daughter, Chiara, brings home her new love, and suddenly Lydia is taken back twenty-eight years to a man she would have done anything for – a man for whom she gave up her future.

In Detail

❧

Chiara's new boyfriend is not Noah. Clearly he can't be. But he looks just like him. After they leave, Lydia is drawn inexorably to her past. Despite her ankle, she clambers up to reach down an olive wood box and looks through the only remains of her life before Italy – her life in England.

Amongst the things in the box is an envelope of photographs, of her parents, and her sister Valerie. One of them is of her and Noah messing around as teenagers, another, creased, torn and worn, is just of Noah. Now Lydia can see the startling similarity between Noah and the man Chiara has fallen in love with. He can only be Noah's son. Lydia always knew that the past would catch up with her one day . . .

It was the ventriloquist's dummy that did it. That was the start of so many years of unhappiness and guilt. With her ninth birthday coming up, Lydia had set her heart on the one in the toy shop window. If only she hadn't gone on so about it to her mother, but everything had changed since that rainy day when her father had been taken from them, and she had to do so much to help her mother. Surely, now, the ventriloquist's dummy wasn't too much to ask for? But it turned out that it was. Her mother got worse and worse until a frightening middle-of-the-night walk ended in the piercing screech of metal wheels trying too late to stop on metal rails. And Lydia and Valerie were sent to live with their grandparents – the same couple who were so bitter about who their son had married, they were glad he was now dead.

Swallowsdale was so much worse than she could ever have thought. Her grandparents were impossibly strict. They were members of The Church of The Brothers and Sisters in Christ and were convinced that Lydia was cursed in the same way that her mother had been. They couldn't punish her mother for taking their son from them, but they could hurt Lydia. And they did. Small windows of light shone into Lydia's world: Pastor John seemed kind, and batty Sister Lottie was good to her, but it wasn't until the arrival of a new boy at school that Lydia found a focus in her life. Noah was an outsider like her, and an alliance grew.

Over the years they drew closer and closer together, and made plans for the future – until one awful night when the simmering violence in Swallowsdale exploded and Lydia ran away. She'd started running and never really stopped . . .

About the Author

Erica James grew up on Hayling Island in Hampshire, and has since lived in Oxford, Yorkshire and Belgium. She is the author of eleven bestselling books, and says her main qualification for writing is that she's 'a nosy devil and loves watching and eavesdropping on other people's conversations'.

She now lives in Cheshire.

For Discussion

- If you're a child of the seventies, were you transported back? How does the author achieve this? How does she recreate the past?

- 'Since Marcello died, seldom did she close the shutters as well. She didn't like to shut out too much of the world.' Doesn't she? Why would Lydia want to see what was outside her apartment?

- How does the author use water in the novel?

- 'In fact, we're all so abnormal we're completely normal.' If Lydia had realised this earlier, how do you think her life would have been different?

- How is the concept of sanctuary used in *Tell it to the Skies*?

- Lydia believes she is 'a lightning conductor of bad things'. Is she? Is any of it her fault? Could she have made her life better by making different decisions or behaving differently?

- What do you think the author thinks about religion?

- 'Keeping relentlessly busy was the answer, she'd found. Leave herself with no time to dwell on those old memories and she was able to put it out of her mind.' Does this save Lydia, or curse her never to move forward?

- Why do you think the author named Noah's son Ishmael?

- *Tell it to the Skies* is a novel of consequences. As a tale of those 'roads not taken', whose lives could have been different?

Suggested Further Reading

Pillow Talk by Freya North

A Gathering Light by Jennifer Donnelly

Starter For Ten by David Nicholls

The Pact by Jodie Picoult

A Party in San Niccolò by Christobel Kent

The Villa in Italy by Elizabeth Edmondson

VENICE AND THE ROLE IT PLAYED IN THE WRITING OF *TELL IT TO THE SKIES*.

Although the vast majority of *Tell it to the Skies* takes place in Yorkshire, Venice played a crucial part in pulling together the story. In fact, it was the trigger for writing the book in the first place.

I had written eleven books in as many years and reached the point when I needed time out to recharge my creative batteries. I knew I needed to step back from my writing because when I came to the end of the book I was then working on – *Gardens of Delight* – I didn't know what I was going to write next. Usually I know exactly

what I want to write next but, scarily, my mind was blank this time round. So I decided I would go and stay in my favourite city for a month. I was also in the mood for a bit of an adventure. And where better to do that than Venice?

I had already been having Italian lessons but, conscious that I had a long way to go yet in learning the language, I signed up for a week's course at the Istituto Venezia – the language school in Campo Santa Margherita – which in due course became the language school where Noah's son Ishmael takes lessons.

Just about every other person in Venice seems to be a

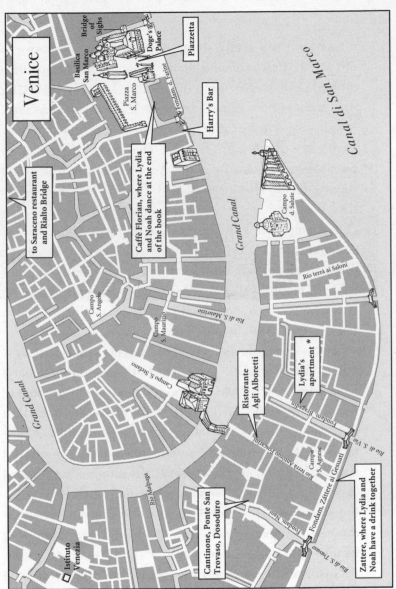

Venice

Bridge of Sighs

Basilica San Marco

Piazza S. Marco

Doge's Palace

Piazzetta

Harry's Bar

Fondam. L. Farine

to Saraceno restaurant and Rialto Bridge

Caffè Florian, where Lydia and Noah dance at the end of the book

Canal di San Marco

Grand Canal

Campo d. Salute

Rio terrà ai Saloni

Campo S. Angelo

Campo S. Maurizio

Campo S. Stefano

Rio di S. Maurizio

Lydia's apartment *

Ristorante Agii Alboretti

Rio terra Antonio Foscarini

Fondam. Bragadin

Campo S. Agnese

Rio di S. Vio

Grand Canal

Rio Malpaga

Fondam. Nani

Fondam. Zattere ai Gesuati

Rio di S. Trovaso

Cantinone, Ponte San Trovaso, Dosoduro

Zattere, where Lydia and Noah have a drink together

Istituto Venezia

* There isn't a specific building which I used, just the row/area

writer and so it really shouldn't have been a surprise to me on my first morning at the language school to turn around in the registration queue and find myself looking at a crime writer I knew from back home. He was later responsible for introducing me to a great cicheti bar, Cantinone, Ponte San Trovaso, Dosoduro, as well as an excellent restaurant near the Accademia, the Ristorante Agli Alboretti (Dosoduro 882, Rio Terà Foscarini), where they serve the most excellent baccala and offer the best cheese selection I've ever eaten in Italy. Much to my embarrassment, during a recent visit I got stuck in the toilet in that particular restaurant, but that's another story! It was also through this crime writer that I met an American woman who taught English for a living, which later gave me the idea for how Lydia meets Marcello.

It was once I had survived the rigours of the language school that I applied myself to the challenge of what I would write next. I was sitting in the Saraceno restaurant next to the Rialto Bridge, when the first glimmer of an idea came to me. It was mid October, the light was fading and the weather had turned unexpectedly cold and wintry. I started to think of all the things that I loved about Venice, how it can be enchantingly seductive yet at the same time quite sinister, giving the impression that there is so much more hidden behind the crumbling facades than at first appears. I thought of the proud resilience of the city and its people, how against all the

*Erica on the Rialto Bridge, with the Saraceno restaurant
in the background*

odds Venice was still standing. I thought how claustrophobic the city can be with the narrow *calli* jam-packed
with tourists, but then how late at night one could have

Detail of the Rialto Bridge

the place practically to oneself, catching little more than
a shadowy glimpse of a solitary, ghost-like figure walking home.

My thoughts had just moved on to thinking how
melancholy and secretive the city can feel when I suddenly pictured a woman about the same age as me living
there and having a secret that she had never shared with
anyone. I held on tight to this thought and reflected how
easy it would be to lose oneself in Venice. The more I
thought about this, the more I could imagine that this
was the perfect place for someone with a secret, a person

who had a very real reason to hide from their past.

A glass of wine later, I had a strong mental image of my central character stumbling on the steps of the Rialto Bridge after she catches sight of a face in the crowd. From then on, there was no stopping the ideas, they kept on coming.

Over the following weeks, I became a regular at the Saraceno. I felt it was a 'lucky' place for me and returned again and again, notepad and pen in hand. The waiters, once they realised I was a writer, were great and never hustled me on to make room for other diners, despite the restaurant always being busy. It's a restaurant I still like to visit as it now holds very special memories for me. Plus, the waiters are always so charming!

✧✧✧

Before I can really start writing a new book, I have to experience an emotional pull to the characters and the setting. Venice instilled within me a strong sensation of sadness and loss – which essentially sets the tone of the novel, that and a sense of mystery – and to underpin this feeling, when I was back at home and writing in my study, I listened endlessly to the following pieces of music:

Waltz from Georgi Sviridov's *Snowstorm*
Onegin's Theme from the soundtrack to the film
    Onegin

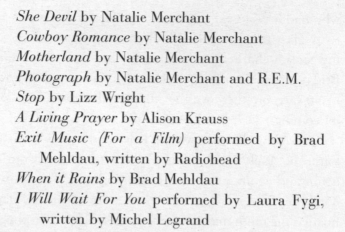

She Devil by Natalie Merchant
Cowboy Romance by Natalie Merchant
Motherland by Natalie Merchant
Photograph by Natalie Merchant and R.E.M.
Stop by Lizz Wright
A Living Prayer by Alison Krauss
Exit Music (For a Film) performed by Brad
    Mehldau, written by Radiohead
When it Rains by Brad Mehldau
I Will Wait For You performed by Laura Fygi,
    written by Michel Legrand

It's an eclectic mix but what these tracks all have in common, whether it's through the melody of the singer's voice or the lyrics, is an air of mournful longing, bitter regret and melancholy. They conjure an atmosphere that is haunting and dreamlike. Just as Venice does.

On the whole, my books are known for having a feel-good quality to them – admittedly that takes a long time to happen in *Tell it to the Skies* – and consequently people tend to think that to write books with a happy ending I must be of a permanently sunny disposition. It always comes as a surprise when I reveal the darker side to my nature, in that I feel things acutely and have a natural inclination to tap into those gloomier and more sombre emotions and explore them through my characters. I think that's why I feel so at home in Venice; I'm able to

Erica outside the Basilica San Marco

connect with the place, recognising that beneath the surface of faded grandeur and fairy-tale beauty, there lurks a very different soul. There's an intriguing sense of drama and tragedy about Venice; why else would so many crime writers choose the city as the setting for their novels?

But Venice isn't all gloom and mystery. There's plenty of fun to be had. Venetians have a raucous sense of humour and many would claim they need it, given the challenges they face on a daily basis, whether it's coping with the hoards of tourists that descend on the city, or the increasing threat of *acqua alta*.

For a fun night out, one of my favourite places to eat is Harry's Bar (San Marco 1323, Calle Vallaresso). It really isn't the tourist trap people think it is. Yes, a lot of Americans have it on their 'must do' list, but on the occasions I've been there Italians have always outnumbered foreigners. I've eaten the best risotto of my life in this restaurant. But a word of warning, it is colossally expensive. I burst out with near hysterical laughter when I first ate there and asked for the bill afterwards. 'I only wanted to pay for my meal, not everybody else's,' I felt like saying. It's by no means large inside and the décor is nothing to write home about, but there's always a fantastic buzz to the place. I'd advise booking ahead and dressing smartly. Definitely no shorts or flip flops! Personally I'm not a huge fan of the Bellini cocktail the bar is

The Piazzetta

famous for, and prefer a glass of Prosecco or a vodka martini.

Another favourite place of mine is Florian's (Caffè Florian, San Marco 56–59, Piazza San Marco). How could it not be? After all, it is *the* place in the Piazza San Marco. The toasted sandwiches are sublime as is afternoon tea. The cosy interior is excessively kitsch and is the perfect place to people-watch when it's too cold to sit outside. Again, it's off-the-chart expensive but somehow I can always justify it. Especially when the musicians are playing their repertoire of catchy crowd pleasers. I'm a total sucker for anything cheesy or romantic.

The Bridge of Sighs

I had written about a quarter of *Tell it to the Skies* when I pictured the final scene with Lydia and Noah dancing in the Piazza. One of the artistic liberties I had to take with that particular scene was having the musicians playing when strictly speaking they wouldn't be there until a few months later when the weather is warmer. What few people realise is that the musicians who play in the Piazza aren't Italian, let alone Venetian. They're from Eastern Europe, all classically trained but unable to find work at home. Request a Russian piece of music and see their faces light up.

There's a lot of snobbery regarding Venice. The so-called experts will tell you to avoid any of the tourist spots to eat, drink or shop. But frankly, I'll eat, drink and shop exactly where I feel most comfortable. Nor do I try to put as many ticks as possible in the cultural boxes each time I visit. In my view, Venice is like a large box of very rich chocolates – eat too much in one go and the pleasure is spoilt. I like to pace myself, knowing that I have a store of new gems to enjoy on a return trip. I hate it when people look at me in horror and say, 'What do you mean you haven't seen the Carpaccios at the Scuola di San Giorgio degli Schiavoni?' Which, for the record, I have now seen.

There have been so many books written about Venice, and the ones I've enjoyed the most are:

The City of Falling Angels by John Berendt
A Thousand Days in Venice by Marlena De Blasi
Miss Garnet's Angel by Salley Vickers
Venice by Francesco da Mosto
Venice Revealed: An Intimate Portrait by Paolo Barbaro

It would be presumptuous of me to align myself with any of these authors, but it would be nice to think that my own book might tempt someone who hasn't yet been to Venice to go there and discover for themselves just how unique a place it is.

With very best wishes
Erica James

Lose yourself
in a good book with Galaxy

Curled up on the sofa,
Sunday morning in pyjamas,
just before bed,
in the bath or
on the way to work?

Wherever, whenever,
you can escape
with a good book!

So go on...
indulge yourself with
a good read and the
smooth taste of
Galaxy chocolate